ABOUT THE AUTHOR

Philip Photiou was born and lives in Plymouth and is the author of two books, *Plymouth's Forgotten War*, a non-fiction work and the *Wrath of Kings*, a novel set during the Wars of the Roses. Philip's passion for history covers many periods and he lectures to groups on several subjects in and around his home town. He is also involved in the production of short historic podcasts which are very popular.

Research has taken Philip all over England and he is now in the process of writing his next novel which covers the turbulent years of late fifteenth-century England.

PHILIP PHOTIOU

The Lamb of God

AUSTIN MACAULEY PUBLISHERS™

LONDON • CAMBRIDGE • NEW YORK • SHARJAH

Copyright © Philip Photiou 2022

The right of Philip Photiou to be identified as author of this work has been asserted in accordance with section 77 and 78 of the Copyright, Designs and Patents Act 1988.

All rights reserved. No part of this publication may be reproduced, stored in a retrieval system, or transmitted in any form or by any means, electronic, mechanical, photocopying, recording, or otherwise, without the prior permission of the publishers.

Any person who commits any unauthorised act in relation to this publication may be liable to criminal prosecution and civil claims for damages.

A CIP catalogue record for this title is available from the British Library.

ISBN 9781398461642 (Paperback)
ISBN 9781398461659 (Hardback)
ISBN 9781398461666 (ePub e-book)

www.austinmacauley.com

First Published 2022
Austin Macauley Publishers Ltd
1 Canada Square
Canary Wharf
London E14 5AA

DEDICATION

This book is dedicated to my family and friends,
and the many helpful people I have met during my research.

ACKNOWLEDGEMENTS

Mr Graham Turner – Artist

Dr Tobias Capwell – Wallace Collection

Mr John Clark – Museum of London

Miss Julia Snelling – Royal Archives Windsor

Mr Stephen Goodchild – Tewkesbury

Mrs Susan Skedd – Barnett

Mrs Mary Cosh – Islington

Mr Jo Wisdom – St Paul's Cathedral

Staff & Guides at York minster

Staff & Guides at Westminster Abbey

Tower of London Guides

Guildhall Library London

Mr Bill Callaghan – Alnwick

Mr John Jefferys – Tewkesbury Abbey

Michelle Klein – Houses of Parliament

Robert Wynn Jones – Lost City of London

Sarah Moulden – Curator of Collections London & East
English Heritage

Staff at Lambeth Palace

Prologue

WHEN BAMBURGH CASTLE surrendered to the Earl of Warwick in July 1464, Harlech, in Wales, was the last place holding out for the displaced Lancastrian King Henry VI. On and off for the past nine years, the royal houses of York and Lancaster slaughtered each other for the crown; now, finally, Edward IV felt secure enough to consider marriage. His cousin and mentor, Richard Neville, Earl of Warwick, was already negotiating with King Louis XI of France for the hand of Louis' sister-in-law, the Lady Bona of Savoy. Eager to meet with the French king, Warwick hurriedly dismantled his camp outside Bamburgh and made preparations to go to France.

Chapter 1

Crouching on a limestone ledge near the bottom of a steep, narrow valley, Philip Neville deliberately reduced his breathing. Carefully removing his spurs, he silently motioned for the two men kneeling behind him to follow his example.

A thirty-year-old manorial knight indentured to his cousin Richard, Earl of Warwick, Philip was outspoken, aggressive and oozed resentment, symptoms nurtured by the murder of his father, the loss of the woman he loved to another and the death of his brother at Bamburgh. His dark, intense eyes blazed expressively and his cheeks would pulsate when he was aroused. Rash and opinionated, Philip was true to his cousin King Edward and held a deep-seated hatred for all his enemies. Philip's faith in God was constant but he despised the Church for its hypocrisy and abuses.

With an undetermined number of enemy soldiers below, Philip knew he must put aside his personal feelings and concentrate on the task at hand. Drawing his arming sword from its scabbard, he winced at the scraping sound the steel made as it cleared the locket. Wiping his damp palm on his crimson tunic, he nodded to his companions.

Philip had been straining since dawn to see below the low-lying mist and assess the enemy's strength. Through the fog, he finally caught a glimpse of someone in a yellow and blue livery coat: the colours of Thomas Lord Roos, a Lancastrian noble executed at Hexham. Leaderless and with nowhere to go, these diehards were out on a looting spree and Philip could only speculate whether they would stand or run. Bringing along several women from nearby Helmsley, Roos' men had spent the previous night drinking and fornicating. The coarse comments and slurred laughter reverberating through the valley convinced Philip they were in no state to fight and he decided not to bring up the rest of his company.

As the sun rose higher, a thin ribbon of smoke from the campfire filtered through the mist and hovered lazily above the trees. Without a word, Philip crept towards the lip of the ledge and parted the prickly branches of a hawthorn shrub sprouting from its precipice. Peering through the white flowers and bright red berries, he counted five horses tied between two trees, which until now had been obscured by the dense fog. The sun's rays began to spear down through the trees, spotlighting the dark, heavily wooded valley floor and warming Philip's back. Raising a hand he showed the fingers to his fellow knights, indicating the number of men below, before allowing the shrub to close over.

"Five," he confirmed to his companions, Sir John Middleton and Sir Thomas Talbot. "And two women."

"Will they fight?" Middleton asked.

"They've been swiving all night," Philip sneered, watching one of the women walk delicately to the fire. "It'll be easy."

"Roos' men," Sir Thomas revealed. "That gutless bastard."

Such vulgar language grated on the more sensitive Middleton, who disliked profanity in any form.

"We'll hit them while they break their fast," Philip said, as the mist began to dissipate.

"I'll fetch the horses –" Talbot suggested.

"No," Philip hissed, "we go on foot."

"But –"

"Quiet," Philip cut him off.

Talbot lurched forward angrily but Middleton put a hand out to calm his temper.

"They're not expecting us," Philip leered. "We'll come at them from the trees," he added, curving an arm out to indicate the direction they were to go.

"I'll bring up the others?" Middleton suggested.

"There's no time," Philip insisted, taking a last look at the camp. "The mist will be gone soon."

Eager to see, Talbot crawled past Philip and pushed his face into the prickly shrub.

"Stay down," Philip barked, dragging him back by the shoulder.

Talbot gripped the handle of his sword and glowered at the back of Philip's head, outrage twisting his features into a snarl.

Thomas Talbot had been allocated to Philip by Lord Warwick because of his hostile nature. When informed of the assignment, Talbot, two years Philip's senior, boasted he would sooner boil his own head than serve such a lowly knight. Talbot's haughty attitude was evident in his cold, unblinking eyes, deep brows and firm mouth. Philip's second reluctant companion, John Middleton, was in his mid-forties with dark, thinning hair, greying at the temples. Sagging cheeks drew his mouth down, giving him a dour demeanour. Despite capturing and executing the late Duke of Somerset, Middleton was sent to Philip because of his protestations to Warwick's Herald for the way Philip and his brother were forced to fight at Bamburgh.

"Ready –" Philip sniffed, as the men below were served food by the women.

Struggling to rise, he limped down from the ledge accompanied by his fellow knights. Keeping the trees between himself and the river, Philip bent low and careened forward, breathing heavily as he skirted hawthorn and hazel, and zig-zagged between birch, ash and rowan. Stopping suddenly he dropped onto one knee and waited for Talbot and Middleton to catch up. When they knelt beside him all three listened to the frivolous banter of the enemy. Oblivious to the moisture in the soil penetrating his woollen hose, Philip held his sword tight for the final dash.

"Now!" he yelled, kissing the cross-bar of his sword and bounding forward.

Confused by the thrashing noise coming from the woods behind them, the men and women, lolling in the tall grass, were bewildered by the sight of three screaming madmen bursting out of the trees. Tossing aside plates and cups, they scattered: several splashed across the slow-flowing River Rye; another charged off in the direction of Helmsley. Two, how-ever, chose to stand their ground. Talbot pursued the Lan-castrians across the river, while Philip and Middleton moved against the men who elected to fight.

"Come back, you codheads," Talbot yelled, wading through the water and cursing their cowardice, "and fight me!"

Wearing faded yellow and blue livery coats, the two men-of-arms standing their ground grabbed swords and took up a defensive stance. Middleton moved to the left and Philip drew the second man's attention by circling the point of his arming sword in his face.

Roos' men stood almost back to back as the two knights closed in. Philip, his heart pounding, looked into his oppo-nent's worried eyes. While the man nervously wiped irritating perspiration from his eyes and raised his blade, Philip swung his weapon up and brought it down on his bare head. The Lancastrian parried the strike and the two swords clanged together, the sound echoing through the quiet valley. Philip went for a quick kill but Middleton preferred to take his man alive. Striking again and again, Philip gave his opponent no chance; it was too easy years of experience guided his arm as he hacked away from all angles.

"Drop it!" he demanded, his sword screeching down his opponent's badly-burred blade and striking the crossbar with force enough to bump him back. "Do it now."

The Lancastrian thrust his sword at Philip's groin, but he evaded the stroke, the metal thwacking his knuckles.

"Goddamn you!" he spat, swinging his weapon in hard. "I'll kill you for that."

Caught off balance, the Lancastrian knew he was a dead man. "Mercy," he whimpered.

"Too late!" Philip snarled, slicing the lower end of his blade against the side of the man's head and cutting off part of the top like an egg.

Blood and bone splinters sprayed Philip's tunic and as his victim crumpled, he closed his eyes, relishing the sudden hot wetness on his face and the tingling sensation gushing through his veins. As blood ran down Philip's tanned face and trickled into his mouth, the rich, meaty taste briefly sated his bloodlust.

Having displayed all the valour of a trussed chicken and terrified by the death of his companion, Middleton's opponent dropped his sword like a hot coal and fell on his knees. Dragging him up by the scruff of his neck, Sir John held on to him.

"The dogs ran too fast," Talbot coughed, returning empty-handed.

"You were too slow," Middleton grinned, shaking his prisoner. "What'll we do with this one?"

"Hang him!" Talbot suggested, lunging threateningly at the two harlots huddled together.

The whimpering women looked at Philip and pointed to several sacks concealed in the long grass.

"They belong t' them!" one of them exclaimed, her voice as rough as her prematurely aged face.

Arbroth and the rest of Philip's men now appeared with the horses.

"Take a look!" Philip told his Scottish retainer, sleeving blood from his chin.

Removing a dagger from his belt, Arbroth sliced open one of the sacks and Philip moved towards the man held by Middleton.

"Here, mah lord," Arbroth chirped up, rummaging through the bag and producing a gold chalice and silver cross. "Thay 'ave pilfered this from a church, tha devils!"

Philip glared at Arbroth, for the Scot had done no less in France many years ago. Arbroth shrugged off the memory of a severe whipping he received on that occasion and turned his attention to the sacks' contents. Philip stepped up to the prisoner and looked him straight in the eye. Encouraged by the man's terrified bearing, Philip demanded to know the whereabouts of the old king. The captive stared into the wide-eyed, blood-streaked face of his inquisitor.

"I wouldn't tell thee if I knew," he sniffed, overcome by a surge of courage.

"He's found his balls," Talbot chuckled, leaning against a tree and folding his arms across his chest. "Cut them off and be done with it."

Philip sheathed his sword and rubbed his throbbing knuckles.

"My friend, you have robbed a church," he tutted, tracing an invisible cross on the man's face.

"So?"

"Shut your mouth!" Middleton snapped, shaking him violently by his collar.

Before the man could speak, Philip grabbed his cheeks with his sore hand and squeezed. Using his good hand he again drew his sword and thrust its point up into his bristly chin.

"Another word and it'll be your last," he vowed, the sharp tip forcing the prisoner to stretch his neck back.

"Kill the son of a bitch and be done with it," Talbot jeered, deliberately inflaming the situation.

"Don't listen to him," Middleton pleaded, as Philip eased his grip but kept the sword in place.

"Enough!" he hissed, glaring at the prisoner. "Where is Henry?"

The Lancastrian coughed and spittle flew from his mouth.

"Answer me?" Philip repeated.

"Go to the Dev –"

Before he could finish, Philip thrust the sword point up into his lower jaw. Gurgling blood and broken teeth, the Lancastrian fell forward. Middleton let him go.

"God save us," he gasped, turning aside.

"Too late for this one," Philip grunted, as blood ran down the steel and stained his hands.

With a sardonic grin, he let the man's weight drive the sword further into his head until it burst out of the skull. As the man's body slumped to the ground Philip stepped on his twitching neck and jerked the blade free. In a moment of blind rage, he had released all the pent-up anger bottled inside him since the cruel death of his brother. Closing his eyes Philip raised his bloody face to the sun and exhaled; killing always inspired a thrilling moment of surreal intoxication.

"You'd better kill them," Talbot sniffed, meaning the women.

"No!" Sir John objected.

"Have it your own way," Philip huffed, turning to the cowering harlots. "Where did they get it?" he asked, referring to the plunder.

The terrified woman looked at each other and shrugged their shoulders, while Robert Harrington took a towel from one of the packhorses and soaked it in the river.

Handing his sword to the teenager, Philip snatched the towel and pressed it against his hot, stinging face; and the water cooled his skin and calmed his temper.

"Go home," he told the women, rubbing blood and sweat from his face and hands, "and tell the people of Helmsley to come and bury these fools."

They nodded their understanding and looked at the sacks.

"Leave it," Talbot growled.

Raising their skirts, they bared their wool to Sir Thomas and ran off, cackling.

"Ugly crones," he scoffed.

"What's tah be done we-is?" Arbroth asked, searching through the sacks.

"Take anything of value and leave the rest," Talbot suggested, before Philip could respond.

"Return it to the church," Middleton objected. "They can –"

"It's booty," Philip said, sheathing his sword. "If you want your share, take it but make haste… We cannot tarry here: those who got away will be back, with others."

Walking to the river, Philip knelt down on the bank and plunged his head under the water. Holding his breath he swished his tangled, dusty hair in the cold, clear liquid before drawing it out with a spluttering gasp.

"Hurry!" he urged, dabbing his eyes dry and massaging his aching knuckles, while his men plundered the dead.

"Nearly ready," Philip's esquire said, walking over to his horse.

"What's up with him?" Philip asked, nudging his chin at Middleton, who was sitting sullenly in the saddle.

"Who knows?" Sir John's esquire replied.

"Mount!" Philip barked, swinging a leg over the saddle and wedging his arse in the hard curve.

"He's no' a happy man," Arbroth commented, coming up

beside his master, while his esquire attached Philip's spurs to his boots.

"I don't give a fig," Philip huffed, steering his palfrey out of the deathly silent camp.

The three knights, their esquires, retainers and servants, rode out of the valley and rode to Doncaster.

One week later

Despite the unseasonably humid weather, the lepers hobbling down the Great North Rd to Doncaster were dressed in heavy woollen cloaks, their heads and faces covered. A six-foot pole topped with a brass crucifix was carried out front as a warning for others to stay away. The pace was slow: it had taken them five days to travel the short distance from York to Pontefract, and Doncaster was still three leagues away. The leader of the group raised a bandaged hand, bringing his flock to a shuffling halt. Exploiting an inherent intuition, he leaned on his quarter staff and peered hard at the tree-lined curve in the road ahead. His perceptive hearing picked out the thud of horse hooves accompanied by the tinny, jangle of equine furnishings. Waiting until the sound became more distinct, he flagged a hand up and down, a signal for the others to get off the road. In a near panic, they dragged their disease-wracked bodies onto the grass verge.

Philip Neville and his company were riding north on the same stretch of road, having failed to find the old king in Doncaster. A lattice of overhanging branches covered in dense foliage formed a natural canopy over lengthy sections of the road, blocking out the sun and cooling the perspiration on their faces. Attired in a dark, red linen tunic and black hose, Philip rode beside his esquire, sweat dripping from his hair and coursing down his face in tickling rivulets. Slouched limply in the saddle, his head bobbed loosely, while the sword at his side thumped annoyingly against his thigh. Michael's murder, his failure to find Henry and the slaughter of Lord Roos' men near Helmsley were pushed to the back of his mind. Now he was tormented by the idea that if he did not ask his friend Francis for the hand of his sister, Isobel, another would come along and snatch her up, as had happened with Elizabeth Percy, a concern that forced the pace.

As he led his company out of the shady tunnel, Philip spotted pedestrians struggling to get off the road. Straightening himself in the saddle he shook the indolence from his mind and picked out the ominous clacking sound. Using his knees and a light touch of the reins, he brought his eleven-hundred-pound chestnut palfrey from a canter to a cautious trot, gesturing for those behind to slow down. The man waving the clapper above his head was issuing a warning for the horsemen to keep away, but curiosity drew them on. When they were barely two horse-lengths away, the lepers raised shallow wooden bowls that dangled from their rope belts.

"Charity, my Lords?" they wailed.

Their words and bandaged faces put the fear of God into Philip and he jerked his reins hard to the left. Fighting against the sharp pain in its jaw, his palfrey Clovis turned off the road, followed by the others who covered their mouths with a sleeve and crossed themselves. Once clear, Philip curved his horse back onto the old Roman road while the lepers lowered their bowls and congregated back on the highway. Philip's company came to a halt and he trotted back alone, watched by his bewildered men. As he approached the lepers they huddled together and drew their head coverings closer to hide the embarrassing lesions. The man with the clapper lifted it above his head and rotated it passionately, but Philip defied the warning until another thrust out a hand, imploring the inquisitive knight to come no nearer.

The leader of the group casually leaned on his staff, making no attempt to deter the horseman. Fearing trouble he fingered the outline of a dagger hidden beneath his cloak.

"Stay back my Lord. Do ye not see tha signs? We are unclean."

Philip allowed his palfrey to walk on until the animal's sensitive nostrils caught the tang of decay and baulked. Pressing his knees into Clovis's heaving ribcage, he patted its sweaty neck to soothe the anxious beast. Trying not to stare, Philip found his eyes drawn to the bandaged features of the hooded man standing before him.

"I mean you no harm," he said, using the back of his glove to wipe perspiration from his neck. "My name is Sir Philip Neville and I am on the king's business."

"What business does tha king have with the likes of us?"

"I seek the fugitive Henry of Lancaster."

Waving a hand across his mouth to rid himself of an irritating fly, the wary leper noted the white bear and ragged staff badge over Philip's left breast.

"Lord Warwick's man?" he asked, lowering the dirty bandage from his mouth.

Philip nodded, resting his hands on the pommel and winced at the chafing to his thighs, a condition caused by the abrasive edge of his velvet-covered wood saddle.

"I was an archer in his Lordship's retinue, and served his father afore him. 'Twas I who wounded tha Duke of Somerset's standard-bearer on St Albans field," the leper recalled proudly, smiling at the distant memory, but the moment was fleeting and with a reminiscent sigh he lifted the stained bandage back over his scabby mouth.

"What name are you called?" Philip asked, combing his fingers through Clovis's dusty mane.

"Ranulph... I was once the finest bowman in Calais," he

said proudly, lifting his right hand to reveal only a thumb and little finger. "Now I am nothing."

Philip flinched at the gruesome exhibit and Ranulph continued, his voice full of bitterness.

"I cut them off tah stop corruption from eating m' whole arm," he sneered, lowering his hand and allowing the long sleeve of his habit to cover the mangled stump. "Now I must beg for a piece of mouldy bread."

"But…" Philip began, only to be stopped by Ranulph's intolerant gaze.

"His Lordship dismissed me when he learned of my condition," he explained, anticipating the question and looking back at his flock. "These people took pity on me." He continued. "We're called unclean and sinful, and are forbidden tah enter a church," he whined, his tone hostile. "We are dying a little more each day, yet there's no sympathy for us."

Philip drew his legs away from the saddle to ease the stinging and cringed at the soreness, but showed no compassion for Ranulph's predicament.

"Where are you bound?"

"Tha shrine of St Thomas a Becket, at Canterbury," Ranulph revealed, drawing the damp bandage from his mouth. "We have not seen tha one you seek."

"That may be, but I must look you over," he said. "A thousand men are searching for Henry… The man's as slippery as an eel."

"Do what tha must," said Ranulph, his swollen feet forcing him to constantly shift his weight to relieve the agony.

"I'll not cause your people distress," Philip promised, clicking his tongue against the roof of his mouth as Ranulph stepped aside.

Philip wove a slow path through the lepers and they shuffled aside, allowing the warhorse to pass between them. Prudently holding his breath, he indicated for each member of the group to reveal his or her face before moving on to the next. The three women huddled together for safety and he tried to imagine what they might have looked like before the disease took hold. When lepers appeared in public, people would give money but only to be rid of them. They noticed the same look on the face of this reticent warrior, who inspected them with empathy-laced contempt.

Having checked half the group, he eased Clovis back to Ranulph who flipped the hood from his head. Pricking Clovis gently with his spurs, Philip tried not to show he was holding his breath. Struggling to stand still, Ranulph was helped by the leper carrying the cross-staff, but his badly deformed feet were nothing more than lumps of tortured flesh and the attempt was excruciatingly painful. Nevertheless, he inched his body up in a mute declaration of pride.

"You don't have tah fear us," he exclaimed, observing Philip leaning back in the saddle.

"'Tis not you I fear, only the pestilence you bear."

"Then tha know only a fool would join us."

"A fool," Philip said, dabbing a dew-drop of sweat from his chin, "or a desperate man."

"Some say Henry is blessed?" Ranulph revealed, crossing himself.

"Yes, and others say he is insane."

"Blessed or insane, he is a good man."

During the conversation with Ranulph, Philip kept a suspicious eye on his clan, looking for anything amiss.

"Tha look troubled, friend?" Ranulph said, noting his agitated posture.

"My troubles are nothing compared to yours," Philip replied, scratching his wet hair.

"We are all affected by this cousins' war," Ranulph said, signalling for his flock to prepare to leave.

"Arbroth!" Philip called gruffly, twisting his body in the

tight saddle and suffering a sharp twinge in the lower back for his trouble.

"Mah lord?"

"Fetch bread and wine!"

Jumping from his scruffy rouncey, Arbroth crossed to a pair of heavily laden sumpters, untied a bag and removed the requested items. Glaring at Philip's smirking esquire, he swept the tacky hair from his eyes and walked warily down the road, deliberately avoiding the lepers who watched him with tittering amusement.

Short and wiry, his round face and broken nose shrouded by a head of wild twisted hair, Arbroth had served Philip since fate threw them together during the French wars. A resourceful Scot who could find water in a desert, Philip relied on him to cover his back. Despite his gambling, disgusting personal habits and a penchant for cheating, Philip valued his loyalty.

Reaching his master, Arbroth offered up the items.

"It's not for me," he said, trying not to laugh.

Drawing a deep breath, Arbroth held it as he laid the food on the grass.

"Tha'll not catch it," Ranulph teased, poking a finger beneath the bandage around his face and scratching a festering sore under his right ear.

"God save us," Philip tutted at his behaviour. "Go back to the others."

"Do not rebuke him, m'Lord," said Ranulph, as the Scot scurried away. "What we don't know frightens us."

"When you reach Canterbury, find a priest and ask him to offer forty masses for my brother's soul," Philip said, opening his gloved hand to reveal a Rose Noble. "And this is for your trouble," he added, producing a second gold coin.

Lifting the bowl hanging from his waist, Ranulph held it for Philip to drop the coins in.

"God bless thee," he nodded.

Winding the reins around his left hand, Philip watched Ranulph secure the money before thrusting his arm out.

"Do you have the courage tah take it?"

Blinking nervously Philip eyed the scab-swamped, two-fingered stump and reacted without thinking. Clamping the end of his fingers of his right hand between his teeth, he yanked the glove free and shook the diseased hand. Ranulph saw his features contort and grinned.

"May St Christopher guide you on your journey," Philip said, drawing his hand away diplomatically before steering Clovis back to his waiting retainers.

"Godspeed!" Ranulph called after him.

Rejoining his entourage, Philip leapt from the saddle and hurried over to Arbroth, holding out his right hand, fingers splayed.

"Quickly," he hissed. "Do we have vinegar?"

"Aye," Arbroth nodded, looking confused at the rest of the men idling beside their mounts.

"Then get it!" Philip snapped. "And hurry."

The Scot feverishly untied several straps on one of the bags and removed a small brown jug. Tugging the wood stopper free, he offered it to Philip.

"I don't want to drink it, you cod-head, pour it on my hand!"

Sprinkling the brown, acidic liquid over Philip's extended fingers, Arbroth muttered under his breath as he wiped off the excess with a towel.

"My Lord, you can only catch leprosy from swiving an infected woman," one of his mounted men-of-arms chirped.

"Don't talk shit!" Talbot countered. "'Tis a punishment from God."

"For an educated man you sound like a fool," Middleton scoffed, a comment that spawned an argument.

"Enough!" Philip snapped, rubbing the area between

thumb and forefinger, and examining his hand for signs of corruption. "Mount up."

While the knights and their retinues regrouped on the road, Ranulph shepherded his people southwards. The donation from Philip would allow them to find shelter and eat for a month. As they set off, the man holding the brass crucifix adjusted the bandage covering his nose and mouth.

"Come," Ranulph said, laying a fatherly hand on his shoulder. Jerking his hand off, he stood watching the horsemen ride away.

"We must go," Ranulph insisted.

"He did not know me?"

"Praise God," Ranulph said. "Do we use the money to pay for a priest to say mass for his brother?"

"Why waste it?"

The two men joined their friends and they continued their journey to Doncaster. Leading his companions in the opposite direction, Philip glanced over his shoulder, convinced he had missed something. Shrugging the thought from his mind, he allowed his memory to slip back eight weeks and the reason why he was on such a wild goose chase.

When Bamburgh surrendered in July, Philip's brother Michael, a Lancastrian knight, disguised himself to blend in with the other prisoners. When these men were released, Michael headed west. Informed by the garrison priest of Michael's presence among the prisoners, Lord Warwick sent a detachment of horse in hot pursuit. Forced back to Bamburgh, Michael found himself cornered below the north wall. Given the option to fight his brother Philip in single combat or face trial and execution, Michael had no other choice. The brothers fought until a crossbow bolt, fired from the wall, killed Michael.

Warwick's herald, Davy Griffiths, swore he had received written instructions from his lordship that Michael must not live, but the Earl denied issuing such an order. Griffiths said Michael was killed by a Burgundian crossbowman and swore Lord Warwick had sanctioned the execution. After watching Michael's body float out to sea, Philip stormed off in a rage. Warwick had the assassin swiftly executed and dispatched his herald to Calais for his own safety. Later he sent a message, through his brother John, for Philip to leave Bamburgh and pursue the fugitive King Henry. To boost his command, two recalcitrant knights were assigned to him. Philip's page, Ashley Dean, was ordered to Sheriff Hutton for training, but he was permitted to keep his esquire.

The onus of telling Lady Joan Beaufort of her son's death was taken up by Philip's friend, Francis Talbot. Dreading having to face his mother, Philip gratefully accepted the offer. Arbroth was sent to York to sell part of the Bamburgh plunder and, for the next seven weeks, Philip and his companions criss-crossed northern England in search of the royal fugitive but found no sign of him.

In late August, Philip was reunited with Arbroth at the royal castle of Conisborough, near Doncaster, and was told something that sent him into a fit of pique. After hearing the heart-breaking news of Michael's slaying, Philip's mother had joined her husband at Whitby. Arbroth rode hard to catch her but arrived too late: Lady Joan and Sir William had sailed for France.

When he heard this news, Philip walked over to a water trough, placed his hands against the wall for leverage and lashed out, kicking the trough into kindling. Unable to comprehend such gratuitous violence, Middleton exchanged a concerned look with Thomas Talbot. Later that day, Philip and his men left Conisborough in silence and headed for Helmsley, where they slaughtered Lord Roos' men several days later.

As the lepers limped south on the Doncaster road, Philip

led his party north and spent the night at Pontefract Castle. Next morning he set off to continue the search for Henry. After eight back-breaking days in the saddle, Philip offered Middleton and Talbot leave to visit their families. Disturbed by his increasing volatility, they accepted, and the group disbanded in Newcastle. Philip took his retainers to Seward House, his mother's home ten miles south of York, where he planned to divvy up the remaining spoils looted from Bamburgh. The morning after that, he moved to Claremont Hall, the family townhouse in York.

During his time in the city, Philip paid several visits to the Talbots for news of Isobel, but with Francis overseeing repairs to Bamburgh, he knew she would not leave her home in Ashby-de-la-Zouch. Without his mother and brother Thomas, Claremont Hall was a damp, soulless house, forcing Philip to spend his evenings at the Sign of the Bull, a tavern in Coney Street. Unemployed soldiers from the Calais garrison made the Bull their haunt and frittered away the time drinking, playing cards and putting the world to right. Recognising the white bear and ragged staff badge on his red livery coat, they invited Philip to join them, and in the dimly lit main hall they reminisced and re-fought old battles. Philip's exhausted mind easily surrendered to the mind-numbing effects of strong wine and the conversation eventually drifted into slurred nonsense. Soon most of those at the table were sprawled face down in spilt wine and cold food. This ritual was repeated every night for several weeks.

Chapter 2

BY THE END of the first week of October, Philip Neville was ready to leave York. Men and horses were rested and the last of the Bamburgh plunder had been sold or swapped. Some of the men bought clothes or boots, others wasted their share gambling and drinking, but everyone felt revitalized. Standing beside his palfrey, Philip watched his hooknosed groom Daniel tighten the leather girth strap, while his mounted esquire chatted with the recently arrived retainers of Middleton and Talbot.

Robert Harrington's roving eye latched on to several maidens on their way to the Tuesday butter market, near St Martin's Church, but his poor attempt at flirting failed when they ignored him and walked on. With his cheeks aglow and Arbroth grinning at his humiliation, he tried to cover his embarrassment by drawing his hair down to conceal the deep forehead scar, caused by a kick from a horse when he was a page.

"Let's go," Philip commanded, locking the fingers of his hands together and stretching his arms before mounting.

The herd of palfreys, rounceys and sumpters shuffled and snorted, throwing horsehair and fine dust in the air. The animals were quickly brought under control and Philip's groom wound the reins of the packhorse around his fingers. Using words that would send a Bishop into a fit, he forced the overloaded sumpters to submit to his authority.

As the animals were pushed and slapped into line, Philip's men noticed a distinct pealing of bells. While they waited for the order to move, the dull clanging rose in volume until an inconsistent opus filled the air. The group turned to Philip for an answer but he was equally perplexed.

"Perhaps they ring an elegy for the late archbishop?" the kindly Middleton suggested, referring to the recently deceased Archbishop of York, William Booth, who had died a few weeks before.

"Perhaps?" Philip contemplated crossing his chest.

"That's no funereal dirge," Sir Thomas commented.

"You there!" Philip barked at a passer-by.

The bony-faced rat catcher, his dirt-ingrained clothing coated in a greasy film, stopped abruptly.

"Yeh?" he scowled, allowing the bulging sack to slip from his hunched shoulder.

"What's happening?"

Tugging hard on a rope leash to stop his mangy cat tearing the sack open, the rat-catcher frowned.

"The bells, you rogue!" Harrington shouted above the reverberations. "Why do they ring?"

"For king's marriage," the man huffed.

"The king's marriage?" Middleton echoed, surprised. "Whom has the king married?"

The rat catcher wiped his nose in his frayed cuff, leaving a three-inch trail of slime on the garment.

"A widow woman."

"You lying toad!" Talbot barked.

"'Tis true!" the rat catcher insisted, grinding up a gobbet of phlegm from his lungs, pursing his lips and firing the thick, dark liquid at his annoying cat.

"Get about your business," Philip hissed, dismissing him with a flick of his wrist, while his cat rolled around in the dust.

"My Christ's blood," Middleton gasped.

"What'll we do?" Harrington appended, goaded into speaking by Talbot.

Philip's features broadened into a grin, as the rat-man swung the sack up over his shoulder and dragged his cat away.

"My Lord?" said Harrington, perplexed by Philip's smugness.

"My cousin Warwick seeks the hand of the fairest princess in all Europe for the king, and Edward is wedded a widow?" he said, dismounting.

"What do we do?" Middleton sniffed.

"I don't know about you but I'm for Neville's Inn," Philip declared, referring to Warwick's townhouse in Walmgate. "I must know more; we'll leave here tomorrow."

The three knights and their esquires walked to Neville's Inn while their men took the horses to the castle stables before dispersing, happy to spend another day in the taverns. Removing their swords, Philip and his companions congregated around a long table in a room on the first floor of the hostelry, where they were served food and wine by the steward.

"Where's your master?" Middleton asked, referring to Warwick.

"My *new master* is with the king," the haughty steward replied, directing a server to fill the wooden cups set on the table.

"Where?" Philip snapped, frowning at his hostility.

"Reading."

"Reading, 'my Lord'!" Philip growled.

Talbot decided to have a little fun at a young server's expense: as the lad hurried around the table to fill his cup, he deliberately jerked his arm back, causing the server to spill his wine.

"Clumsy oaf!" Talbot bellowed, flicking red wine into the server's terrified face and jumping to his feet.

"Forgive me, my Lord…," he spluttered, visibly scared and dabbing Sir Thomas's fingers with a towel.

"You snivelling wretch," Talbot said, pushing the server away and grinning at Harrington. "Look what you've done."

The esquire was unimpressed and thought he should have grown out of such teasing.

"Enough, my Lord," Philip sighed, as the waiter tried to compose himself and wiped the floor. "Do you measure your courage by abusing a poor fool who cannot defend himself?"

Talbot glowered at Philip, while Middleton shook his head. Snatching up his cup Sir Thomas downed the wine in one long gulp, belched loudly and looked around, defying anyone to object.

Philip was about to leap out of his seat when the door opened, culling the tension.

"Apologies, gentlemen!" an unexpected visitor shouted.

"John Boon?" Philip gasped, barely recognising the dusty stranger.

"Well, well, Philip Neville?" the other responded.

A quiet, innocuous fellow, John Boon posed as a horse trader but kept his real work of spying for the Earl of Warwick secret. Philip knew Boon as an amusing conversationalist with a keen eye for fine horses and married women.

"I heard you were in France?" Philip said, after introducing his companions.

"I was." Boon yawned, removing his hat and using it to slap dust from his sweat-stained coat, before drawing up a chair. "I hear York has widows aplenty; there'll be rich picking for a man with a yard as big as mine," he boasted.

"These Lancastrian whores will slit your throat as soon as look at you," Talbot warned.

Boon sniggered at this comment, snatched Harrington's cup and filled it to overflowing. Channelling the contents between his parched, cracked lips, he closed his eyes and released a somnolent gasp.

"I needed that." He coughed harshly, rubbing his tired, bloodshot eyes and looking at those around the table. "What do we have here... a plot?"

"No plot, sir," Harrington said, miffed by his curtness.

"We seek Henry of Lancaster," Philip revealed, glancing at his esquire and signalling him not to react.

"You'll not find him in the bottom of a cup," Boon smirked.

"Has anyone told you you're not funny?" Philip sniffed.

"Many times,"

"They were right," Philip chuckled. "Why are you here?"

"I come from the council at Reading with a message for Lord Warwick's brother, Sir John," he explained. Exhaustion was causing his eyelids to droop but he rallied enough to add a scathing indictment. "The king has married a woman not fit to be queen."

"By St George!" Talbot growled, jumping to his feet. "Then it's true."

"Who is this woman?" Philip asked.

"Elizabeth Woodville."

"But her husband died fighting for Henry of Lancaster," Talbot revealed.

"This unholy union will stir up a storm that will reach into every corner of the kingdom," Middleton predicted.

Opinions on the king's marriage were bounced across the table like tennis balls, but Philip was eager to know more and demanded silence.

"Before the king revealed his news he assembled his council," Boon explained, reaching around to scratch an irritating wart on the back of his neck while his audience waited. "At that council, Lord Warwick explained the need for a treaty with France, but many doubted Louis's sincerity, and proof of a French plot against this realm was unveiled."

"Go on," Talbot pressed, captivated by Boon's west-country dialect.

"Lord Warwick said it was all lies and their evidence should be sent to Louis for him to prove or disprove, the council agreed."

Everyone at the table was mesmerized by Boon's revelations; even the steward was listening in.

"Someone asked the king for his thoughts on marriage," he continued. "Edward replied that he desired to be wed but that his choice of bride might not please everyone. The council thought he was in jest and Lord Warwick asked which lady caught his fancy."

Boon sated his thirst before continuing and Philip sat back, folded his arms and tried to imagine the scene.

"'Elizabeth Woodville,' Edward said and the chamber went silent. His Grace the Archbishop of Canterbury agreed that the Lady Elizabeth was indeed beautiful and virtuous, but she was neither the daughter of a prince nor a duke, and he reminded Edward she had two sons by her first husband. The king urged his uncle to sit and Lord Warwick said he had been working hard to find the king a wife fit to be his queen."

Boon's narrative was interrupted by a hacking cough and he waved for the server to refill his cup.

Alarmed by Boon's startling disclosures, Philip absorbed it all but kept silent. Wiping the spillage off his grizzled chin, the drowsy messenger continued.

"Sir John Wenlock was agitated, for he was in negotiation with the French king for the hand of his sister-in-law, the Lady Bona of Savoy, as the ideal choice for Edward. The archbishop begged his nephew to reconsider."

Philip's esquire sneezed and apologised, and Boon was set to unfold the most dramatic moment of the royal council.

"The king said it was all too late; that he was married and had been for several months. Lord Warwick's anger was plain to see. The archbishop asked the name of Edward's wife, but all now knew it. When he confirmed their fears, an atmosphere of betrayal swept through the room. The councillors looked to Lord Warwick for guidance but he was still in shock."

Philip was appalled by the king's choice, but Edward had defied Warwick and made him look foolish in front of the council. Sipping wine, he smirked into his cup, for it was Warwick who had initiated the breakdown of his own relationship with Elizabeth Percy.

"By the holy relics," Middleton gasped, as the news sank in.

"Calm yourself, my Lord," Boon advised. "On Michaelmas day lord Warwick presented the queen to the council at Reading Abbey, and she received the homage of the lords."

"I wish I could have been there," Philip chuckled.

"It is said the king's mother scolded him for his choice of bride," Boon added.

"God bless her," Philip smirked.

"Gentlemen, I am in much need of sleep," Boon yawned, "for I have another long ride on the morrow."

Philip nodded and John Boon stood up, his shaky legs barely able to support his weight.

"What news!" Philip smiled as Boon left the room, but there was very little reaction; everyone at the table looked stunned.

When John Boon left the next morning, Philip had his esquire round up the men and horses. After a short delay, the company assembled in the tiny courtyard of Claremont Hall. As the Minster bells rang out the hour of Sext, 9.30 a.m., Philip led the mounted column through the crowded streets and out of Micklegate Bar a day later than planned. He would spend the next three months riding across the North Country, brooding over personal anxieties. Dissatisfaction sprinkled with antipathy caused arguments between the knights and their retainers, most of whom blamed Philip for keeping them on the road. His familial affiliation with the king and the brutal slaying of Roos' men at Helmsley were enough to quell any thought of mutiny.

Late on Christmas Eve 1464, a bedraggled, strung-out column of horsemen and a single wagon crossed Canongate Burn, a shallow tributary of the River Aln. Trotting through the narrow streets of Alnwick, in the county of Northumberland, they rode along Balliffgate up to the well-lit barbican of the Castle. Wrapped in heavy cloaks and furs stiff with ice, their boots and hose caked in frozen mud, they were challenged by a guard looking down from the Barbican. Dehydrated and exhausted, Philip painfully sat upright in the saddle to announce himself, and the great gates groaned open. Thomas Talbot motioned for the driver of the cart, holding four shivering prisoners, to move.

As the cart trundled forward, its iron-rimmed wheels skidded on the ice covering the drawbridge. Dragging a sleeve under his sore, red nose, Philip nudged his trembling horse on. Crossing the drawbridge he remembered his last visit to Alnwick. It was the day his cousin Warwick took him to see a captive, Elizabeth Percy, and the moment their future together died. When the outer doors slammed shut, an inner set grated open and Philip came back to the present. The steward, waiting in the inner bailey, signalled an attendant to take Philip's bridle.

"Welcome to Alnwick." The steward shivered, blowing on his hands to keep out the chill. "I am Thomas Archer. Sir John bids thee welcome and invites thee to spend Christmastide with him."

"I have prisoners," Philip managed, struggling to articulate his numb, cracked lips, while the cart disgorged its miserable cargo.

"What is their crime?" Archer asked, watching the driver aggressively poke the captives from the wagon with a pole.

"They deny Edward his kingship."

"They do?" The steward tutted, turning to several guards sheltering near the doors of the Great Tower, and flicking a finger. "Then they will live to regret it."

The guards drew their swords and crunched over the frosty courtyard.

"Take them to the *Oublier!*" Archer commanded.

"The what?" Philip coughed, dabbing his lips.

"A basement with neither door nor window, nor candle and reached only through a trapdoor. Once that door is shut they'll have time to reflect on their treachery."

Roped together, hands tied in front, the captives were shoved towards the Great Tower by the guards.

"What do you wish done with them?" Archer asked. "We cannot keep them here for long."

"Interrogate them, Mr Archer, interrogate them hard and send them on to Lord Warwick," Philip said, removing his riding gloves and scratching his frozen whiskers.

The steward, his untidy brows cutting a dark brooding line across his forehead, nodded.

"Where is his Lordship?" Philip enquired.

"At prayer," Archer revealed, pointing to the Chapel, a building on the far side of the Castle in front of the Constable's Tower. "Rooms have been prepared and there's a fire to warm you."

"Good." Philip coughed. "My yard is frozen to my bollocks," he said, dismounting delicately.

Grateful to be out of the saddle, Philip pulled the wet hose away from his legs and ordered his groom to attend to the horses. The steward escorted the three knights and their esquires to a pair of octagonal towers guarding a series of buildings known as the Great Keep. Once in his assigned chamber, Philip, with the help of a servant, removed his clothes. Using a block of soap and hot water, he scrubbed the caked sweat and entrenched dirt from his skin. After drying he moisturised his lips with a balm given to him by his mother before wrapping a towel around his aching body and collapsing onto a bed. After a short nap, he put on a fresh shirt and dressed in his damp doublet and hose, which had been brushed down, partly dried and sprayed with scent. Reluctantly he shuffled out of the warm room and joined his knightly companions in the Great Hall for a supper of bream, herrings, eel and codling; Christmas Eve being a fasting day, no meat was served.

Sir John Neville was attending Angel's or Midnight Mass, in the Church of St Michael and St Mary's, Alnwick, but he left orders for Philip to join him on Christmas morning for the Shepherd's Mass. For his victory at Hexham Warwick's brother was endowed with the title 'Earl of Northumberland' and given most of the confiscated Percy estates. With his pregnant wife and young son, he settled down in Alnwick to enjoy his new life.

Shortly after dawn next morning, the Earl of Northumberland, his wife Isabel and a full congregation stood waiting impatiently in the Castle Chapel. Despite several blazing braziers placed outside the door, the wind found its way in and breached the cloaks and furs of even the best dressed. A commotion outside drew all attention to the door, which suddenly flew open allowing cold air to blow in.

"Close it!" the agitated priest barked.

Before the door could be shut, Philip's esquire tripped over the threshold, followed by Philip and his two knights. After waking late they bolted to the chapel, drawing on belts and hooking up doublets as they went.

Thomas Talbot slammed the door behind him and bowed apologetically to the Chaplain.

"Welcome!" The elderly clergyman offered, his breath cloudy in the cold atmosphere. "Find a place, and quickly."

Philip dipped his fingers in the holy water stoup, inside the door, went down on one knee and touched the freezing liquid to his forehead and both breasts. His companions did the same and followed him as he forced his way through the disgruntled crowd to a spot behind his cousin. The priest grabbed the sides of the altar and shook his head intolerantly while the latecomers switched places several times before settling.

"Are we ready?" he huffed, straightening the white altar cloth and staring at Philip.

Philip responded with a sharp nod and the Chaplain muttered something under his breath before continuing.

The service consisted of readings from the gospels, the homily and the Eucharist, liberally sprinkled with prayers. Philip stood for what seemed hours, bored by it all, and his mind began to wander. He thought of his men slaughtered in the Forest of Galtres, on his order, and compared it to the killing of Roos' men near Helmsley. Looking up at the ceiling, he recalled the death of his brother at Bamburgh and his father's still unresolved murder. Blowing on his hands, he ground his teeth and muttered to himself. Shaking his head, he began conjuring up lustful images in his mind. He knew he shouldn't have such thoughts on this, the holiest of days, but he couldn't help himself. Shuffling uneasily, he felt the pressure building in his hose as he mentally undressed Isobel Talbot.

"Dear God," he sighed, unintentionally.

Those standing in front turned and tutted at his disrespect.

"Forgive me," he whispered awkwardly.

The priest frowned at the interruption before continuing with Mass, but Philip quickly returned to his carnal imagery. A sharp dig in the ribs from Middleton caused him to cough, and he silently apologised to the elderly knight. Spotting the incident the chaplain tutted at the continuing disturbance but refused to break his stride. The service went on and Philip grew more disinterested. He folded his arms, he unfolded them; he shifted from foot to foot and blew his intolerance through lacerated lips. His ennui finally ended when the Chaplain finished the service with a Latin blessing.

"*Benedicat vos omnipotens deus pater, et filius, et spiritus sanctus,* Amen!"

"Amen," the congregation echoed, crossing themselves.

"Amen," Philip gasped, swiftly tracing a cross on his chest. "Thanks be –"

Standing in front of Philip, Lady Isabel looked at her husband and raised her eyebrows at their guest's irreverence.

"What now, my Lord?" Philip asked, tapping the Earl's shoulder.

"First we eat, then you and I will pay a visit to some of my tenants," he grinned.

"My Lord?" Philip questioned, rolling his eyes at his grinning esquire while the congregation filed out of the Chapel.

"I need to show these people that I can be as generous as their old master. My poor Isabel has not recovered from giving birth to our daughter, so you will take her place," he explained, lovingly wrapping an arm around his wife's shoulder. "The people of Alnwick have much affection for their old Percy overlords but show me nothing but contempt."

"Hang a few and the rest will kiss your feet," Philip said, his proposal causing Isabel to frown. "My lady." He apologised.

John tried not to smile at his wife's discomfort, as the cold December air blew the taste of incense into Philip's throat, causing him to cough.

"To the food," Northumberland announced, pointing at the Chaplain. "And you, Father, will join us."

"Thank you, my son," the grateful cleric said, before frowning at Philip.

While the Earl and his guests quickly crossed the middle bailey to the Great Hall, they could hear the bells of St Michael and St Mary tolling down in the town.

"What do I tell the men?" Harrington asked.

"Tell them they may do as they please today," Philip replied. "But no gambling."

The esquire bowed low to the Earl of Northumberland, and backed out.

After a late breakfast-early lunch of wild boar, pork, chicken, goose, custards and tarts, washed down with jugs of wine, Northumberland, his wife and their guests watched a play presenting the story of Christ and performed by a group of masked mummers. While the audience booed King Herod, Philip and his cousin left the hall, cocooned themselves in thick cloaks and walked out into a fresh fall of snow. Mounting their horses, they trotted to the gatehouse accompanied by six men-at-arms.

"Snow?" Philip mused, staring up at the low, leaden sky.

Guiding his party out through the barbican, Northumberland headed for a stone bridge that spanned the Aln. As they approached the bridge, several pedestrians pressed their bodies into one of the passing recesses and waited for the horsemen to cross.

The eight mounted men trotted over the bridge in pairs.

"What did you say?" Philip snapped, jerking his head around and drawing up his horse.

"Nothing," one of the men on foot sneered.

"You god-damned knave!" Philip barked, reversing Clovis back to the middle of the bridge.

"Leave it," Northumberland groaned.

Ignoring his cousin, Philip nudged his palfrey in close and forced the two men against the hard, V-shaped stone alcove.

"What say you now?" he scowled, as Clovis's dilated nostrils snorted a cloud of moist breath in their terrified faces. "You craven dogs!"

The cowering men tried to push the warhorse back, but Philip tapped spurs to flanks. Snatching the velvet hat off his head, he used it to annoy Clovis's tail, causing him to rear up.

"Cousin!" Northumberland yelled, frustrated by his behaviour. "Stop, I say."

The terrified men raised their hands to shield their faces from the deadly hooves until Philip was satisfied and trotted on.

"Merry Christmas," he called back, weaving his horse onto the slippery north bank and coming up beside his annoyed cousin.

"I do my best to win these people over and you come along and destroy my work," Sir John complained.

"You must not show weakness, my Lord."

"And you must learn to obey," Philip's cousin fumed, urging his horse on.

"My Lord!"

"Have a care, cousin, have a care."

Following the river, the party rode on to Alnwick Abbey, half a mile away. En route they stopped at a dozen cottages where the Earl presented his tenants with a monetary gift and offered seasonal greetings. The snow soon began falling harder, bringing memories of Towton back to Philip. Touching his left shoulder, he winced at the moment a poleaxe sliced deep into his flesh and groaned as the psychological pain of that day returned.

"Are you unwell?" Northumberland asked, noting his hurt expression.

"No, my Lord, 'tis nought but the cold."

"Tomorrow I entertain my tenants," Sir John revealed. "'Twould be better if you leave in the morning…"

"As you wish, my Lord," Philip agreed, looking over a landscape covered with a blanket of white.

Burdened with snow the branches of evergreen trees were bending and cracking under the strain, while glistening icicles hung from their lower limbs. As they rode on the rushing waters of the River Aln had a strange effect on Philip. For him winter was not a good time; the land was stark, silent and empty, and a constant ache bored deep into his bones and stayed there until spring.

At first glance, the differences between Philip and John were not obvious. Both were well dressed and looked the same age, and both rode horses in prime condition; but here the similarities ended. Indentured to Northumberland's older brother Warwick, Philip's two manors lay in ruins, generating very little income for him to pay his retainers. The twelve soldiers and servants he commanded vowed to stay with him as long as their families could survive. The sixty marks a year paid him by Warwick and his share of the Bamburgh plunder temporarily alleviated his tenant's distress. Since losing Elizabeth, through the efforts of Warwick and the king's chamberlain, Philip had found a new love but his thoughts kept drifting back to his former sweetheart.

Unlike Philip, John Neville had received the highest accolades for his service to the crown. Knighted at Greenwich, he was created Lord Montague eleven years later, and Knight of the Garter shortly thereafter. Devoted to his brother and loyal to Edward, John was a fearsome warrior with a swarthy complexion, firm jaw and untrusting eyes. Twice captured in combat, he later fought and won the battles of Hedgeley Moor, and Hexham, for which he was elevated to the Earldom of Northumberland. During the march to Hedgeley Moor, John Neville survived an ambush only through Philip's timely intervention.

The Earl of Northumberland soon ran out of money.

"The goose was too rich," he belched, spitting a gobbet of sour bile onto the snow.

"Perhaps it was too much wine, my Lord," Philip grinned, flicking water off his nose.

"The king's marriage has angered my brother beyond measure," John said, groaning at the burning sensation in his stomach. "But I couldn't give a fig; Edward will never stay true to one woman and when the widow's belly is full he will bed another – and who knows?"

"I fear the Nevilles will suffer for the king's patronage of the Woodvilles," Philip warned, dabbing his stinging lips.

Northumberland twisted in the saddle and gestured through the curtain of falling snow for his dawdling men-at-arms to close up.

"What will Richard do?" Philip asked.

"I don't know. Since the king's marriage, the Woodville tree has blossomed."

"They are nothing but a brood of bastards who will seduce our cousin," Philip said.

"They must be stopped," John warned, as they passed Alnwick Abbey and rode on to Monks Bridge, half a mile distant. "The queen is planning to wed her kin to the highest in the land," he added. "'Tis rumoured her brother John is to wed our aunt, Katherine."

"But she is thrice his age!" Philip gasped, dragging back the reins and forcing Clovis to shake his wet mane violently. "And such a union will make him our uncle."

Realising his error Philip released his grip and gently patted Clovis's neck.

Northumberland pointed to a distant bridge and slapped powdery snow from his hat.

"We'll cross there and return home."

As the insipid sun began to set and the temperature

dropped markedly, Philip and his cousin nudged their horses into a canter, making the return trip much quicker.

As he crossed Alnwick's drawbridge a familiar sound caught Philip's ear. Before he could react, Clovis's forelegs buckled and the beast fell and skidded, tipping him out of the saddle. Crashing heavily to the ground, he slid on the ice, grazing his arms. Recovering, he jumped up to conceal his embarrassment and cursed the guards smirking at his misfortune?

"Are you hurt?" Northumberland yelled, while Philip's shaken charger got to its feet, screaming.

"Only my pride," he lied, wiping muddy slush from his hose and massaging his scraped elbows.

One of the guards grabbed Clovis's bridle and calmed the panicking beast while Philip dabbed his freshly bleeding lips.

"M'lord," another guard announced. "See here?" he said, pointing to a crossbow bolt sticking out of Clovis's trembling rump.

Northumberland leapt from his horse and he and Philip examined the injury.

"Find him now!" the Earl demanded, while Philip removed his gloves and rubbed his throbbing fingers.

"I'll have your horse taken care of."

"Don't concern yourself, my Lord," Philip countered. "My groom will see to him."

"I want him alive!" Northumberland yelled, as a dozen armed men scattered in search of the would-be assassin.

While Clovis was led off to the stables, Philip and his cousin joined the guests, seated on several rising tiers of benches, inside the decorated hall. In the warm, wine-soaked atmosphere Philip soon forgot his troubles; drinking too much wine, he gasped at the synchronised tumbling of acrobats and snoozed as balladeers sang. Believing the bolt was meant for his cousin, Philip put the incident from his mind. Soon he was laughing raucously at a pair of performers, who jumped through hoops, trying – and failing – not to break the eggs balanced on their heads.

Chapter 3

ON 29 DECEMBER, the feast day of St Thomas à Becket, Philip Neville, riding a sturdy, long-haired rouncey, led his men out of Alnwick Castle. Clovis, his wound cleaned and stitched, would recover; but the assailant was never found.

For the next three months, Philip pursued one cold trail after another. Tempers frayed and arguments between the three knights became the norm. Finally, on a windy spring day near Scarborough on the Yorkshire coast, Thomas Talbot had had enough.

"I'm leaving," he snapped, waving his retainers out of line, "and taking my men with me!"

"You can go to Hell for all I care!" Philip yelled after him, angrily squeezing the handle of his sword.

"I'll wait for you there!" Talbot scoffed, riding away.

"Son of a bitch!" Philip spat, his words diminished by the roar of the sea. "He'll pay for this."

"Let him go," Middleton said, attempting to calm the situation. "We're better off without him."

"This is a waste of time; no one's seen hide nor hair of Henry," Philip hissed, palming the sweat of aggravation from his face. "And we're wearing out horses for nothing."

"We have no choice."

"None whatsoever," Philip groaned, leading the reduced column up the coast to Whitby.

While Philip and his men wore themselves out, spring

turned to summer, new shoots appeared on bare branches and fresh grass sprouted from the wet ground. A refreshingly warm breeze dried muddy trails and blew away the cobwebs. To sleep on soft, fragrant grass and wake under the rays of a warm sun was a pleasant change for men used to shivering beneath damp blankets. Decent food and clean clothes boosted morale and an air of confidence cheered the group, but it didn't last. By the end of the first week in July, Philip was leading his dusty company through Bootham Bar and into York, having achieved nothing. Rumours of a rift between Warwick and his cousin the king abounded: the talk was that they had argued bitterly, with Warwick refusing to attend the queen's coronation. The gossip proved false. Edward and Warwick had fallen out briefly but by the time the king revealed Elizabeth to his council at Reading, they had made up. Warwick missed the queen's coronation only because Edward sent him to Calais.

Riding along High Petergate into the heart of York, Philip had an epiphany and stopped suddenly.

"I must speak to the king," he told Middleton. "And tell him Henry has gone from these shores."

"I'll go home. I've wasted a year of my life," Middleton said, his voice as broken down as the horse between his legs, "and I'm not getting any younger."

The two knights shook hands and parted company. Turning into St Saviourgate, Philip dismounted and led his horse the rest of the way. Arriving at Claremont Hall, the family home, he sent most of the men to Seward House to rest, but insisted they return on Lammas Day, 1 August.

"Stable the horses," he told his Scot, pushing open the gate that led into a tiny courtyard.

Arbroth acknowledged the order by tapping his forehead. Arching his back, Philip stretched out his arms and turned to his armourer, Walter.

"Clean the rust from my armour," he said, handing Walter his blade, "and sharpen this."

The bushy-browed, grizzled armourer laid Philip's sword in the crook of his muscular arm and motioned for all weapons to be handed over. With a full load, Walter kicked open the door of the shuttered forge and entered. While his Scot took the horses to be stabled in York Castle, Philip tried the front door but found it locked. Making a fist, he pummelled the oak until he heard a metallic click. The door opened, but something behind it stopped him entering.

"Open up."

A suspicious eye and a shadowy strip of pock-marked cheek appeared in the gap.

"M'lord?" the young servant gasped, opening the door fully.

"What's going on here, Gilbert?" Philip demanded, looking suspiciously inside.

"'Tis not safe, sir," he answered nervously. "Tha city is full o' rogues."

"Don't worry about them," Philip scoffed, gesturing for his esquire. "Tell cook to prepare food."

"'Tis only me an Arthur here, some of tha servants are at Seward House, tha rest went with Lady Joan and…"

Philip cut Gilbert off with an angry glare before he mentioned William Beaufort by name.

"I know, lad," he said, his tone less abrasive. "Throw something in a pot and warm it up. I'm so hungry I could eat my horse."

Walking through the dark hall, Philip looked around mournfully, while outside Clovis gave a belligerent whinny.

"Is that old goat still alive?" he asked, smirking at his palfrey's reaction and referring to Arthur, the oldest member of the household. "He must be a hundred."

"'Undred and one, m'Lord," Gilbert grinned. "Sir Francis is in town."

"Have you heard from your mistress?"

"Lady Joan and tha brother Thomas 'ave gone ta France…"

Philip sniffed and paced, his irritated footsteps echoing off the panelled walls.

"Well, don't stand out there!" he commanded, shouting at his esquire lurking in the doorway. "Come on in."

Philip went upstairs to his old room and removed his heavily soiled clothes, before washing weeks of dust, dirt and horsehair from his body. Eyeing the ugly wound he sustained at Towton, he ran a finger over the puckered, scarred tissue that ran down to a point beneath his left shoulder. After a rest, he dressed and went downstairs to share a suckling pig with his esquire.

"I'm going to pay a visit to Francis," he announced.

"Shall I go with you?"

"No, he'll boor the braies off you," Philip sighed, deliberately placing his napkin on the table and rising. "You can use my brother's room."

Robert gave a tight-lipped nod before moping up his gravy with a chunk of bread.

"By the saints!" Philip gasped at the severe ache in his back as he turned to Gilbert. "Don't lock me out."

The pock-marked servant nodded and Philip stepped away from the table.

"Keep some for Walter," he commanded, watching his esquire greedily spooning another portion onto his plate.

Harrington guiltily scrapped some of the food back into the pan as he left.

Philip knocked on the door of the Talbot home, a house nestled at the end of a narrow alley in Stonegate, as the church bells tolled the hour of Vespers, 7 p.m.

"Dear friend!" Francis beamed delightfully, escorting his unexpected visitor to the parlour. "Come through."

Philip grinned at Lady Margaret as she hobbled out of the kitchen, wiping her podgy fingers in her apron.

"Look who's here, sweetheart," Francis declared.

"I can see," she smiled, limping forward to kiss Philip.

"How long have you been home?" Francis asked.

"Only today," he answered. "Has Isobel...?" he began hesitantly.

Margaret and Francis exchanged a knowing look and Philip blushed.

"No," Francis smirked, shaking him warmly by the hand.

Philip's shoulders slumped forward and Margaret beckoned him to sit.

"Did she receive my letter?" he asked, nervously.

"Yes," Margaret said, sitting beside him and taking hold of his hand.

"She gave me several letters for you, but no one knew where to find you," Francis explained.

"Has she...?"

"No," Francis anticipated.

"Then...."

"Calm thyself, dear friend," Francis grinned, motioning for a servant to fetch a jug. "Wine?"

Seated on a bench before the table, Philip accepted a cup of Gascony wine, while Lady Margaret limped out to the kitchen.

The same age as Philip, Francis's thin face, pale skin and wispy goatee made him look much older. In comparison, his short, plump, dimpled wife Margaret, was ten years his senior yet she looked younger. The Talbots had no children but were devoted to each other.

"Good health!" Francis toasted passionately, raising his cup.

"Good health," Philip echoed, with less enthusiasm.

Downing the wine, Philip licked his lips, shuddered and drew a sleeve across his mouth.

"You look…well?" Francis fibbed, noting the deep lines on his tanned face.

"I've been looking for Henry of Lancaster for nigh on a whole year," Philip frowned, massaging his deeply ploughed brow.

Francis purposefully sipped his wine and scrutinized Philip's troubled demeanour.

"How was my mother when she heard the news of Michael's death?" Philip asked.

"Margaret told me she remained calm and made the sign of the cross, but shed not one tear."

Philip swallowed his guilt and nodded appreciatively.

"What will you do now?" Francis enquired.

"'Tis as if Henry never existed," he sighed. "We'll go out again and ride our horses into the ground, but I am convinced he has left England."

"Do you have a mind to ask for my sister's hand?" Francis asked, taking Philip completely by surprise.

Caught off guard, Philip downed the rest of his wine,

"If so, I ask that you do it soon," Francis urged, his voice unusually excitable.

"Is she coming here to York?" Philip asked, expectantly.

"No she is in Exeter with my aunt; will you ask for her hand?" Francis repeated.

"I would but I have little to offer a wife."

"Put such thoughts from thy mind, we already have her dowry."

"And her trousseau," Margaret called from the kitchen area.

"But I…," Philip spluttered, sensing himself being pushed into a corner.

Francis smiled as his wife returned to the table bearing a bowl of apples and pears.

"We have been blessed with good fortune," she smiled proudly, "and my dear husband is raised to the royal household."

Philip took an apple from the bowl, held it in his hand and stared at Francis.

"I don't know what to say," he gasped, trying not to show envy. "Why?"

"Why?" Francis gasped.

"'Tis about time," Philip said, but the question he wanted to ask was: *Why would Edward raise a mediocre knight to such a privileged position?*

"Perhaps it is for my uncle's service to the crown," Francis suggested. "He was killed at Castillon, you know."

"I know, I was there with my brother; 'twas our first fight," Philip recalled, turning to Margaret. "My lady, I thank you for thy kindness you showed to my mother," he added. "I could not bear to see her anguish."

Margaret kissed his cheek lovingly and left the room.

"You have come into funds?" Philip whispered, noticing his pristine black satin tunic and large ring on the middle finger of Francis' right hand.

"My uncle had much property in Calais," Francis explained. "When it was sold a handsome share was left to me."

"Lord Talbot has been dead these twelve years."

"His bequest has only now been released."

"I am pleased for you," Philip lied.

"The least we can do is to give my sister a fair dowry."

"You are too generous."

"When will you marry?"

"Twelve months from our engagement, if the king is agreeable?"

"October next year would be better."

52

"If it pleaseth thee," Philip smiled, "October it shall be."

"Good," Francis nodded. "Margaret and I will make all the arrangements."

"You are too kind," Philip said, relieved. "I don't know when I shall see you next."

"You must go to Isobel and ask for her hand; that we cannot do for you."

"Will she accept my suit?" Philip asked, pessimistically.

"Yes," Francis assured him. "Come and visit us when you're next in London, but I beg you not to leave it too long."

Philip acknowledged his suggestion with a nod and plucked a pear from the bowl.

"What will you do now?" Francis asked, repeating his earlier question.

"Take my ease," Philip announced, sinking his teeth into the bruised fruit.

"We leave for Exeter within the week but I shall go on to London," Francis exclaimed, stroking his threadbare goatee. "My wife and sister are to join me there once I have secured lodgings."

Francis wanted to ask Philip about Michael but steered the conversation into calmer waters.

"How did you get along with Thomas Talbot?" he asked, watching his friend turn the core between his teeth and gnaw the sweet flesh.

Philip suddenly stopped eating.

"We have parted company, the man is a turd," he huffed, dropping the core into a voider and taking a sip of wine. "I must leave you now."

"If my sister agrees to everything I'll arrange for the reading of the banns," Francis chirped, escorting him to the door.

"If?"

"Philip!" Margaret called, waving several letters tied with a thin ribbon. "These are yours."

"Thank you," he smiled, taking the letters and kissing her hand. "We'll talk again soon."

Philip stuffed the letters inside his tunic and bade them goodnight.

"Wait!" Francis said as an afterthought, while a servant thoughtfully appeared with a lantern. "'Tis past curfew: you'll need this, but be on your guard," he warned, "these streets are dangerous."

"It's been raining," Philip said, stepping out into the wet street.

When the faint, yellow candle, flickering inside the lantern disappeared round the corner, Francis closed the door.

Walking below jettied houses bowing precariously in over Stonegate from both sides of the street and dripping rain-water, Philip curled a fist around the handle of the dagger in his belt. Turning into Petergate, he noticed several drunks congregated in the road. When they saw him they assumed he was a watchman and scattered.

Near Grope Lane, a narrow alley overgrown with bushes and the notorious haunt of prostitutes, he stopped. A rustling sound drew his attention to the dark, sinister lane and warned him to beware. Shining the pale light into the blackness, Philip tightened his grip on the dagger and listened. The plopping of water and a strong smell of damp added to the tension. Satisfied there was nothing, he turned to leave when he heard a familiar buzzing sound; but he was too slow. A crossbow bolt thudded into his left arm, spinning him around and sending the lantern clattering to the ground.

"Jesus!" he yelped, regaining his balance and grabbing the leather flight lodged in his arm above the elbow. "What the?"

A shadow leapt out of the bushes a dozen paces down the alley and was swallowed up by the night.

"Come back!" Philip bellowed, falling against a boarded shop front. "You bastard."

Recovering from the initial shock he staggered a few paces into the lane drawing his dagger.

"I'm here if you want me!" he gasped, spitting angrily. "Cunnnnt!"

With the would-be assassin's footsteps echoing down Swinegate, Philip snorted at the pain in his arm. Clamping a hand over the bloody wound, he stumbled back to Claremont Hall, cursing his clumsiness.

Reaching the house he pummelled on the door until it opened.

"M'lord?" Gilbert gasped, shocked to see the bolt protruding from Philip's upper arm.

"I told you not to lock the God-damned door!" he yelled, pushing the startled servant aside, his words accompanied by a liberal amount of spittle.

"I –" Gilbert blurted.

"Go and fetch Tobias," Philip growled, falling heavily into a chair.

Gilbert lit a lantern and left the house.

Living in a small rented cottage in Goodramgate with his wife and children, Tobias the family smith did not appreciate being woken in the middle of the night. Rising groggily from his bed, he drew back the wooden latch and picked up a large mallet.

"Who's there?" he hissed, placing an ear to the door.

"Gilbert!"

"What does tha want?"

"You must come," he insisted, nervously swinging the lantern at shadows in the street.

Dressing quickly, the burly smith grabbed a leather bag off the table and followed Gilbert back to Claremont Hall.

Seated on a chair in the poorly-lit parlour Philip, his bloody shirt lying on the floor, groaned at the feathered shaft stuck in his arm and guzzled wine by the cupful.

"I'll 'ave tah pull it out," Tobias frowned, while Arthur held a candle for him. "This should 'ave gone straight through," he continued, moving behind Philip and looking at Harrington. "Tha'll 'ave t' 'old 'im."

"Do what you must do and do it quick –" Philip snarled aggressively, only to yell and jump up from the chair gripping his injured limb. "Goddamned pig-fucker!"

Tobias had yanked the bolt out before Philip was ready.

"Ohh," Philip moaned, biting his fist to channel the pain. "That hurt!"

"Someone wanted thee dead," Tobias surmised, scrutinizing the flights.

"You think?" Philip sniffed, while Gilbert tenderly washed the bleeding wound with watered-down wine.

"Good," Tobias nodded, checking the boy's handiwork. "Tha's no splintering on shaft; it should heal…but go see a physic on tha morrow."

As the pain eased, Philip remembered the incident at Alnwick and realised it must have been an earlier attempt on his life.

"'Tis tha Devil's weapon," old Arthur sniffed, snatching the bloody bolt from Tobias and fingering its diamond-shaped head. "Shall I fetch spider's web?"

Philip remembered the day his mother sewed up his ghastly Towton gash and shook his head.

"Grope Lane's a dangerous place, mah lord," Gilbert declared, wiping up the blood on the floor.

"'Ee's right," Tobias confirmed. "If tha picks a wrong un tha'll find thyself in trouble."

"I wasn't looking for any whore."

"I wish Lady Joan was 'ere," Arthur muttered.

"Well she's not," Philip coughed, wiping spit from his chin and handing Tobias a coin. "I'm obliged to you."

The smith took the coin, tapped his head and left.

Next morning Philip paid a visit to a physician who ruthlessly probed the wound for bone splinters. Satisfied the bolt had damaged only flesh and muscle and there was no sign of infection, he sutured the hole and re-dressed the wound. Philip rested for a week and mulled over who might want him dead: the list was surprisingly long, from the husband of a lowly kitchen maid to the Earl of Warwick. While his arm healed, Philip's paranoia increased, but when he read Isobel's letters, her flowery prose eased his anxiety. Reading through the lines told him she would accept his suit, but his lack of confidence brought on a bout of pessimism. Some nights he paced his bedchamber massaging his arm and wondering if he was ready for marriage. He hoped his obsession for Elizabeth would fade, but sensed it growing stronger.

On St Swithin's day, 15 July, Philip was sat relaxing when Arbroth burst in.

"Slow down," Philip growled, while the sweating Scot puffed and wheezed.

"Mah lord, ah have news," he gasped.

"What news?"

"Ah canna read," he said, handing over a badly crumpled letter, "'Tis from tha Archbishop."

Identifying the broken wax seal as belonging to his cousin, John, Earl of Northumberland, Philip looked surprised and read the note.

"Henry has been found," he announced, with much relief.

"Mah Lord… Tha archbishop said Sir Thomas Talbot was with tha party who took him," Arbroth appended in a low voice.

"Talbot?" Philip hissed, reading on. "That bastard."

Henry of Lancaster was captured not through the skill of his pursuers but by bad luck. Whilst dining at Waddington Hall, in Lancashire, his host's Yorkist brother burst in with a group of armed men. In the confusion, Henry escaped but was taken as he crossed the River Ribble. The old king was allowed to rest before being escorted to York, over twenty leagues away. With Warwick in Calais, the news was delivered to his brother John, who scribbled instructions for Philip through his brother George, the new Archbishop of York.

The letter described Henry's capture and commanded Philip to take charge of the prisoner when he arrived at York, and convey him on to London. The note also revealed that a detachment of Northumberland men would be sent to reinforce him en route.

"Is it true?" his esquire asked, entering the room after listening outside.

"Yes," Philip confirmed. "Henry is on his way here and I am to take him to London."

"By St Peter!" Harrington gasped.

"Henry is to be lodged in St Mary's Abbey but no one must know he's here."

"What will you say to him?" Robert asked, running a finger over the faded scar on his forehead.

"I'll not talk to the man," Philip vowed, snatching a goblet of wine and drawing the dark red liquid through his teeth, producing a slurping sound.

"Henry has much support here; if his presence is made known we'll have trouble."

"Say nothing, to anyone," Philip insisted. "When he arrives I am to dismiss his escort and take him into my custody. He comes by way of Skipton. Tomorrow we'll ride out and meet them on the Knaresborough road," he added pensively. "Go to Seward House and bring back the others."

Harrington acknowledged the order while Philip finished his wine.

"Tell no one," he reiterated, wiping his mouth with a surnape. "I mean it."

"The men'll be suspicious."

"Say nothing," Philip insisted, as his esquire left. "Why do I get the shit tasks?" he groaned.

Next morning Philip, his esquire and retainers went to retrieve their horses from York Castle. Riding out through the north gate, they rattled over the drawbridge and continued along Castlegate and Coney Street before turning into Stonegate. Swinging into High Petergate, they left the city through Bootham Bar. Cantering between a row of houses and the north wall and towers of St Mary's Abbey, they rode out to a point where the road crossed a small stream half a mile from York.

"Does anyone know what Henry looks like, besides me?" he asked, slowing his horse.

One of the archers looked around before warily raising a hand.

"Ride out a way and when you see him, come back; but be certain it is him."

The archer, his sheathed bow slung over his back, trotted on alone.

"We'll wait here," Philip commanded, sliding from the saddle and handing the reins to his groom Daniel.

After securing Clovis to a nearby tree, Daniel joined the rest of the men.

Sitting on the bank, Philip pondered over his daunting responsibility. Picking up a stone, he tossed it into the shallow stream, an action that sent a sharp pain through his injured arm.

"'Tis Ralph!" one of the men-at-arms shouted, pointing up the road.

Philip looked to see his archer galloping back.

"My Lord!" the archer gasped, drawing up in a cloud of dust. "The king," he announced.

"He is not the king and you will not show him such courtesy," Philip warned, standing and brushing dirt from his arse, while Ralph's horse slurped avidly from the trickling stream. "Is Sir Thomas with them?"

"Yes, m'Lord," the archer nodded.

"Mount!" Philip commanded, taking the reins from his hook-nose groom and leaping into the saddle. "Talbot." He grimaced at his esquire.

"Talbot," Robert echoed.

Philip and his men waited at the side of the road, watching carts full of farm produce and pedestrians make their way to the city. After a frustrating delay, Philip looked at the archer who brought the news.

"Perhaps they have taken a different road?" Harrington suggested.

"That'll be just like Talbot," he fumed, rubbing his chin.

Suddenly a group of horsemen appeared in the distance moving slowly along the road.

"There!" the relieved archer yelped.

Philip nudged Clovis to the middle of the highway and had his men post themselves on either side of him, effectively blocking the road.

When the distance between the two groups was no more than several horse lengths the antagonism of the two knights was obvious. Both offered a grudging nod of recognition and each waited for the other to speak. After a strained silence, Philip turned to his esquire.

"Give this to Sir Thomas," he said, handing him the letter from his cousin Northumberland.

Harrington took the well-folded note and passed it to Talbot, who eyed the esquire disdainfully.

"What is it?" he sniffed.

"Read it," said Philip, with equal insolence. "And you'll find out."

While Talbot perused the message, Philip was drawn to the sad, dishevelled prisoner, mounted on a short, light-brown hackney and sandwiched between two guards. His brief study revealed a hunched figure, whose pale drawn face made him look much older than his forty-three years. Henry's light-brown hair needed a wash and cut and several of his front teeth were missing. Dressed in black doublet, brown hose and flat velvet cap, Henry of Lancaster bore no resemblance to his noble status. As their curiosity got the better of them, Philip's men began to whisper amongst themselves.

"This is an outrage!" Talbot exploded, crumpling the letter. "I caught him and I am denied the right to take him to London; by God, I'll not give him up!"

Philip sighed and switched his attention from Henry to Sir Thomas.

"You will hand over your prisoner," he demanded.

"Try and take him," Talbot responded menacingly.

"You refuse to obey an order from his lordship?"

"Wipe your arse with it," Sir Thomas snarled, throwing the note away. "You Nevilles…"

"Do you think I want him?" Philip countered, indicating for someone to retrieve the letter and for his esquire to take the reins of Henry's horse.

Talbot inched his hand towards the handle of his sword.

When Philip mirrored his movement Sir Thomas thought better of it. Drawing his hand away, he scratched his cheek in frustration.

"This isn't over," he warned.

"Have a care, my Lord," Philip countered, as Harrington took the reins of Henry's hackney and led him away.

While the two rivals glared at one another their men drew apart.

Sir Thomas snapped the reins sharply and cantered back the way he had come, while Philip trotted off in the opposite direction. Near the hospital of St Mary's Magdalene, he caught up with his men who were waiting for a party of blind priests to cross the road.

"You have made another enemy, my Lord," his esquire said when Philip caught up.

"They're lining up these days," he said, indicating for his men to turn right at St Mary's Tower and head down to the abbey gatehouse. "That way."

St Mary's Abbey abutted onto York's north-west wall. From Bootham Bar the abbey's long crenulated perimeter wall ran out to the circular tower of St Mary's before angling down to the Ouze. Close to the river the wall turned sharply back towards the city, paralleling the north bank all the way to Lendal Tower.

"Open the gates!" Harrington yelled, cupping a hand to his mouth, to amplify his voice.

"Who makes such a demand?" someone called back from beyond the abbey gatehouse.

Harrington turned to look at Philip, who came forward and repeated the order with more authority.

"Open up in the name of John Neville, Earl of Northumberland!"

After a moment's hesitation, the heavy, wooden doors slowly opened and Philip led his party into the cluttered abbey grounds.

"His lordship has no authority here," a black-robed monk said defiantly, looking at the visitors suspiciously.

"I have a prisoner who is ordered to be confined here," Philip explained.

"This is a monastery, not a gaol," the annoyed Benedictine retorted, his work apron and hands caked in mud.

"This is no ordinary prisoner," Philip snapped at the haughty monk, resting his arms on the pommel of his saddle.

"Wait here and I'll fetch my lord Abbot."

"Then make haste, I don't have all day."

The monk went off as fast as sandaled feet permitted, muttering under his breath. He returned shortly with a middle-aged man, whose demeanour and unhurried gait were indicative of authority and superiority.

"Arrogant little friar," Philip muttered, crossing his arms, and grinning at his esquire.

"Welcome to St Mary's, my son," the Abbot nodded, trying to see the prisoner. "I am Thomas Bothe."

"My Lord Abbot," Philip responded, tipping his head.

"What is it you want here?"

"I have a letter from the Earl of Northumberland," Philip revealed, as his esquire held out the folded note, "it commands me to leave a prisoner in your care, but you are to tell no one of his presence."

Thomas Bothe took the letter and lifted it to his heavily ploughed face, while his funnelled sleeves slipped down to the elbows, exposing unusually hairy arms. After perusing the letter the Abbot craned his neck at the captive and his jaw dropped when he recognised the sullen figure, sitting astride a sorry nag.

"Why have you brought him here?" he gasped, glancing around nervously. "We have troubles enough without this."

"I have my orders, you have yours."

The Abbot shook his head fretfully.

"I'll have rooms prepared in the gatehouse. How long?"

"I'll come for him tomorrow."

The Abbot stepped forward and Philip followed him with cold, menacing eyes. As the Abbot neared the old king, he looked into his cheerless face and fell to his knees.

"Your Grace," he lamented, bowing his head.

Henry snapped out of his gloom, looked at the ecclesiastic with a heavy heart and placed a hand on his head.

Philip was about to scold the Abbot when Harrington touched his arm, urging him not to object.

Rising slowly to his feet with the aid of a monk, the Abbot turned to Philip.

"This man is exhausted. Permit him time to rest and he will be fit to travel."

"I thought you had enough troubles?" he said, patting Clovis's thick mane.

Thomas Bothe looked apologetically at Henry.

"Please."

"As you wish, my Lord Abbot," Philip relented. "He may rest today and tomorrow, but have him ready when I return."

"God bless you."

"Yes, yes," Philip sniffed. "No one is to know he is here, you are responsible for their silence," he warned, nudging his chin at the monks, looking on curiously.

The abbot agreed and Philip signalled his men to leave.

Harrington passed the reins of the king's horse to one of the Benedictines and followed.

Philip Neville and his esquire spent the next morning over a table in the parlour of Claremont Hall, scrutinising a rough map of the roads between York and London. They studiously examined the towns and villages along the route until noon, when Philip made his decision.

"We'll ride to Pontefract and follow this route," he said, drawing a finger down the paper. "Doncaster, Grantham, Peterborough, Hatfield, London."

"What about supplies?" Harrington asked.

"We'll take what we can load on two sumpters and purchase more on the way," he said.

Tapping a forefinger against his lips, the pressure became too much; added to the humidity and the stink of a smouldering tallow candle, Philip suddenly cursed Henry of Lancaster.

"Damn his eyes!" he spat, thumping the table. "Send Arbroth and two men to watch the abbey; if anyone leaves, follow them."

"We'll need Middleton's men."

"No, a large party will attract too much attention."

His esquire agreed and left to find Arbroth, leaving Philip slumped in a chair, his face nestled in his clammy palms.

"God help me," he moaned, rubbing his head in frustration.

Before leaving Claremont Hall, Robert Harrington sent the servants to the Pavement market, to purchase oats, bread, corn and meat, while Daniel and Walter walked to the castle, to check on the horses and collect weapons.

Chapter 4

SHORTLY BEFORE NOON on 18 July, Philip, his men and horses were congregated under Micklegate Bar. Their presence in the narrow gatehouse forced visitors and tradesmen to skirt the mass of snorting horseflesh blocking the entrance. This and the unbearable heat brought on an explosive exchange and several wardens had to intervene to prevent a fight.

"We'll wait outside," Philip fumed, removing a foot from the stirrup and lashing out at a carpenter, who was trying to push his cart through the narrow gateway. "Get out of the road!"

Philip jabbed his spurs into Clovis's flanks and the palfrey reared, sending the carpenter, his apprentice, and their handcart crashing against the wall. Slipping on a pile of freshly dumped horse shit, the carpenter fell heavily to the ground.

"Soldiers!" he griped. "Tha don't give a fig!"

Philip's retainers cheered his embarrassment as they rode out over the drawbridge. Re-assembling at nearby St Thomas's hospital, the group waited for Harrington, who had been sent to fetch Henry from the Abbey. As time went on and the midday sun beat down, Philip grew uneasy: perhaps the Abbot had refused to give him up?

"I should have gone myself," he groaned as irritating perspiration tickled his neck. "What can a boy do?"

"Ye were a laddie once, mah lord," Arbroth sniffed. "Give him a chance."

"I was fighting the French at his age."

"Aye."

"Here they come!" one of his archers announced.

Philip gave his esquire a relieved nod as he led the old king out through Micklegate, his face concealed with a hood.

"Any trouble?" he asked, looking at the prisoner.

"No, my Lord," the youngster replied, confidently, while the company formed in a column of twos. "He came peacefully."

"Has he spoken?" Philip pressed, setting off along the Tadcaster road.

"Not a word," Harrington replied. "The Abbot said he spent his time at prayer."

"Praying will not help him."

"My Lord," Harrington gasped, concerned by his hostility.

"Send one of the men on to Pontefract…to secure lodgings for tonight," Philip commanded, ignoring his esquire's empathy.

Robert relayed his instructions to one of the men-at-arms, who steered his horse out of line and galloped away.

Riding through the village of Tadcaster a few miles west of York, Philip's party attracted hostile looks from the locals, who despised all soldiers for the slaughter and looting perpetrated after Towton. One villager stared intently at the rider wearing a thin cloak with a hood concealing his face and fell to his knees dramatically.

"Highness?" he gasped, bowing his head and raising his clasped hands to Henry.

"Ride on," Philip barked, touching spur to flank.

As they cantered down the London Road, which cut through the Towton battlefield, an eerie silence descended over the sacred ground, broken only by the snorting of nervous horses and the cawing of crows hopping over the field. Philip prudently looked over at the landscape and was surprised that so little evidence of the fighting remained. The area had been gleaned of arrows, discarded armour and weapons, and the dead slept in pits beneath mounds of verdant grass, now thick with colourful flowers.

Those of Philip's men who fought that day conjured up grim images they had spent the past four years trying to forget.

"My Lord?" Harrington whispered, concerned by his reticent horse.

"I'll feel better when we're clear of this graveyard," Philip answered, crossing his chest and patting his baulking horse's neck. "They can smell it?"

"Smell what?"

"Blood...the air is tainted with it," Philip said, turning to those behind. "We showed them that day," he chirped, aiming his comment at the old king, "eh?"

His words received a hearty cheer from several of his men.

Looking over to the right, Philip spotted a distant tree-line, where the ground beyond dipped sharply down to the River Cock.

"I feel the ghosts of the dead are watching us," a trembling archer declared, kissing the silver cross dangling from his neck.

"There are no ghosts," Philip said, unsure if he believed it himself. "It's only the wind in the trees."

Crossing the River Aire at Ferrybridge the column followed an ancient road for several miles and approached Pontefract as the sun began to set. Sited on a high hill overlooking the river, Pontefract was a magnificent royal fortress built of yellow magnesian limestone and grey sandstone, its massive trefoil-shaped Great Tower dominating the countryside for miles.

Once through the Barbican and West Gate, Philip's party

entered the upper outer bailey and found it cluttered with sheep, pigs and carts. Riding through the Gatehouse Tower, they dismounted in the inner bailey.

"Brush down the horses and feed them," Philip commanded, looking around at the extensive rebuilding work going on. "And watch our supplies."

"Mah lord," Arbroth interrupted. "Tha prisoner asks tah pray at tha tomb of Thomas o' Lancaster."

Philip huffed at Henry's piety but relented.

"Go with him and don't let him out of your sight...take someone with you!"

While his men unpacked the sumpters and Arbroth escorted Henry to the Priory of St John the Evangelist, a short walk from the castle, Philip turned to his esquire.

"Find the steward."

"This must be him," Robert answered, pointing at a confident character coming towards them.

The caretaker of Pontefract Castle was an ageing warrior who as a lad survived the French slaughter of the baggage guard at Agincourt. Now well into old age, he resented not being able to fight, but King Edward kept him employed for his service to three English monarchs.

"And you are?" The steward asked warily, his thin, grey hair tied back to reveal well-defined features and busy eyes.

"Philip Neville, cousin to the king," he said proudly. "We seek shelter for the night."

"Hum," the steward huffed, unimpressed by Philip's lineage. "Your man told me you were on your way... How long?"

"One night."

"Where is your prisoner?"

"Does everyone know?" Philip groaned, glancing at his esquire.

"He prays at the tomb of Thomas of Lancaster," Harrington answered.

"'Tis said the tomb has the power to cure," the steward revealed. "Henry's father was a great warrior but his son... huh."

"How did you know?" Philip asked, wondering if the man he sent on ahead had blabbed.

"The news of Henry's capture has spread like the plague. One of my people recognised him when you came through Tadcaster and rode here to tell me, but beware your route and destination are not difficult to plot."

"God damn it," Philip growled, rubbing his temples in frustration.

"I fear your journey will not be an easy one," the steward said, forced to raise his voice above the hammering of stonemasons working on a new tower. "I invite you and your royal prisoner to dine with me and my daughters this night."

Philip accepted and the steward left to order his cooks to prepare extra food.

Without finishing supper, Philip, irritated by the almost indecent flirting of the steward's unattractive daughters, retired to his bed-chamber, on the first floor of the Great Tower. Having eaten frugally and in silence, Henry was lodged in an adjacent room. Despite the guards posted outside the old king's room, Philip stayed awake for most of the night. Occasionally a nocturnal noise startled him and he rushed to the window expecting to see a rope dangling from Henry's room.

When he returned to his bed, Philip fretted over the perilous journey ahead. He knew Doncaster, the next town on his route, would be hostile, as Ralph Grey and Roger de Gravett were executed there after Bamburgh's surrender. De Gravett was a favourite with the townsfolk and many a tear was shed when his head fell.

After breakfast next morning, Philip's men sat on their horses in the inner Bailey watching workmen lime-wash the walls of the steward's lodgings. They were waiting for Henry who was in the castle's chapel praying. When Henry finished he gave the steward a small ring and thanked him for his hospitality.

Philip shook his head intolerantly while Arbroth helped Henry to mount.

"You spoil him," Philip tutted.

"Mah lord, he wears a hair shirt next tah his skin," the Scot gasped, a comment that caused Philip to scratch unconsciously.

"Why do men inflict such torment on themselves?" he huffed, flipping the reins to straighten them out and acknowledging the steward, standing beside one of his daughters, grateful his visitors were leaving. "I shall never understand it."

Arbroth shrugged his shoulders.

"Walk on," Philip commanded, nudging Clovis down to the gatehouse and out of Pontefract Castle. "My God, the poor man has three daughters and every one of them ugly."

"Aye, mah lord, but tha ugly ones are good in bed," the Scot sniggered, bowing his head at one of the girls, who blushed and gave him an impish grin.

"You didn't?"

"Ah did," he boasted.

"Then you're a braver man than I."

Half a league from Doncaster, the column swung off the main road and passed the town without incident. Camping that night near Retford on the River Idle, Philip looked for the reinforcements promised by his cousin. Early next morning the column broke camp and went splashing across the river, the hooves of their horses stirring up the clay bed and adding a red tinge to the foaming waters. Struggling up the slippery far bank, they rode to Grantham, forty miles further on. By early evening they were camped near Elton, a hamlet on the

River Nene, eight miles beyond Peterborough. Once again Philip looked longingly back up the road for the expected reinforcements.

The horses were secured to a rope-line beside a crumbling farmhouse close to the river, and a fire was started in one of the dilapidated rooms. The old king stood apart from the others, his head bowed in contemplation, and as the iridescent sun shimmered down beyond the hills to the west, Philip shared his concerns with his esquire.

"We should have been reinforced by now."

"Some of the men are on edge," Harrington warned, squinting at the fading orange sun, while outside the tethered horses snorted, shuffled and tugged at the line. "The horses sense something is amiss."

"I don't like it," Philip confessed, spitting out trail dust.

"They might have taken a different road?"

"Perhaps," Philip said, using a finger to wipe dirt from his ears. "I think we're being followed."

"I'll take the men and…"

"No –"

"My Lord," his varlet interrupted, "two of the horses have lost shoes and we only have enough oats for one day."

"We're close to Fotheringhay," Philip said, referring to the Northamptonshire home of his aunt Cecily, the king's mother.

Each horse needed at least ten pounds of hay or five pounds of oats per day, as well as forty pounds of green forage and straw.

Turning to his esquire, Philip announced a change of plan.

"Ride to Fotheringhay and buy what we need," he said, handing him a purse. "Hide this on your person…and take Walter, and the horses that need shoeing."

"What if they run into outlaws?" Arbroth asked, watching them ride away.

"Then our horses will eat grass," he said coldly.

"Ah could ride tah Elton and –" Arbroth suggested.

"No," Philip countered. "You'll only get drunk."

"Mah lord, I have never given ye reason tah doot me, do ye think ah would be so foolish?" He pouted, walking away, deliberately scuffing his shoes.

"Arbroth!"

The Scot looked back and Philip stared at him, an apology of sorts, which he accepted with a sharp nod.

Being a Saturday, and with the old king present, the two servants prepared a fish bake.

"Fish?" Philip moaned at the smell of salt ling and hake sizzling on the grid-iron. "Great."

"Mutton's gone sour, my Lord," the cook apologised, wiping his hands in his greasy apron. "We have a little rabbit and pottage?"

"Put the rabbit in the pottage, I'll eat that."

Philip's esquire and armourer returned an hour after sunset.

"Ah, food," Walter said, slapping his lips as he entered the derelict farmhouse to be greeted by the smoky aroma of cooking fish.

"Any luck?" Philip asked, scrutinizing the dark countryside.

"The horses are done but we could only get two sacks of oats," his esquire said.

"That won't last half a day," Philip groaned, looking at his Scot. "I should have sent *him*."

"It's all they had," Robert apologised.

"It'll have to do," Philip sighed, peering into the darkness. "Go and eat, I shall stay awake and keep watch this night."

"My Lord?"

"Do as I say, I can not lose the prisoner."

Harrington slouched over and joined Walter by the crackling fire. Scrapping a portion of crumbled, over-baked fish off the griddle and onto a plate, he sat down and tucked in.

Worried by the lack of reinforcements, Philip tried to stay alert through the night. With the mournful glow of the moon his sole companion, his hearing became attuned to the sounds of the night. The soft plopping sound of water dripping from the trees was amplified and small animals darting through the underbrush transformed in his mind to outlaws lurking in the shadows. Slowly drawing his sword he looked at the snoring forms huddled beneath their blankets and sneered at the old king. Secure in the knowledge that he was not alone, he re-housed the blade.

The annoying hoot of an owl, somewhere deep in the forest, caused Philip to poke his head out of a glassless window. Suddenly his face was enmeshed in the thread of a spider and he leapt back, frantically scrapping the fine mesh from his eyes and mouth. Exhausted, he sat down and struggled to stay awake. Resting back against the rough stone wall his heavy eyelids closed, his head drooped and he began snoring. Henry lay awake, fretting over the safety of his queen and young son but pretending to be asleep. Sitting up he looked at the low flames of the dying fire and noticed Philip slumped in the corner. Picking up his blanket, he tiptoed over and laid it over Philip's legs before returning to his place.

When the first rays of the sun kissed his face, Philip's eyes blinked open and he crawled to his feet. Using a forefinger to knead sleep from bleary eyes he looked around and snorted mucus from his nose. When he saw Henry rubbing his arthritic hips, he yawned loudly and smacked his lips together. Frowning at the crumpled blanket near his feet he wondered who was responsible.

"Wake up!" he yelled, angry with himself.

Slowly his men groaned into consciousness, massaged aching joints, scratched themselves and coughed foul phlegm from their lungs. Shuffling past Philip, Arbroth bent his knees and farted.

"Sorry, mah lord!"

"Start a fire," Philip growled, slapping the back of his head. "You pig!"

Raking up a pile of dry kindling, Arbroth sprinkled it over the smoky remains of the old fire.

"Feed the horses," Philip commanded, nudging his chin at the groom and turning to his esquire.

"Did you sleep?"

"Did you?" he countered, rolling up his blanket.

"You should have woken me."

Philip huffed at Henry as he delicately cleaned his teeth with a cloth, his pathetic deportment shooting a pang of remorse through his heart and softening his expression.

After an early breakfast, Philip's men joined Henry in prayer. Being the feast day of St Mary Magdalene and a Sunday, Henry begged Harrington to ask Philip for a day of rest and prayer. He refused.

"I'll not pander to his superstitions," he sniffed, climbing into the saddle and shifting his weight. "To horse!"

With a heavy heart, Henry mounted his hackney and slouched in the saddle. Philip's men showed their resentment at his response to the old king's request. Despite Henry's years of misrule, many ordinary people respected him and Harrington passed the prisoner a sympathetic smile as they set off. Philip took a last look back hoping to see the fabled reinforcements, but the road was empty.

At midday, the sun was at its highest and the heat shimmered and danced above the old Roman road, and Philip narrowed his eyes and saw distorted black shapes in the distance. Unable to see clearly he raised a hand and brought the column to a halt. Wiping sweat from his eyes with thumb and forefinger, he took a drink of ale to wash the dust from his throat.

Swishing the warm liquid around his mouth, he leaned out of the saddle and spat.

"'Tis hot, mah lord," Arbroth griped, dismounting and wiping his wet face on his horse's mane.

"Like a forge," Philip blew, swigging another mouthful of ale and ignoring the spillage trickling down his chin.

"Horses," Arbroth confirmed, stroking his rouncey's steaming neck. "Do ye wish tah rest?"

With his attention locked on the riders approaching from the south, Philip wiped his mouth on his sleeve. The intense heat hit the road and the horsemen appeared to hover several feet above the ground.

"We go on," he announced, nudging his horse. "Stay sharp!"

Philip's retainers made sure their weapons were in reach and the servants edged closer to the prisoner for mutual protection.

"They're in a hurry," his esquire warned, easing his horse up next to Clovis. "Northumberland's men?"

"They're running their horses into the ground," Philip said, unable to take his eyes off them as they closed in. "If I draw sword, kill them all." He commanded, looking back at Henry, "Cover his face."

Easing his right hand over the pommel of his arming sword, resting against his left thigh, Philip felt a painful twinge in his arm where the crossbow bolt had struck two weeks before.

Wearing Northumberland's red and black livery, with its distinctive Griffin badge, the approaching horsemen drew up their foam-flecked mounts. One nudged his panting horse forward until the animal's bristly wet nose almost touched Clovis's face.

"Mark Fulkerston," he panted, sweating heavily. "We have ridden hard to catch up with you."

"Philip Neville and you are late," Philip answered, eyeing

the dusty, lightly bearded knight, his spacious front teeth barely visible beneath a dense moustache.

"We did not know which road you would take," Fulkerston revealed breathlessly, the dripping perspiration on his forehead causing his eyelids to flicker.

"Only eight of you?" Philip frowned, observing how they tried to conceal their faces.

"His Lordship thought a large force would draw too much attention."

Philip sniffed and circled his left arm to relieve the dull ache.

"Is that him?" Fulkerston coughed, rising in the stirrups to look at the hunched figure at the back.

Philip acknowledged Henry's presence with a nod and made a cursory examination of Fulkerston's sweat-stained, ill-fitting tunic and lathered mount.

"Has he given you cause for concern?" Fulkerston asked.

Philip shook his head while gauging Fulkerston's potential. At a glance he noted the man's confident posture and large hands. Several faded scars on his face told Philip he was a warrior, but he wore his sword on the right hip; he knew if Fulkerston moved first, Philip would have the advantage.

"Shall we ride on?" Fulkerston suggested, extending an arm out.

"Fall your men in."

Fulkerston's company merged in with Philip's and the extended column moved on.

After several miles, the road cut through a swathe of densely wooded country, where the lush burgundy leaves of a copper beech stood out vividly from the mass of green. Blooming yellow, white and blue flowers growing in clusters on the forest floor stretched their petals for a share of the limited sunlight.

"How is my cousin?" Philip asked, holding the reins loosely in his left hand and resting the other on his thigh.

"He prays we reach London without incident," Fulkerston sniffed, the plodding gait of their horses causing both men to rock drowsily in the saddle.

"Have you served his lordship long?"

"We were captured together on St Albans field," Fulkerston revealed. "I was held captive until Lord Somerset's execution."

"So long?"

"I killed an esquire during an escape attempt…he was the duke's favourite. That mistake cost me my freedom for three years," he explained. "His Grace wanted my head. 'Twas fortunate my family has money."

"How are his lordship's sons?"

"Ah…" he smiled, Philip's sudden chatty manner lulling him into a sense of ease, "they are in fine health."

"So the baby has recovered?"

"Yes," he nodded convincingly.

Fulkerston's response sent a shiver down Philip's spine and he tensed himself.

"We'll rest there," he suggested, pointing to a rocky outcrop where the road curved before sloping down to a shallow creek and scratching his head, the pre-arranged signal for his Scot to join him.

"We're still a fair way from London," Fulkerston frowned, while Philip greeted Arbroth as he came up on Fulkerston's blind side, ready to distract him.

"Arbroth, I want you to…" Philip began. "Now!" he yelled as Fulkerston looked at the Scot, surprised to see him there.

Philip drew his blade and Fulkerston seemed confused as its sharp point tore his throat open. Slapping a hand to the gaping wound Fulkerston gurgled something incomprehensible. The two men stared at each other as blood poured between the fingers of Fulkerston's riding glove. The mortally wounded knight swayed and toppled from his horse, blood from the severed carotid artery splashing his palfrey's neck and terrifying the animal.

Before Fulkerston's men could respond they found themselves savagely attacked by Philip's retainers, who leapt from their mounts and slaughtered them with sword and dagger. It was over in the blink of an eye, Fulkerston and most of his men were dead. One poor wretch lay in the long grass, a wedge of bone chopped cleanly out of his forehead.

"This one's alive!" Robert called out, kneeling at his side.

"Finish him off," Philip commanded.

An archer gave a sardonic leer and drew his dagger, but was suddenly stopped by Philip.

"Ask him who sent them," he demanded, ripping up a handful of grass and using it to wipe the blood off his blade.

The wounded soldier muttered a few words, his exposed brain causing his arms to twitch uncontrollably.

"They're Lord Roos's," Harrington revealed, bending down and putting an ear to the dying man's mouth.

"What happened to those whose coats they wear?" Philip asked, dropping his sword into its casing.

The esquire listened intently while the man spluttered something.

"Dead," he confirmed.

"You would have done the same to us," Philip snarled. "Why did you not come at night?"

The Lancastrian's lips moved and he tried to speak, forcing Philip's esquire to lay his blood-splattered ear closer.

"They feared harming the king," he explained.

"Anyone hurt?" Philip asked, watching his men dragging the bodies off the road.

"No, my Lord!"

The mortally wounded Lancastrian convulsed once and his body went limp.

"Craven dog," Philip hissed.

"This one has a purse," Arbroth called out, rifling Fulkerston's bloody corpse.

"How much?" Philip asked, as the Scot emptied the contents into his palm.

"Two poonds," he chirped, counting the coins.

"We'll share it out later."

"My Lord, there are only seven here," one of his archers warned.

Philip cautiously unsheathed his sword and placed a finger to his lips, urging silence. Holding his breath, he looked furtively around but the nervous shuffling and neighing horses broke his concentration.

"How did we miss him?" Arbroth whispered.

"Quiet," Philip urged.

While his men gathered up the horses, Philip scanned the trees west of the road. Glancing over his shoulder, he tutted at Henry, who was moving among the dead, praying over them as if he were a priest. The muffled thud of horse hooves snapped his attention back to the woods.

"Look to your weapons," he urged, peering into the foliage.

Glancing up, Philip saw beams of sunlight streaming down through the hazy leafy green mesh and lowered his eyes to spears of vivid purple foxgloves blossoming in clumps on the forest floor. His distraction ended when he glimpsed a dark shadow among the trees.

"Here he comes!" he bellowed.

Resting against the tree trunk, Philip watched the horseman weave through the underbrush, coming closer with every twist and turn.

The lone rider drew his blade and charged and as he thundered past the tree, Philip brought his arming sword up.

Bending low the horseman made a sharp turn and evaded the strike. Abandoning his cover, Philip backed up as horse and rider galloped towards him. To avoid being run down, he flung himself to the side and hit the ground heavily. As he struggled to his feet, the horseman leapt from his horse.

With his arms and legs partly armoured, and face concealed by a scarf, the warrior raised his bastard sword above his head with both hands and ran at Philip. Pulling the twisted scabbard from between his legs and cursing his clumsiness, Philip lifted his weapon to parry the blow. The blades collided and the resulting clang reverberated through the forest. Shearing apart, the weapons struck again and again, both men taking it in turns to attack and defend, each seeking an advantage. Distressed by the pain in his upper left arm and the determination in his opponent's penetrating eyes, Philip struggled to conceal his fear.

"Son of a bitch!" he spat, backing against a tree and using the sole of his boot to force his opponent back. "Fuck off."

The kick failed to give Philip the time he needed to recover and perspiration ran down his face, adding to his discomposure. The combat continued and the silent, faceless assailant showed no sign of tiring. Several archers manoeuvred to use their bows but were unable to get a shot.

"Stay back!" Philip coughed, levering himself off the trunk and swinging his sword wildly, hoping to put off his opponent.

Roos' man came at him again and again, each assault more punishing than the previous one. Philip was fighting for his life; he kicked, he punched and he cursed, but fatigue was etched clearly on his face and his opponent pressed the attack with more verve. Growling like an angry bear, he brought his fluted blade down harder and steel splinters prickled Philip's face, but his unhealed arm throbbed painfully and every blow increased his despair.

Falling on a grassy bank, Philip crossed his sword barely a thumb's width from his eyes only to see it knocked from his sweaty grasp.

"Jesus," he spluttered, closing his eyes.

Before his assailant could strike the fatal blow, Arbroth leapt on his back and plunged a dagger into his side. The narrow point tore through his doublet and penetrated near the lowest rib. Sucking in air, Roos' man dropped his sword and slewed away, trying with all his might to extract the dagger wedged in his side. Dropping to his knees, his eyes blinked and the scarf went rapidly in and out as he struggled to force air into his lungs. Tracing a cross on his chest he finally fell forward into the dirt.

"Ah have killed him, mah lord," Arbroth announced.

"If you hadn't he'd have killed me," Philip gasped, the savagery of the attack terrifying him.

Arbroth turned the dead man over, yanked the scarf from his mouth and frowned at his twisted features.

Philip spat out a gobbet of bloody phlegm and tried to compose himself.

"He was a handsome rogue," Harrington said.

"He'll be worm food soon," Philip coughed, resting his palms on his knees to control the trembling. "Put him with the others."

"He went fer ye, mah lord," Arbroth puffed, taking one of the dead man's feet and dragging him off the road with the aid of an archer. "Ah saw tha look in his eyes, he wanted ye dead."

Philip poured a skin of water over his head and gasped at the shock.

"How did you know they were not Sir John's men?" his esquire asked. "They wear his livery."

"The coat he wore was too big for him and my cousin has only one son; his second-born was a girl. Neither of them was sick the last I heard."

"Ah!" Harrington smiled knowingly.

"His armour is foreign," Arbroth announced, removing and examining the decorated cuisse from the assassin's thigh. "French?"

"Frog bastard!" Philip exploded, kicking the body.

"Mah lord –" Arbroth objected, but a menacing glare ended his protest.

"He has caused my wound to flair," he growled, retrieving his sword. "Cover them up… I need to shit," he said, tearing a handful of leaves from the ground and limping into the underbrush.

Fearing another ambush, Philip, having washed off the blood, led his retinue down the road to Huntingdon. After sleeping in the open on a night fraught with false alarms, Philip pushed his tired men through Huntingdon and across the Great Ouze River. The thirty-five-mile ride to Letchworth was uneventful but those in the rear spent a tense day looking over their shoulders. That night Philip paced in agitated silence, his wound aching and his nerves on edge while Arbroth and the others lounged around the fire, showing off their plunder. Henry sat alone.

Chapter 5

ON THE SIXTH day out of York, Henry rose, prayed, broke his fast and frowned at his dingy attire before greeting his horse. Several of Philip's retainers were relieving themselves against a tree, each competing to see who could piss the highest. When they set off for the last leg of their journey, morale improved and the men began to relax. After only a few miles Robert Harrington lurched in the saddle, jerked his head to the side and vomited. As he slid from the saddle spewing his guts up, the column shuffled to a halt.

"What is it now?" Philip groaned, hearing violent gagging.

Irritated by the heat he trotted back down the line, accompanied by Arbroth.

Harrington indicated with a wave that he was fine, which was quickly followed by a further discharge of vomit.

"The laddie musta eaten summat bad," Arbroth surmised.

"Fetch wine," Philip grimaced, the sour smell steaming off the pool of sick making him urge. "Hurry!"

Arbroth dismounted and forced his way through to the pack horses near the rear while Philip backed Clovis up.

The Scot offered the pale esquire a skin of wine but he wanted water.

"Water?" Arbroth questioned, as Harrington, holding his cramping stomach, leant against his horse for support.

One of the servants dismounted, poured a cup of water and handed it to the tremulous esquire.

"Thanks," he gasped, pouring the liquid between his chattering teeth.

Squirting the water around inside his mouth to loosen gunk, he spat and repeated the process several times before the bitterness subsided. Noting his pallid complexion Philip ordered him to the front.

"But…"

"Don't argue. I'll ride with the prisoner."

The esquire gratefully obeyed, for the Henry rarely spoke except to ask for an occasional drink of water.

While Harrington remounted his jittery horse, Philip nudged his palfrey up next to Henry's nag. Once the column was reformed, Robert glanced over his shoulder and Philip waved him on. For the next few miles, Philip kept his own company, refusing even to look at the prisoner. Unconsciously massaging his painful left arm he cogitated on the recent attack on his person and who might hate him enough to employ an assassin to do the job? Staring ahead, he muttered to himself, while his riding companion struggled not to stare for fear of drawing an abusive response.

Sensing he was being watched, Philip looked at the old king.

"Do you wish to stop?" he asked, annoyed with himself for showing weakness.

Henry shook his head and Philip acknowledged his answer with a tight-lipped nod. They were less than twelve leagues from London and the build-up of traffic was beginning to be a nuisance. Philip's party was forced to relinquish the road a dozen times to allow carts to pass. After reforming on the road for the umpteenth time a few miles beyond Stevenage, Henry leaned back and closed his eyes, allowing his face to soak up the sun's warmth. Philip took the opportunity to scrutinise Henry's gaunt, deeply-lined features and unkempt hair, which stuck out unkindly from under his hat, and his lower lip protruding like that of a chastised child.

"Yes?" Henry said, opening his eyes.

"Nothing," Philip sniffed, miffed at being caught.

"I remember your father and your brother; they were two of my most loyal men."

"Yes," Philip mused, irked by Henry's velvety voice. "And both are now dead."

"I wish it could have been otherwise. Michael was a good knight," Henry explained, his face full of remorse.

"And my father was murdered, by Lord Somerset," Philip asserted.

"You are wrong," Henry said, grabbing the wooden crucifix resting on his chest and touching it to his lips. "I swear by the Virgin Mary, Edmund Beaufort had no part by thought or deed in your father's murder. I saw his face when your father's body was brought to Westminster; it was not the face of a guilty man."

Philip tried to shake the notion that he might have been wrong all these years from his mind. Since boyhood, he firmly believed that Edmund, Second Duke of Somerset, was responsible for his father's murder and so far no one had been able to sway his conviction. Henry's declaration came from the heart, and cracks now appeared in Philip's ideology. Had his mother been truthful all these years? Too pig-headed to admit he could be wrong, he pushed it from his mind and clung to his perspective like a man hanging onto a cliff by his fingertips.

"Your mother is much loved in France," Henry said, diverting the conversation.

"As she was in Scotland," Philip huffed, clamping his lips together. "Though my mother is wedded to a Beaufort, she will always be a Neville," he added passionately.

"William is a good man and his loathing for politics is notorious," Henry explained. "When he and your mother came to court they were in a world of their own. You should not hate him, for he seeks neither fame nor fortune and judges men only on merit."

Philip shielded his eyes and looked at the road ahead, tenderly rubbing the muscles in his upper left arm.

"Are you hurt?" Henry asked, his concern sparking a sense of humanity in Philip.

"No," Philip snapped, instantly regretting his tone. "I have spent a year looking for you."

"We were always a small group, constantly on the move, never staying in one place for more than a day or two. When they found us we were dining with friends. 'Twas a monk who betrayed me," Henry revealed. "The black-robed villain recognised me and sent word to my host's brother, who was Edward's man. I thought nothing amiss until they broke in and demanded my name."

The happy warbling of sparrows flitting in and out of the tress on both sides of the road distracted Philip and he was only half-listening.

"My companions held them off while I fled into the forest with my chamberlain," Henry continued. "I was taken shortly after whilst crossing a river. When Sir Thomas Talbot arrived he threatened to kill me if I did not do as he said. Oh, he is not a pleasant fellow."

"Huh," Philip scoffed. "You are too generous; Thomas Talbot is a cunt."

"You are most profane," Henry gasped, horrified by the brutal expletive.

Philip raised his eyebrows at Henry's sensitivity.

"Forgive me," he apologised.

Henry looked down and crossed himself.

"When I was a child I wanted to be king more than anything in this world, but my dreams were quickly crushed. My family

87

quarrelled and turned against me, and the common people piled all their woes upon my shoulders. No matter what I did, I was bound to offend one party or the other," Henry revealed. "I am tired of it all and pray my cousin Edward will allow me to live out my days in peace."

"You are not solely to blame; the Beauforts have destroyed the crown's integrity and lost us France."

"If my father had lived but a few years more," Henry sighed woefully, shifting in the saddle. "He was a worthy king who ruled with a strong hand, but God took him too soon. I wish I had some of his strength."

"Do not languish in the past."

"Perhaps, but what does the future hold for me and my son Edward?"

"Your son is safe in France."

"He'll never be safe," Henry moped.

"Edward is a compassionate king –"

"You are naïve to think so," Henry sighed. "As long as I live I am a threat," he said, squinting up at the sun. "I know my wife will fight to the death to put our son on the throne."

"She must not do it…Edward is powerful; some of his 'new men' were only yesterday in your service."

"Should Edward meet defeat in battle, his support would wither as swiftly as mine has."

"Then we must pray that no such calamity befalls him," Philip frowned. "Too many have died fighting for the crown."

"There's always enough for one more killing," Henry reminded him. "When there is no foreign enemy to fight, we English turn on each other like mad dogs. When I am gone, Edward will seek out a new war. Do you not wish an end to all this suffering?"

"What is there for a soldier?" Philip sniffed. "When the French wars ended, did the people of England welcome us home? They did not; bad harvests, no work and starvation were their reward. Nobody wanted thousands of armed men roaming the country…so don't be too quick to promote peace."

"You have your brother's spirit," Henry smiled, remembering Michael's snub to the Duke of Somerset after Hedgeley Moor, "and your father's capricious temperament."

"Bishop's Hatfield over tha rise, mah lord!" Arbroth announced, returning to the column after scouting the road ahead.

Shielding his eyes from the sun, Philip looked and gauged the time to be around mid-morning, and guessed they were only eight leagues from London. The closer they got to the capital, the more Henry withdrew into himself and Philip could see his turmoil in his hunched posture.

Riding alongside an ancient boundary bank, topped by a thick hedge, the column came to a junction where the Great North and St Albans roads met. From here they cantered uphill, passing a moated manor house and trotted through Barnet. Cantering down the opposite slope, they dodged children, pigs and rotting waste, dumped in the street. Around Barnet, the country opened out into broad heathland and cultivated fields, and the sweet warbling of birds was replaced by snorting pigs and the bleating of scruffy sheep. Sensing the long journey was coming to an end, Henry began to brood on his fate. When Arbroth rode on ahead, Philip attempted to alleviate his anxiety.

"Not far now," he said, pushing a hand down into the gap between the hard saddle and his sweaty lower back and moaning at the grinding pain.

Henry gave a passive smile and gazed up at the few formless clouds drifting aimlessly across an azure sky.

With the sun high, Philip led his party through the Bishop of London's hunting estate and up steeply wooded Highgate hill. From the crest, he could see London in the distance, its extensive skyline dominated by hundreds of church spires. Head and shoulders above them all was St Paul's, the iconic landmark for all visitors to the capital, its great steeple pointing almost five hundred feet into the sky. Standing in the stirrups, Philip saw his Scot riding back up the road.

"Nothing warms the heart more than the sweet smell of the country," Henry sighed, drawing the fragrant aroma of wildflowers in through his nostrils.

"Horseshit," Philip scoffed rudely, concerned by the way Arbroth was lashing his horse, "is what I smell."

"Mah lord!" Arbroth yelped, yanking back on the reins.

Philip halted the company while the Scot drew up his frazzled rouncey in a cloud of billowing dirt.

"Tha Earl o' Warwick is waiting for ye!" he spluttered, pointing to the village of Islington. "Doon thar!"

"What?" Philip coughed, flapping dust from his face.

"Tha Earl –"

"I heard you!" Philip frowned, looking at his mystified esquire.

"You are mistaken; his lordship is in Calais," Harrington piped up.

"Ah dinnah know aboot that, laddie; all ah know is what ah have seen," he confirmed.

"I know why he's here," Philip growled, scratching his wet neck and pointing his chin at Henry. "He wants *him*."

"But –" his esquire objected.

Philip shook his head and channelled his frustration into one long exhalation.

"That –"

"My Lord!" Robert cut him off before he said something he would regret.

"By Christ's blood," Philip spluttered, recalling Thomas Talbot's reaction when he took Henry from him at York. "We do the work and my cousin reaps the glory!"

"Perhaps he is here to applaud your good fortune?" Harrington suggested.

"Yes and I'm a dog's arse."

"What will you do?" Harrington asked, as Philip edged his horse forward and looked at the last village before London.

"I don't know," he sighed gloomily, hoping his Scot might be mistaken. "Where is he?"

"Mah lord?" Arbroth said, coming up beside him.

Closing his eyes, Philip drew a breath and held it briefly.

"Forget it," he gasped. "Go to my cousin…" he continued, looking at his esquire. "And tell him…tell him I'm coming in."

Harrington tapped his forehead and spurred his horse away.

"Stay with Henry," Philip told Arbroth. "Let's get this over with."

Falling in beside the old king he bowed respectfully while Philip carped at the state of his sweat-stained tunic before leading the column down Highgate Hill.

Islington lay between two roads which came together at the far end of the village. The houses, inns and several moated manors of Islington were interspersed with patches of wasteland, the most famous being the 'Green'. Trotting towards the southern end of the village, Philip strained to see around a bend in the road. With soldiers on their doorsteps, the locals chose to stay indoors.

Passing the last houses obstructing his view, Philip turned the corner and was greeted by a crowd of knights, men-at-arms and archers, gathered around the maypole on the Green. Warwick's huge banner, held aloft by his banneret, dashed any doubt Philip had that Arbroth may have been wrong. Looking back at his Scot, he rolled his eyes, and brought the column to a halt.

Sitting on a well-groomed horse, in the shade of a tree, the

Earl of Warwick offered his cousin a curt nod. Compared to his grimy, sweaty, bewhiskered kinsman, Warwick, five years Philip's senior, sported a crimson velvet doublet fastened with gold buttons and studded with precious stones. Clean-shaven, his dark brown hair cropped to the lobs, he oozed wealth, power and above all arrogance.

Richard Neville, cousin to the king, Knight of the Garter, Great Chamberlain of England, and Captain of Calais – to name but a few of his many titles – was the most influential nobleman in the land. Many said he ruled England while Edward merely sat on the throne, but this was nothing more than jealousy.

Philip climbed down from his horse and walked over to his cousin, flapping dust from his tunic with his gloves. Sliding easily from the saddle, Warwick motioned for one of his knights to take charge of Henry.

When Philip was face to face with his cousin, those who knew of their recent poor relationship watched with bated breath. Standing before Warwick, Philip waited while he took a step towards him, placed both hands on his shoulders and gave him the kiss of peace.

"Philip," he said sadly, while a knight took Henry's bridle and led him to the maypole through crowds of awed soldiers. "It has been too long."

"My Lord," Philip responded, bowing his head and looking contemptuously at Warwick's dog, Mongo.

"The King will be pleased to hear of your safe arrival... Where is the rest of your escort?"

"My retinue is small, my Lord."

"My brother was to send you reinforcements?"

"We met a detachment wearing Sir John's livery, but they were not his men."

"How could you know?"

"Their captain called himself Mark Fulkerston, I knew him

neither by name nor face, and his answers pleased me not. Wishing to lose neither prisoner nor my life, I ordered my men to kill them."

"Oh," Warwick said, looking at Henry pensively. "Did he attempt to escape?"

"No," Philip sniffed, using his rolled gloves to wipe beads of gritty sweat from his forehead. "I thought you were in Calais, my Lord."

"I finished my business there and returned home," Warwick revealed, miffed by his insolent question, "The king ordered me to take charge of the prisoner and escort him to the Tower."

"Huh," Philip snorted curtly and Warwick spoke quietly in his ear.

"Change your manner or you will join Henry in the Tower."

During their conversation Warwick's men crowded around the old king, reverently touching his clothes and crossing themselves. Resting against the black, deeply-fissured trunk of a poplar tree, Warwick grew frustrated at the attention his men were showing the prisoner.

"Look at those fools," he scoffed, cupping a hand to his mouth. "Stop that, he is no longer your king!"

One of Warwick's esquires led a detachment of men-at-arms to force back the crowd.

"Unbelievable," Warwick huffed.

Irked by his cousin's threat, Philip looked at Robert Harrington, who was stroking Warwick's caparisoned palfrey.

"You will ride with me to London," Warwick commanded.

"As you wish, my Lord," Philip agreed.

"Tie him on!" Warwick shouted at the men guarding the old king.

Several archers roughly tied Henry to his saddle, removed his spurs and bound his feet together under the horse's belly.

As a final insult, one of them snatched the velvet cap from his head and replaced it with a straw hat.

"There, your highness!" the man bowed mockingly. "Now you are king again."

"Enough!" Warwick growled, observing the discontented murmurings of the majority of his men. "Get them on the road!"

Warwick's officers pushed and prodded the soldiers off the Green and lined them up for the short march to London.

Lord Warwick and his knights led the way, passing the Priory of St John's Clerkenwell and the monastery at Charterhouse before moving through West Smithfield. During the journey Henry rode alone behind Warwick's knights, while Philip and his retinue followed, dragging the extra horses taken from Fulkerston's party. Warwick's foot soldiers tramped along in their wake, griping at having to eat dust.

The procession entered London through Newgate, which had been built to relieve the congestion around St Paul's. Filing under the gatehouse, they passed the Greyfriars, Newgate market and St Nicholas shambles, where an angry crowd had gathered, ready to pelt the Henry with fruit and vegetables.

"Why did we come this way?" Philip's esquire asked. "Aldersgate would have been an easier route."

"Don't you see? My cousin has set this up, it's part of the act," Philip scowled, angry with Richard for relegating him to ride behind the prisoner. "The mighty Earl of Warwick needs an audience to show off his trophy. Hah, he thinks he is Caesar."

Riding at the head of the column, Warwick soaked up the adoration thrown at him like a sponge.

"See how easy it is to please these sheep," he told his banneret.

"Aye, my Lord."

"Look at him!" someone shouted, pointing at Henry from an upstairs window. "Get off and milk it!"

The comment brought howls of derisive laughter from the crowd and several men stepped forward to bare their arses, Henry did not react.

"This is no' right," Arbroth complained, shaking his head as a badly bruised pear flew past Henry's head and splattered in the street.

"What can I do?" Philip said. "They blame him for all their woes."

"Your wife is a whore!" Someone yelled, as Warwick's great hairy dog Mongo escaped his leash and weaved back through the column, barking at Clovis.

"And your son is a bastard!" an old woman cackled, her words causing the old king's head to slump forward.

"They should not treat him this way; he's like a lost lamb," Harrington announced.

"*Domine Deus, Agnus Dei*," Philip said thoughtfully.

"The lamb of God?" Harrington translated.

"Some call him that."

His esquire made the sign of the cross.

The insults and flying fruit increased as prisoner and escort progressed through the slippery, fly-infested butcher's shambles and entered Cheapside. Near the Cheap Cross, a beautifully-carved monument to Eleanor, wife of Edward I, its niches full of iconic statuary, Philip gingerly massaged his sore arm and looked at the two painted stone shields on the memorial, one bearing the arms of England the other those of Eleanor's birthplace Castile.

"Is your arm painful?" Harrington asked.

"No," he lied.

"His lordship knows how to stir up these fools," his esquire commented as they passed the Church of St Mary-le-Bow.

"Have you and his lordship resolved your differences? I saw him kiss you."

"Did Judas not kiss Jesus before betraying him?"

Harrington said no more.

At the Great Conduit, a huge cistern of drinking water carried underground by lead pipes from Tyburn, a number of Warwick's retainers broke ranks and rushed to the fountain. The roofed-over water tank, set below ground on the south side of the street, near the junction of Cheapside and Le Poultry, was a popular spot for locals and traders to collect clean water.

"Stop wasting it!" the agitated warden shouted, as a dozen thirsty, dust-laden soldiers crowded around the stone basin at the end of the conduit.

Philip tutted as Warwick's men fought for the water cock and used their palms to scoop up the cool, refreshing liquid.

"*Peysans*," he sneered, using the French word for country folk.

"Get back, I say!" the warden growled, thwacking the unruly men with a stick to force them away.

A wagon carrying two large water barrels set off from the conduit just as a young child tottered into the street. Startled by the cold water splashing their legs, the oxen stampeded, sending the cart slewing sideways on the wet street. The cooing infant sat down to pick up a stone in the road and a heavy cartwheel rolled over his body, crushing him to death. The sharp cracking of bones and the sight of mashed flesh blended with a demented mother's high-pitched screams. When the cart bumped off the child, the mother carefully picked up the bloody, muddy bundle and collapsed on the ground.

"My God," the warden gasped, trembling.

Alerted by the commotion behind him, Warwick turned

and commanded one of his sergeants to get the men back in line.

"What happened?" he demanded.

"A child's been killed, my Lord," one of his knights said casually.

"Give the mother a purse for her loss."

The knight cantered back to the distressed parent, sat in the dirt rocking her dead infant, and callously tossed her a small leather pouch.

"Life is cheap?" Philip's esquire mused as the column set off.

Riding on, Philip watched his cousin wave his hat in the air, goading the crowd to cheer him more loudly and insult the prisoner more passionately.

"Hey Harry, what's your wife doing in France?" A baker yelled, nipping out of the crowd and slapping Henry's horse on the rump.

The animal lashed out with his back legs and the old king wobbled in his saddle, before the procession moved into Le Poultry.

"Get back!" Philip barked, slipping a foot out of the stirrup and kicking the baker into a draper's stall.

"Where's Margaret?" an old crone asked.

"On her back being swiven by frogs!" a patron of the Cardinal's Hat obliged, standing outside the tavern, close to where Le Poultry divided into Cornhull and Bradstreet.

Philip pressed his knees into Clovis's ribs, steering him to trample Warwick's annoying dog, which continuously raced up and down the column barking at the horses. Unable to see the hound, Clovis's hooves nipped its tail and the animal bounded off along Cornhull yelping in pain. Near Longhornes Alley, Mongo ran up to a vintner, locked in a pillory for selling bad wine. The felon had been showered with his own product and forced to drink the tainted brew. Mongo jumped up licking wine off the prisoner's face and barked furiously, while his master yelled at his dog-handler to leash the mutt.

"Damned dog," Philip scoffed, as Mongo rolled in the wine, staining his hairy coat.

"He wears Lord Warwick's colours," Arbroth commented, bringing a smile to Philip's face.

Clammy heat, the warm stench, a baying crowd and Warwick's intimidating standard combined to aggravate Philip. Rubbing his wet neck, he looked at the ugly faces of the crowd and pouted at their misguided anger.

"Why are they so mad?" his esquire asked.

"Can't you smell the ale amongst all this piss and shit?" He sighed. "His lordship's people have done their work well."

"My Lord?"

"I've had enough," Philip hissed. "We'll take our leave," he said, pointing to where Bishopsgate St bisected Cornhull. "There."

"His lordship won't like it."

"He's too far up his own arse to notice. We'll go and visit my manors," he said, "what's left of them."

"Shall I inform –?" his esquire suggested.

"No," Philip cut him off.

"With respect, my Lord –"

"No!"

Near a small water conduit at the crossroads, the Earl of Warwick steered his horse south into Grasche St, while Philip rode off in the opposite direction, waving for his men to follow.

"I am going to be wed," he announced out of the blue as they trotted along Bishopsgate Street.

"Mistress Talbot?" his esquire asked, placing a hand on his hip.

"Mistress Talbot," Philip confirmed, with a wicked leer.

"Not a night goes by that I do not think of her," he said, an impression of Isobel's naked body in his mind.

"Happy thoughts, my Lord?"

"The happiest," he sighed longingly.

"Grope Lane's no far away, mah lord!" Arbroth called out, listening in.

Philip looked at him and chuckled.

"We can find a couple o' Flemish whores; they know how tah satisfy a man."

"Their cunnis hair's as thick as a Northman's beard," Philip cringed.

"Aye," Arbroth beamed, licking his lips. "There's nothing ah like better than tah bury ma yard in a moist bush o' Flemish wool."

Laughing at Robert's discomfort, Philip nudged Clovis into a canter as they approached Bishopsgate and the crenulated city wall spreading out on either side. Passing through the gatehouse they followed the road out into the country.

Philip Neville led his company to his manor at North Marston by way of Barnet. By the time they reached St Albans, he was asleep in the saddle, and his trembling, frothing horse was on its last legs. In a single day, they had ridden over sixty miles but could go no further. As Clovis scuffed up to where Sopwell Lane and Holywell Hill met, the faint sounds of a battle fought long ago echoed once more inside Philip's head. In his insentient state he saw images of himself, ten years earlier, smashing through a house with Sir Robert Ogle, as they broke into the town.

While these events absorbed Philip's thoughts, his palfrey's tremulous gait took him up Holywell hill to the marketplace. Between Eleanor Cross and the clock tower, the column shunted to a halt and Clovis snorted defiantly, refusing to go on. Rubbing his numb face, Philip looked at the clock tower and remembered the soulful clang of its bell 'Gabriel', as a prelude to the first battle of St Albans.

"My Lord?" his esquire said.

"What?" Philip yawned, fingering his heavy, bloodshot eyes.

"Which way?"

"Seek lodgings, there," he groaned, indicating a long two-storey, half-timbered building that was split into two separate inns, the upper floor bowing into the lower one.

Harrington nodded and Philip persuaded Clovis to walk the last few yards. Threading his way between the market stalls, he turned into Church Street and dismounted at the Swan Inn, grimacing at the pulsating pain raging from his neck to his knees.

"See what you can get for the spare horses," he told Arbroth.

"Mah lord, they serve good ale here," he announced, pointing to a nearby alehouse with a green bough outside, indicating a fresh brew.

"Feed and brush down our horses first."

Arbroth tapped his forehead and led the captured herd away in search of a buyer.

"I need sleep," Philip muttered, sniffing his tunic. "Phew," he grimaced, as Robert entered the inn in search of lodgings.

With no bath available, Philip settled for a wash and shave. Too tired to eat, he guzzled several cups of wine and staggered downstairs to his room. Leaving the door ajar he collapsed on the low bed and fell asleep. Arbroth followed moments later and found his master in a deep sleep. After removing his boots, he left.

At breakfast next day, a revived Philip Neville divvied up the money Arbroth received from the sale of the horses and what he found on Fulkerston's body. Keeping five pounds for himself, he shared the rest amongst the men. After a lazy morning, he led his retinue to Aylesbury, twenty-five miles further on.

Trotting into the quiet market town, their arrival was accompanied by St Mary's Church bells tolling the canonical hour of Vespers, 7.00 p.m. With the sun setting Philip pushed on the final nine miles to North Marston, dropping off his men at their homes along the way, until he was left with Arbroth and Robert. After negotiating a tangle of low branches jutting out over the dark, weed-choked path, Philip was relieved to see the silhouette of his home. Throwing a blanket on the ground, he bedded down for the night.

Rising to the dawn chorus, Philip tossed aside the damp blanket, sucked in enough air to fill his lungs and vigorously rubbed his arthritic elbows. North Marston and Stratton Audley had been bequeathed to Philip by his father, but the farmland around the house was mainly heavy clay that baked hard in the summer and turned to sticky mud in winter. Poor drainage allowed isolated pools of water to stagnate, turning much of the land to marsh. When Queen Margaret marched on London in February 1461, a marauding band of Lancastrians raided the area and burned down the two manors along with the mill at Long Marston and his tenant's cottages. A few small farms escaped the destruction, but they barely produced enough food for their own use.

Philip silently surveyed the collapsed timbers and ivy-strangled limestone walls and looked sadly at the rising sun. The first hint of daylight gave the grey clouds a pink tinge and sent rays of light shooting through the trees, breathing life into a new day and banishing the uncertainty of night. For Philip the early morning was a favourite time. In the low-lying, viscous mist fogging the countryside during that mysterious grey period between fading night and dawning day, nature stirred into life.

"Mah lord?" Arbroth interrupted, grinding up a ball of phlegm and spitting as he emerged from the ruins.

"Cold?" Philip asked, his serene thoughts shattered.

"Aye," the Scot shivered, drawing the blanket around his shoulders.

"You're becoming an old woman," Philip scoffed, as a light breeze rustled the leaves in the trees.

"Ah feel mah age in tha mornings."

"Look at this place," Philip tutted, finally able to see the damage. "Goddamned French whore."

Arbroth struggled to keep the blanket on his shoulders when Robert Harrington popped his head over the wall.

"Hello," he yawned, his youthful exuberance irritating.

In his late teens, Robert Harrington was a quick learner, though he lacked confidence and at times would lapse into a dark mood; he never got over his mother's early death. A fine esquire, Robert yearned for what he believed was his overdue knighthood.

"Start a fire," Philip told his Scot. "We'll look around."

After a sobering inspection of his property, Philip and Robert returned to the house. Shortly before noon they sat down to a meal of pea and onion soup, seasoned with sugar and salt, and wine. With a full belly, Philip picked up a dead branch and used it to beat down some of the weeds smothering the front wall and examined the stonework. Arbroth, meanwhile, brushed down Clovis and inspected his lower legs.

"He needs rest," Philip announced.

"Aye…and he has tha sore back," Arbroth said, running a hand over the palfrey and sensing the animal's pain as it whinnied and snorted.

"Ride to Aylesbury and find me a good rouncey," Philip told his esquire. "I need money to rebuild this," he blew, tossing the branch aside angrily.

Arbroth overheard the conversation and joined them.

"Robbie, would ye take them for a wee walk?"

The esquire obliged and when he was out of earshot, Arbroth turned to Philip.

"Ah can fetch up some o' tha money," he whispered, referring to the five hundred pounds meant for the Duke of Somerset but taken by Philip and squirrelled away in the Forest of Galtres.

"No," Philip said, crossing himself, "that money is cursed."

"But ye need it," Arbroth insisted. "What's tha use o' leaving it buried?"

Philip stared at the caved-in roof and blinked vacantly as he remembered the men murdered at his command, for him to get one over on Somerset.

"No," he insisted.

"My Lord!" his esquire called excitedly, leading the horses in a genteel walk and pointing to a rider cantering up the track.

The three men watched the horseman dismount and walk toward them, dragging his snorting horse.

"This is not a good omen," Philip muttered.

"I seek Sir Philip Neville?" he panted.

"You've found him."

The sweating courier reached into a satchel attached to his belt and thrust a letter at Philip.

"Oh?" he frowned, recognising the king's seal.

While he read the letter, the messenger took a long drink from a flask slung over his shoulder and shared it with his horse.

"I am to return to London," Philip told his esquire before addressing the courier. "How did you find me?"

"Lord Warwick told the king you had deserted him," the courier explained, wiping his hand in his sleeve. "His grace said you might come to this place."

"Deserted?" Harrington gasped.

"I'm in the shit," Philip groaned, putting a hand under his chin to stress the depth, "up to here."

"Mah lord?"

"Go to Aylesbury and find me a fresh horse," Philip told his Scot, removing several coins from a purse. "Tell the men to stay home and plough their fields… I'll send word when I need them."

Arbroth took the money and listened while Philip explained what he should do.

"When Clovis is rested take him to York; I'll send for you, if I am at liberty."

"Yea'll be fine," Arbroth said. "Tha king's a fair man."

"Perhaps, but I've stretched his good graces of late."

"Ye have that," he agreed, bouncing the coins in his hand.

"Tell the king I will come to London," Philip told the messenger. "But I have to wait for a horse."

The courier remounted his horse and trotted away. When Arbroth was set to leave Philip called after him.

"And don't forget my change!"

Chapter 6

AFTER A TWO-DAY ride, Philip and his esquire arrived at Eltham Palace, one of the king's residences, eight miles from London, and were escorted to the royal apartments. While waiting for the king, Philip walked along the bookshelves and ran his fingertips lightly over the spines of the leather-bound volumes. Pulling out several books, he flipped through the pages and was impressed by the colourful illustrations. Engrossed in *La grant hystoire Cesar*, he failed to hear the king enter. Philip's esquire managed a meaningful cough as a warning and he quickly replaced the book.

"Your Grace," he grovelled, dropping to one knee and bowing his head.

"Cousin," Edward sniffed, noting Philip's dusty attire. "You have done well."

"Sire?" he said, confused, his attention focused on the king's shiny red leather boots.

"A present," Edward smiled, aware of his interest as he extended his hand, "from his Excellency the Spanish ambassador."

Philip took his hand and kissed the blood-red ruby set in a thick gold band on his middle finger.

Standing six feet four inches tall and wearing a white silk shirt and black hose, Edward's great height was impressive. His long flowing chestnut hair, finely sculpted features, bejewelled fingers and manicured nails were indicative of his newfound passion for style. This 'most handsome of Princes' loved fine clothes, jewellery and fighting, and his sexual appetite was legendary. Criticised for allowing his wife's relatives to marry into the noblest families, Edward tried to show a sense of fairness. Regardless of his faults, Philip was proud of their shared bloodline. Since the queen's coronation, in May 1465, Edward had worked hard to persuade his people to accept her.

"How may I please you, your Grace?" Philip asked.

"You admire my books?"

"Yes, sire."

"My brother Richard is the reader of the family," Edward said, dismissing Harrington and steering Philip through a door that led to a gallery via the queen's lodgings. "Come, walk with me."

A second door opened onto an inner courtyard and Philip struggled to keep pace with Edward's giant strides. While crossing a stone bridge over the moat, Philip looked back and saw four armed guards following at a distance.

"How was your journey from York?"

"There was only one attempt to free Henry," Philip smirked. "Which we foiled."

"'Twould have been better for us all if Henry had never reached London," Edward muttered.

"Your Grace?" Philip questioned, as they passed through the gatehouse and entered a walled orchard.

"Nothing," he sniffed. "I come here for solitude." Edward sighed, waiting for a chair. "Here I am able to lay aside the burden of kingship for a brief moment," he explained, while half a dozen servants marched into the orchard bearing a padded, brightly painted chair and a canopy of embroidered gold cloth, which was propped up on spears above the seat to protect the king from a glaring sun. "How shall we mend this?"

"Your Grace?"

"You and Richard," he said, sitting and indicating for Philip to be seated on a stone bench.

"I left his lordship –" Philip began, while the servants knelt to wait on the king's pleasure.

"This rift between you causes me great concern," Edward stopped him.

"I believe in my heart that he ordered my brother's execution," Philip said, almost shamefully.

"I have spoken to Richard on this matter; he swears he is innocent of such slander."

"Sire…. I –"

"He demands your arrest, but I have calmed his temper, for now."

Philip nodded his gratitude.

"I want an end to it," Edward insisted. "I'll not allow another private feud to turn this kingdom upside down."

"But your Grace –"

"My cousin covets an alliance with Louis of France, though he knows my mind is set on a treaty with Burgundy," Edward revealed. "In my heart I know he will never forgive me for my choice of bride and this distorts his judgement," he continued. "Yet for all his scheming I am willing to forgive him; were it anyone else I would have his head on a spike. I want to forget the bad blood between us, but how long should I put up with his arrogance? I fear one day he will push me too far."

"You must do what you think best," Philip responded guardedly.

"Your impertinent advice is not helpful," said Edward, while a servant picked up a cushion and placed it behind his back.

"Sire, you are surrounded by knaves who give you fealty in return for favours; regardless of our differences, I know Lord Warwick is true to the House of York."

"Govern thy tongue, cousin!" Edward warned. "I am not as naive as you presume."

"Forgive me, sire," he apologized.

"You are much too candid," Edward huffed. "And that is your downfall."

"May I ask a boon?"

"Tell me and I will consider it," Edward said, surprised by his audaciousness.

"I seek your permission to wed."

"You?" he gasped. "Whom do you wish to wed?"

Philip hesitated and a whistle of anxiety fluted from his nose.

"Speak up," Edward pressed, curiously.

"The sister of Sir Francis Talbot."

"Isobel?" The king mused. "She is a beauty."

"And such sweetness of voice," Philip sighed, recalling the day they met in York.

"The language of love does not become you."

Philip blushed and cleared his throat.

"Has she accepted your suit?" Edward asked.

"Not yet, but she will not refuse."

"Your confidence does you credit," the king smirked. "We are finished here, you will accompany me to Westminster."

"Now?"

"Now."

"But your Grace, I am without funds."

"All who had a part in finding Henry and bringing him to London will be rewarded for their efforts," Edward announced. "And you will serve me as a knight of the body?"

Philip was speechless; service to the king would remove him from Warwick's sphere, but it would bring him into contact with his old flame, Elizabeth Percy, now a lady-in-waiting to the queen, and wife of Ralph Hastings, brother to the King's chamberlain.

"Well?" Edward sniffed, irritated by Philip's delay in answering. "What say you?"

"Sire…" He gasped, dropping to his knees. "I am overwhelmed by your Grace's trust."

Edward looked down at Philip's greasy, tangled dark hair and sniffed.

"Rise," he commanded.

Philip tried to show gratitude as he sat back on the bench.

"You have the royal consent to marry."

"But I *am* indentured to Lord Warwick," he reminded the king.

"All men owe allegiance to their king above any other; you shall wear your own colours and serve me. I will smooth Richard's ruffled feathers. For bringing Henry to London your properties shall be restored and you will be paid the sum of thirty pounds for one hundred and fifty days' service."

"You are most generous, sire,"

"There is the question of a thousand pounds," Edward continued. "Meant for the Duke of Somerset and lost while in your charge?"

"Your Grace, we were attacked in the night by outlaws," he said nervously. "My men were massacred and the money taken."

Philip's nervously flickering eyes and blushing face betrayed his guilt.

"Lord Warwick told me a villain came to him," Edward said, "and revealed a plot by one of your own men to waylay the coach in the Forest of Galtres."

"But every man was killed."

"All but one."

"I was badly injured and left for dead –"

Edward raised a hand to stop him, but he continued.

"Your Grace, I will swear on the Holy book if such a declaration will prove my innocence," Philip blurted.

"Your word is enough," Edward said casually. "Did Henry complain during the ride from York?" he asked, while a servant approached with a jug of wine.

"No, sire."

Edward nodded and waved the servant away.

"He bore his suffering in silence," Philip explained. "Yet at Islington Lord Warwick had him tied to a horse and led through the streets of London in abject humiliation."

"Henry is the cause of all the misery in this land, and he will be confined until I decide his fate…" Edward explained. "You have sympathy for him?"

"Not sympathy, sire, compassion."

"I must speak with my Secretary; we leave here within the hour."

The Guards and servants bowed their heads as Edward walked back to the palace alone. Philip stayed in the orchard for a while, contemplating his good fortune and enjoying the silence. From now on, his life was to be closely linked with the king's.

After a short rest, Philip and his esquire collected their horses and joined Edward's entourage in the outer court. Soon the king and his banneret were leading a column of knights, foot soldiers and servants back to Westminster. As they passed Charing Cross and the bright, white lime-washed walls of the Chapel and hospital of St Mary's Rounceval, Edward looked over his shoulder at his cousin.

"Tonight we eat and drink until we are fit to burst," he announced, slapping his standard-bearer on the back, "and get very merry."

"His grace is in good humour," Harrington said.

"What of the queen, sire?" Philip dared, the odour of bad water rising from a series of ditches that drained into the Thames, strong.

"The queen chooses to stay at Eltham," Edward quipped.

Philip exchanged a knowing grin with his esquire.

Passing the Hermitage of St Katherine's and an area of open land known as Scot land, the column made its way along King Street. Out in front, the murrey-and-blue royal standard, bearing the quartered emblems of England and France, danced around its pole, producing an hypnotic effect on Philip which filled his chest with pride. With a growing population, London had burst out of its old walls and was spreading in all directions. The area along the river between the city and Westminster was no different; new houses and tenements were creeping ever closer to the palace.

Built of Kentish ragstone and Reigate freestone, Westminster lay sandwiched between the ancient abbey and the Thames. Protected by high walls and the river, the royal residence was dominated by its Great Hall, the largest in all Europe. Next to the Great Hall was St Stephen's Chapel and beyond that the royal apartments. In the far southwest corner of the cluttered palace lay the Jewel House, an 'L' shaped, partially moated tower, which held the king's plate and jewels.

The royal party entered the palace through a gatehouse and was greeted by a fanfare of trumpets.

"By the Holy Ghost," Philip gasped, slapping a hand to his ear.

"The King's trumpeters are in much need of some practice," his esquire squirmed.

Edward acknowledged the guards, who stood ready to disarm those who were to accompany him inside.

"Why should I give up my blade?" Philip complained, grudgingly unsheathing his arming sword. "Surely my new position entitles me to keep it?"

Harrington shrugged his shoulders as he received Philip's blade and passed it, along with his own, to the guard.

"My Lord, I beg thee…do not offend the king, he has been most generous."

Philip huffed at Robert's comment, while Edward dismounted and made his way to the king's chamber. The soldiers, household officers and servants dispersed to carry out their duties.

Philip and his esquire were taken to a small chamber near the royal apartments. With so many courtiers, craftsmen and soldiers at the palace, lodgings were at a premium. Forcing open the jammed door of his assigned room, Philip lurched back.

"Phew," he gasped, as the strong odour of stale reeds wafted out, "it stinks."

Devoid of furniture, the undersized chamber consisted of a small fireplace and one tiny window.

"No garderobe?" Philip complained.

"Latrines is outside," his escort explained. "You're lucky to 'ave a room; the king's chamberlain rents a house in the city."

"When was the last time this place was occupied?" Philip groused. "And where's the furniture?"

"You buys yer own."

"Buy my own? My wage will barely pay for the care of my horses," He gasped, turning to his esquire. "Go and see what you can find," he told him. "I'll need a bed, candles and a pot to piss in, and anything else you can find to make this…tomb liveable."

"I'll need money."

"Here," Philip said, tossing him a purse.

"Where am I to lodge?" Harrington asked.

"'Why, 'ere," the guard said surprised, rubbing his thick nose.

"Here?" Harrington echoed, looking inside. "There's barely room for one."

The esquire kicked out at the layer of dusty reeds.

"Open the window," Philip commanded, angry at being forced to share. "And clean up this shit."

"I'm not a servant," Robert pouted.

"No?" Philip hissed, looking at the guard. "What about food?"

"The Lord Chamberlain allocates food, drink and firewood for those lodging at the palace," he said before leaving.

"Hastings," Philip hissed, shaking his head.

Philip's esquire found a threadbare broom behind the door and aggressively swept out the rotting reeds covering the floor. Coughing on the choking dust, Philip went off to explore the palace. Once the apartment was swept clean, Harrington purchased the items needed to make their lodgings bearable. When he returned, he was permitted to rest before leaving for York, to fetch Philip's horses, armour, clothes, and Arbroth.

That evening, Philip Neville, still miffed over the accommodation, and wearing his Warwick livery, entered the Great Hall through its south entrance. Decorated with huge, rich tapestries and colourful bunting, and lit by hundreds of iridescent candles, the hall radiated warmth and opulence. After a sumptuous supper, the tables were packed away but Philip struggled to conceal his loneliness. Scuffing his boots on the dark marble floor, he tried, and failed, to attract the attention of several ladies. The white bear and ragged staff badge, sewn over his left breast, was a slap in the face to those who disliked Warwick, yet despite their strained relationship, Philip enjoyed flaunting the symbol of Neville power. Sensing hostility from the anti-Warwick faction, he deliberately downed a goblet of sweet vernage wine in one swift gulp and deliberately rubbed the badge.

While half a dozen musicians played a medley of popular songs and several couples danced, Philip, his stomach bloated from too much goose and stuffing, snatched another cup of wine and raised it to one of the absent queen's maids of honour, in an attempt to catch her eye. Frowning at his impudence, she stuck her nose in the air and walked away. Sniffing the sleeve of his doublet, which had been sprinkled with sweet water to conceal the smell of stale sweat, he looked up and saw Henry Brandon, steward of the royal household, and Thomas Lord Stanley looking at him. Narrowing his eyes, Philip scowled in their direction. Stanley was the older brother of Sir William Stanley, the knight who found Philip's drunken abuse towards the Bishop of Durham, at Bamburgh, offensive. To counter Philip's hostility, the tall, long-haired Lord Stanley turned his back.

"Mr Brandon, there was a time when a Knight of the Body was a title worthy of merit," he said loud enough for Philip to hear.

"Aye my Lord," Brandon, agreed, glancing sympathetically at Philip.

Drawing a deep breath in through his nostrils, Philip slapped a hand to where his sword should have been and passed them a curt nod. Walking over to the king, standing with his beautiful nineteen-year-old sister Margaret, he asked permission to retire. Edward accepted his plea of tiredness and Philip bowed graciously, but a tap on his shoulder delayed his departure.

"Good evening, Philip," William Hastings announced cheerfully, his soft, satirical voice irritating.

With Edward and his sister present, he knew he could only respond with courtesy.

"My Lord."

"I must congratulate you for bringing Henry safely to London."

"Thank you," he managed, bowing and smirking at William's ridiculously long pointed shoes, the pikes extending more than a foot out from the toes and secured to his bony knees by thin silver chains.

As Edward's chief advisor, Will Hastings had been well

rewarded for his service to the crown. Tall, spindly, his face dominated by arching brows, high cheekbones, a long sharp nose and steel blue eyes, Hastings was obsessed with his appearance. Despite a soft voice, William spoke from the heart, adding passion to his words with exaggerated hand gestures.

"Will," Edward smiled. "I have taken my dear cousin into my household."

"A munificent act, sire," he grovelled before turning back to Philip. "Dear friend, I would embrace thee but I know you would shy away from such affection."

"I thank my lord chamberlain for his indulgence," Philip replied. "By your leave sire," he added, bowing to the king and his sister before walking away. "Poser," he hissed softly at Sir William.

"He will never learn," Edward told his sister, tutting at his comment.

"Then why indulge him, sire?" Hastings said, spotting a pair of demure damsels curtsying in the background.

"His father was my mother's brother...and she loved him very much." The king smiled, approving of his chamberlain's choice.

Kissing his sister's hand, Edward excused himself and walked away with Lord Hastings.

"Take them to my bedchamber," he whispered discreetly.

William nodded and signalled for the two women to follow him.

Philip stormed back to his room, cursing Hastings as he felt around the dark, unfamiliar surroundings in search of a candle.

"Shit!" he swore, stubbing his toes on the foot of his low bed. "Fuck...."

Removing his boots, Philip held his injured toes until the pain receded; the fresh reeds scented with aromatic herbs helped ease his anguish. Utilizing the pale moonlight beaming in through the tiny window, he sparked a candle and slammed the door. Sitting down on his pallet, a gift from the king, he massaged his foot.

With his esquire on his way to York, Philip was overwhelmed by a sense of isolation. Pondering his new position, he unfastened and removed his tunic and lay down. Staring at the ceiling, he clasped his fingers together under his head and yawned. Closing his heavy eyelids, he thought of Isobel.

"Elizabeth," he mumbled wearily, his eyes snapping open as he realised his mistake. "Treacherous bitch," he spat, turning on his side.

Chapter 7

WITH LITTLE TO do at the palace, Philip sought an outlet to relieve his boredom. His new livery coat would not be ready for several days, thus putting his duties as a knight of the body on hold. Wandering the corridors and yards of the palace, he would smile at the court ladies coming and going, which tormented him to such an extent his appetite for carnal pleasure became unbearable. To douse his lustful yearnings, he took part in a tennis tournament. Using thick gloves, Philip and three fellow knights belted a leather ball stuffed with dog hair back and forth over a net set up in the Great Hall. Several giggling female spectators, watching from the gallery, fuelled Philip's rising ardour and only encouraged him to show off. After several hours he had had enough. Shaking hands with his opponents, he wiped dripping sweat from his face and bowed to the ladies before leaving.

During a calming game of tables later with the steward of the royal household, Philip spoke openly of his urgings. Henry Brandon, the steward and one of Edward's close circle of friends, suggested he pay a visit to the Southwark stews.

"Go to the Rose Inn," he grinned, "and ask for Cherrylips." Leaning over the gaming table and jerking his thick brows up and down, he added: "She'll set thy craving free."

"Cherrylips," Philip frowned. "What kind of name is that?"

"You'll find out," Brandon sniggered. "Go by boat – but

beware, the alleyways of Southwark are infested with thieves and murderers… so go armed and keep your wits about you."

Philip knew of the brothels lining the south bank of the Thames, tempting Londoners to come over and enjoy the fleshpots. Being outside the city, the 'Bankside stews' came under the Bishop of Winchester's jurisdiction, his own residence being cheek by jowl with the brothels.

"I shall take your advice," Philip said.

After accompanying the king to Vespers that evening, Philip returned to his bedchamber. Plopping a flat velvet cap on his head and throwing a short cloak around his shoulders, he retrieved his sword and made his way to the waterfront. At Bridge wharf, a dock extending out into the Thames, he saw a line of boats tied up.

"Hello?" he called out.

The two watermen in the nearest wherry looked up and grudgingly from their game of dice and silently took their seat in the centre of the light, shallow boat.

"Bankside," Philip demanded, dragging his scabbard aside as he stepped aboard and sat in the stern.

"We only go to Coldharbour," a grizzle-faced ferryman sniffed, spitting over the side.

"If you walk from Coldharbour to St Magnus Church and you'll find a ferry to take you over," his more amenable companion suggested.

Philip accepted the offer with a nod and the vessel set off downriver, sped along by an outgoing tide.

Several hundred yards from London Bridge the wherry cut back to the north shore, aiming for Coldharbour Steps. Having paid the fee, Philip walked several hundred yards downriver, his route illuminated by the flames of roaring braziers. At Churchyard Alley, he saw half a dozen men waiting to be ferried over to the south bank. Descending the slippery steps, he rudely forced his way to the front of the queue and boarded the boat first, exposing his old Warwick livery coat to any who objected. Holding his arms out for balance, he took his seat in the back.

"Bankside?" a strapping, frizzy-haired boatman announced, sneering at Philip's gall.

The other passengers traipsed aboard and sat in twos, showing their backs to the ill-mannered knight. None confirmed their destination and the vessel set off for St Mary's landing on the opposite shore.

As the boat cast off, a last-minute fare ran along the jetty and leapt aboard, almost tipping the vessel. Sitting in the prow, the latecomer received a tirade of abuse from both boatmen and passengers.

"You risk our lives for a piece of wool… you donkey!"

Keeping his features shrouded by a cowl, he refused to answer.

With the drama over, Philip relaxed and began to wonder what Cherrylips was like, but the stink of detritus floating out with the tide curtailed his blissful thoughts. As the ferry cut across the Thames, the roar of water surging under London Bridge grew deafening. The structure's twenty arches channelled the turbulent river between rubble-filled starlings, and it was only the skill of the oarsmen that prevented the boat from shooting under the bridge and capsizing in the boiling waters. Hundreds of twinkling lights from buildings on the bridge shimmered off the surface of the river, illuminating the white-washed brothels on the south bank.

"We all going for a-swiving," the smaller, heavily tanned ferryman sang out annoyingly.

"You want a Winchester goose, *sir*?" his bulkier companion asked one embarrassed passenger, laughing at his discomfort. "The 'art's 'orn 'as some good uns."

"What?" Philip hissed.

"Hart's Horn," his grunting associate clarified, emphasising the 'H', his body lunging back and forth with every pull on the oars. "They got a Flemish whore with the biggest breasts; you ask these *gentlemen*, they've been many times afore."

"And 'er teats is like pot lids," his friend added with a leering grin as the boat grated into the sandy shallows before bumping up against St Mary's Dock.

With water squirting up through the gap between the wherry and the submerged steps, Philip paid his penny and followed the others ashore.

"Its tuppence each way and you pays now," one of the ferrymen demanded, grinding up phlegm and snorting it back into his throat. "Or swim back."

"I'll pay when you pick me up," Philip countered, flipping a second coin at the boatman.

"Watch yer step, there's some 'ere who'll cut yer throat for them fine boots you wear'," his mate said. "Curfew bell rings at ten: if ye come out after that, use a torch or the watchmen'll 'ave 'e."

"And come back the same way; if you takes a shortcut along the front, they'll get you for sure."

"When do you stop running?" Philip asked, wiping his wet hands in his hose.

"Ten of the clock."

"Law says we must be tied up on the north shore afore the curfew bell rings, but we makes more money at night... You won't see us but we'll be waitin'," his companion added.

Walking carefully up the slimy steps of St Mary's Dock, Philip watched the boat pull away before following the other passengers down to Maiden Lane. From here they turned west for Horseshoe Alley and followed that narrow, foetid thoroughfare to the stews.

As the bells of St Mary's rang the liturgical hour of Compline, 9.15 pm, Philip found himself standing before a drab building, a huge white rose painted on its front. His fellow passengers had been dropped off at the various brothels fronting the river until Philip found himself alone.

"Come in," a coarse voice called from a well-lit open door.

Philip entered the whorehouse and saw a plump, middle-aged woman seated behind a tall desk, her colourless features hideous in the murky candlelight. He looked at her haggard face and the large hairy birthmark drew his attention to her cheek. Glancing into a side room, its soft yellow light distorting his vision, he spotted several men bouncing semi-clad whores on their laps and laughing.

"Looking to dip yer yard in-ta summit warm 'n' wet?" the woman behind the desk cackled, licking her forefinger and running it down a badly stained sugar loaf.

Philip cringed as she slowly and seductively sucked the sugary finger when movement on his blind side caused him to grip the handle of his sword.

"No 'arm'll come to ye 'ere," she sniffed. "You wanna girl?"

"We 'ave a new un," the gruff stew-holder interjected, but before Philip could answer, he sidled up next to his spouse. "Nearly fifteen and still fresh," he leered, trying to gauge the customer's preference. "Eh, Mrs Collins?"

"Not for me," Philip huffed, scowling at the woman, "and I don't want some old strumpet."

"She's my wife," the offended bawd gasped, fondly pinching her arse, "an' she ain't fer sale at any price."

"Cherrylips," Philip said confidently.

"Cherrylips, Mrs Collins?" the stew-holder mused.

"Cherrylips?" she echoed, baring her few remaining teeth. "She don't come cheap."

"How much?" Philip growled through pursed lips.

"A silver groat."

"A silver groat?" he gasped.

"There's cheaper uns."

"You're nothing but a pair of thieves," Philip snapped.

The stew-holder looked to his burly chucker-out and smirked as the man stepped forward, ready for trouble.

"I'll pay your price, whore-master," Philip growled, as the chucker-out stopped and folded his arms over his barrel chest. "But she'd better be free of the French pox."

"Ye won't find a cleaner whore in all Bankside."

"If I catch the itch, I'll be back," Philip warned, reaching for his purse.

"You pays the girl, but leaves your sword 'ere."

Philip unbuckled his belt and tossed the scabbard at the chucker-out.

"Perhaps my Lord would like two girls –?"

"One's enough at your price."

"'Er room's out back an' up the stairs, red door," Mrs Collins explained, jabbing an elbow in her husband's side, a prompt that he should have asked for more money.

Philip walked through to the back and found himself in an open courtyard. Heading up a set of stairs, he moved along the balcony that went around three sides of the courtyard, passing several painted doors.

Tittering sounds of pleasure interspersed with the grunting of couples locked in carnal rapture, brought a wicked leer to his face as he passed several rooms. Knocking on the red door he suddenly had a vision of some wrinkled old hag waiting on the other side.

"Come in."

Philip opened the door but hesitated.

"Come in," she repeated.

Stepping into the room he saw a shadowy figure standing near the window. Looking around the dimly lit chamber, he made out a chair, a wash basin with a green glazed jug, a cupboard and a bed. Though spartan, the room was tidy except for a broken window which drew in the foul air from the street below and added to the musty smell of mould.

"Have you lain with me before?" she asked, her timbre soothing.

Philip shook his head and tried to see her face, but all he could make out was her dark shape.

"My price is a silver groat," she said almost apologetically, her sweet voice contrary to her harsh profession. "But you are my first tonight."

"Here," he said, removing a groat from his purse. "I hope you're worth it."

"You won't be disappointed," she purred, reaching out to take the money.

"I want to see what I'm getting," he demanded, grabbing her arm and pulling her closer.

"Let go or I'll scream," she threatened, trying to break free, "and you'll be sorry."

Unable to see her face clearly, he released her.

"Do you enjoy hurting women?" she hissed, checking the coin with her teeth.

"Depends on the woman," he parried, removing his hat and unhooking his doublet.

While he undressed, she picked up a towel and stuffed it around the broken window.

"I've asked them to mend this... They never forget to take the rent," she fumed, moving to the bed and sprinkling scented water over the thin sheet.

Draping his doublet and shirt over the chair, he sat down and yanked off his boots and socks while she sparked the pathetic stump of a tallow candle.

"Take your time," she sighed, lying on the bed and edging her body up until her head rested on the horsehair pillow.

"Why are you called Cherrylips?" he asked, feverishly untying his hose.

"You'll find out," she smirked decorously, allowing her robe to fall open. "Perhaps."

"By the saints," he gasped, as his eyes, adjusting to the stuttering candle allowed him to gaze upon her perfect body. What the poor light failed to reveal were the dark rings around her eyes, pallid skin and prominent ribcage, all signs of malnutrition.

"Put out the candle," she whispered.

Philip's heart raced as he studied her from neck to toe. He liked what he saw but her cunnis was obscured by a bent leg. Teasingly she lowered the limb and he focused on the area between her thighs.

"What happened to your wool?" he gasped, startled by her closely cropped cunnis hair as he tried to extinguish the candle with thumb and forefinger.

"I cut it short to keep clean… The candle?" she repeated.

"Forget it," he growled, giving up.

Removing his hose and braies, Philip moved smugly to the bed.

"I see you're ready," she grinned, eyeing his privy parts.

"I've been ready for this a long time," he puffed, climbing onto the bottom of the bed and running his hands up her thin legs.

"Most of my customers keep their stockings on," she chirped, as he inched his way up between her knees, prising them apart as he went.

"Stop talking," he commanded, her sweet scent and the sensual smoothness of her thighs exciting him beyond measure. "For a silver groat I want a feast."

Using his knees to force her legs open, he edged up and blew warm air over her cunnis. She arched her back in pleasurable response and he kissed it softly, his lips barely touching the skin.

"Don't stop," she gasped, grabbing his hair and steering him up towards her bosom.

Suddenly he found what he wanted and forced his yard inside her.

Kissing her forehead, Philip caressed her neck, breasts and shoulders with his tongue and she tried to hold her emotions in check. Finally, she wrapped her arms and legs around him tight and released a frenzied cry that eventually dissolved into a whimper. Before her journey ended, Philip drew in a sharp breath, closed his eyes and released his essence. With his body trembling, he threw back his head and exhaled.

"I did not expect you to be so gentle," she said, as he slid off and lay on his back.

"I could fight a lion," he declared, as she turned on her side and nestled her head in the crook of his arm.

"Am I worth a silver groat?"

He looked at her and they both laughed.

"Again?" she asked.

"Will it cost more?"

"You've paid your money," she smiled. "I'm yours for the night."

"What is your name?" he asked, folding his left arm back under his neck and lightly running the fingers of his right hand over her bony shoulder.

"Portia," she answered, unsure why she was explaining herself to a man who only wanted her for sexual gratification. "I am called Portia."

"Portia? The wife of Brutus was called Portia."

"Brutus?"

"A Roman who murdered Caesar."

"Oh," she said indifferently, tracing a finger over the lumpy, raised skin curving down his left shoulder and under the armpit. "What happened?"

"Towton," he sighed.

"And this?" she pressed, stretching to touch the scabbed-over hole on his upper left arm.

"York."

"Your scars run deep."

"Deep enough to pierce my very soul," he explained.

"Why do you do it?"

"Why do you choose this life?" he countered. "You are not low born."

"My father was an English nobleman wedded to another, and my mother a French seamstress," she revealed. "They met in Normandy but when she fell pregnant he abandoned her."

"The dog."

"The plague took my mother and my father brought me to England, but he died within weeks and his wife left me at a church," she explained. "When I was old enough I was brought here and here I've been ever since."

"Why don't you leave –?"

"I have a little money and one day I shall return to France," she answered.

While he listened, Portia lightly massaged his stomach and the sensation turned his skin hypersensitive. Releasing a pleasurable moan, Philip felt ready for the next course. When he turned to face her, she eased onto her back and raised her arms above her head. Manoeuvring into position, he looked at her face and thought of Elizabeth Hastings. Resting his chin in the cup of his open palm he stared down at her.

"You have a wife?" she asked.

"Not yet," he said thoughtfully, "but soon."

"Do you love her?"

"Love is for fools," he sneered.

"We are all foolish at times… You regret this?"

"No," he smiled, climbing on top of her.

This time Philip was more forceful, pinning her arms, he kissed and bit her neck, breasts and lips. Elated by his sense of superiority, he thrust in and out of her until her moans of pleasure turned to cries of pain.

"You're hurting me," she yelped, as the rope lattice, holding the bed frame together, squeaked and stretched. "Please…"

Aware the guilt he was feeling for betraying Isobel and his antipathy towards Elizabeth Hastings were driving his performance, Philip reined in his anger. This time the act took much longer and was more business-like, and when he finished he rolled off and turned over. Though Elizabeth was no longer his, it was as though he had deceived her, and he cursed himself.

Confused by his frosty silence, Portia touched his back but he jumped off the bed and snatched his clothes. Surprised by his reaction, she pulled on her robe shamefully and moved behind a curtain.

"What's wrong?" she asked, squatting over a piss pot. "You were different."

"Can't you wait to do that?" He groused, screwing his face up at the sound of her pissing in the pot.

"I don't want a child," she answered, moving to the basin and dipping a sponge in a mix of vinegar, rose petals and herbs. "Did I not please you?"

"Yes," he huffed guiltily, quickly tying up his braies.

"You are not like the others."

"Oh yes I am."

"When you leave, take heed: if they know you have money they'll send their man after you," she warned. "Will you come to me again?"

Philip left without another word and thumped heavily downstairs, only to be confronted at the bottom by the lecherous stew-holder.

"Everything to your satisfaction, sir?"

"That's my business," he barked. "My sword."

"If she displeased you, I'll 'ave her beaten."

"She did not displease me."

"There's a fog up, you'll need a torch," he said, handing

Philip his blade. "Go through the garden at the back," he explained. "Watchmen patrol the riverbank at night. They know what goes on 'ere and they sometimes hide nearby."

Philip buckled on his sword belt and the stew-holder went into a side room, only to reappear with a burning torch.

"'Ere," he sniffed. "Now go before you set the place afire."

Philip thanked him with a nod and left the inn. After an anxious walk back to St Mary's Dock he tossed the guttering torch onto the wet sand and looked through the low mist hovering over the river, for the ferry.

"Good night?" asked a smirking waterman seated halfway down the steps, whittling on a piece of driftwood.

"Someone's shadowing me," Philip whispered, edging down the slippery steps and glancing back. "Where's the boat?"

The ferryman pointed his knife at a net-covered mound on the beach, close to the water's edge. The second boatman was scouring the shore for anything of value and when he heard Philip he crunched back to the boat. With the tide turning, he quickly removed the netting and whispered for Philip to wait, but he ignored him and stepped aboard the beached wherry. Cursing his manners, the two boatmen struggled to heave the vessel out of the shallows. Eventually, it scraped free and they jumped aboard. With the vessel drifting into deeper water, Philip looked back and saw a tall, thin man loom out of the mist and stand waiting on the dock.

"Stop," he hissed.

"What is it?"

"There's someone back there."

"We must go on –"

"Turn back," Philip insisted.

One of the ferrymen pointed up at London Bridge.

"If we're caught, we'll lose our licence."

"Do as I say!"

Withdrawing their oars allowed the slow current to slew the vessel around until its prow pointed at the south bank. As the boat turned Philip kept a sharp eye on the shadowy figure onshore.

"Come on," one of the ferrymen whispered, cupping a hand to his mouth and waving.

"'E's the one who jumped in on the way over," his friend reminded him, spotting a burning torch dancing its way through the smoky mist toward the steps.

"D'yah wanna cross or not?" his nervous friend repeated.

"By St Edmund," Philip griped, keeping one eye on the torch-totting bridge guards. "Pick him up," he hissed, noting something familiar in his manner.

"But –"

"Hurry," Philip urged, the approaching torch failing to instil any urgency in the man on the dock.

"He must see us," one of the watermen growled, rowing frantically for the shore.

As the bow bumped over the submerged foreshore Philip glanced up at the bridge, but when he looked back the mysterious man had vanished in the fog.

"Where'd he go?"

"Son of a bitch," Philip spat, circling his finger, while the crew levered the vessel off the bottom with their oars. "Get us out of here."

When the wherry reached midstream, the boatmen relaxed.

"We're safe now," one of them gasped.

Stretching his arms along the stern, Philip exhaled noisily at the memory of his tryst with Portia and then cursed Elizabeth Hastings for ruining the experience. When they heard him the boatmen looked at each other and guffawed.

Chapter 8

PHILIP NEVILLE ENTERED the great Tower of London through the Lion Tower, his glowing conceit clear for all to see. Sitting rigidly in the saddle, reins draped loosely in one hand while the other rested on his hip. The reason for such superciliousness was his recent elevation to knight of the body. To accentuate his egotism, Philip proudly wore his new murrey and blue quartered tunic. The linen doublet, tapering to the waist, fitted nicely over his clean white shirt before flaring slightly at the hips. Sewn on the breast was his personal badge, bearing a rampant silver lion. Black hose fastened to the doublet by ties and a pair of dark brown boots laced on the inside compounded his vanity. Clean-shaven, his hair cropped and washed, Philip felt good about his appearance for the first time in months. His crowning glory was the beautifully balanced arming sword hanging at his side and presented to him by the king.

Philip led a detachment of four mounted men-of-arms under the Garden Tower and into the noisy inner ward, where several masons chipped away at blocks of stone to produce gun stones. The Tower had been turned into a centre for arms production: cannon were being cast, bowyers shaped war-bows and fletchers glued feathers to sheaves of arrows. As he passed the White Tower, Philip was stopped by several guards commanded by a sergeant who asked the reason for his visit.

"I bear a message for the Constable," he shouted above the din, unhooking his doublet and producing the letter.

The suspicious sergeant looked at the seal and frowned at the badge on his jacket.

"Do you recognise the king's mark?" Philip snapped, impatiently.

"You'll find his lordship in there," the sergeant huffed, aiming his chin at the chapel, near the northwest wall, "'tis the Sabbath and he is at prayer."

Philip nudged his palfrey up the gentle slope to the Chapel of St Peter ad Vincula.

"Dismount," he commanded, slipping from the saddle and clearing his throat. "Here," he said, handing the reins to one of his men and removing his riding gloves.

As he approached the chapel a noxious odour assaulted his nostrils. The stench was the result of the tower latrines emptying into the moat and causing the effluence to stagnate until the outgoing tide sluiced it away. Unfortunately, large amounts of excrement and other waste clung to the muddy walls of the moat, and in hot weather the stink became unbearable. Using his sleeve as a mask, Philip approached the church, its lime-washed whiteness blinding.

"I am here to see Sir John Tiptoft," he told the guard standing near the door.

"Sir John is at mass."

"I'll wait," he urged, turning to his escort. "Return to the palace!"

The men-at-arms looked at each other and hesitated, forcing Philip to repeat himself. Leaving his horse they mounted and rode away.

"Where is the old king?" he enquired, looking around at the numerous towers spaced out along the extensive walls.

"Wakefield Tower," the guard responded, pointing to a

large, round structure on the south wall, next to the Garden Tower.

"How does he fare?"

"'E's in the care of Sir Ralph Hastings. 'E's got a priest, servants an' a dog, an' 'e's well-fed: what's 'e got t' worry about?"

"Ralph Hastings," Philip sniffed, waving a hand in front of his face. "How do you live with that stink?"

"You gets used to it," the guard grinned, not wishing to engage in conversation.

"You're a miserable dog," Philip hissed, pacing back and forth.

Wetting his dry lips, he wondered if he had time to take a drink from the flask attached to his saddle, when the chapel doors suddenly opened. Sir John Tiptoft, Constable of England, royal councillor and Constable of the Tower, strode out into the bright sunshine. Despite a reputation for ruthlessness, Tiptoft was one of the most learned and well-travelled men in England. Richly attired in a red and gold tunic, he swept his thick, curly hair back from his rugged face and looked apathetically at Philip.

"Who are you?" he asked, dismissing his attendants with a lazy wave.

"Philip Neville, my Lord," he answered. "I am here on the king's business."

"I know you," said Tiptoft, puzzled. "But you wear different colours now."

"I once served Lord Warwick," Philip explained. "But now I serve the king."

"And what does the king want of me?"

Philip shrugged his shoulders and handed him the letter. Taking the communiqué, Sir John broke the seal, unfolded the paper and held it as if he were about to make a speech. Philip waited for him to disclose the contents of the missive, but once he finished, Sir John refolded the letter along its original creases and looked blank.

"You could have delivered this to my home and saved yourself the ride."

"I was told to hand it to you, my Lord."

"Then you have done your duty," Tiptoft said. "You may go."

Philip bowed smartly and walked to his horse, which was busy nibbling on the long grass.

"Don't eat that," he said, pushing the animal's head away and mounting.

Swinging his palfrey down to the Garden Tower, Philip retraced his route through the Middle Tower and clattered over the drawbridge.

"His Lordship is a puffed-up turd," he told his horse, before steering him up Petit Wales Hill.

Passing rows of tenements, shops, inns and taverns, lining both sides of Tower Street, he mulled over the numerous attempts on his life and tried to make sense of it all.

The coarse voices of traders enticing customers, combined with children laughing, the lamentations of beggars and the grinding rumble of carts, failed to rouse Philip from his thoughts. At the junction of Tower Street and St Dunstan's Lane, he steered his horse to the left and down a narrow alleyway. Emerging into Thames Street, instinct snapped him out of his daydreams and he sensed something was amiss.

Reaching the Church of St Magnus the Martyr, next to London Bridge, Philip dismounted. Taking a sip of wine from his flask, he poured a little into a cupped palm and offered it to his horse. The palfrey greedily lapped up the liquid with its hot, rough tongue and Philip replaced the flask before drawing his sword.

While he studied the faces of people jostling for space, something caught his eye. Amidst the crowd, he spotted a tall man dressed in a long beige habit. A hood concealed his face but Philip continued to watch him weave in and out of the crowd, a sense of urgency in his pace. When he crossed to the south side of Thames Street, he noticed his footwear.

"You are no monk, my friend," he hissed, noting the man's leather boots.

Flattening himself against the west wall of St Magnus, Philip reversed his sword. Gripping the handle and blade, he took a last peek and saw the monkish figure less than ten paces away and coming on fast. Kissing the crossbar he aimed the pommel at the point where he assumed the monk's head would appear. When the friar turned the corner, Philip struck; the heavy scent-bottle-shaped insert in the tang smacked the friar square in the face.

"My God!" he yelped, reeling from the unwarranted assault.

Philip flipped his sword and pushed the tip into the cleric's back as he struggled to staunch the blood pouring from his shattered nose.

"Goddamn you!" the monk gasped, as horrified onlookers shied away. "Goddamn you."

"Why do you follow me?" Philip demanded, jabbing the point into the friar's arse and relishing the pain he inflicted.

"My nose is broken!" he wailed, feverishly drawing a rag from the wide sleeve of his habit and using it to stem the blood. "Bastard."

"Nice words for a man of the cloth," Philip scoffed, prodding his sword in harder and forcing the Benedictine to jerk his hood back. "I'll break more than your nose –" Philip threatened, coming face to face with his young brother.

"Thomas… what the… why this charade?"

"Look at it," Thomas groaned, staring at the blood staining his habit. "Everybody's right, you're fucking mad!"

"I don't care what they says," he growled, sheathing his

blade and producing a handcoverchief glowering at the growing band of shocked spectators.

"By all that is holy," Thomas coughed, using a sleeve to dab his injured nose.

"Where's your horse?" Philip asked, untying his palfrey.

"I have no horse," he exclaimed, "I've been following you on foot."

"Come," Philip said, pushing through the unimpressed crowd and leading his brother up New Fish St Hill. "We'll find somewhere private."

New Fish St Hill went from London Bridge up to Cheapside. At St Margaret's Church halfway up the hill, where Crooked Lane joined New Fish Street from the west, they walked out into the middle of the road to avoid piles of rotting fish entrails tossed carelessly into the street by the fishmongers, whose stalls bordered the church wall. The gagging stench attracted swarms of flies and wasps that terrorised traders and customers alike.

"See that," Philip said, pointing at a large hostelry near the entrance to Crooked Lane.

Thomas rolled his eyes, for he knew what was coming: a lesson in history.

"The Black Bell," Philip revealed. "It once belonged to the Black Prince."

"Where are we going?" Thomas panted, his voice muffled by the bloody rag damming his nose.

Philip looked at Thomas and chuckled.

"What are you laughing at?" Thomas snapped.

"Your nose is big enough to absorb the impact."

"Hah, you should look in a mirror."

"It's not safe for you here," Philip warned.

"I had to come."

Reaching a crossroads, where East Cheap bisected Fish Street Hill, Philip looked at his brother and grew concerned for his safety. It was his mother's wish that Thomas, the youngest of the Neville brothers, should enter the church, but his father defied her by sending him to study law. After several years at Cambridge and an intense engagement, Thomas gave it all up and accompanied Queen Margaret to France. Bored with the bickering of a court in exile, he drifted aimlessly through life at the château of Kouer-la-Petite, near St Mihiel-sur-Bar.

Word of their brother Michael's murder drove Thomas into the arms of Lancaster, but the influence of his mother, who joined him in the summer of 1464, calmed his desire for revenge. To satisfy a need to know the truth, Thomas decided to return to England. Worried his association with Margaret would put his life at risk; he donned the habit of a Carthusian monk and called himself Brother Raphael.

Philip pointed Thomas to a row of covered stalls serving pies, pasties, fish, meat and poultry, as well as ale, cider and sweet pastries. Up to now the brothers barely spoke, each contemplating what to say, but neither knowing where to begin.

"There," Philip said, pointing at a large, tented stall. "They serve the best flesh and fowl in all London."

Securing his horse to a post, Philip approached the only table and squeezed out several customers about to sit. Thomas sat opposite and apologised with his eyes to the disgruntled patrons, who fumed at such bad manners, while Philip chuckled at his brother's discomfort.

"Goose a-pence, rabbit three-pence –!" The stall-holder barked.

"Two plates of goose, some bread and wine," Philip ordered, raising two fingers to emphasise his order.

"Yes sir," the stall-holder acknowledged, slipping a fat-dripping goose off the hook attached to a rack above his head.

The stall-holder hacked the bird in two with a chopper and

placed it on wood trenchers. Slapping a chunk of white bread on the side, he served the food, along with two cups of red wine, a bowl of water and several napkins.

Satisfied his nose had stopped dripping, Thomas gently blew it in his napkin.

"Father," the stall-holder objected. "Please?"

In the process of taking a mouthful of wine, Philip stopped and stared at his host over the rim of his cup, forcing him to wipe the counter. Long jostling queues were beginning to form in front of the stalls along both sides of the street and pleasant chatter soon filled the air.

"The habit of a monk suits you," Philip said sarcastically. "Mother will be proud... do you also wear a hair shirt?"

Thomas scowled and shook his head.

"You should not wear the boots of a gentleman," Philip said.

"They are more comfortable than sandals."

"How did you get here?" Philip asked. "All the ports are being watched."

"I came through Flanders," Thomas explained, "and took a ship at Sluys."

"Where did you come ashore?"

Thomas refused to answer, for fear of incriminating his confederates.

"You are fortunate," Philip said. "Lord Warwick's men are everywhere; he even has a spy in Margaret's court."

"And she has several here," he countered. "How do you think I knew where to find you?"

"Has our mother forgiven me?" Philip sniffed, tearing at the goose and wondering who Margaret's agent could be.

"You should die of shame for the heartbreak you have caused her," Thomas declared.

"I've done nothing but stay loyal to my king!"

"She always said one of you would end up dead," Thomas

sighed, using his fingers to shred the goose into manageable pieces.

"'Twas no fault of mine," he pouted. "I gave him the chance to get away, but he chose to stay and fight me."

Thomas delicately fingered his fragile proboscis.

"If you go to the king, he will forgive you," Philip said. "God knows he has forgiven those who do not deserve his mercy."

"What of William?" Thomas asked, meaning their stepfather Sir William.

"All the Beauforts are treacherous dogs," Philip snarled, banging a fist on the table.

Thomas watched Philip fume inwardly as he tore his bread and threw half on the ground for his horse.

"Edward forgave a Beaufort once before and he betrayed him; he will never trust another," Philip snorted, spitting out slivers of hard chaff. "What happened to the girl you were set to marry?"

"What happened to yours?" Thomas countered.

Philip huffed and picked at his food when a cloud of choking smoke blew into his face.

"Your bread is shit!" he coughed at the stall-holder, leaning over the voider to spit out masticated bread and wheat chaff.

"But the goose is excellent," Thomas added, exasperated by Philip's conduct and puzzled by the badge on his coat. "You no longer serve Lord Warwick?"

"I serve the king," Philip announced, pompously, "My reward for escorting Henry of Lancaster to London."

"Mother has received a letter from Margaret Talbot."

"Oh," Philip moaned, rolling his eyes.

"Do you marry Isobel for love?"

"What other reason is there?" he answered, uncomfortable talking of such things with his young brother, and pointing at the deep gash on his swelling nose. "You have your first battle scar."

"To remind me of your temper," he flashed.

"Fresh goose!" the stall-holder yelled, coming around to refill Philip's cup. "Veal and…"

"Step away," Philip hissed, disgusted at the showering spittle accompanying the man's words.

"How is your shoulder?" Thomas asked, recalling the night after the battle of Towton, when their mother sewed up his ghastly wound.

"Huh," he sniffed, chomping away.

"You have aged," Thomas commented, scrutinizing his brother's weathered face and the crow's feet spreading from the corners of his dark, busy eyes. "If you are not careful, you'll be dead before you're forty."

"I bear a heavy burden," he said, staring into space. "Where do you stay?" he asked, snapping out of his distraction.

"With friends."

Philip watched Thomas lean over the table and scrape his leftovers into the voider.

"I must be on my way soon," Thomas announced, delicately wiping his mouth on the bloody napkin.

"It was you!" Philip gasped, thrusting an accusing finger at him, "In the boat at Southwark… and on the steps later that night?"

Thomas failed to answer.

"Why did you not speak?"

"Why? Look how you acted today!" Thomas growled. "I followed you to the whorehouse and waited, hoping to meet with you alone. When you finally left I kept to the shadows, but I became lost, by the time I reached the shore you were pulling away."

"I came back."

"So did the wardens."

"Do you have funds?"

"Yes," Thomas said, pulling the woollen hood up over his head, while Philip paid the stall-holder.

"Thank eh, sir," he nodded, tapping his sweaty forehead.

"I am on my way to Francis Talbot's, to arrange the marriage contract," Philip announced. "Say a Prayer for me," he said mockingly, "Father?"

Thomas made the sign of the cross at him with equal sarcasm.

"Where do you go now?"

Thomas grinned and extended his hand, which Philip promptly shook before they parted company.

Walking leisurely along East Cheap, Thomas stopped at its junction with Grasche Street. Untying his horse, Philip followed him discreetly on foot, eager to find his brother's safe house and have his associates arrested. Blending in with the crowd, he ducked down when he saw Thomas stop to look around. Satisfied he hadn't seen him, Philip stood up, only to discover his brother had vanished. Dragging his horse along, he looked down Grasche Street as far as he could see.

"Suspicious little shit," he chuckled, mounting up and riding away.

Making his way along Cornhull, Le Poultry and Cheapside, Philip's route took him past the great cathedral of St Paul's, the Bishop of London's Palace, Ave Maria Alley, Ludgate Hill and the Fleet Bridge.

Crossing the reeking Fleet River he rode to the church of St Dunstan in the West and turned into Chancellor Lane. Near to the townhouse of the notorious Clifford family, he dismounted and patted down his windblown hair. Adjusting his doublet he gasped at the churning sensation in his stomach and thumped the door of the modest house. Overcome by the same emotions he felt before going into battle, Philip began to sweat profusely. The front door opened and Francis Talbot appeared with a huge grin on his face.

"Dear friend?" he chirped, stepping aside and rubbing his hands together. "Come in, I've been waiting for you."

Chapter 9

SUNDAY 29 OCTOBER 1466 dawned cold and crisp, and the almost constant rain of the past week had finally stopped. From a near-cloudless sky, the weak autumnal sun broke through and shone down on the parish church of St Margaret's. Built in the shadow of its more illustrious neighbour, Westminster Abbey, St Margaret's was about to host its first wedding of the week. Standing in the walled graveyard, which was carpeted with wet leaves, Philip Neville, wearing his finest livery tunic, waited in nervous contemplation.

Rubbing his forehead, he tried to understand how he had allowed himself to be lured into marriage. Turning the ring on the middle finger of his left hand, he detected a shrill whistling sound fluting in and out of his nostrils. Groaning at the thought of others hearing the aggravating, high-pitched whistle, he sniffed and snorted until his nose was cleared. Looking at the sky through the bare branches of a tree, he closed his eyes.

"What am I doing here?" he groaned.

"'Tis thy wedding day," Sir Thomas Vaughan announced, coming up behind him and squeezing his shoulder to instil courage.

Philip responded with a rueful smile.

"You look like a man going to his own execution," Thomas said.

Thomas Vaughan, treasurer of the king's chamber, was

a Welshman who had recently fallen afoul of the Hastings clan. As a consequence of their mutual dislike of the two brothers, Thomas and Philip became allies. Well past middle age, Vaughan's thin, rugged chin and lower jaw were furred by a fuzzy, greying beard, below which his Adams Apple bobbed prominently whenever he spoke. With Philip's family in France and only a few friends at court, Thomas took him under his fatherly wing.

"'Tis almost time," he announced, his gruff accent grating.

"Do you have it?"

Thomas produced a sealed license, signed by the Archbishop of Canterbury, and waved it triumphantly.

"I paid ten shillings for that piece of paper," Philip carped, as they walked to St Margaret's.

"It would have cost far less if you would only conceal your contempt for the Church."

"Hah," Philip scoffed, watching a group of beggars gathering outside St Margaret's. "They're early."

"They're come for their alms," Vaughan explained.

"They can smell money," Philip growled, as Vaughan, also wearing the king's livery, waved Robert Harrington to the church porch.

Rubbing his temples, Philip knew what he was about to do went against God's laws, but felt compelled to go through with it. He tried to forget Elizabeth Hastings and searched his soul in the hope of resurrecting the intense love he once felt for Isobel, but the only emotion he conjured up was lust.

While his companions entered St Margaret's, Philip recalled the day, fourteen months before, when he proposed. As he sat with Francis Talbot, drinking wine in his London home, Philip had agreed to the dowry. For his part, he promised to leave Isobel one of his manors in his will and swore to love, protect and care for her. The two friends shook hands and Philip was re-introduced to Isobel. Red-faced, he nervously asked her to be his wife. She agreed and Francis offered to arrange for the banns to be read in York and Ashby. Being in the king's service Philip suggested the ceremony be performed in St Margaret's, Francis and Isobel agreed. With both parties residing in London, Philip was forced to apply to the Archbishop of Canterbury for a licence to wed outside their own parishes.

Between engagement and wedding, Philip spent most of his time with the king, who extended his length of service indefinitely. He attended Edward on his travels, escorted him to council and on certain nights, slept on a pallet outside his chamber. After riding to York, Philip's esquire brought Arbroth, his horses, armour, weapons, servants and his armourer to London. Among the group was a nervous nine-year-old, Richard Warren, Philip's newly assigned page. To accommodate his household Philip rented a property in King Street, between Westminster and Charing Cross. Despite a lack of money, Edward kept his promise and work began on Philip's manors.

During the last days of September, Philip breathed a little easier when told his brother Thomas was back in France. The crossbow injury Philip suffered at York had healed, but his Towton wound still bothered him. When not on duty he trained with his esquire in the palace yards. On Wednesday evenings he went to the 'Tavern of the Sun' and got drunk. He continued to visit the Rose Inn, forcing his esquire to remark that he was always in good humour after a night at the stews.

Since the queen's coronation, the relationship between Edward and his cousin Warwick deteriorated. On 28 September 1465, Warwick acted as Steward at his brother George's enthronement as Archbishop of York. Among the two thousand guests at the banquet in York were Lord Hastings and the king's youngest brother, Richard, Duke of Gloucester, but Edward and his queen did not attend. In February 1466 the queen gave birth to her first child with Edward. The King and Warwick patched up their differences and the Earl stood godfather to the new princess. In the spring, Warwick crossed the Channel to negotiate trade agreements with France and Burgundy, and arrange a marriage between Edward's sister and the Duke of Burgundy's son.

In France, the scheming King Louis was planning to extend his authority into Brittany and Burgundy and saw the Earl of Warwick as a potential ally. Aware of Edward's bond with Burgundy, and loathing the rise of the detested Wood-villes, Warwick secretly sided with Louis. When war broke out between France and Brittany, the English ambassadors returned home. During Warwick's absence, the queen had extended her influence by arranging high-profile marriages for her siblings. When he came home to England, Warwick rode to Middleham and spent the next four months brooding and plotting.

"Hey!" Thomas Vaughan shouted at the distracted groom.

Looking up, Philip saw Vaughan pointing at the bridal party clattering through the gatehouse. Solemnly he watched Isobel, elegantly attired in a blue dress, dismount from her fawn mare without assistance. Her soft yellow hair, crowned by a thin, flower-entwined gold circlet, glistened in the brassy sunlight as she straightened her dress. When she pinched her pale cheeks to infuse colour Philip's legs started to buckle.

"Come," Thomas urged, motioning for him to join them at the porch, "We must go."

A slight rush of wind rustled the trees and showered Philip's hair with water droplets. Shaking his head, he kicked a path through the sodden grass and leaves and pretended not to see the Talbots making their way along the narrow path. Squelching through puddles of muddy water, he cursed Elizabeth Hastings for trespassing on his wedding day.

As the two groups came together, Richard Saxilby, the tall,

thin-faced, flinty curate of St Margaret's, waited in the spacious porch. Dressed in a long-sleeved, white alb that reached almost to his feet with a long, narrow cream and green stole around his neck, Saxilby initially refused to perform the service. A friend of the abbot of Westminster, the silver-haired Saxilby resented Philip's hostility towards the church, but a word from the king curtailed his reluctance. Not one to defy the crown, Saxilby agreed to marry the couple, though he insisted on performing the service in the church porch. As a knight, Philip had a right to marry inside the church, and Saxilby hoped he would refuse his conditional offer. Philip cared little for such nonsense – in or out of church; it made no difference to him – so he agreed.

When Philip looked up and saw the Chaplain's stern countenance he passed him a curt nod and smiled at his bride. Holding her brother's arm for support, Isobel Talbot responded with a smile. Stepping into the cold porch Philip, Isobel and Francis stood before the Chaplain, while their respective parties squeezed in behind. Francis's wife sat on the stone bench and massaged her gamy leg, which pained her in damp weather.

Dressed in a tight-fitting murrey and blue velvet gown, the furred collar curving low under her neck and the train gathering dead leaves, Isobel looked stunning. Standing beside Francis, she crossed her dainty hands together in pious repose. Stepping up next to Francis, Philip's brain boiled with anxiety, regret and bewilderment. Looking down at his boots, coated in a mush of mud, shredded sward and rotting leaves, he failed to hear Francis pronounce the dower arrangements.

"The purse," Vaughan hissed, nudging him with his elbow.

Philip fumbled inside his tunic until he felt the purse containing the wedding ring, a handful of gold and silver coins, and thirteen pennies. Emptying the purse onto the bible held by Sir Thomas, he tutted as several coins rolled off and bounced noisily over the stone floor. Thomas Vaughan put a foot out to stop the coins rolling away, scooped them up and gave them to Philip. Placing the money carefully on the bible, Philip passed Francis a frightened grin. The pennies were to be disbursed to the poor after the service, while the gold and silver, and the ring, were for his bride. Saxilby asked if anyone knew of any impediment to the marriage and Philip half-hoped someone would speak up, but except for a couple of boys poking their heads into the porch and giggling there was no objection. Philip's esquire chased the boys away and the ceremony continued.

Francis gave the hand of his nineteen-year-old sister to Philip and stepped back. Nervously taking her cool, tiny hand in his sweaty palm, he gritted his teeth and tried to calm down. Isobel countered his nerviness with a composed smile but her effort failed. Philip was brought back to the solemnity of the occasion by Saxilby's gruff voice requesting him to repeat the vows he was about to administer. Despite the damp, chilly atmosphere, beads of sweat blistered Philip's forehead and trickled down his face. Using a sleeve to dab his chin, he repeated the Chaplain's words.

"I take thee, Isobel Talbot, to my wedded wife... to have and to hold from this day forward; for better, for worse; for richer, for poorer, in sickness and in health, till death us do part, if holy Church it will ordain; and thereto I plight thee my troth."

Ending the traumatic ordeal with a gulp, Philip felt Isobel squeeze his hand supportively. Twisting his neck to alleviate the sweaty discomfort, he was relieved when the Chaplain turned to Isobel. Compared to Philip's bumbling effort, she recited her vows boldly and with clarity.

Saxilby took the ring from the bible held by Vaughan, mumbled a short blessing and made the sign of the cross over the ring. He then guided Philip as he touched the ring to each of the three fingers of Isobel's left hand. As the gold band was passed from finger to finger, Philip offered the following words.

"In the name of the Father, and of the Son, and of the Holy Ghost."

Slipping the ring over her fourth finger, the Chaplain signed the cross a second time and Philip continued.

"With this ring I thee wed."

Saxilby motioned for him to give his wife the gold and silver. Taking the coins, Philip, his hands shaking, looked imploringly at Vaughan. Dropping the money into a small silk purse, he snapped the drawstrings and presented it to his new wife.

"With this gold I thee honour," he began. "This gold and silver I give thee. With my body I thee worship. And with this dowry I thee endow."

"The gold and silver given here this day signify that this woman shall have her dower and goods if she abides after thy decease," Saxilby declared.

Closing his eyes, the Chaplain gave a short prayer and a blessing for the young couple's future before shepherding everyone inside the church.

"Silence!" he snapped, aiming his warning at a group of chattering women.

Philip fumbled for Isobel's hand and led her into the Nave, where the couple were ordered to lie face down on the stone floor and Saxilby prayed over their prostrate forms. Rising, Philip and Isobel followed the ecclesiastic into the Quire for the nuptial mass. After the Sanctus, Saxilby motioned for the couple to prostrate themselves once again, while several of their male friends came forward and held the nuptial veil over them. Philip found it difficult to conceal his disdain for such drivel and when he caught Isobel looking at him he rolled his eyes.

Finally, they stood up and Philip received the kiss of peace from Saxilby, which he relayed to his new wife. After a final communion, the Chaplain gave a brief sermon on the sanctity of marriage and, for Philip's benefit, the duty of man to God and his Church, and the ceremony was over.

Philip, his wife, their friends and family left St Margaret's as the choir chanted the Agnus Dei. Outside, Isobel distributed the thirteen pennies to the poor before the wedding party rode back to the Talbot residence for the feast. The largest room in the house had been gaily decorated for the occasion and three long tables were squeezed in to accommodate thirty guests. The reed-covered, earth-packed floor was strewn with saffron and rosemary and exuded a pleasing aroma when walked over. Philip and his lady sat on the top table, with Francis, his wife and Sir Thomas and Lady Vaughan; the rest of the guests were seated on the two tables extending out. The newlyweds opened the proceedings by drinking from the loving cup, a two-handed silver chalice, to the clapping of hands. During the feast, each guest came forward and offered their gifts.

With the stress of the church service behind him, Philip relaxed, and the congenial atmosphere and flowing wine helped him forget the experience, and Elizabeth. With his inhibitions fading away, he began to fawn over his young bride: he kissed her hands, looked into her eyes and flattered her; he even toasted the Chaplain. Though invited, none of the royal family attended; then, halfway through dinner, there was a sharp rap on the front door. Silence filled the room and everyone's eyes followed a servant as he walked to the door; those same eyes tracked his return.

"My Lord," he whispered in his master's ear.

"What is it, Mathew?" Francis asked, gnawing a rabbit bone.

"The King's secretary is here."

"What?"

"The King's secretary –"

"Show him in," Talbot spluttered, jumping up and wiping his mouth on a surnape. "Show him in at once."

The servant bowed apologetically and hurried to obey.

"My God, what is the man thinking?" Francis groaned at Philip. "He told the king's secretary to wait!" he gasped, nervously dabbing his forehead. "Some of my servants have turnips for brains."

The King's secretary and his four companions entered and walked straight to the top table. Stopping before Philip and his wife, the official removed his hat and bowed low.

"Welcome Mr Both," Philip said, tipping his head in recognition.

"My Lord," he responded. "The king congratulates you on your marriage this day and prays you and your good lady will forgive his absence. He offers this gift in recompense."

Isobel could barely hold back her excitement when the secretary presented her with a velvet-covered cushion edged in fine gold thread.

"For you, madam."

With hands atremble, Isobel took the gift and carefully lifted the flap of soft red velvet to reveal a gold ring surmounted by a cluster of emeralds.

"'Tis the most beautiful thing I have ever seen," she gasped, slapping a hand to her bosom and showing the ring to her sister-in-law.

"Please convey our thanks to his Grace," Philip said, "and tell his Highness there is nothing to forgive."

The secretary turned and left, leaving the guests talking excitedly among themselves. Feeling left out, Philip wished his mother and brother could have been present; he knew they would accept his bride, for Joan Neville and Lady Talbot were old friends. Glancing at Arbroth and his esquire, Philip grinned as they sat propping each other up, having made merry with too much wine. As the afternoon wore on, the food disappeared, more drink arrived and the guests were becoming rowdy. Philip soon slipped into boredom and found himself drinking for the sake of it.

When Isobel leaned over to speak with her young sister, he discreetly picked up the boar's head, set in the middle of the table, and raised it up to the back of her head. When she turned he shook the bristly snout in her face and squealed loudly. Releasing a piercing shriek, Isobel pushed herself back into her seat. The room suddenly went quiet and then everyone burst out laughing. After the initial shock, Isobel put a hand to her heart and giggled hysterically while Philip impishly replaced the boar's head.

"Back you go, Ralph," he said.

"Ralph?" Vaughan questioned.

"I have named this boar Ralph in honour of Ralph Hastings."

"Why?"

"Because he's a boor."

"Ah!" Vaughan chuckled.

The wedding feast continued long after the church bells sounded the hour of Compline.

While the guests continued eating and drinking, the Chaplain followed Philip and his bride up to their bedchamber. When Saxilby spotted Philip brazenly squeeze Isobel's arse he shook his head and deliberately huffed his disapproval. The Chaplain blessed the nuptial bed and sprinkled the sheets with Holy water.

"Bless, O Lord, this marriage bed and grant the young couple a fruitful union," he declared, making the sign of the cross.

"I hope so," Philip slurred.

"Heavenly Father, hear my prayer," Saxilby ended, with a wistful sigh.

With a disapproving sniff the cleric left, frowning at the groom as he did so.

"Silly old fool," Philip scoffed.

"My Lord," Isobel frowned, shocked by his disrespect, "he heard you."

"I don't give a fig," he grinned.

For Philip the wedding night failed to live up to expectation; too much wine and the long day left him exhausted. Struggling to undress he fell back almost naked on the bed and no sooner did his head hit the soft, feather pillow than he was asleep. Waking next day to the bells of St Dunstan in the West ringing out the hour of Terce, around 9 a.m. he shuffled over to a small cupboard. Scooping water from a bowl with his hands, he rubbed it into his face and gasped at the shock. Grabbing a towel he dabbed his face and grimaced at the foul taste in his mouth. Massaging his aching neck he looked at his young wife sleeping like an angel, her long golden hair lying across her cheek and curling down over her white, slender neck.

Taking hold of a small jar Philip lifted the lid and sniffed the mixture of sage, salt and water. Winding the corner of a towel around his forefinger, he dipped it in the paste and cleaned his teeth. Needing to empty his bladder, he dropped his braies and pissed into a pot.

"Brrrr," he twitched, the early morning chill sending a shiver through his body.

As he pushed the pot under the bed, a soft murmur fled from his wife's lips and he quickly removed his braies and slipped back into bed.

"Good morning, my lady," he said softly.

"My Lord," she yawned, stretching all four limbs.

Aroused by the shape of Isobel's body beneath her taut nightdress, he edged closer, ready to consummate the marriage.

"Your scent is intoxicating," he whispered.

Isobel unexpectedly backed away and he put an arm out to stop her.

"Are you sick?" he asked, stroking the soft coney edging of her nightdress.

She shook her head and he drew her nearer, but as he kissed her lips she brought an arm over to shield her chest. Sensing her anxiety Philip gently pushed her hand away and loosened the ties holding her nightdress together. When she resisted, he snapped.

"Lay still," he hissed, the threat in his voice enough to make her obey. "What are you afraid of?" he asked, his tone softer.

"I am told the act of love is hurtful," she bleated.

Philip rested his chin in his palm and looked into her innocent eyes.

"I would never hurt you."

She looked unconvinced and her body went rigid.

"At first there is pain, but it is fleeting and the pleasure that follows will make you forget," he smiled, kissing her forehead.

Drawing the nightdress open, Philip laid bare her bosom and released a gratifying sigh. Ready to enjoy his wife, he bent to kiss her again, but she turned away. Ignoring her concerns, he pushed his fingers inside her inner sanctum and drew them out. Sniffing the sweetness of her cunnis he moved on top of her and forced his way in. Isobel closed her eyes and pressed her cheek into the pillow while he had his way; though he was gentle he felt her body stiffen but was unable to stop. Having released his essence, Philip blew a groan of contentment tinted with frustration. Observing the distressed expression on her face he lay down beside her. Wiping a tear from Isobel's cheek he tried to comfort her but she turned over, put her head down into her chest and brought her knees up.

"I..." he began apologetically, only to change his mind;

after all, she was his wife and he had a right to enjoy her. "Forget it."

Since the day Philip first saw Isobel in York, they had met only occasionally, and she always brought a chaperon; such moments barely gave the couple time to exchange more than a few words. Long anticipating this night, Philip fumed at her reaction. Moving to the edge of the bed he sat up, grunted and rubbed his face vigorously.

"You're a woman now," he said coldly. "Find a matriarch and ask her to instruct you on a wife's duties and how she must please her husband." He added, retrieving his braies, "Go to my house in King's Street and take your trousseau."

Dressing quickly, Philip heard her sobbing but ignored it.

"I'll not touch you again until you are ready," he said, belting on his sword. "But do not keep me waiting; I am not known for my tolerance."

"Why did you marry me?" she whined.

"Where does this come from?"

"You spoke her name in your sleep."

"Whose name?"

"You know of whom I speak."

"Am I responsible for my dreams?"

"Do you still love her?"

"No!" he snapped. "I must go now… good day, madam."

Leaving the room Philip went downstairs thinking of Elizabeth and muttering to himself.

"Women!" he scoffed at the surprised servant holding the front door open for him.

Chapter 10

THE GREAT COURT of Eltham Palace was packed with hundreds of guests showing off their finest clothes. While they chatted and pruned their feathers, scores of servants rushed to finish laying the tables. The noise of so many eclectic conversations echoed up into the roof, yet the forced smiles of those who despised one another failed to completely gloss over their veiled loathing. Velvets, satins and silks edged with plush fur were flaunted, while gold finger rings, peppered with precious gems, glittered in the shimmering candlelight. Bandsmen, seated up in the balcony, tuned their instruments and sheepish latecomers rushed into the hall, relieved to have made it before the king.

Each time the doors opened, a wave of cold air cut through the room like a knife and those who loitered near the entrance, hoping to be first to greet their sovereign lord, groaned in disappointment as yet another latecomer arrived. The walls of the hall were lavishly decorated with seasonal tapestries, cloth of gold, colourful banners, armour and weapons. An over-abundance of holly, ivy and mistletoe and bunches of red berries dripped from every window and doorway, while heat from the great fire and clusters of candles teased out the fragrance of rosemary. The king's Christmas banquet was eagerly anticipated by all those invited.

It was this raucous, redolent atmosphere that greeted Philip when he entered the Great Court with his wife, shortly after midday. Swinging the short cape from his shoulders, he helped Isobel out of her heavier cloak and handed both to a servant. Wearing a fitted murrey and blue doublet over a clean white shirt, he escorted her inside.

"I know none of these people," she said excitedly, looking agog at the richly decorated walls and holding Philip's arm tight as he led her through the crowd.

Since the strained consummation of their marriage, Philip and Isobel had grown closer. The painful ordeal of losing her virginity was forgotten and she looked forward to her husband's by-weekly visits to her bed. When he was off duty, they rode out to the country or visited her family. Isobel's dramatic transformation helped Philip forget Elizabeth Hastings, and the Rose Inn.

Wearing a dark blue dress, its tight bodice hugging her shapely figure and showing off just enough bosom to tease, Isobel looked dazzling. Her light, yellow hair was tied up at the back and secured by a half-moon silver comb. As they walked slowly she attracted envious looks from several older women and lecherous stares from their husbands.

"Am I dreaming?" she mooned, intoxicated by the atmosphere.

"Methinks *they* would like to know you," he whispered, offering a smug nod at several male courtiers ogling his wife.

Isobel giggled at his comment as the hall fell silent and everyone looked to the doors.

"Pray silence for Edward, by the grace of God, king of England and France, and lord of Ireland, and his most gracious queen!"

Richly adorned in a suit of blue velvet, lined with white satin and embroidered with gold ribbon, Edward entered the Great Court. Each of his long fingers bore an oversized stone-studded ring and the crown of St Edward rested on his head. Queen Elizabeth walked beside her husband, well aware some of her enemies would be present. The disparity in their heights brought a smirk to Philip's face, and as the royal couple strolled between two lines of guests, they nodded and smiled. The crowd bowed low at their approach only rising once they had passed.

Philip watched the train of Elizabeth's long green velvet dress slither by and sensed he was being watched.

"What's wrong?" Isobel asked, trying to see the cause of his distraction.

"Nothing," he sniffed, fixated on someone way down the line.

"Tell me," she whined, standing on tiptoes to see, though she had no idea who or what she was looking at.

"Be silent."

While the king and his leading nobles moved to the top table, Isobel shook Philip's arm to break the spell.

"Enough," he growled, aggravated by her persistence.

The king, his queen, the Archbishop of Canterbury and half a dozen leading nobles, stepped up onto the raised dais and stood in front of their allotted seats at the king's table. Ushers signalled for the other guests to sit at the long tables spreading out below the High Table, the king visible to all. Those of status and wealth were seated closest to their sovereign, the rest filtered down the line in order of importance. With each guest at their assigned place, the king and queen took their seats. One of the first to sit, Philip plonked his arse heavily on the bench reserved for Knights of the Body and their ladies. Folding in her long skirt Isobel sat next to her husband, miffed by his stony silence. The annoying scrape and screech of bench legs being dragged over the floor briefly filled the room.

"Who has put thee in such bad humour?" Isobel asked, licking her thumb and brushing down his left eyebrow, which stuck out untidily.

"Leave it," he growled, drawing away.

Pouting at his snappy retort, she watched as Philip angrily twisted the base of his empty goblet into the white linen table-cloth.

"Tell me," she pressed.

"Hush," he hissed, flattening out the scrunched up table-cloth before flicking a surnape over his shoulder.

"Philip," Thomas Vaughan chirped, sitting down opposite him.

"Thomas," Philip said, surprised his tone unintentionally abrasive.

"My lady," Vaughan added, in his strongest Welsh accent, smiling at Isobel.

"Sir," she answered. "Lady Eleanor."

Vaughan's homely wife sat down between her husband and another knight and touched Isobel's hand in friendship.

"'Tis said the queen is ill-disposed towards Lord Hastings," Vaughan revealed, "and blames him for taking Edward from her bed, and setting him on a path of wantonness."

Philip sniffed indifferently and craned his neck to look at the top table,

"I don't see Lord Warwick."

"He keeps Christmas at Coventry," a fellow knight offered.

"The queen has forbidden the court to mention him by name until Christmastide is over," Eleanor revealed, wiggling a loose front tooth to see if it was ready to come out.

"I thought Edward ruled in England," Philip scoffed, grimacing at the way Eleanor tugged at her tooth, "not his wife."

"Her wish is the king's command," Vaughan nodded.

Philip looked over the tables until he found what he was looking for and locked in on someone seated three tables away.

"Ralph Hastings," he muttered.

"What about him?" Vaughan asked.

"He's here."

Conscious of Philip's loathing for the brother of Lord Hastings, Isobel exchanged an anxious glance with Thomas. She knew of the pre-contract between Philip and Elizabeth, and how she was forced to marry Ralph Hastings. Taking Philip's hand, she prised his fingers open and gently rubbed the tensed muscle in his arm, to soothe his angst. Her pleasant touch had the desired effect and his temper ebbed.

A blare of trumpets was followed by four cooks marching into the hall carrying a boar's head on a silver tray. Scoured of its hair the animal had been cleaned and cooked and an apple stuffed in its mouth. The arrival of the boar was greeted with applause and the king nodded appreciatively as it was placed before him on the high table. The Clerk of the Kitchens gave a sharp clap and a line of servers traipsed out bearing huge silver platters of food. Several swans, slaughtered by royal consent, skinned, cooked and re-dressed, were paraded around the room to the gasps of the guests. Venison, beef, chicken, mutton, pheasant, dressed peacock and birds baked in pies followed. With the table groaning under the weight of so much food, the Clerk of the Kitchens pointed for the servitors to begin distributing dishes to the guests in order of rank.

The first course – sixteen plates of beef, mutton, fish, fowl, birds and other delicacies – was set out before each set of six guests, but before the eating could begin, Thomas Bouchier, Archbishop of Canterbury and the king's uncle, rose from his chair. Holding his hands out, he blessed the royal couple and all present and offered a prayer for the bountiful feast. During the archbishop's monologue, Philip laid his knife on the table and tried not to look at the man who stole his first love, but the temptation was irresistible. When he saw Elizabeth by his side, he felt as if a dagger had been plunged into his heart and twisted, and was consumed with jealousy. Servers now distributed several large, glazed pies to each table.

"Christmas Pie," Isobel hummed, as Sir Thomas pushed the delicacy in front of her.

She graciously refused and Philip smiled at Eleanor.

"You must accept the first slice, my lady," he told his wife.

Isobel looked confused. "Why?"

"Tradition," Eleanor revealed. "You take the first bite and make a wish."

"If you refuse bad luck will follow you all year," Thomas warned.

Isobel removed the hard pastry lid, spooned out a portion of savoury mince and spiced fruit, and nibbled away like a mouse, to the delight of all.

The banquet proved a gut-busting experience, but with so much rich food and drink, many would suffer later for their excesses. After three hours of eating, those full up but unable to resist such sumptuous offerings left to take an emetic and returned to continue gorging themselves. At one point the queen's brother, Anthony Lord Scales, rose from his seat just below the top table, while he struggled to maintain his balance he offered a slurred toast to his sister.

"*Elisabetha…Reginae Anglorum, salus et vita!*"

"The pup forgets his place," Vaughan scoffed.

"Drunken fool," Philip growled. "I remember him at Woodstock, the arrogant whoremaster."

The queen acknowledged her brother's salute with a pleasant smile as he slumped down on his seat.

"It is said the queen usually dines alone and her ladies must kneel in silence until ordered to rise," Isobel said, using a surnape to wipe juice from her lips.

"'Tis true," Vaughan confirmed. "The king and queen rarely share a table."

"Or a bed," Philip sniggered, stabbing a capon with his knife, dragging it onto his plate and tearing the succulent meat apart with his fingers.

"You're in a strange mood," Vaughan said.

Isobel thanked him for confirming what she already knew but Philip brushed it off.

"How do you cope with managing a household?" Eleanor asked, chewing her food slowly to avoid loosening the tooth further.

"There's so much to remember it makes my head spin," Isobel replied, licking her sticky fingers.

"You'll get used to it."

With the servers rushed off their feet trying to empty void-ers, the diners began to discard bones and leftovers on the table. When most of the food was eaten, the guests washed their fingers and watched the wealthiest nobles approach the king and queen, kneel and offer presents. Pleased with this show of devotion, Edward rose from his chair and thanked everyone for making this the best Christmas yet.

"I understood presents were given out on New Year's Day," Sir Thomas whispered.

"The King and queen will be spending New Year at Windsor, alone," Philip said, taking the napkin from his shoulder and drying his hands.

"My queen and I thank you for your gifts and good wishes," Edward said, as his lords returned to their seats. "Now clear the room!"

The guests stood up and backed away while a bevy of servants, wearing red tunics, flitted between the tables, removing bone boxes, tablecloths and soiled napkins. The benches were then folded up and trestle tables moved away, and when the room was clear the master of the king's music received his cue from the steward of the household. Responding with an eloquent bow to the royals he motioned for his musicians to begin.

"Come!" said Edward, stepping down from the dais and

making his way to the centre of the room, "Everyone in the centre, no exceptions."

Philip groaned, for though he excelled on the field of battle, on the dance floor he was a clod. The rare occasions he did indulge, his performance was akin to a plodding cart horse.

"'Tis easy, my love," Isobel whispered, trying to boost his confidence. "Follow my steps."

Philip knew he could not disobey the king, who was busy herding his more reluctant guests away from the walls. Observing Philip's hesitation, he bore down on him.

"Your Grace," Philip said, trying to deflect him from his purpose, "may I present my wife?"

"You may indeed," he smiled. "So this is the maid who will calm my cousin's tempestuous nature?"

"I shall try, your Grace," she curtsied.

"Rise, my lady," Edward commanded, his towering frame intimidating. "I see why you did not bring this rare flower to court before; she has much light and fire in her eyes."

"Thank you for the gift," she said, thrusting the fingers of her left hand under his nose, "'Tis most exquisite."

"I know what it looks like," Edward laughed, kissing her hand. "*Elle est très jeune et très jolie.*"

"Thank you, your Grace," she blushed.

Philip put a hand to his mouth and coughed discreetly, irked by the king's attraction.

"Philip?" Edward said, moving the gold, jewel-encrusted crown enough to scratch his head. "I hear work on your property is under way?"

"Yes, sire –"

Their conversation abruptly ended when William Hastings appeared.

"Your Grace," Hastings whispered in the royal ear, "my brother has a special gift for thee."

"Ah," Edward mused, rubbing his hands together. "More presents."

"A pair of the finest Norwegian falcons," he announced, "He will bring them to your apartments later."

Edward's face lit up, for he loved falconry and Norwegian falcons were his favourite birds.

Philip and Hastings traded strained good wishes before the latter ushered the king away.

"*Everyone* dances," Edward reminded his cousin.

"Yes sire," Philip managed, rubbing his bloated stomach.

"Oh," Isobel sighed, clasping her hands together and stroking the ring, "the king kissed my hand."

"Son of a bitch," Philip growled through his teeth, only to receive a look of abhorrence from the offended Archbishop of Canterbury, who happened by at that moment and misread the intended target of Philip's ire.

"Forgive me, your Grace," he bowed, pointing his chin at the object of his abuse.

The Archbishop silently reprimanded Philip by making the sign of the cross at him and moving on.

With the musicians ready to play, a file of young boys, dressed in white robes and red caps, entered and formed two lines. The room went quiet and the king, his queen and their guests drank in a heart-warming choral version of John Plummer's composition, *Tota pulchra es*, 'My love is wholly beautiful.' When the music ended the choristers bowed and filed out, and the bandsmen prepared to liven up the evening with a saucy number, *Branles Des Pois*.

Formed into groups of twelve alternating couples, the men bowed to the women and all held hands. When the music opened they began to dance in circles. Over-thinking, Philip failed to negotiate the simple steps and his embarrassment was noticeable. Sweat gushed from every pore and his face turned bright red, increasing his anxiety. The more he concentrated the more erratic his movements became until he found himself being dragged along by the woman on either side. *Branles Des Pois* was followed by a Pavane, after which his ordeal came to a thankful end. A flustered Philip Neville bowed to the ladies and blew his relief through pursed lips, but tittering laughter from a nearby circle of dancers caught his ear. Snapping his head round, he saw Ralph Hastings whisper in a lady's ear and the entire group tittered.

Ten years younger than his brother, Ralph could thank filial connection for his position at court. Tall and long-limbed with an elongated face, wide blue eyes, high curving brows and the classic Hastings nose, Ralph was not as particular in his dress as William. Clothes never sat well on his lean frame and he brushed his light, flat hair forward, yet he was custodian of the king's lions and owned land in more than six counties.

Convinced young Hastings and his cronies were laughing at his clumsiness, Philip saw red. Breaking the circle, he moved to confront Ralph but Thomas Vaughan interceded.

"Now is not the time," he warned, grabbing Philip's arm and looking at the guards spaced along the walls, each armed with a halberd.

Philip jerked his arm free and lunged forward.

"Think, I beg thee," Sir Thomas hissed, blocking his path. "Your time will come."

Closing his eyes, Philip routed his anger into his balled fists.

"I am becalmed," he sighed.

Isobel knew her husband still had strong feelings for Elizabeth Hastings despite his denials. Given time, she hoped to wean him off her but after his behaviour today she wasn't so sure.

"We should mix," she suggested, taking him by the arm and thanking Sir Thomas, for his intervention.

"Philip," Thomas called after him, pointing a stern finger, "remember."

"Who's that?" Isobel asked, observing a tall, elegant woman dressed in crimson velvet and surrounded by a clutch of young noble men and women.

"The king's mother-in-law and her damned brood," Philip sneered, steering his wife in the opposite direction, "Leeches, every one of them."

"We should leave."

"Why?"

"If you don't know, I'm not going to tell you."

"You leave if you wish."

"Come with me," she pleaded.

"I cannot until I am dismissed by the king," he explained, looking into her fretful face and hooking several strands of hair over her ears. "I have to stay."

"Please," she pined, her hurt expression playing on his emotions.

"Why?"

"You are angry, I fear –"

"I'll not offend his highness."

"Promise me," she urged, looking into his eyes.

Isobel's spirit amused Philip, but on occasion it could incite a hostile retort.

"I shall play the part of a saint," he smiled, laying a hand over his heart and catching sight of Ralph Hastings out of the corner of his eye.

"You cannot help yourself," she groaned, watching his eyes follow Ralph like a predator stalking its prey. "What am I to do?"

"Wait," he commanded, grabbing her arm as she turned to leave. "I gave you my word."

Before she could speak, an usher stepped up onto the dais in front of the top table and banged his staff against the floor.

Joining him on the dais, the king's chamberlain demanded silence and the noise in the room gradually diminished to nothing more than an occasional cough.

"Pray silence for the king!" Hastings screeched, his high-pitched voice breaking up, forcing him to put a hand to his throat.

Edward stepped onto the platform and looked his guests over.

During the pause, Philip and Isobel shuffled forward to get a better view.

"My children," Edward began, his bright eyes brimming with joy, "again, we thank you for your gifts and good wishes, and extend an invitation to all –" He paused to stifle a belch that threatened to embarrass him. "I invite every man here to join me on a deer hunt. We meet at my hunting lodge in Waltham Forest the morning after twelfth night. Bring your bows and spears, for I promise it will be a day to remember."

The men in the crowd responded with roars of approval and Ralph Hastings raised his cup to toast the king's largesse.

"And what of the ladies, husband?" the queen asked.

"Why, the ladies may join their husbands, if they so wish."

"I've never attended a hunt," Isobel whispered.

"There's nothing like it," Philip sighed, rubbing his hands excitedly. "But 'tis no place for women," he warned, annoyed with Edward for suggesting such a thing just to please his wife.

"Why?" she pouted.

"'Tis too dangerous."

"Huh."

"Remember the bear pit? You covered your eyes through the whole performance," Philip said, keeping his voice low so as not to interrupt the king.

"That was different; the poor beast was chained up and torn to pieces –"

"That old bear killed six dogs before they got him down."

"It's not fair –"

"Shush," someone in the crowd hissed.

Philip was about to snap back but Isobel stopped him.

The king concluded his invitation with a hope that Harlech Castle would surrender soon and left the dais. The queen now approached Philip and Isobel, accompanied by half a dozen of her ladies-in-waiting.

"Sir Philip."

"Your Grace?" he responded, bowing sharply, concerned by the curious way the queen looked at his wife.

"Lady Neville?" she said in a kindly tone. "You are a most beautiful and charming young woman; I know your brother and his wife. Come, walk with me."

While the crowd applauded the king's speech, Isobel strolled with the queen and several of her ladies-in-waiting.

Though he despised Edward's choice of consort, Philip appreciated her womanly virtues. Elizabeth's exquisite good looks and poise were beyond compare. Her long fair hair was swept back from a high, shaven forehead and bundled up at the back, and her shiny pale face was covered with a transparent, gold-edged veil. Elizabeth's only jewellery was a thin necklace, wedding ring and a small crown which fitted perfectly. Her flawless complexion was offset by dark eyes, faint, nearly invisible brows and perfect red lips.

"Don't let the king catch you staring," Thomas Vaughan whispered, coming up beside him.

Philip grinned but the aggravating tone of Ralph Hastings' voice in the background cut the smile from his face.

"By the blood of St George," Philip spat, "I would gladly pound his face to a pulp."

"Philip –" Vaughan groaned, only to be interrupted by one of the king's secretaries.

"Sir Thomas!"

"Mr Both?"

"I need your opinion."

Reluctant to leave his uptight friend, Thomas walked away, looking ruefully over his shoulder, but Philip had already disappeared in the crowd. Fortified by wine, Philip tried hard to control his anger but when he saw Ralph Hastings making his way to a table alone, to refill his goblet, he felt compelled to act. Pushing through the masses, he made straight for the table.

"What do you want?" Ralph demanded, as Philip approached with menace in his eyes.

Philip physically forced him into an alcove and slapped his hands on the wall, one either side of his head. Leaning in, Philip stared hard into his eyes.

"Know this," he opened, his wine-laden breath forcing Ralph to turn his face away. "I will rip –" he continued, only to see the king coming across, accompanied by an elegantly dressed companion.

Lowering his hands from the wall, Philip stepped back and both men bowed to the king.

"Is this a private conversation?" Edward frowned, noting Ralph's distress.

"No sire," Philip said.

"Do you take me for a fool?" Edward hissed, turning to the Burgundian ambassador. "You see, your Excellency, my court is full of deceivers. You will excuse me?"

Bowing low the ambassador threw his arms out in a show of flowery obsequiousness and backed away, and Edward saw a slight smirk on his cousin's face.

"Leave us," he told Ralph, turning to Philip. "Will you ever learn?"

"Sire I –" he blurted, afraid of unleashing the infamous Plantagenet temper.

Edward shot a hand up to silence him and for a moment Philip feared for his life.

"If you intimidate or threaten my chamberlain or his brother, you will find yourself arrested, cousin," Edward promised.

Out of the corner of his eye, Philip noticed a group of spectators looking on and whispering.

"Tell me you know my mind so there is no misunderstanding."

"I am your Grace's humble and obedient servant," Philip said as the king stormed away.

Philip lowered his head and forced a path through the crowd. Spotting his wife and the queen, he waited impatiently for them to finish their conversation and when Isobel finally withdrew, he stepped up and took her hand.

"What did she want?" he demanded.

"*Her Grace* asked if I am happy with married life."

"Does she want you for a lady-in-waiting?"

"No," she answered, surprised. "Why?"

"I would forbid such a thing."

"But how could I refuse?"

He scoffed at her response.

"There was no talk of it," she confirmed.

"Do you wish to dance?" he asked, as the musicians began to play again.

Isobel shook her head and with the annoying nasally wailing of a tambour echoing in his ears Philip realised the evening was over. Laying Isobel's hand on his, he led her to the king who was back in conversation with the ambassador and begged forgiveness for the intrusion.

"Well?" Edward asked curtly, smiling at Isobel.

Philip announced that his wife wished to leave and the king's demeanour softened. Excusing himself from his companion, Edward kissed her hand.

"Lady Neville, you must come to the palace more often," he said, looking to make sure the queen was out of earshot. "Burgundy may boast the finest court in all Europe," he told the ambassador, "but England has the fairest maidens."

Isobel blushed and put her hands to her cheeks to cover her embarrassment. Nodding at a clutch of elderly matriarchs, Edward winked at Isobel.

"Those old hens are the exception," he said, bowing and smiling in their direction and receiving a round of curtsies and immature giggles in return. "You may take your wife home," he announced, amused by her discomfiture. "I won't need you tonight."

"Sire," Philip nodded, bowing to the Burgundian ambassador, "Excellency."

Withdrawing backwards from the king's presence, Philip turned and led Isobel through the crowd. On the way out he detoured to speak briefly with Thomas Vaughan.

"Farewell, Thomas."

"You're leaving?"

"The king does not need me this night."

"Then I will see you on the morrow."

Philip shook hands with his friend and guided his wife to the exit.

His behaviour had spoilt the evening and Isobel looked at him with mixed feelings as he signalled for a servant to bring their coats.

"Brrrr," she trembled, as the doors opened and a cutting wind blew in.

"Come," Philip said, bundling her up in a thick cloak and escorting her to the stables.

A week after the Christmas banquet, Philip Neville marched purposefully through the draughty corridors of Westminster, indignation etched deeply on his face. His left hand was balled into a fist while in his right was a brocaded leather gauntlet; the reason for his angst, the king's refusal to allow him to join the hunt. After Philip's confrontation with Ralph Hastings at Eltham Palace, Edward thought it wiser to keep them apart. Philip was drinking with friends at The Mermaid in Bread Street when told he would not be attending the hunt. The messenger who broke the news revealed that Ralph was making disparaging remarks about Isobel's fidelity.

Returning to the palace, Philip took a gauntlet from the armoury and went looking for Ralph.

"Where can I find the lord chamberlain's brother?" he demanded of an esquire in the king's cloister.

"I saw him a moment ago in the old yard," the teenager replied.

Cutting through the Lesser Hall, Philip opened a door that led out into an enclosed area known as Old Palace Yard. Spotting a couple locked in a loving embrace near the Black Princes' old palace, he stopped and stared, his temper rising. Eventually, they separated and strolled on, oblivious to Philip's smouldering gaze. Moving to intercept them, Philip deliberately stomped on the frozen ground until they heard him.

"What do you want?" Ralph asked, as Philip came up and stood in front of them.

Philip glowered at Elizabeth and turned to her husband, the milky whiteness of his foul breath billowing in his face.

"Well?" Ralph huffed impatiently, as Philip's proximity forced him to take a step back.

Shoving the gauntlet under his nose Philip threw it to the ground. He wanted to slap Ralph's face with it but the rules of chivalry denied him such a pleasure.

"What's this?" Elizabeth gasped.

"Pick it up," Philip commanded, ignoring her reaction.

"Don't," she bleated, touching her husband's arm.

"Pick it up!" he repeated. "Or be called coward."

"I am no coward," Ralph said, offended by the accusation.

"Please!" Elizabeth begged.

"No!" Ralph snapped, snatching up the gauntlet. "He has insulted me for the last time.

"When?" Ralph barked.

"Tomorrow," Philip snapped back.

"Where?"

"Smithfield, eight of the clock."

"I'll be there."

"Why do you do this?" Elizabeth pled.

"You know," Philip countered.

"But you have a fine wife," she said incredulously.

"We were promised to each other," Philip reminded her.

"We exchanged words in a field, nothing more."

"'Twas a contract nonetheless," he growled.

"My uncle would never have allowed me to marry a Neville," she countered, referring to her deceased guardian, Henry Percy, Third Earl of Northumberland.

"I did not know," Ralph gulped.

"You did not know?" Philip mimicked.

"The King will hear of this," Elizabeth said.

"Let him be a man for once," Philip said.

"My husband does not need a sword to prove himself –" she parried.

"Be silent!" Philip barked.

Elizabeth looked aghast and stepped back, and Philip nodded at Ralph before walking away with a satisfied smirk on his face. Pleased with himself, he looked forward to visiting his wife's bed. When he saw several workmen urinating against a wall, he shouted at them.

"Use the latrine, you dogs!"

Chapter 11

WEDNESDAY 15 JUNE 1467 was hot and sultry and the trapped muggy heat inside the tent nurtured a rising irritability in Philip that compounded a loathing for confined spaces. While his esquire and page unpacked armour, sweat ran down his face, forcing him to scratch his itchy neck. Wearing a linen arming doublet with mail voiders sewn on to protect armpits and elbows, he waited impatiently for the dressing. When he saw his page looking perplexed at the steel harness, Philip released his frustration in one long exhalation.

"Fetch Walter," he hissed.

Lamenting the loss of his former page, Philip rolled his eyes at his esquire. Sensing his aggravation, Robert ushered the page out.

"Give him a chance, my Lord," Harrington said. "He'll learn."

It had been five months since Philip threw down the gauntlet to Ralph Hastings, and after a strongly worded reprimand the king hoped the incident would be forgotten. How wrong he was: Philip's burning hatred blossomed after missing the New Year hunt. Despite every attempt to calm his fiery temperament, nothing could stop Philip's demand for satisfaction. Lord Hastings went to his friend the king, who again rebuked both men, to no avail; Philip meant to punish Ralph for coaxing Elizabeth Percy to his bed and insulting his wife, or so it was alleged.

On St George's Day, the king was informed of a further clash between his courtiers, near the fountain in New Palace Yard. To make matters worse, the verbal confrontation was witnessed by the queen and several terrified ladies-in-waiting. With a tournament planned to celebrate a visit by the Duke of Burgundy's bastard son, Antoine, a frustrated Edward told William Hastings it would be a good thing for Philip and Ralph to settle their differences at the tilt. Philip's reputation forced William to remonstrate with the king, even offering to take his brother's place. The king refused. The great tournament was calendared for June and a directive issued for both men to appear on the field of arms with horses, armour and weapons.

The political situation in England was also causing the king concern. Warwick was eager for an alliance with France, and Edward knew the Bastard of Burgundy's visit would create a problem. To avoid an international incident, he decided to send his cousin overseas. Warwick sailed for Honfleur on 28 May and the following day Edward met Antoine at Chelsea. When Warwick's brother, George Neville the Archbishop of York and Chancellor of England, learned of Antoine's arrival he refused to attend the opening of parliament. Several days later Edward rode to the Archbishop's residence at Charing Cross and relieved him of the chancellorship.

Philip's armourer entered the tent, followed by his worried page.

"Field armour, m'Lord?" Walter questioned, looking at the harness laid out on the ground.

"I have no other," Philip answered, lamenting his lack of means.

"Tha'll need a shield."

"Shield and lances are provided by the king," his esquire chirped, joining them.

"Huh," Walter sniffed. "M'lord, do tha wish t' do this?"

"I have waited long for this," Philip sighed.

Harrington laced up Philip's satin-lined arming doublet and checked his leggings down to the cordwain shoes. Elbowing the esquire aside, Walter examined the linen arming points to make sure the mail gussets attached to the doublet, covered those areas likely to be exposed through the joints.

Locking the steel gorget around Philip's neck, Walter shook his head and muttered. The gorget was old-fashioned and most knights used a wrapper for better protection, but Philip preferred a gorget and had his armour adapted.

"Easy," he hissed.

"You must wear a helmet or tha'll not be allowed t' fight," Walter warned.

Philip nodded and his armourer pointed to a stool.

Young Richard Warren drew the seat over for Philip and picked up the sallet while his esquire grabbed the sabatons.

"'Tis hot," Philip blew, as the sabatons were secured to his shoes.

The tops of the sabatons were constructed of overlapping metal plates to protect the upper part of the foot. Once they were buckled on, his esquire stepped back and Walter indicated for Philip to stand. His page snatched the stool away and watched fascinated as armourer and esquire work together. The mail skirt was wrapped around Philip's waist, next the greaves and cuisse were strapped to his lower legs, knees and thighs. Breast and back plates were then fastened and finally vambraces and couters were attached to arms and elbows.

"All good?" Walter asked.

"Feels tight," Philip sniffed.

"Tha've gained weight."

Philip huffed at his comment while the linen ties were tightened under his armpits and he twisted his torso to test flexibility.

"Ow's it now?" Walter asked, thumping him on the back.

"Hum," Philip grunted, forcing his chin down into the metal collar to see the words '*Fides et Honore*' hammered onto the metal near the top of the breastplate and fire-gilded.

"Keep tha head low and shield up."

Philip acknowledged Walter's advice while he made the final checks, and Harrington strapped his spurs to the back of the sabatons before leaving to fetch his horse. Walking out of the tent, Philip's face was bathed in glorious sunshine. Careful not to trip over the guide ropes, he slapped his sides.

"I'm as fat as a bishop," he chuckled, winking at his page.

The crowd was in festive mood; musicians, jugglers, fire-breathers and acrobats encouraged endless cheering, laughter and applause.

Drawing the plated gauntlets on over his lining gloves, Philip's mind rolled back ten years to a tournament in Coventry, when he was unhorsed by Ralph Percy. The pain and humiliation of that day returned, but he hoped for better results here.

The first five days of the tournament witnessed the highlight of the event, an exciting '*Pas d'armes*' between the queen's brother, Anthony Woodville, Lord Scales, and the Bastard of Burgundy, which lasted two days. Sunday was set aside for feasting, but the crowds returned on Monday eager for more mayhem. On Tuesday the king and queen attended a banquet at Grocer's Hall and Wednesday's opening bout was postponed after an accusation of cheating. To please his guests and placate the muttering crowd, Edward ordered the deed of arms between Philip and Ralph brought forward.

The fairgrounds of St Bartholomew's Priory, Smithfield, was the venue chosen by the king for the tournament. People normally came to 'Smithfield' to buy and sell livestock, or attend the annual four-day fair in August. The fairgrounds had been transformed into an arena, one hundred eight paces long by seventy-two wide, with a six-foot-high, unpainted, planked tilt running down the middle.

East of the tilt, at its midpoint rose a two-tiered grandstand or tabernacle. Constructed at great expense and hung with dark blue silk cloth, decorated with gold fleur-de-lys and the word 'Forever' on numerous scrolls. The upper viewing area was carpeted and could be reached by a set of steps, at the bottom of which were two chairs, one for the Constable, Sir John Tiptoft, the other for Sir John Howard, Duke of Norfolk and Marshall. In the centre of the upper floor was the king's ornately-carved chair of estate, painted red and upholstered in velvet with gold and silver heraldic symbols. Tasselled cushions were placed on the seat and an awning of gold cloth was stretched above. Beside the king's chair was the queen's much smaller seat, while ten plain chairs fanned out on either side.

Less elaborate stands were constructed around the arena for the mayor of London and his guests, knights, esquires and the royal archers. The thousands of commoners who attended were crowded behind a rough fence 'erected around the inside of the arena. As guests of the king, the wives of Philip Neville and Ralph Hastings sat at opposite ends of the royal box. Fixed to the front of the stand were a number of colourful shields bearing the arms of noble English and French families, while from the roof a dozen banners bearing the black bull and white boar, symbols of King Edward and his brothers, drifted in the light wind.

"My Lord!" Harrington shrieked, struggling to control Hotspur.

Sensing the esquire's anxiety, Philip's warhorse reared and bucked.

"Where is my wife's favour?" he asked, taking the helmet from his page and wedging it in the crook of his arm.

"Aha!" Harrington said, gratefully handing the reins to

a groom, and producing a white silk handcoverchief from inside his tunic as if by magic.

"Tie it above the elbow," Philip commanded, eyeing the crowd. "He senses your fear," he said, referring to his horse, while Robert secured the favour to his left arm. "Show him kindness and he'll eat out of your hand."

"There's blood here, my Lord," his page interjected, pointing dramatically to a dark stain in the compacted earth.

"Aye," Philip grinned at his esquire, "Any bones?"

"Why, yes!" he gasped, shocked at what he believed were human bone fragments, but were really small stones.

"There," Harrington declared, snapping the knot tight.

Philip nodded and his esquire approached Hotspur gingerly, took the reins from the grinning groom and followed his master to the royal stand, led by Lord Tiptoft, wearing leg armour, a gorget and a cloth-of-gold, sleeveless tabard. Ralph Hastings emerged from a tent at the far end of the field, saw Philip heading for the royal box and set off, his charger being led by an esquire.

Walking behind Tiptoft, Philip grew apprehensive over his courser's minimal protection. A thick, leather trapper covered its body from head to tail, surmounted by a full-length red and white silk caparison emblazoned with four silver lions. Hotspur's only armour was a steel chanfron, salvaged from a dead horse at Towton. The chanfron shielded the stallion's face and eyes but gave no defence to the rest of its body.

"Bollocks!" Philip cursed, treading in a pile of horse droppings.

"You'll have good fortune," Harrington grinned, while Tiptoft shuddered in disgust and Philip shook his foot to shake off the shit sticking to his sabatons.

The contestants and their horses drew up before the royal stand and the two knights faced their king, while his guests craned their necks to see.

Standing straight, Philip noted the curious looks of those on the balcony. Recognising the queen, Lord and Lady Hastings and the king's brothers George and Richard, his focus was drawn to the far end of the stand. Catching sight of Elizabeth Hastings, before she drew back, brought a growl from his throat and a churning sensation in his stomach. When he saw the smirk on Lord Herbert's face he narrowed his eyes.

Like Warwick, Philip despised William Lord Herbert, a cold-hearted knight who had been overly rewarded for subduing Wales. Philip remembered Herbert at the council of York, after Towton, when he sat near the king, staring contemptuously at him.

"You can look," he muttered, narrowing his eyes at the rugged Welshman before acknowledging his cousin, Richard Duke of Gloucester, with a kindly nod.

The King's fourteen-year-old brother combed a hand through his long brown hair but his mind seemed elsewhere.

Switching his attention to the other end of the stand, Philip acknowledged his wife Isobel with a nod. Edward, his high chair giving him a panoramic view, looked as the contenders bowed respectfully. Miffed at Philip's insistence on going ahead with the duel, and his own weakness for allowing it, Edward accepted the salute.

Both men walked to their respective mounting blocks and sat for the fitting of their helmets. As Harrington lowered the sallet over Philip's head, he held his breath.

"Make it secure," he barked unnecessarily, as the helm was strapped under his chin and the padded lining hugged his sweaty face.

Peering through the slit in his visor took Philip back to the second battle of St Albans. On that cold February day during Warwick's chaotic retreat, a disoriented Philip Neville fell in a ditch and was attacked. Wedged in the bottom of the dark, wet trench, his head was forced down into the brackish water and he struggled for breath. Coughing and spluttering as foul, icy water gushed into his mouth he punched his fists into the mud and forced his head up. The tinny clicking of daggers thrust into gaps in his armour made him panic.

"Roll the son of a bitch!" someone yelled.

Philip's head was twisted violently and one of the assailants tried to stab his face through holes in his visor. Fortunately, the blade was too thick and before it could find a way in, Arbroth and several men-of-arms arrived and butchered the assailants. Badly shaken, Philip was hauled from the ditch, his sallet was removed and he gasped air into his lungs. He never forgot the experience.

"Ready?" Philip's esquire asked.

Coming back to the present, he calmed down and noticed a narrow yellow scarf flying from the crest of Hastings' helm.

"I'll cut that favour from his helm and take the head with it," he vowed.

Philip asked God to protect him and traced a cross on his breastplate, while his esquire held Hotspur steady. Thrusting his left foot through the stirrup, he swung his right leg over the cantle, settled his arse in the saddle curve and patted his courser's neck.

"Easy," he said, as his warhorse pawed at the hard ground.

Harrington held the bridle until the beast grew accustomed to the weight on its back.

Philip looked down the tilt at his opponent and both men instinctively nudged their steeds towards the royal stand. Bowing, they saluted the king, and half-heartedly each other.

"This deed of arms between Philip Neville and Ralph Hastings is fought here this day to settle a matter of honour," the marshal announced, loud enough for all to hear. "Six lances will be broken!"

"To the death," Philip dared.

"What say you?" the king demanded, leaning forward.

"Nothing, sire," Philip cringed.

"Insolent knave," Edward gasped, slumping back and turning to his chamberlain. "What am I to do with him?"

Will Hastings shrugged his shoulders. Fearing his brother would be made to look a fool, or worse, he raised his pinched, colourless face to the heavens and closed his eyes, while the two knights trotted back to their respective pavilions.

The blare of the royal trumpets hushed the crowd and a herald, wearing a long coat showing the arms of Edward IV on the front, back and sleeves, stepped forward.

"Six courses are agreed!" he reiterated, bowing to the king and withdrawing.

"No one is to approach the lists!" another herald addressed the crowd, "Upon pain of imprisonment."

Philip bent his head and his esquire passed him a wooden jousting shield covered in thick, painted linen. Slipping the leather strap over his head, he drew the concave shield into his chest and left shoulder. Passing his arm through the enarme stabilised the shield and allowed him to take the reins in the same hand. Walter now came forward carrying a lance cut and shaped from a young pine tree stripped of its bark and branches and painted bright red, its tip fitted with a steel coronal. Satisfied with the position of the shield Philip lowered his visor.

"Keep tha head down," Walter repeated, handing him the ten-foot lance, "or he'll break tha neck."

Philip adjusted his balance to compensate for the weight of the lance.

Walter's warning was followed by the clarion call of a single trumpet, a red square pennant bearing three golden lions hanging from its stem, and the two knights prepared to charge.

Holding his lance up, Philip looked down the tilt at his opponent as six royal trumpeters sounded the signal to begin.

Releasing a grunt, he tapped the rowels of his spurs against Hotspur's flanks and the courser cantered down the right side of the tilt, keeping close to the barrier. As the distance closed, both men lowered their lances, the iron tynes of Hastings coronal pointing straight at Philip's chest. Ignoring the warning some of the crowd began to cheer, which merged with the thudding hoof beats as the horses broke into a charge. At the last moment, Philip levelled his lance over the barrier, put his head down and leaned forward. Both lances struck shield simultaneously and the impact sent a painful jolt through Philip's upper body. His lance snapped with a loud crack and wood splinters shot twenty feet in the air. Re-balancing, he tossed aside his broken lance and slowed his horse.

"By the blood of Christ," he coughed, repositioning his shield.

While a herald marked his score cheque both men took fresh lances and prepared for another run. Philip shunted the new lance forward and nudged his charger into a gallop. Hotspur sped down the tilt and Philip aimed his lance over the barrier behind the courser's nodding head. The coronal hit Hastings' levelled weapon and skidded down the shaft almost to the vamplate protecting his hand, before Philip was able to disentangle and ride on.

"You bastard!" he spat, the curse echoing inside his helmet.

Trotting back to his waiting esquire, Philip flipped open his visor.

"Son of a bitch," he snorted, using the soft leather under-fingers of his glove to wipe sweat from his eyes. "Not so many here today?" he commented, glancing around at the empty spaces in the mayoral stand.

"There's pestilence in the city," Harrington said.

"Watch 'im, m'Lord," Walter warned, checking Philip's shield.

"You worry too much," Philip retorted, taking a wet towel

from his esquire and pressing it against his hot face. "I'll get him this time."

"Aim for his neck."

"Yes, yes," Philip said, impatient to be away, while a groom ran his hands over Philip's horse looking for signs of injury.

"Mah lord, dinna let yer temper blind ye," Arbroth hissed, having just arrived.

Philip threw the wet towel at him, closed his visor and took another lance from his esquire. Couching it tightly under his arm he manoeuvred into position. The next run ended with neither knight gaining an advantage and Philip released a snort of frustration as he accelerated into a fourth charge. The lances hit with a resounding crack but this time the steel coronal of Hastings' spear struck the centre of Philip's shield and shattered it. Shocked by the blow Philip rode back to his esquire with the irritating cheers of Hastings supporters echoing in his ears.

"Get it off!" he barked, dragging the strap over his head and discarding the shivered shield. "Give it to me," he demanded, meaning a new lance.

"But my Lord, you have no shield!" his esquire yelled, as Philip lashed Hotspur away down the tilt. "My Lord!"

Thrilled by the excitement of the bout, the king's guests broke the rules and were on the edge of their seats, while the marshal frantically waved Philip back. Blinded by rage, he ignored the warning and forgot his vows of chivalry. Hastings counter-charged, aiming the point of his spear a little higher this time. Dropping his lance over the tilt, Philip thrust the tip hard against Ralph's shield. The lance bent and broke, throwing splintered shards into the air. With no shield, the metal studs of Hastings's coronal caught Philip under the pauldron and violently wrenched his head backwards. His feet slipped out of the stirrups and he fell off his horse.

"Oh," he groaned, hitting the ground in a state of shock, pain and confusion.

The crowd released a coordinated 'Ooh!' and those in the stands leapt to their feet. Hotspur let out a terrified scream and careered around the arena. Thumping into the tilt, Philip closed his eyes, rolled his body into the foetal position and prayed not to be stomped on. After a while he turned onto his back and looked through the dust at the lucent blue sky. Slowly moving his hands, feet, arms and legs he was relieved no bones appeared broken. The marshal hurried over and stood over the prostrated knight lest his opponent take advantage.

"By the blood of Christ," Philip gasped, attempting to rise, despite Sir John Howard demanding he stay down.

When it was safe to do so, Philip rattled to his feet, coughing harshly, and shoved his visor open.

"Goddamn it!" he spat.

Witnessing her husband's fall, Isobel buried her head in her hands, only looking when told he was alive. Snorting bloody mucus back through his nose, Philip waved to assure her he was unhurt. Relieved, Isobel lowered her fingers from her face and turned to the king, who was also thankful his cousin was alright. For weeks Isobel had pleaded with her husband not to go through with this insanity, but he refused to even listen.

"Hotspur?" Philip hissed, concerned, while his courser was secured by several grooms and men-of-arms.

"Ee's fine," Walter said, nodding in Lady Isobel's direction to confirm her husband was uninjured, "A little shaken, nothing more."

Philip scoffed at Ralph Hastings as he trotted down the tilt waving to the cheering spectators. Drawing his horse up before the royal stand, Ralph bowed to the king.

For dismounting his opponent, the queen presented

Hastings with a golden spur. Graciously accepting the gift he saluted the royal couple.

"They gloat at my misfortune," Philip hissed, as Tiptoft's men demanded silence from the crowd.

"Who?" his confused esquire asked.

"Will Hastings and that Welsh whoremaster."

"No, my Lord."

"Yes," he fumed, twisting his neck from side to side to relieve the pain.

"Tha was lucky," Walter exclaimed, running a finger over the dents in his breastplate where the steel tynes struck.

"I thought my head had come off," Philip chuckled, twisting his aching neck.

"Dinna let him get ta ye –" Arbroth reiterated, watching Ralph Hastings trot conceitedly around the arena.

"I won't," Philip vowed, narrowing his eyes.

William Hastings applauded his brother's success while John Smert, the middle-aged Gloucestershire lawyer and Garter King of Arms, offered his advice to Edward, who had appointed himself judge for the day.

"Pair of dog's bollocks," Philip sneered, tweaking his lower jaw and wincing at the pain.

"I can fix this," Walter said, fingering the damage to his breastplate.

Philip watched Edward and Garter King of Arms conversing.

"That overdressed little shit is full of shit," he huffed.

"After five passes Sir Ralph has unhorsed his opponent!" a herald announced.

Examining his scoring cheque, he added up the strikes and nodded at the king who was about to declare Hastings the winner.

"Your Grace, 'twas a foul blow!" Philip called out, to the

dismay of all, tossing his cup aside and limping towards the royal stand.

"There was no foul, sir!" Sir John Howard countered, exasperated by Philip's outrageous impertinence.

Edward felt the bony fingers of Lord Hastings on his arm.

"Sire," William announced, "my brother has won and fairly so."

The King looked at Howard, who seemed stunned by Philip's objection. Shrugging off his chamberlain's hand, Edward looked at Philip's wife, the veil of her coned hat concealing her distress.

"You will accept the decision gracefully," Edward commanded.

Philip bowed to the king and withdrew.

"Gentlemen," Sir John Howard announced, "prepare for foot combat."

While the two knights refreshed themselves before the next bout, jugglers, musicians and acrobats once again took to the field to perform for the crowd.

Chapter 12

HAVING WON THE first round, Ralph Hastings was offered the choice of weapons; he selected poleaxe, sword and dagger.

"I choose the same," Philip said sullenly.

"The first to strike his opponent five times with each weapon shall be adjudged the winner!" the herald declared.

Two pursuivants, apprentices to the heralds, led the antagonists into the Champ Clos, a fenced circular area below the royal box better known as the 'stockade'. Taking the four-foot-long poleaxe from his esquire, Philip relished this next phase of the combat. A lethal weapon in the hands of an expert, the poleaxe had a spike at the top for thrusting and, just below, on opposite sides, a hammer and axe head. Armour was no deterrent to a warrior trained in the use of such a weapon, as Philip found out at Towton. The hammer could crack steel and cause horrendous injury to flesh and bone, the axe was for piercing an opponent or dragging him off balance, while the spike was for thrusting.

Philip lowered his visor and spun the poleaxe confidently in his hands.

"Come on," he hissed, glaring at Ralph through the slit in his visor and deliberately provoking him.

The two men watched the herald raise his hand and drop it swiftly.

With adrenalin coursing through his veins, Philip violently

thrust his weapon forward. Unable to cope with the speed of the attack, Ralph managed to parry each strike, but Philip was out for revenge. His poleaxe swung in from all angles, first the hammer, then the axe, then the hammer again. Assailed by a barrage of blows, Ralph defended himself as best he could; it was not good enough.

"Three strikes to Sir Philip Neville!" the surprised herald announced, marking his cheque.

Philip came on again, twisting his weapon and snagging Hastings' visor with the axe-head. Using his strength he dragged him off balance and sent him crashing into the fence. Philip was prevented from bringing the hammer down on his head by a man-of-arms, who interposed his halberd between them and shoved Philip back. The herald looked to the marshal, who silently approved of his actions.

"Points again go to Sir Philip Neville!" he declared.

While Ralph caught his breath, Philip, the cheers of the crowd music to his ears, swapped the poleaxe for a sword.

Holding the blade before his eyes, he released a snort of satisfaction and kissed the crossbar.

Once recovered, Ralph waited while his armour was examined by an esquire, a delay that irritated Philip and gave his opponent time to catch his breath.

"Get on with it," he growled.

When he was ready to resume, Ralph was handed a huge sword and the crowd let out a gasp of disbelief. The bastard sword was much heavier and almost twelve inches longer than Philip's arming sword and its keen edge could cleave a man in two. As Ralph confidently walked around the Champ Clos swinging the blade ostentatiously, Philip scoffed at his pretentious display.

"Is that allowed?" the king asked Garter King of Arms.

Wearing the long tabard of his office, its front, back and

sleeves emblazoned with the king's colours, he shrugged his shoulders.

"Mah Lord," Arbroth whispered, looking over the fence, "wear him oot."

Philip was confident he could defeat Ralph, even if he brought along a cannon. When both men were ready Philip stared at Ralph, aiming to unnerve him. John Howard and a man-at-arms joined the two contestants as they strutted around the arena like peacocks. The two knights continued swaggering until the marshal could bear it no longer.

"I'll stop the contest if this nonsense continues!" Howard warned, indicating for his men-at-arms, lined up below the royal box, to intervene if either man broke the rules. Rolling up his list, Sir John Howard left the Champ Clos, bowed to the king and took his seat at the foot of the steps leading up to the royal stand.

Slamming his visor down Philip assumed a defensive pose and brought his weapon to the side of his head. The earlier tumble from his horse produced an ache in his neck which spread down and across his shoulders, but he tried to focus. After a period of dramatic side-stepping, Philip lunged at his opponent. Hastings blocked the assault with his much heavier sword, but Philip continued the offensive. The loud grunts and groans, and the clanging and scraping of swords hushed the crowd.

Against the flow of play Hastings suddenly swung his great sword in a circle above his head and brought it down on Philip's sallet. Reacting sluggishly, Philip parried the blow but the weight of the Bastard sword jarred his wrists and almost knocked the blade from his hands. Both men stepped back to seek an opening but it was Ralph who came on first, swiping his sword in from the side, the weapon missed its target and glanced off the thin metal ribs protecting Philip's pauldron. Curling his lighter sword up in an arc he thwacked the crest of Hastings' helmet. Bellowing profanely, Ralph pushed his blade forward but the heavy metal hit air and spun him around.

"You dog!" he spat acerbically, as Philip's supporters cheered.

The herald marked his cheque and directed the man-of-arms to be ready. Recovering, Hastings looked for a chance to level the score.

"Arse face!" Philip yelled.

"Varlet!" Ralph puffed his strength flagging.

Before the joust, Lord Hastings had warned his brother of Philip's volatile temperament.

Remembering his s words, Ralph took two quick steps forward, left and right, aiming for Philip's helm. The blow was deflected and struck Philip's upper arm, snapping off a rivet and loosening another shoulder rib.

"I'll kill you for that!" Philip raged.

"Try it!" Hastings spat.

Philip's blood boiled and he ran at Ralph, aiming to smash his sword down on his head. Ralph avoided the first blow and the second, but the third caught him above the visor.

"Ah!" he yelped, staggering back and waving his sword blindly in front of his face.

Following in, Philip knocked his sword aside and thumped him back with his breastplate. Ralph's long spurs, which his esquire had forgotten to remove, tripped him and he fell. Philip elbowed aside the man-of-arms as he tried to keep them apart and deliberately stamped on Ralph's sword arm at the wrist. Pressing his weight down until his hand was forced open he snatched the bastard sword from his grip and held it up triumphantly.

Opening up his visor, Philip stared down at his defeated foe.

"Next time you choose to fight with such a weapon, learn how to use it first," he crowed.

"You can go to Hell and damnation!"

Philip tossed Ralph's sword aside and bent down to whisper in his ear.

"Know this: I took your wife's maidenhood!" he deliberately lied, glancing at the man-of-arms, daring him to intercede. "And she panted for more."

"You lie!" Ralph barked, knocking his damaged visor up.

"Ask her," he smirked, glancing at the royal box. "And when you do, look into her eyes… for then you will see the truth."

"'Tis a falsehood!"

"Step away!" Lord Howard commanded, while the man-of-arms thumped his pole against his chest, forcing him to back off.

Philip swung his sword up as if to strike.

"No!" a woman yelped from the royal stand.

Philip lowered the blade and tapped Ralph's broken visor with it, just enough to knock it closed. With a glazed look in his eyes he thrust the point of his sword under the mail skirt protecting Ralph's privy parts.

With the frenzied crowd chanting for blood, Philip contemplated slicing off Ralph's bollocks. The spectators goaded him on and he looked at the king, who sat with the forefingers of his clasped hands pressed to his lips.

"Stand back!" Sir John Howard repeated.

Philip withdrew his sword but lunged forward and tore the scarf from the crest of his helmet. Screwing up the yellow silk he threw it to the ground before laying his sword in the crook of his arm and bowing to the king. Stepping back, he smiled courteously at Isobel and rubbed her favour.

"For the third time the mark goes to Philip Neville!" the herald declared.

Hastings punched his visor open and seethed.

"The dagger," William Hastings reminded Edward, aware his brother had already lost the contest.

The king looked sympathetically at his friend.

"Do you wish to prolong his embarrassment?"

"No, sire," he sighed submissively.

"Then it is finished."

Handing his damaged sword to his esquire, Philip leaned against the fencing to catch his breath while Ralph was helped to his feet.

"By order of the king, this deed of arms is over," the herald announced.

Edward leaned over the stand and spoke down with the marshal. After their brief exchange, Sir John nodded and the king resumed his seat.

"The King declares this contest a tie!" he announced.

"A tie," Philip huffed.

"Come forward and claim your prize, sir knight!" Howard said sharply.

Philip left the Champ Clos and walked to the royal box.

Pretending not to see Ralph Hastings, he deliberately knocked against him with his shoulder on the way out. This sly move did not go unnoticed by the king, whose disapproval was clear.

Sweeping his arm across his stomach as an apology, Philip waited. Rising from her seat, Queen Elizabeth opened an oblong velvet box, removed a gold-handled dagger and gave it to Sir William Hastings. Determined not to show displeasure the chamberlain clumped down the stairs and gave the dagger to Sir John to present.

"Your prize, sir," Howard said, offering the dagger, his disapproval obvious.

Philip accepted the gift, thanked the royal couple and exhibited the dagger to his cheering supporters before rejoining his retainers. Looking at Isobel, he kissed the prize to show he had won it for her. Lifting her veil, she acknowledged his salute with a charming smile that lit up her face.

"Ye showed him," Arbroth smirked, patting his back, while his esquire removed his helmet.

"A fair result, my Lord," Harrington commented.

"I should have killed him," he spat as his sallet was removed.

"My Lord," Harrington said, detaching the helmet from the gorget.

Philip wiped his eyes in a towel and spotted Edward leading his guests down from the royal box.

"He's coming this way," Harrington said, panicking.

"What now?" Philip groaned, handing the towel to his page.

Philip's men bowed and backed away, leaving him alone, while Will Hastings, his sister-in-law and Lord Herbert broke off and headed over to Ralph's tent.

"Something's afoot," Philip whispered, but his men had already withdrawn. "Dogs," he hissed out of the corner of his mouth.

"Your Graces," Philip smiled, bowing to the royal party.

"Rise, cousin," Edward commanded.

"My lady?" Philip said, addressing his wife, who accompanied the king, his queen and the Duke of Gloucester.

"'Twas a fair joust," Edward decreed. "What say you, brother?"

"Yes. sire," Richard agreed.

"Poor William, I thought he would die of apoplexy," Edward chuckled, referring to his chamberlain.

Wary of offending the king, Philip made no comment and the queen motioned for Isobel to stand with her husband.

"I hope this has put an end to your differences."

"Yes, sire."

Edward read the lie in his eyes and raised his eyebrows.

"Your Grace, this day has given me a thirst for battle," Philip said, surprising his wife.

"You prefer the mud and filth of campaigning in a foreign land to serving your king?"

"My life at court is tedious and a waste of my martial talents," he boasted. "There are still many enemies, in Wales."

"You are a knight of the body and your place is here," Edward emphasized, pointing down at the ground and smiling at Isobel.

"Yes, your Grace," Philip frowned.

"But you," said Edward, motioning for Robert Harrington to come forward, "you are released from service as an esquire. You have earned your spurs; you will join my brother Richards retinue."

"Your Grace," Harrington stammered, kneeling and lowering his head.

Edward took his sword, which was handed to him by a man-at-arms, and knighted the youngster.

"Arise Sir Robert, knight of the realm, and be recognised," he declared, tapping the flat of the blade onto each of the esquire's shoulders. "Fear not, I'll find you another to take his place," Edward promised Philip, while an esquire came forward and attached a set of spurs to Robert's heels.

Passing the sword back to the man-at-arms, Edward walked his wife to the royal stand, accompanied by prolonged cheering from the crowd.

"I am pleased for you," Philip fibbed, "'tis no more than you deserve."

"My Lord," Harrington gasped, overjoyed at receiving his long-awaited knighthood.

Philip extended a hand which was grasped firmly by the youngster, who was still in shock.

With an expression of regret laced with annoyance, Philip watched his esquire show off his spurs to his friends.

"Dear lady," he said, taking the dagger from his page, "this is for you."

"What will I do with such a thing?"

"Keep it," he sniffed, looking discreetly at Elizabeth Hastings.

"But you won it, my Lord."

"I care nothing for such trinkets."

"But."

"Madam, if you do not want it then give it away," he cut her off. "I don't care."

"I…" she gasped, shocked by his tone.

"Tha lad deserves it," Arbroth said, attempting to ease Philip's irritation.

"Aye," Walter agreed, smirking at the sight of Hotspur nipping Robert Warren's fair hair as he tried to untie the animal.

"The King promises me an esquire, but I need a good page too," Philip sighed, frowning at the boy's failure to control the powerful charger. "With Robert gone, who will rein in my temper?" he groaned, staring at Ralph Hastings.

"Sir Thomas Vaughan?" Arbroth suggested.

"Thomas?" he scoffed. "He spends too much time with the Woodvilles," he added. "You know he was once Henry's man."

"Mah lord, most o' tha fools at court were once Henry's men," Arbroth explained. "You yerself said he was no a bad mon…Ye canna fight tha whole world. Sir Thomas has been a good friend tah ye."

"'Tis hot," Isobel gasped using a hand to fan her face. "I feel faint."

"I'll have you taken home, but stay in the house: pestilence is rife in London again."

"'Tis tha bloody flux this time," Arbroth interjected, cupping a hand to Philip's ear. "Ah have seen men and women dying doon by tha river, blood squirting oot o' their arses. Ah hear tell carters are refusing tah take away tha dead."

Isobel shuddered at his frankness. Sensing her distress, Philip ordered Arbroth to be silent and take her home.

"Aye, m'Lord."

"Help me out of this," he told Walter, kissing his wife goodbye. "And bring my horse."

Walter was a powerful man with massive hands and a head of scraggly hair that was usually tied back, revealing tanned, rugged features. Hotspur knew better than to defy Walter and walked with him obediently.

Before having his armour removed, Philip took one last look at the Hastings clan gathered outside his marquee at the far end of the tilt and looking his way.

"Goddamned codheads!" he spat deliberately, before drawing open the tent flap and disappearing inside.

Chapter 13

THE GREAT TOURNAMENT ended when news reached London that the Duke of Burgundy had died, forcing his son Antoine to curtail his visit. Shortly after Antoine's departure the Earl of Warwick landed back in England with a French embassy but the king's frosty reception boded ill for any relationship with that country. Angered by Edward's attitude and the sacking of his brother George from the chancellorship, Warwick left London. With his cousin away, Edward cemented the alliance with Burgundy by engaging his sister Margaret to the new Duke, Charles.

Around this time a courier from the exiled Queen Margaret was captured near Harlech. Startled by his confessions, Lord Herbert sent him to London where he revealed that Warwick was sympathetic to Henry of Lancaster. Edward ordered his premier Earl to court but he ignored the summons. Not sure what to believe, Edward sent the prisoner to Warwick, but when they came face to face, the man retracted his statement. With growing opposition to rising taxes Edward feared a rebellion, and decided to move the court to Coventry for Christmas. Early in January Edward demanded that Warwick join him, but again he failed to appear.

Frustrated by his performance at Smithfield, Philip Neville quickly fell out with Thomas Vaughan over his friendship with the Woodvilles. A week after Michaelmas, 29 September, several of Philip's retainers joined him in London bringing arms, equipment and his palfrey. The house in King's Street was too small to accommodate everyone and he was forced to rent a more suitable property in the Strand.

During the nights Philip was on duty at the palace, he slept on an uncomfortable wheeled pallet in the corridor outside the king's chamber. Such nights were long and sleepless and the days cold and damp. The back-stabbing, frivolity and boredom of court life gave him time to dwell on matters best left alone. The high point of Philip's days was when he secretly followed Elizabeth Hastings as she escorted the queen on her walks around New Palace Yard. Drawn to her like a moth to a flame, he would linger and watch, and languish in self-pity. When Edward and his wife left London to spend Christmas at Coventry, Philip went with them. Away from Isobel, his former infatuation with Elizabeth was rekindled. Her image dominated his thoughts during the day and haunted his dreams at night. To douse his passion he asked the king again, to be sent to Wales. Despite his insubordinate nature, Philip was one of the few men Edward trusted and he promised to think on the matter. His answer gave him a glimmer of hope as he rode north with the king and his enormous entourage.

In the great Chapter House of the Benedictine Priory and Cathedral Church of St Mary, Coventry, Philip rested against the wall near the west doors. With his damp clothes clinging to his skin, he folded his arms over his chest and listened to the incessant rain beating down on the roof. Watching the king pace impatiently, he let out a weary sigh, removed his gloves and massaged his knuckles, to relieve the arthritic ache.

"My bones soak up this rain like a sponge," he complained.

A fellow knight shook his head and blew his boredom through his lips.

Woodhouse, the annoying royal fool, dressed in red and sporting a paper crown, walked behind the king imitating his gait and forcing the bodyguards to conceal their mirth, but Edward suddenly lashed out.

"Begone, fool!" he thundered, his booming voice bouncing off the high vaulted ceiling of the Chapter House. "Begone, I say."

As the terrified fool fled to the exit, Philip stopped smirking and stood to attention when the king's gaze fell on him.

Before leaving, Woodhouse scowled at Philip, who he knew disliked him, and looked back at the king.

"Your Grace!" he said. "I am a fool and I know it to be true."

Edward looked blank.

"But some here are fools and they don't know it," Woodhouse explained, grinning at Philip.

Edward chuckled as his cousin craftily jabbed the sharp, pointed metal chape at the end of his scabbard, into Woodhouse's arse.

"You little turd," Philip hissed.

Woodhouse yelped and was helped on his way out by another knight who also despised the obnoxious fool, and the door was slammed shut. A black-robed Benedictine sitting in a nearby alcove shook his head at their irreverence.

Startled by the cry, Edward looked sternly at his innocuous-looking guards before continuing to walk up and down uneasily.

"I am not happy here," he growled. "Seven years ago my father was attainted in this very chamber by Henry and his council of devils."

"Craven dogs," Philip growled.

"Shush," another knight warned.

"Why are we standing here scratching our balls?" Philip muttered.

"You are in a holy place, sir knight," a companion reminded him.

"Where is he?" the king griped, his patience waning, "By the saints!"

Suddenly the doors shrieked open on their rusty hinges and a courier strode into the Chapter House.

"Your Grace!" he announced enthusiastically, removing his hat, throwing back his wet cloak and going down on bended knee.

"Speak?" Edward barked, unimpressed by his pompous style.

"Sire, the Earl of Warwick demands an audience with thee," he announced, dripping rainwater over the green and orange tiles to reveal an embossed checker-board pattern of Flowers, Fleur-de-lys and rampant Lions.

"The Earl of Warwick is in no position to make demands of the king," Lord Hastings interceded, seated on a stone bench, one of many set in alcoves along three of the walls.

"I apologise, my Lord," the messenger grovelled, bowing his head. "Lord Warwick begs an audience with your Grace."

Edward gave a reluctant nod and the messenger reversed out of the chamber.

Outside the rain had stopped and sunshine slanted in through the painted windows of the Chapter House, lighting up the inside. Philip's mind began to wander and he looked curiously at the detailed faces of the twenty-four elders of the Apocalypse, painted in the decorated arches around the walls. Each figure was clothed in white with a crown of gold and Philip surprised himself when he recognised John the Divine by the halo over his head and a bright red book in his hand.

The sound of heavy footsteps drew his attention to the doors of the Chapter House and he stepped back. The king had been waiting for Warwick since early January; now, almost six weeks on, he was here and Philip wondered how Edward would react. When the doors were thrown open and a bedraggled Earl of Warwick entered, his haughty bearing was plain for all to see. Philip and his companions bowed respectfully as he stopped briefly between them.

Aware of Philip's presence, Warwick narrowed his cold, blue eyes and unsheathed his sword.

"Cousin," he sniffed brusquely, handing him his blade.

"My Lord."

Though resenting Warwick for Michael's death and his treatment of Henry of Lancaster, Philip empathised with his kinsman's declining popularity.

Snatching the dark blue velvet cap from his head, Richard Neville walked up to the king and knelt before him. Taking Edward's hand, he touched his cold lips to the ring on his middle finger.

"Dread sovereign, I crave thy indulgence."

When her father's manor at Maidstone was plundered, reputedly on Warwick's order, the queen pressed her husband to publicly chastise the arrogant earl. Edward promised he would do so, but only to shut her up. Now, as he knelt before him, he remembered the old fellowship. Warwick's years of loyal service were weighed against his hostility to the queen's family, an obsession with a French alliance and the hope of marrying his two daughters to Edward's brothers.

As the king looked down at Richard's dark, flat hair, grey at the sides, his anger receded and nostalgia saddened his countenance.

"Rise, gentle cousin," he said, his voice quivering emotionally. "It has been too long."

Warwick stood and the two men embraced lovingly before Edward kissed his cheek. Philip folded his arms, embarrassed by their emotive clinch, but knew it was only familial theatrics. At the urging of his brother, the Archbishop of York, Warwick agreed to bury the hatchet with Lord Herbert, but refused to consider reconciliation with the Woodvilles.

"Welcome," Edward said, noting Warwick's pallid complexion and heavily furrowed forehead.

"Your Grace," he bowed.

"We must forget what has gone before and revive a friendship that brought us victory on so many bloody fields," Edward said. "We were always good together; let it be so again."

"I would like nothing better, sire," Warwick agreed, with a smile that smoothed out his rutted brow and brought colour to his cheeks.

Conscious of his cousin's calculating ways, Philip raised his eyebrows in surprise. Both Richard and Edward were focused on their own separate agendas: Edward was being coaxed by his wife, her family and the anti-Warwick faction at court, Warwick by Louis of France and his own ego.

"The Archbishop of York has made this day possible," Edward declared.

"My brother always did have *savoir-faire*," Warwick responded, a nagging doubt in the back of his mind that Edward might be plotting his arrest.

Philip could not believe his ears. Archbishop Neville had been robbed of his Chancellorship by the king, and Warwick, despite all his intrigue and blustering, was back in the royal fold. The scenario was reminiscent of the Duke of Somerset's double-dealings and he knew it wouldn't end well. His years with Warwick gave Philip a fair insight into the power-hungry and proud nobleman.

"This is a farce," a knight whispered. "Lord Warwick has put his head in the lion's mouth."

"That lion will, one day, snap its jaws shut and cut it off," Philip prophesied as Edward and Richard linked arms and left the Chapter House for a banquet.

"Make way for the king!" an usher announced, banging his staff on the tiled floor.

Edward's knights formed a double line and bowed as the king and his cousin walked out together. Philip received a sly glance from Warwick as he passed through and snatched his sword back.

"Lord Warwick has marked thee," one of the knights warned.

Philip scoffed and followed them out but his cheek began to twitch nervously.

The dawn of a new York-Neville partnership was on the horizon; or was it? While Edward basked in the mistaken belief that Warwick knew his place, the earl was already plotting his next move.

In late June Warwick escorted Edward's sister Margaret to Stratford Langthorne, in Essex, for the first leg of a journey that would end with her marriage to Burgundy. Despite their new-found harmony, Edward knew Warwick would oppose his plan to ally England with Burgundy and Brittany against France.

When the royal party returned to London, Philip went home to his wife, who was not the same woman he left behind in December. Sweet, slender Isobel had gained weight, her once beautiful soft face was spotty and her golden hair was lank and lacked patina. Believing she had lost interest in herself, he threatened divorce if she did not regain her former allure. It was only when informed that she was with child that his manner softened.

"Sit!" he commanded, grabbing a chair for her and crouching on his haunches before laying a hand on her stomach. "I knew nothing," he apologised, his tone sweet and sympathetic. "Are you certain? Your belly is not big."

"Yes..." she puffed.

"Why was I not told?" he bellowed, glaring at her maid.

"I made them promise," Isobel cut him off. "I did not wish to burden thee..."

"Burden me?" he gasped, rubbing his forehead, "Oh, foolish wife."

"My lady refused to lie in until you returned," her maid Kate said.

"Why was I not told?" he repeated, turning to Arbroth, who looked down at the floor.

"We did not know…" Kate apologised. "There were no signs."

"No signs?" he huffed. "Look at her face."

Isobel blushed at his unintended slight.

"My Lord her piss was clear," a male servant offered.

"They are not to blame," Isobel insisted, taking Philip's hand to calm him. "I only knew myself when I felt movement."

"The quickening came swiftly," young Kate revealed, ringing out a wet towel into a bowl of cold water and pressing it to Isobel's forehead.

"You must lie in," Philip insisted, caressing her left hand and noting the rings cutting into her swollen fingers, "For your sake and the child's."

"'Tis too soon," she smiled.

"Don't leave it too long," he warned, arching his back.

"Do you love me?"

"Why do you ask?" he frowned, embarrassed by such things being spoken of in front of servants.

"Because I feel fat and ugly."

"You look radiant," he said, raising his eyebrows at her maid.

Isobel knew he was lying and buried her face in her hands. Philip looked to Arbroth for help but he shrugged his shoulders and Isobel began to sob. Unnerved by her emotional state, he signalled for Kate to come and comfort her.

"I must return to the palace," he explained, rising slowly to counter the pain in his knees and waving for Arbroth to join him. "But I will return, soon."

Stepping out into the busy street, Philip drew on his riding gloves, while a groom held his rouncey.

"Watch over her," he told his Scot.

"Aye, m'Lord," he saluted. "Will ye come home tonight?"

"I cannot deal with childbirth," Philip said, riding to Westminster Palace, followed by his page on a horse that was far too big for him.

The summer of 1468 was a season of much discontent for King Edward. A Lancastrian force under Jasper Tudor had sailed from France, landed on the Welsh coast and burned Denbigh. Pursued by Lord Herbert, the raiders fled back to their ships. Around this time, another of Queen Margaret's agents was caught. Under torture he revealed a list of names, which included a servant of Warwick's friend Sir John Wenlock, but Edward refused to believe his cousin was involved in any conspiracy. Several of the accused, including a number of London merchants, were tortured and executed and Edward's popularity in the city plummeted. To make matters worse, the price of food and lodgings in the capital rose dramatically. To many the king was alienating his friends to curry favour with his hated in-laws.

Shortly before noon on the final day of August, Philip left Portia's bed, the harlot he'd been swiving since his wife's lying in, and walked out of The Rose Inn. Strolling along the path to a set of steps leading down to the river, he watched an armada of merchant ships, small boats and wherry's struggling against the outgoing tide.

Philip believed 1468 would be a turning point in his life, but so far it had failed to live up to expectations. Any hope of going to Wales ended when Harlech surrendered in August and Isobel's pregnancy was growing more difficult every day. She hated being confined to her bed in a dark room with only her maid for companionship. Her illness and constant complaints forced Philip to spend more time in the tavern or whorehouse.

Shuffling along the shore, Philip sighed as he recalled the erotic passion of his night with Portia. Watching the brown foaming waters of the Thames swirl and roar through the arches of London Bridge, he chuckled at the sensitivity in his balls. Rubbing his itchy palm on the scent-bottle-shaped pommel of his sword, he wondered when his new esquire would arrive. Edward had promised him one more than a year ago but he was still waiting. This was partly his own fault: the king had proposed several candidates, but Philip was too particular. The one bright spot in his life was the restoration of his manors, which were beginning to show a profit, enabling him to increase his retinue to twelve.

Distracted by a party of soldiers escorting a line of prisoners, roped together and making their way up Goat Lane, Philip sneezed aloud. With hands manacled, the captives were being prodded along by sword point.

"What is their crime?" Philip enquired.

"They planned to riot in Southwark last night," the sergeant in charge revealed.

"To what end?"

"To burn out the Flemish weavers."

"And cut off their thumbs," another added.

"Aye and we would 'ave done it," one of the prisoners lamented, tugging at the coarse rope halter rubbing his neck raw, "but we was betrayed."

"Why?" Philip asked.

"Bloody foreigners come here an' take the bread from our mouths!" he sneered.

"'Tis said the Earl of Warwick is behind it," the sergeant said with conviction.

"His lordship is blamed for every indiscretion these days," Philip huffed, "'Tis the Woodvilles who are the traitors here. Am I the only one who sees it?"

"By your leave, sir," the sergeant said, as prisoners and escort shuffled on, and Philip made his way onto London Bridge.

Walking through the great stone gateway and onto the bridge, he weaved a way through rushing pedestrians. Passing over the drawbridge and beneath a second gatehouse, he stopped to wipe the sweat off his face. Looking up at the battlements he saw several long poles pointing skyward, each topped with the rotting head of a traitor.

"Phew," he gasped, staring at the strands of hair adhering to the weathered skulls and dancing in the breeze.

Philip moved on between the tall, overhanging houses on both sides of the bridge, which frowned inwards and blocked out most of the light. The ground floors of the buildings were occupied by tradesmen, their lowered counters further reducing the twelve-foot wide roadbed. With traffic and angry pedestrians almost at a standstill, he pushed on to the Chapel of St Thomas of Canterbury. After zig-zagging through grousing apprentices, argumentative customers and irate carters, he reached the north end of the bridge.

When he stepped off the bridge, Philip was relieved as cool air blowing down the river valley dried the perspiration on his face. Turning west at the Church of St Magnus the Martyr, he walked along Thames Street to the Blackfriars Monastery, where he was to attend the king.

"Shit!" he swore, as the bells of St Pauls tolled the hour of 'None', around 12.40 p.m.

Conscious the king disapproved of unpunctuality, Philip ran as fast as his legs would go. Passing quickly over the Walbrook Stream, he criss-crossed the street to avoid the crowds. Short of breath, he turned down to the river but the gagging stench of decaying waste, washing into Queenshithe, forced him back up to Thames Street. The wind blowing up the Thames failed to penetrate the streets away from the river and the intolerable heat was debilitating. Gasping for air, he found his progress was painfully slow.

Reaching the north side of Baynards Castle he hurried up Athelyng Street to its junction with Carters Lane. Near the King's Wardrobe, he turned left and followed the bright lime-washed wall of the Dominican Friary, around to its north gate.

Entering the monastery Philip gasped at a friar and begged to be taken to the king. Without a word the monk led him down between rows of tenements and beautifully manicured gardens to a two-storey building. Blackfriars covered a vast area from the Thames as far north as Ludgate, and from the Fleet River in the west to the King's Wardrobe in the east. It was the wealthiest and most politically important of the five London friaries. The top story of the building was, on occasions, used for parliamentary business.

"You don't say much, friar," Philip teased, when the monk pointed to the building, the ground floor of which was used as the abbey infirmary.

Philip chuckled as he walked up the stairs to the hall on the first floor. Approaching the guarded doorway he heard the unmistakable booming voice of his cousin, the king. Exchanging a pained nod with the guards, he was about to knock on the door.

"No one is to pass," one of them warned, lowering his pole-axe to bar access.

"His Grace is in bad humour," a second guard added, removing his pot helmet and wiping his brow. "He's kicking his hat around in there."

Philip knew that when Edward used his hat as a football, it was better to stay away.

"Who's in there with him?"

"Lords Herbert," the guard began, "Rivers and Norfolk, and others…"

Philip dragged his sticky hair off his forehead and paced.

"I will be king in my kingdom!" Edward bellowed, "All he asks for, for I have given him… Ever-thing!"

Philip and the guards looked at each other.

"Yet the commons hold him in higher esteem than their king!" Edward continued to rage. "I respect the citizens of London but they shower him with praise: why?"

"The people of England fear another war with France," a calm voice countered, one that Philip recognised as belonging to Archbishop Neville. "The best of six generations have been sacrificed for the wars with France."

"Lord Warwick seeks a treaty with Louis that will end centuries of conflict," another added, but Philip failed to identify him.

"Burgundy still refuses to revoke the ban on English cloth, your Grace," Robert Stillington, Bishop of Bath and Wells exclaimed.

"My Lords, France has invaded Brittany, and we are bound by treaty to go to her aid," Lord Rivers chipped in. "My son is raising an army as we speak."

Philip stepped between the guards and put an ear to the door.

"Where is this mythical army," Edward demanded, "that drains my treasury?"

"Sire," Hastings interjected, his soft voice making it difficult for Philip to hear, "it takes time. Lord Scales is arranging the required indentures…"

"Why does everything take so long?" Edward whinged.

"He's not a happy king today," Philip smiled.

"Your Grace," Lord Herbert spoke up, "Brittany will be lost before we can cross the Channel."

"You are my advisors," Edward barked impatiently, "so advise me!"

A moment of silence was followed by the king addressing his cousin, the Archbishop of York.

"Your Grace, tell your brother to cease his conspiracies against me or I will forget our kinship," he warned. "When he came to me at Coventry, I believed the bad blood between us was past, but I am too compassionate; Well, no more! Richard will support me or I'll destroy him!"

"Your Grace –" the Archbishop objected.

"No!" Edward snapped. "That is my final word."

Philip rolled his eyes at the guards and tutted.

"The church should have no say in the governance of this realm," he muttered.

The command 'All rise for the king' was followed by the doors opening, forcing Philip to step aside as three armed knights marched out followed by the king. Catching sight of his cousin, Edward snapped at him as he traipsed down the stairs without breaking his stride.

"You are late!"

"Forgive me sire but –" Philip apologised, struggling to keep up with the king as he hastened down Water Lane to Blackfriars stairs on the Thames, where the lavishly decorated royal barge was moored.

Edward stepped aboard the rocking vessel and sat in the curtained off stern, on a pile of cushions, where he was joined by Lord Herbert. Philip and William Hastings sat together in the centre, though both were uneasy at the pairing. The nobles and bodyguards sat in twos from the middle of the boat to the front. With limited space, most of the guards walked back to Westminster. As the barge rowed up the Thames, the red and blue quartered banner of England fluttering from the helm, and Edward sipped a goblet of wine.

"Why were you late?" he asked, staring at Philip's back.

"I…" he stuttered, aware the king was addressing him.

"Say nothing," Edward warned. "I know where you were and with whom."

Philip glanced red-faced at Lord Hastings whose own countenance was slowly turning green.

"My Lord chamberlain does not travel well on water, sire," Philip teased, aiming to lighten the mood.

"While you were swiving a harlot, your wife has given you a child," Edward said, ignoring his attempt at humour.

Philip's heart thumped excitedly.

"You have a son," Hastings groaned, delicately rubbing his stomach.

"A son?" Philip gasped.

"When we reach the palace, wash the stench of the whorehouse from your flesh and go to her," Edward commanded. "We will talk later."

"Yes, your Grace," he answered, relieved.

Resting an arm on the back of Hastings' chair, Philip looked at the north shore, through the smartly dressed rowers straining at the oars, and wondered why he felt strangely detached.

"Will you tell him, my Lord?" Herbert whispered in the royal ear.

"No."

Chapter 14

WHEN THE ROYAL barge tied up at Westminster and the king disembarked, Philip went to his chamber, sat on his low bed and brooded on how the birth of a son would affect his life. After visiting a barber, he left the palace and rode along King Street. Taking the right fork at Charing Cross, he cantered along the Strand until he reached his home, a double-fronted jettied house opposite the Bishop of Chester's Inn. Dismounting with a grunt, he stared at the door while his rouncey snorted and switched its tail.

The stone and timber build belonged to a wine merchant and consisted of rooms on two floors, with a hall, kitchen, cellar and courtyard. Knocking on the door, Philip tried to understand why the initial euphoria he felt at the news of his son's birth had so quickly faded and been replaced by ambiguity.

He thumped the door hard until it was eventually opened by the tearful wife of his friend Francis Talbot, whose own home was close by.

"Margaret?" he frowned, puzzled by her distress. "What is it?"

Blowing her nose in her handcoverchief, she sobbed hysterically. Unable to speak, she waved him in and led the way along a narrow passage and up the stairs to an unlit chamber, its shuttered window and low candlelight creating a deathly ambience.

While his eyes adjusted to the poor light, a bundle was unceremoniously thrust into his arms.

"What's this?"

"Your son," was the response from the shadows.

"My son?" he gasped, squinting at a dark figure standing near the shuttered window. "Francis?"

"Yes," he answered, his voice croaky,

The tightly swaddled lump in his arms moved slightly and Philip looked horrified, but when a thin beam of sunlight shone through a gap in the shutters revealing his son's angelic face, his heart melted.

"By the Holy Ghost," he managed, awkwardly balancing the infant in his arms so as not to drop him.

"Don't put your dirty fingers near his face," the midwife scolded, taking the child from him and shattering his confidence. "He's been washed and oiled."

"Why is everyone so miserable?" Philip said cheerfully. "This is a joyous occasion… open the windows, let in the light. Well?" he snapped, irritated by the continuing silence. "Francis?"

Talbot said nothing and Philip tried to make sense of the melancholic mood.

"Where is my wife?" he demanded, the sound of soft sobbing and the odour of blood in the air, worrying, "Where is she?"

"Lady Isobel is –" Arbroth began, coming forward.

"She is what?"

"She is dead, mah lord… we have laid her in another room."

Philip balled his fists and stormed out.

Pacing the courtyard in brooding detachment, he blamed the tragedy on everyone but himself. While he whored the morning away, Isobel lay dying in childbirth.

"God forgive me," he groaned, disgusted with himself.

After a while, Lady Margaret came into the yard.

"We did all we could to prolong her life until you returned," she sniffed, looking at the colourful flowers in front of the wall. "Where were you?"

"What happened?" he answered, avoiding the question.

"She laboured in great pain for more than a day. We gave her inhalations and moved her from the groaning chair to the bed," Margaret explained, dabbing her puffy, red eyes. "But we could not stop the bleeding," she lamented. "I loosened her hair and administered tonics but she worsened… Isobel died without seeing the child."

"Did she say anything…?"

"She begged your forgiveness and asked that you not blame the child."

Philip stared out over the wall at a piece of open pasture and Margaret left him with his grief.

"Mah lord, we sent for a priest and had tha baaby baptised as soon as it appeared," Arbroth said quietly, joining him. "We dinna know if he would survive; we named him George after yer father."

"The God-parents?"

"Sir Francis and Lady Margaret."

Philip nodded approvingly, his guilt vividly portrayed in his tormented features.

"Well?" he hissed, irritated by the intrusion.

"Do ye wish tah see tha baaby?"

"I've seen him."

"But, mah lord?"

"Leave me with my thoughts."

Arbroth tiptoed away and Philip was left alone in the vegetable and herb garden, where the chirping of starlings, chasing each other in and out of the bushes, was a palliative to his sorrow. He remained wrapped in his memories until he heard the bells of St Mary and the Innocents tolling the hour of

Vespers. With a long woeful sigh he rubbed his damp eyes and dragged himself back inside.

Watching his master through a gap in the window, Arbroth went out to meet him in the passage. Enticing him into a side room, he placed a finger to his lips.

"Mah lord, Sir Francis and Lady Margaret canna cope we it."

"It's all my fault."

"No one's blaming ye but they know aboot yer visits… ta, Bankside."

Philip's head drooped until his chin touched his chest.

"Ah told them it were no' true and tha messengers were sent but couldna find ye."

Philip allowed Arbroth to continue.

"Ye must make arrangements for tha funeral."

"I can't think of that now," he groaned. "Why did this have to happen?"

"Ye must, mah lord…ye have a son ta think aboot."

"What do I know about babies…? That's women's work," he snapped. "I don't want to be burdened with it."

"Perhaps Lady Joan…?"

"My mother?" Philip huffed. "She'll blame me for everything and curse the day I was born."

Living in self-appointed exile in France, with her husband William Beaufort, Philip's mother was eagerly awaiting the birth of her first grandchild since news of Isobel's pregnancy first filtered across the Channel.

"You look after it!" Philip barked. "And don't look at me like that or I'll punch you in the head!"

"*It's called George*," Arbroth growled, storming off.

"Come back here," Philip barked in frustration.

Ignoring his master, Arbroth left the house, slamming the front door, and traipsed to the nearest tavern.

"Stubborn arse," Philip muttered.

After a moment of contemplative silence, a door rasped open and Lady Margaret hobbled out into the passage holding the infant close to her chest.

"See how calm he is?" she mewed, joining Philip and hoping to bring out his paternal instinct. "His eyes follow you."

"You're moving him."

"We must arrange the funeral," she said, her mouth twitching pitifully.

Margaret offered the child again but Philip stepped back as if it had the plague.

"I can't think of that now," he said, kissing his son's forehead. "I must return to the palace."

Lady Margaret drew the baby to her cheek and gently rocked him.

"All will be well," she promised the infant, as Philip left the house.

With her husband inconsolable and Philip dispassionate, Margaret knew she must be the strong one.

Several days after the funeral Philip was laid on his bed at the palace, fingers locked behind his head, mulling over her burial. The weather had been wet and overcast, a perfect adjunct for such a sad occasion. Contrary to her brother's wishes, Philip insisted on Isobel being interned in the same church where they were married less than two years before. Francis wanted her buried in Ashby-de-la Zouch, but Philip refused to travel all the way to Leicestershire and suffer the cost of such a trip. After Isobel was laid to rest, he paid a priest to chant a mass for her soul every day for a year, and then drank himself into a stupor.

A knock on the door jolted Philip out of his grief.

"What?" he hissed rudely.

The door opened and a well-dressed young dandy entered.

Expecting Arbroth, Philip raised himself up on one elbow and frowned at the visitor, who flicked hair out of his eyes.

"Who are you?"

The teenager put a hand to his mouth and coughed deliberately.

"Speak up," Philip growled. "I'm in no mood for games."

"Do you not know me, my Lord?" the young man questioned, stepping into the room.

Philip narrowed his eyes and scrutinized the thin, pale face dominated by a bent nose and bright blue eyes.

"Ash?" he guessed.

"Aye," he beamed.

"I do confess I did not know thee," Philip smiled, leaping off his pallet. "You look taller, but your face… have you seen battle?"

"No my Lord, I was taught the use of weapons by one who enjoyed inflicting pain on his students."

"Why are you in London?"

"I am your new esquire."

"Ah good," Philip said, patting him on the shoulder. "I am glad."

"I heard the sad news of Lady Isobel."

"Don't concern yourself, she is in the ground and I have said my farewells," Philip sighed. "I have a new page," he chirped, "but one who is easily distracted."

Since leaving Philip's service, Ashley Dean spent his time at Middleham and Sheriff Hutton, learning the art of becoming an esquire. Shortly after his seventeenth birthday, the king ordered Warwick to return him to Philip.

"I have little money –" Philip began.

"I have money, my Lord," he grinned, producing a purse from his tunic and rattling the coins.

"Keep your money," Philip said. "But don't let Arbroth know you have it."

Ashley sniggered at the inference and stowed his purse.

"Did my cousin treat you fair?"

"I saw his Lordship only when I served him at table, or at chapel."

Philip walked to the tiny window and looked out.

"I have a son."

"My Lord?"

"Nothing," he sniffed, snapping out of his heartache. "You'll perform the duties of an esquire."

"Yes sir."

"We must find you a sword."

"I have a sword, a gift from Lord Warwick," Ashley beamed. "And a fine horse too."

"Well, well, my cousin is most generous," Philip commented. "Come, we'll celebrate your return."

"My Lord, while I was at Middleham I overheard treason spoken…" he revealed, lowering his voice.

Taking his belt from a nail on the wall, Philip motioned for Ashley to close the door.

"Shush, we are surrounded by traitors here," he warned. "We'll talk later, but now my throat's as dry an old maid's cunt."

Embarrassed by the crude analogy, Ashley's face reddened and Philip laughed at his discomfort.

"You have a lot to learn."

The Tavern of the Sun was a popular haunt for those working at the palace and was only a stone's throw from Westminster. The rowdy, lewd, badly-lit watering hole was notorious for its brawls, usually between the king's supporters and Lord Warwick's men. Philip and his esquire entered the tavern and found an empty table. As they took their seats a woman shuffled over and used a mucky cloth to sweep everything off the table bar the candle.

When she slouched away Philip looked around and saw Sir John Howard playing cards, insensible to the rowdy atmosphere.

"My Lord?" Philip offered the sixty-year-old Treasurer of the king's household and his two companions, "Gentlemen."

The long-haired, pompous knight poked his aquiline nose over the top of his cards and nodded.

"Old whistlehose," Philip muttered, under his breath.

"Is it safe to talk?" asked Ashley.

"Calm yourself," Philip smiled. "More treason is debated in the taverns of London than anywhere."

A female servitor came over and pressed her ample chest into Philip's face.

"Wine, sir?" she offered lackadaisically.

"Ale," he countered, admiring her breasts, which unfortunately detracted from her ugly face.

When Philip saw her toothless, sucked in features he cringed. Offended by his reaction, she stormed away.

"And bring us fresh ale!" he demanded.

"She'll spit in our cups," Ashley groaned.

Convinced the boisterous chatter and raucous laughter in the crowded hostelry would cover their conversation, Philip urged his esquire to tell what he knew. Fearful of being overheard, the teenager jerked his head around nervously.

"For God's sake, be still," Philip hissed, slapping the table and causing those nearby to look over.

Aware he was being watched, Philip responded with a sickly, apologetic grin. Smoke from the foul-smelling tallow candle made him cough and he waved his esquire to continue.

"I was serving wine to Lord Warwick and two gentlemen who came to Middleham late one night and did not wish to be recognised," he began, cupping a hand to his mouth, which drew curious glances.

"You're drawing attention to us," Philip grimaced. "Lower your hand and sit back."

Before Ashley could continue, the woman returned,

banged a jug of ale and two cups down and snatched the coin off the table.

"Miserable shrew," Philip sneered, while Ashley filled his cup and slurped the ale. "Calm down," he commanded, "and talk as if we are having an ordinary conversation."

"When I finished filling the cups Lord Warwick dismissed the servants, but I was curious and waited behind a door near the stairs."

"Do you know who my cousin's companions were?"

"Master Thomas Kent and Sir John Conyers."

"Ah," Philip mused, stroking his chin and leaning back. "Go on."

"They spoke of their hatred for the Woodvilles and of raising an army to fight against the king."

Philip knew Warwick was opposed to Edward's policies and suspected him of plotting to take the crown and placing it on the head of Edward's brother George, but he said nothing.

"My Lord?" Ashley offered, unconsciously digging at the candle wax.

"Go on."

"I heard footsteps on the stairs and left... will you tell the king?"

"He will not believe it."

"I saw letters marked with the seal of the king of France."

"Did you have a chance to read them?"

"No, my Lord."

"I cannot go to the king with such evidence," Philip said, disturbed by his esquire's revelations. "Tomorrow we'll begin your training," he explained, glancing at Sir John Howard and lowering his voice. "Tell no one what you have told me; if the king hears of it things might go bad for you, and if they go bad for you they'll be worse for me."

"Yes sir."

The two men finished their ale and Philip stood up, inclined his body at Sir John Howard, who reciprocated with a curt nod.

"He is a most unpleasant fellow," Howard told his drinking cronies, as Philip left the tavern.

For the next twelve months, Philip put the loss of his wife and the birth of a son to the back of his mind. He was only able to do this because the Talbots took the child into their care. When not on duty, Philip tutored his esquire and page and in his free time he visited his manors or hunted. Mindful of the attempts on his life, he was accompanied on such trips by several armed retainers.

Lady Joan was overjoyed to learn she had become a grandmother, but when Philip fobbed the boy off on the Talbots, she penned a scathing letter reminding him of his duty as a father and vented her fury by comparing him to his reckless father. Scrunching up the letter, he tossed it into the fire and fisted the wall, bruising his knuckles. Sexual relief came from nocturnal visits to Portia, where, after sating his lust, he spoke of his brother's murder and Isobel's death. Acting the part of confessor, she listened and soothed his conscience.

By the time Edward was ready to cross the Channel and aid his allies, in September 1468, it was too late. Brittany had come to terms with Louis and Burgundy was preparing to sign a treaty, leaving the English king with a deep hole in his exchequer. Two months later, a conspiracy involving the Earls of Oxford and Devon was exposed. Devon was executed, but Oxford reeled off a list of Lancastrian agents and was released. Oxford was Warwick's brother-in-law, and the Earl believed Edward was persecuting his relatives.

In April 1469 John Neville, the Earl of Northumberland, crushed two rebellions which broke out in Yorkshire, much to his brother, Warwick's chagrin. Two months later, while on a pilgrimage to Bury St Edmunds, the king learned of a fresh uprising in Yorkshire, this time he planned to deal with it personally. Confident of victory, Edward moved north; but his progress was slow. On 9 July he was told that Robin of Redesdale, alias Sir John Conyers, another Warwick relative, was marching south with a rebel army.

Warwick, meanwhile, was spending much time flitting back and forth across the Channel, accompanied by the king's brother, George, Duke of Clarence. From Calais, Warwick denounced Edward for allowing his kingdom to fall into misery and poverty? When told the king was in the Midlands, Warwick sailed for home. Marching on London, he spread rumours concerning Edward's illegitimacy and quickly set off for Coventry, hoping to link up with Robin of Redesdale.

When he heard Warwick was back in England, Edward was in Nottingham awaiting reinforcements. Adding to his woes the king was told his brother George had betrayed him by marrying Warwick's eldest daughter. With the news that Redesdale was closing in from the north and Warwick marching up from the south, Edward fell into apathy. On 26 July, Redesdale destroyed Edward's reinforcements at Edgecote, near Banbury, capturing Lord Herbert. Brought to Warwick at Northampton, William Herbert was swiftly beheaded. Oblivious to the destruction of his allies, Edward left Nottingham three days later and moved south to Northampton.

Chapter 15

AT NOON ON 2 August, Philip Neville cantered into the quiet village of Olney, twelve miles south-east of Northampton, leading a detachment sent on ahead by the king to scout the crossing of the Great Ouze River. Drawing his palfrey up in the marketplace, Philip signalled his men to halt. Turning his horse in a slow circle, Philip eyed the houses along both sides of the street. Without a word he jabbed two fingers towards the bridge on the edge of the village.

"Ah don't like it," Arbroth whispered, coming up beside Philip, as two men trotted off to check the bridge.

With most of his armour on its way to London, Philip wore only arm and leg protection.

"It's too quiet," he commented, biting his lower lip anxiously. "Search the whole village."

"Ah cannah believe tha King has allowed Lord Warwick tah go so far."

"He's too trusting," Philip said. "Two of you that way," he commanded, indicating an alley to his right, "two more down there," pointing to a side street on the left.

While his men dispersed to search the village, a wooden shutter creaked open on the first floor of a house above a barn and a young head popped up.

Philip dropped a hand over his sword.

"Are you from Lord Warwick?" the boy chirped.

"No," he answered, relaxing. "We are the king's men."

"Is the king coming here?" he asked, straining to look up the road.

Philip nodded.

"They say there was a big fight at Banbury," the boy revealed gleefully.

"We heard," Philip said. "What do you know of it?"

"They say the royal soldiers were beaten and Lord Warwick's on his way to Coventry."

"Then it's true?" Arbroth gasped.

Philip put a hand out to stop him as the men returned from the bridge.

"Crossing's clear, sir," one of the scouts confirmed.

"You are well informed," Philip said, addressing the youngster.

"Some of Lord Herbert's men came through here," he beamed, waving a shiny sallet. "Look what I got."

"'Tis a fine piece," Arbroth growled jealously.

"Have you seen any rebels?" Philip asked, nudging his palfrey towards the barn.

"Many soldiers have come this way but I don't know who they serve."

"Here!" Philip sniffed, flicking a coin in his direction.

"Thank ee sir!" the boy grinned, scooping it out of the air with his sallet and pointing northwest. "The last lot went that way."

"My Lord," one of Philip's retainers called out, pointing to the Northampton Road, "the king!"

Philip looked back to see King Edward riding in from the north.

"Behold, here comes tha best-dressed man in England," Arbroth smirked, spotting Lord Hastings with the party.

"Pity he has no backbone," Philip scoffed, nudging Clovis forward.

The king halted his dusty, sweaty column with a weary wave.

"Your Grace," Philip bowed from the saddle, alarmed at Edward's much-reduced army. "The village is secure, but I sense the enemy is close."

"Cousin," a worried Edward responded anxiously. "Anyone here who shouldn't be?"

"No sire, but I believe Lord Herbert has met with disaster."

"I fear it is so," Edward confirmed. "We must return to London."

"Where are the wagons and the rest of the army, your Grace?"

"Word of Lord Herbert's defeat has demoralised the men," the immaculately dressed William Hastings announced, his red, baggy eyes and pale gaunt features underlining his concern. "Desertions have greatly reduced our numbers."

"Damned cowards!" the king's spirited sixteen-year-old brother barked.

"Govern thy tongue, Richard," Edward said. "Many of those men served me well in the past."

"Sire… you have barely fifty men?" Philip gasped, counting heads.

"Better fifty good men than a thousand who would flee at the first sight of the enemy," Hastings interjected.

"They seem nervous," Philip commented, noting the strain on their grim, dusty faces.

"They fear God has abandoned us," Gloucester said.

The low thrum of approaching horses drew Philip's attention to the bridge and a sinking sensation gripped his gut when he saw his cousin, George Neville, clatter into the village.

"What's he doing here?" Hastings groaned.

"And why does he bring such a large escort?" Edward frowned.

Philip nudged Clovis up next to Edward's foam-flecked horse and gripped his sword, while Arbroth and the rest of the men fell in behind. Dressed all in black, a large silver crucifix dangling from the chain round his neck, Archbishop Neville trotted forward alone. Dismounting, he dropped to his knees, bowed his head, removed his hat and stretched out his arms.

"Your highness," he grovelled. "I am here to take you to my brother at Coventry."

"Why?" Gloucester snapped, controlling his jittery mount.

"For your safety, your Grace, the country is alive with armed rebels."

George Neville, Archbishop of York, was as cunning and ambitious as his brother Warwick, but nowhere near as ruthless. Tall and thin, with a florid complexion crowned by dark brown hair, he had a passion to wear a Cardinal's hat.

"My Lord Archbishop, your brother has a strange way of showing his loyalty to the crown," Edward remarked, glancing at Philip. "He professes fidelity yet defies me by marrying his daughter to *my brother* and raises the north against me. These rebels have destroyed an army sent to break up their unlawful progress. Does he plan to take my crown and place it on the head of my treacherous brother George?"

"Sire, Lord Warwick has nothing but love for and harbours no thought of replacing you as king."

"Rise, your Grace," Edward sniffed, unimpressed.

The Archbishop stood, but in his mind he had no intention of forgiving Edward for robbing him of the chancellorship.

"Your Grace," the ecclesiastic bowed, acknowledging his cousin Gloucester.

"My Lord," Richard answered curtly, before deliberately looking away.

"Is Lord Rivers not here?" the Archbishop enquired, looking over the group.

The king responded with a vacant stare.

Lord Rivers' absence was a blow to the Archbishop, but he managed to conceal his disappointment.

"You may dismiss your men, sire; we will escort from here on," he said.

Edward signalled for his men to fall out.

"Your Grace –" Philip protested.

"If Lord Warwick wishes to see me, I shall not disappoint him," Edward said apathetically.

"You are the king, he should come to you!" Gloucester spat. "By God."

"Enough!" Edward sighed. "Richard will not harm me."

Gloucester looked at Philip but both knew they were powerless to change his mind.

The young Duke fumed, bowed to his brother and swung his horse away.

Hastings bade Edward farewell and followed Gloucester, motioning for the king's men to join him. The archbishop formed his men in two lines behind the king but Philip stubbornly remained until forced to move. Swinging Clovis out, he drew his sword and glared at the escort.

"I'll take you one at a time or all together, it makes no difference!"

The archbishop's men looked on his bravado with restrained humour but no one took him seriously.

"Put away your blade," Edward commanded, amused by his absurd challenge.

"Yes sire…" he demurred, thrusting his sword into its scabbard. "I hold you responsible for his grace's life," Philip warned, pointing a finger at the archbishop. "If he should meet with an accident I will seek you out, cousin."

"You dare to threaten me?" Archbishop Neville gasped.

Philip bowed to the king, nodded insolently at the ecclesiastic and galloped away.

Terrified of running into the rebels and ending up like Lord Herbert, Will Hastings followed the north bank of the Great Ouze south and then turned west, reaching Banbury two days later. Philip suggested they turn back and try to rescue the king, but Hastings, miffed by his impertinence, insisted they obey their orders and ride on to London. Philip begged him to at least try, but he refused, believing that to do so would endanger Edward's life.

"Then I shall go alone," Philip snapped, waving for his own retainers to fall out.

"You obey my orders as you would the king's," Hastings said, shocked by his insubordination.

"I will not leave my cousin to be devoured by his enemies!" Philip exaggerated as he rode out of Banbury.

"Coventry?" Arbroth said.

"Coventry," Philip confirmed.

"All six of us?" his esquire gasped.

"Be silent."

"We're no far from North Marston, mah lord...we have no food and –"

"Forget your belly," Philip barked.

"Come back!" Hastings yelled hysterically, his high-pitched voice cracking.

"I cannot hear you," Philip shouted, leading his men up a narrow path. "My Lord!"

"Tha mon sings like a nightingale," Arbroth chirped, slipping his rouncey in behind Clovis.

"Keep your eyes open."

For two days they rode north, keeping to the forest where possible and avoiding Warwick Castle. Philip halted his company at a farmhouse near Kenilworth, less than five miles from Coventry, the incessant complaints over food forcing his hand.

"We'll rest awhile Philip said, sliding from the saddle. "See if you can find any food."

Dismounting, the men dragged their horses through the long grass to a nearby brook.

"Do ye have a plan, mah lord?" Arbroth asked, feverishly untying his hose and braies, and showering his relief over a bush.

Before Philip could reply, half a dozen armed men, wearing red livery, spilled out of the cottage.

"Don't touch your weapons!" a smartly dressed knight commanded, aiming the point of his sword at Philip.

Recognising the white bear and ragged staff badge of Warwick, Philip ignored the command and slowly drew his sword.

"Dinna do it, mah lord," Arbroth warned, panicking to re-tie his braies as more soldiers appeared from the underbrush.

"I am on the king's most urgent business," Philip warned, shoving the blade back in its scabbard.

"Show me," the young knight demanded, thrusting a hand out.

"I don't take orders from you," Philip sneered.

"We've been following you since Banbury," the knight smirked, lowering his sword.

"To what purpose?"

"Lord Warwick wishes to see you."

"You have no right to interfere with a man on the king's business."

"Then show me your authority, sir."

"I wear the king's colours," Philip spat, pointing to his murrey and blue tunic. "Can you see?"

"His lordship said you would not come easily," the knight countered. "That's why I have twenty good men at my back. So, hand over your sword, my Lord, and take that horse," he added, pointing to a chestnut rouncey with a dark, shaggy mane. "Your men can go," the knight said, accepting Philip's blade.

"My horses need forage."

"That's no concern of mine."

"My Lord?" Ashley cut in.

"Do as he says," Philip sneered, mounting up. "Return to London."

As his retainers rode south Philip trotted off in the opposite direction, heavily guarded.

Coventry was a city in turmoil: a succession of mounted couriers dashed to and fro on foam-flecked mounts, and hundreds of soldiers were milling about the streets. After being intercepted at Olney, the king was taken to Coventry where Warwick told him he was there for his safety, but Edward refused to dignify his cousin with an answer. The Earl, however, was in a dilemma: what should he do with his distinguished prisoner? Coventry was not secure enough to hold such a powerful captive, so Warwick decided to move him.

Philip and his captors arrived at Coventry two days after Edward and as he looked up at the twelve-foot-high sandstone city walls, his heart sank, for he had been unable to escape. He was led through the Greyfriars Gate, up Warwick Lane and into busy Pepper Lane until they reached the Bishop's palace, close to the cathedral church of St Mary. Left outside, while the knight in charge went in search of Warwick, Philip dismounted and wilted in the airless heat, made worse by a foul smell of tanning leather. While he waited Philip watched a gaggle of noisy children kicking a ball, made of a pig's bladder.

"We go on to Middleham," the returning knight huffed, tightening his saddle girth, his lazy eyes and quiet nature making it difficult for Philip to judge his temperament.

"Middleham?" Philip groaned, rubbing the small of his back.

"Lord Warwick fears there may be an attempt to rescue the king."

"Am I a prisoner?"

"No…"

"Then I shall bid thee adieu," Philip smirked, climbing into the saddle and taking up the reins.

"Lord Warwick demands you attend him."

"Then I *am* a prisoner."

"Believe what you wish."

The party rode out of Coventry through Bishops Gate and headed north, and as soon as they cleared the gate Philip was thinking of escape.

It took seven days to cover the hundred and seventy miles to Middleham Castle, in Richmondshire, and it was a dusty, straggling group of men, on foam-flecked, steaming horses that eventually clattered over the drawbridge in the middle of the night. As the portcullis rumbled down heavily behind him Philip was disappointed; he had been too closely guarded during the ride to slip away. Dismounting before the Constable, he patted his broken-down rouncey's soapy neck and sighed.

"Sir Philip, you have the freedom of the castle," the Constable announced, recognising him. "But you must not go beyond the walls."

Familiar with Middleham from his youth, Philip looked up at the dark Great Tower and a sense of helplessness overwhelmed him.

"Am I a prisoner?"

"You are his lordship's guest," the Constable insisted.

"With limitations?"

"Conditions."

"I want my sword… it was a gift, from the king."

"You shall have your sword."

Philip was led to an apartment in the south-east tower, and

his blade and pieces of armour were returned. With nothing but the clothes on his back, he demanded, and received, a clean shirt and underwear.

For the next two weeks, he used the time to hone his skills, but his aggressiveness alienated his partners and many refused to spar with him. In the evenings he would dine with the constable and other knights, which, on occasion, ended in a drunken argument. Philip would spend many hours innocuously walking the ramparts and making mental notes for an escape, but the guards watched him constantly. One day, a rumour reached Middleham that Warwick had captured and executed Lord Rivers and one of his sons and was divvying up the offices of the late Lord Herbert.

The sound of someone rushing past his room one night and frenetic shouting woke Philip. Stepping out into the darkness, he rubbed his bleary eyes and saw the shadows running along the battlements.

"Are we attacked?" he called out.

"No!" A man-of-arms replied, his ghostly face distorted by the flaming torch in his hand. "His Lordship has brought the king here."

Philip stifled a yawn and returned to his bed.

Next morning he dressed and made sure he looked respectable before opening the door to his chamber, only to find it locked.

"Open this door!" he demanded. "Open up, I say."

Eventually a key clunked in the lock and the door opened.

"Why was I locked in?"

"Orders," the guard answered.

"Whose orders?"

"Lord Warwick's."

"Huh."

"I am to take you to him."

"What does *his highness* want?"

The guard made no comment and Philip followed him out and along the parapet of the south wall. Passing through the Lady Chamber, they turned right into a covered gallery that bridged the South Courtyard, before entering the Great Tower. Leading the way down a flight of stone steps into the Great Chamber, the guard stood back, allowing Philip in.

The Great Chamber, its lime-mortared, white-washed walls hung with stunning tapestries, was divided into two rooms by an ornate wood-panelled partition. Several wheel-candelabras, suspended from the high ceiling, and half a dozen blocks of beeswax illuminated the chamber, which was dominated by its cavernous fireplace. Alone at the head of a long table sat the Earl of Warwick, his hairy hound Mongo at his feet and a goblet of wine in his hand.

"Come in," he said.

Philip stepped into the Great Chamber, its carpeted wood floor warped by heat rising from the kitchen below.

"Cousin," Warwick offered as he entered.

"My Lord," Philip replied warily, noting hostility in his expression.

Mongo shuffled to his feet, bared his teeth and growled at the visitor, but a reassuring pat from his master mollified his temperament.

"You're a thorn in my side," Warwick sighed, as Mongo settled down.

"If you say so, my Lord?"

"Is that all you have to say?"

Philip looked vacant and Warwick continued.

"Our dear cousin the king is within these walls."

Philip frowned.

"He is here for one reason," Warwick continued. "To keep him safe from the rebels."

"You have cut off the heads of Lord Herbert and the king's father-in-law?" Philip dared.

"I had no other choice. William Herbert was a knave who wormed his way into the king's favour and was rewarded with offices and titles that are mine by right," he revealed, banging the walnut table. "The Woodvilles have divided this realm and set the king against me."

Philip thought of his brother and looked down at the floor, but Warwick knew what was in his mind.

"You hold me accountable for what happened at Bamburgh?" Richard said.

"With respect, my Lord, did you not order Michael's execution."

"You presume to know much, yet you know nothing!" Warwick bellowed, leaping out of his chair, ready to order his churlish kinsman thrown into the deepest dungeon. "He is not dead."

A strange numbness fuzzed Philip's brain and it took a while for the words to sink in.

"I don't believe it," he gasped.

"I gain nothing by making such a false statement."

"I saw him die…" Philip insisted, indicating with a finger where the crossbow bolt lodged in Michael's chest. "And watched his body –"

"He was sorely wounded and rescued by fishermen who left him with the monks on Holy Isle."

Philip stared at his cousin and took a moment to regain his composure.

"Praise God," he gasped, crossing his chest, "Why was I not told? I have borne such guilt all these years."

"I did not know."

"What of my family?"

"My agent in Calais told me your brother fled to France… so they must have known."

Philip's legs trembled and he leaned on the table for support.

"Thomas knew… and never told me."

"Thomas?"

"Yes, he came to see me, but said nothing," Philip frowned. "How many others know?"

"The king?" Warwick guessed.

"No?"

"The crossbowmen at Bamburgh… were they not Burgundian's, loaned to me by the king?"

Philip blinked vacantly.

"Davy Griffiths was your man," Philip countered, referring to the herald who swore he had a written order from Lord Warwick to execute Michael.

"I gave no such an order."

Gradually absorbing the news, Philip rubbed his forehead in frustration.

"I had you brought here to tell you this," Warwick explained. "I would have told you when we rode through London with Henry, but you left without a word."

"My Lord, I have been attacked by assassins and now I am your prisoner, what am I to think?"

"You have my permission to leave here whenever you wish."

"I must speak with the king."

"No," Warwick said, emphatically. "But know this, were it not for the blood we share you would have been dead long ago, though not by my hand. Lord Hastings and the Woodvilles have the king's ear: look to them for the cause of all your misfortunes, was it not Hastings who stole away your Elizabeth," he explained. "Forget the past and let it be between us as it was before; help me to save Edward from himself."

"What must I do?"

"Burgundy's agents are stirring the people of London against me; I have sent my son-in-law to calm the situation until I can go there myself."

"His grace is not popular in the city, my Lord," Philip

warned, referring to Edward's brother George. "As for me... I regret I cannot betray the king."

"I do not ask you to betray him," Warwick frowned. "I have sacrificed much to make Edward king, do you think I would give it all up if there was any other way?" he said, agitated. "You'll never understand this game we play. Now go; we'll talk again later."

"I will not change my mind."

"Go, I said," Warwick hissed angrily, emphasising the command with a flick of his wrist.

Bowing to his cousin, Philip left exhilarated by the news that his brother was alive. As he exited the chamber he heard Mongo barking, followed by a thud and a yelp of pain: Richard had taken his frustration out on the dog.

Despite Warwick's statement that Philip and the king were not prisoners, they were kept apart for the next four weeks. During this time, Warwick tried and failed to get the backing of parliament and Edward realised it was only a matter of time before his cousin would be forced to release him.

Chapter 16

WHEN SIR HUMPHREY Neville learned of the king's capture he raised rebellion on the northern border in the name of Henry of Lancaster. Warwick asked his brother the Archbishop of York to seek Edward's counsel. Surprised by Warwick's request, Edward promised to support Warwick if he set him at liberty. With England falling apart, Warwick had no choice and released the king. Once free, Edward rode to York, where he received the homage of both lords and commoners. The king kept his promise to Warwick and helped him smash the uprising, he then set about re-establishing his authority by summoning his brother Richard and those trusted members of his council, to join him.

Standing beside the king in the grounds of York Castle, Philip Neville, who accompanied Edward from Middleham, watched the executioner's axe slice off Humphrey Neville's head in one neat blow. The headless body twitched as it slithered down behind the block, blood pouring from the neck.

"His backside won't trouble him anymore, your Grace," he smirked, remembering Sir Humphrey's bad attack of haemorrhoids at Bamburgh, and his suspicion that almost cost Philip his life.

Edward made the sign of the cross on his chest and sniffed imperiously, before nodding at the waiting executioner.

"He betrayed his friends at Bamburgh to save his own neck," Philip recalled.

The masked axe-man picked up the severed head by its bloody hair and thrust its face forward to the unusually muted crowd.

"Behold tha head of a traitor!"

His words were followed by an apathetic cheer from the lacklustre spectators.

"They don't look happy," Philip commented, sensing disapproval.

"Sir Humphrey was much beloved here in the north."

With the execution over, Edward mounted his palfrey and cantered away. Philip and the escort ran for their horses and caught up as he trotted along Castlegate.

"Some are calling me a bastard," Edward revealed, waving at the crowd gathered near St Michael's Church, eager to catch a glimpse of the king, "and some say my wife's mother is a witch."

Philip knew the story of an English archer rumoured to be Edward's father but ignored it.

"Idle gossip, sire," he scoffed, steering his rouncey to avoid hitting those stretching out their hands to touch the king for luck.

"I'll be glad to leave this place," Edward said, leading the way along Coney Street, before turning down to Ouze Bridge.

Philip kept an eye on anyone who came too close and sneered at those whose demonstrations of loyalty did not satisfy him.

After leaving York, Edward rode to Pontefract under a threatening sky, hoping to rendezvous with his supporters.

As they trotted south rain began to fall, damping Philip's clothes but not his spirits. Looking at the king he observed confidence in his bearing.

"Sire?" he dared, fighting the urge to ask what he knew of his brother.

"What?"

"Lord Warwick would never harm thee."

"No? When my father marched on London eighteen summers ago, he was betrayed by Richard's father, Lord Salisbury," Edward said. "My father's army was camped near Dartford, but he was not there to fight, but to demand the arrest of Lord Somerset. Salisbury promised Somerset would be dismissed if my father dispersed his army. He did as they asked, for as he said, he was not there to fight the king. When my father presented himself to King Henry, Somerset was by his side." Pausing a moment, Edward's cheeks pulsated with anger. "My father was arrested and forced to swear on oath that he would never again rebel against the king."

"I did not know," Philip said, palming rain from his face, "What will you do?"

"Warwick would have had my crown if the council and commons supported him."

"Who can we trust?"

"Only my fool," Edward joked.

Philip frowned at his response and the king sensed his hurt.

"Fear not, cousin, I have never doubted your loyalty."

Philip felt a pang of remorse for the deceitful way he helped manipulate the Duke of Somerset's downfall, but the emotion quickly vanished. Sweeping his wet hair back, he looked at the muddy road disintegrating beneath the hooves of their horses.

"'Tis cold, sire," he shivered.

Edward did not answer and the rest of the journey continued in silence.

While Edward waited at Pontefract Castle for those he sent for to arrive he visited nearby Pontefract Priory and prayed over the graves of his father and brother. When Gloucester, Lord Hastings and the others rode in, he set off immediately for London. King Edward entered his capital on a bright autumnal day in mid-October and was met by the mayor, his aldermen and a near hysterical crowd. Despite the disaster at Edgecote and Warwick's actions, Edward refused to denigrate his brother George, and declared Lord Warwick to be his dear friend and kinsman.

Returning to his home in The Strand in the early evening, Philip found the place empty and closed the door behind him shutting out the world. Unbuckling his sword, he dragged himself to an unlit room and slumped down in a cushioned chair. In the dark silence, his thoughts fluctuated between Isobel, Michael, his son and Elizabeth, until exhaustive sleep blocked them out.

"Who's there?" a puzzled voice with a recognisable Scottish twang demanded.

Philip opened his eyes and saw Arbroth standing in the doorway.

"Mah Lord?" he gasped, glad to see his master home safe.

Philip slapped his lips and grunted, having slept through the whole night without waking.

"How is my son?" he mumbled.

"He's a bonny laddie!" Arbroth grinned, opening the shutters and flooding the room with light. "Tha Talbot's have him at Ashby."

"Ashby?" he groaned, shielding his eyes against the hurtful brightness.

"Aye, Sir Francis's service with tha king is over, he does-na like London, 'tis no a good place tah raise a child."

Philip knew Francis and his wife would care for his son.

"Did you have any trouble after we parted company?" he asked.

"Nay, mah lord, we rested fer a day afore riding home."

"How's the youngster?"

"Ashley has taken him under his wing. Tha boy is slow-witted, but he'll learn."

Philip gave a wide, jaw-crunching yawn that ended with a loud crack.

"I need a wash," he said opening and closing his mouth. "Ouch."

"Mah lord, may lady's maid is still here."

"Why?"

"She's nowhere tah go," he frowned, furiously scratching his head.

"Lice?"

The Scot gave a rueful nod and Philip waved him away.

"Cut it off," he commanded.

"Aye, mah lord."

"Fill a tub first, the hotter the better."

"Aye."

"Fetch some wine and have my horse cared for, I left him tied up outside last night."

"If he's still there," he said.

When Arbroth left, Philip nestled down in the chair and fell back to sleep.

"Bath's ready, mah lord," Arbroth came in and whispered in his ear.

Philip opened his eyes and sighed heavily, but as he stood up his weeks in the saddle crippled him. When the pain slowly receded, he limped to the kitchen where a tub, lined with a sheet and half filled, was set before the fire.

Philip moaned pleasantly at the steam rising off the water.

"Leave me."

Arbroth placed a cup of wine on a chair within reach, bowed and left.

Removing his doublet and hose, Philip stripped off his foul underwear and stepped cautiously into the tub. Once his feet were used to the heat, he edged down and reached for the cup.

"By the saints!" he gasped as the hot water turned the submerged parts of his body red.

Using a shampoo of vine stalks, fern, ash and egg whites, he washed his hair. Dunking his head under the water to rinse out the shampoo, he sat up and dragged the hair from his forehead. Once his badly scarred body was used to the temperature, the heat and wine sent him in and out of sleep until he was brought to by a sharp knock

"What?" he hissed angrily, wiping his face in a towel.

A maiden entered carrying a glass jar and Philip's imagination began to work.

Curtsying she waited, embarrassed at the sight of his naked shoulders.

"Speak up?" he said, eyeing the shape of her body beneath the apron.

"I…" she gasped, averting her gaze. "I have salts to relieve your aches, sir… Mistress Isobel always…"

Using thumb and forefinger to wipe the water running down his face and dripping off his nose he felt a familiar stirring in his loins.

"Pour it in."

The blushing maid edged closer, removed the stopper and emptied the powdery contents into the tub, trying hard not to look at him.

"Kate…" he said, relishing her discomfort. "Why don't you join me?"

"My Lord, I…" she stammered, before fleeing red-faced from the kitchen.

Philip threw his head back and laughed at her humiliation, before settling down with his wine.

"You won't regret it!" he shouted after her.

When the water lost its soothing heat, Philip finished off the wine and climbed out of the tub. Towelling himself dry, he put on clean underwear, a fresh doublet and hose, and sought out a barber.

The house was a sad reminder of Isobel's suffering, and his

infidelity and he decided it was better to stay at Westminster. The tedious routine of court life didn't help his conscience and he soon found himself floundering in a sea of self-pity which could only be alleviated by drink.

King Edward welcomed his errant brother and his cousin back to the fold, but he would never forget their treachery. Warwick was forced to give up the offices he took from the late Lord Herbert and, to rub salt into his wounds, Anthony Woodville inherited his father's title, and Henry Percy was released from the Tower, where he had languished since his disinheritance. In the spring of 1470 rebellion was reported in Lincolnshire, and once again Edward ordered his lords and knights to assemble their retainers. Warwick went to Yorkshire to raise his affinity for the king, but the crafty Earl had a different agenda in mind.

Standing on the parapet of the Flint Tower, on the north-west inner wall of the Tower of London, Philip placed his hands on the merlons and stared out at Tower Hill. Commanded by the king to remain in the city and help secure London, while he marched north, Philip sensed a battle was imminent and fumed at being left behind. Stocked with cannon, powder, bows and armour, the Tower also held an important prisoner, Henry of Lancaster. Fearing an attempt might be made to release him, Edward needed men he could rely on and Philip was among that number.

The rumbling wind howling up the river blew Philip's hair into a tangled mess and he finally gave up trying to keep it in place. Looking at the scaffold set up on Tower Hill, he contemplated the fate of the rebels once they were defeated, as they surely must be. They would be dragged through the crowded streets of London, executed on the Tower Hill and their heads impaled on spikes.

"God-damn," he hissed, snorting snot into his throat and spitting it out.

Looking at the crumbling remains of the city's Roman wall he wondered what those early Londoners were like.

"My Lord?" A gruff voice intruded, breaking his train of thought.

"What is it?" he growled, annoyed at the interruption.

"Lady askin' t' see ya," a billman announced.

"What lady?"

The soldier sniffed and shrugged his shoulders.

"Send her up."

"She wants you to go to her."

"By the bones of Saint Edward," he grumbled, stomping down the narrow, winding steps to the ground floor. "Who does she think she is? Where is this... *lady*?"

"In the chapel," the soldier said, pointing at the building below.

Philip walked softly into St Peter ad Vincula and saw a woman knelt in front of the altar. Sensing his presence, she quickly finished prayers and stood but did not turn round.

"You wish to see me, my lady?" he whispered, still annoyed as he walked leisurely up the aisle.

When she looked around, he stopped dead in his tracks.

"Yes," she answered.

"What do you want," he fumed, "*Madam*."

"I must speak to you."

Elizabeth Hastings' pleading irritated, but he felt compelled to hear her out.

"What could you possibly say to me that I would wish to hear?"

"I have been a fool," she said, embarrassed.

Her words grated on him but he allowed her to continue.

"There are some on the king's council who plot to humiliate the Nevilles and force them into rebellion."

"Why do you tell me this?"

"My husband is one," she revealed, "He no longer lies with me and has taken a mistress."

Philip folded his arms over his chest and sniffed impassively.

"When you told him that you had lain with me, your words poisoned him, though I swore I was a maiden when we married, he did not believe me."

Elizabeth's revelation was music to his ears and the urge to crow was suppressed only with great restraint.

"You deserve everything you get," he scoffed.

"I, I don't understand –"

"You betrayed me," he cut her off. "What is there not to understand?"

Elizabeth's head flopped forward and her distress touched his heart. Lifting her chin, he looked into her eyes only to be beguiled by her sorrow.

"After everything…" he began, the inability to control his emotions causing him to ramble.

"When you saw me at Bamburgh you called me a whore, yet at Smithfield I feared for your life more than my husbands."

"You could have refused to marry him; by God, how I despise the whole Hastings brood."

"Did you love Isobel?"

"Yes," he sighed, massaging a sudden dull ache in his chest.

"As you once loved me?"

"No," he stammered, petulantly, "What we had was different."

"I never loved Ralph." she declared.

"You gave a good imitation of it."

"I wish…"

"'Tis too late for regrets."

"Forgive me," she bleated, reaching out to him.

She sensed he was about to reach out and take her in his arms her but he stepped back instead.

"No," he hissed.

His answer stunned her and she turned to the altar, knelt, crossed herself and rushed out of the chapel in tears. Philip tried to make sense of what had happened; failing, he blew his frustration through his lips and left.

Next morning he woke to the pealing of the city's church bells and someone pummelling on the door.

"What the hell's going on?" he shouted, burying his face in the pillow.

"Mah Lord!"

"Yes?"

"Tha king has won a great victory!" Arbroth shouted through the door, lingering on the 'g'.

"What?" Philip demanded, sitting up. "Where?"

"Near Stamford."

"Don't stand out there yelling, come in."

The Scot entered the room to see Philip vigorously rubbing sleep from his face.

"Go on."

"Tha king has destroyed tha rebels."

"And I'm stuck here," he moaned, the foul taste in his mouth accentuating his grimace.

Rising from his bed, Philip slouched and snorted his way to a wash basin and dunked his face in the water. Blowing into the liquid caused bubbles to surface and burst against his face. When he could no longer hold his breath he yanked his head up and shook off the excess water.

"Anything else?" he gasped, drying his face in a towel.

"It is said that afore tha fight tha rebels cheered for Lord Warwick and tha Duke o' Clarence."

"Lies!" he barked throwing the towel down. "All lies."

"Ah dinna believe it, either."

"Is the king coming here?"

"Nay, mah lord," Arbroth confirmed, "'Tis said Lord Warwick and tha Duke must disband their army and join Edward, but they hav'na done it yet."

Philip angrily knocked the basin off its stand.

"Why is my cousin so foolish?" he snarled, meaning Warwick.

Arbroth jerked his shoulders and rubbed his short, cropped hair.

"There are enough men here to hold the Tower," Philip declared. "Fetch my horses and have the men meet me at twelve of the clock…and bring my armour."

By leaving his post Philip knew he was disobeying his king but put the thought from his mind. Strung out behind him on the road were his esquire, page, twelve soldiers and servants, a cart containing armour, weapons and supplies, and a string of horses. Arbroth galloped ahead of the group, seeking the king and was to meet Philip in Grantham, where Edward was last seen.

After nine days in the saddle, Philip caught up with the royal party at York on Sunday 25 March. When he presented himself, King Edward scathingly censured him for flouting his orders. After soaking up the rebuke, Philip was dismissed and skulked off to Claremont Hall. After the battle of Empingham, in which they took no part, Warwick and Clarence rejected the king's offer to join him and instead marched north. While heralds rode between the two camps, with messages, Edward's strength increased but Warwick's diminished.

Late in March, the king offered to pardon his brother and cousin if they would submit to him. Warwick demanded safe conduct but Edward refused and ordered them both to come in unconditionally. After failing to gain the support they needed, Warwick and Clarence decided to run for the coast and turned south, Edward made preparations to pursue.

Out in the courtyard of Claremont Hall, Philip chatted with his esquire, when old Arthur deliberately coughed.

"Well?" Philip said.

"Someone comin', m'Lord," he slurped, slapping his toothless gums together.

Philip looked to see the Earl of Northumberland dismounting.

"My Lord?" he bowed, surprised by his cousin's unannounced visit.

"I have supported Edward with all my heart!" an angry John Neville yelled. "And how does he repay me? By robbing me of my title and giving it to a mere boy whose father fought with Henry."

"My Lord?"

"The King has given it all to Henry Percy," he fumed, throwing his arms in the air angrily. "I have defied my brother for this king and he robs my son of his future, for what, a Marquisate? God forgive me for what is in my mind."

"'Tis a fair title," Philip ventured, while his men continued to pack.

"By God, I shall –"

"My Lord, you must not," Philip warned, anticipating his threat to turn against Edward.

"Fear not, cousin… I shall not betray him," John said hesitantly, "Though he does not deserve such a loyal servant."

While loading the sumpters, Arbroth eavesdropped on their conversation; Sir John's tirade made it difficult for anyone in the yard not to hear.

"Why has he done this to me?" John whined.

"My Lord, we must be on our way," Philip said, waving for his men to mount. "We join his highness."

"To what end?"

Philip shrugged his shoulders.

"Edward promises to forgive my brother but I fear he will not do it."

"What will you do now?"

"I don't know," he groaned, rubbing his brow. "I must go… God-speed, cousin."

"My Lord."

"There goes a very angry mon," Arbroth commented, as John Neville galloped off.

"Everything packed?" Philip asked, mounting his palfrey.

"Aye."

Lightly tapping the rowels of his spurs against Clovis' flanks, Philip led his men to the rendezvous with Edward. Arthur and Gilbert stood in the doorway, relieved to see them go; the house was always a mess when Philip came home.

Having assembled a great army, Edward left York on 27 March, and went in pursuit of his brother and cousin. Warwick, Clarence, his pregnant wife and a few loyal followers reached Dartmouth on 9 April and boarded several ships.

Hoping to cut off their escape, the king sent a mounted detachment, which included Philip, south under his brother Richard. Having covered more than four hundred miles in less than four weeks, a saddle-sore Philip Neville drew up on the high ground overlooking Dartmouth.

"Are there any strangers down there?" he demanded of a passing shepherd, pointing down at the town.

"No sir, there was but they left more'un five days ago… took boats and sailed away they did," the heavily bewhiskered local revealed, just as Gloucester's main body appeared.

"Have we missed him?" the Duke gasped, drawing his lathered horse to a halt.

"Yes, your Grace," Philip said.

"The King will not be happy."

"Damn his good fortune," Philip spat as they trotted down to the port.

Warwick arrived off Calais on 16 April, but the garrison had orders to fire on him if he attempted to land. Though the Calais troops were for the king, the commander, Sir John Wenlock, was Warwick's man. Unwilling to go against the king, Wenlock rowed out and advised his friend to go on to France where he would be welcome. Warwick sailed away and on May Day he dropped anchor in Honfleur.

With his rebellious cousin overseas, Edward believed his crown was safe, but Warwick would prove more dangerous abroad than at home. Louis of France was already planning to ally Warwick with the exiled Queen Margaret, and place Henry of Lancaster back on the throne. The York-Burgundy partnership was detrimental to French interests and Louis wanted that unholy alliance severed.

Chapter 17

EARLY IN OCTOBER 1470, the Earl of Warwick was back in England and on his way to London. To induce panic, his agents in the city opened the prisons, allowing the inmates to run riot. They were aided by Kentishmen loyal to Warwick, who looted and burned parts of Southwark. The Mayor of London closed all the city gates, called out the militia and placed cannon on the north end of London Bridge.

Several months earlier King Edward had crushed yet another insurrection in the north, this time led by Warwick's brother-in-law, Henry Lord Fitzhugh. The king's council suspected this was a plot to lure Edward away from his capital and believed Warwick was only awaiting news of his departure before launching an invasion of England. To alleviate the council's concerns, Edward sent an Anglo-Burgundian fleet to blockade Warwick's ships in the Seine. Urged by Louis to ally himself with Margaret, Warwick agreed and knelt before her, kissed her hand and promised to rescue her husband, Henry, from the Tower. To seal the contract, Warwick's youngest daughter Anne was betrothed to her son, Prince Edward. In the first week of September a violent storm scattered the English blockading fleet and two days later Warwick, accompanied by Clarence and a number of Lancastrian lords, set sail for England.

After defeating the northern rebellion, Edward lingered in York and was still there when Warwick landed at Dartmouth.

Informed his cousin was marching on Coventry, Edward moved south and ordered Warwick's brother to join him. Simmering over his disinheritance, John Neville left Pontefract with a strong force but during the march he suddenly declared for his brother. Outnumbered and with his army shrinking daily, Edward fled to Bishop's Lynn on the Norfolk coast and took ship for the continent.

While London descended into lawlessness Lord Tiptoft, Earl of Worcester and Constable of the Tower, ordered Philip Neville to escort the queen, her mother and three daughters to the sanctuary of Westminster Abbey. Hoping to get out of London, Philip cringed at being picked for such a dangerous assignment but knew he could not refuse. With enemy cannon on the south bank, travel by boat was not viable, so using his own men and a company of Tower guards he bundled the queen, her family, Lady Elizabeth Hastings and their servants into three carriages. Drawing the curtains, Philip led his charges on a hair-raising ride through the streets of London. When they reached Westminster Abbey, the heavily pregnant queen tried to retain her composure but the sobbing of her terrified daughters shredded her resolve.

Philip's men escorted the queen and her companions into the abbot's lodgings, near the west doors of the abbey.

"I am ordered to return to the Tower, your Grace," Philip announced, while his men unloaded the queen's baggage.

"You are abandoning us?" she gasped, using both hands to support the unborn child in her stomach. "Lord Warwick will have me taken from this place and paraded through the streets of London."

"Your Grace, Lord Warwick will not harm you," He assured her, motioning for his men to bring a chair.

"Lord Warwick is no friend to the king," Elizabeth Hastings commented, still hurting from their last encounter.

"And where is *your* husband, my lady?" he scoffed; aware Ralph Hastings had fled with Edward.

"Sir knight, I implore thee, please stay here and give us your protection," the Queen pled, wringing her hands. "We are defenceless."

"Lord Warwick will not break sanctuary, I give you my word… your Grace, I must go and find the king."

"You will not find him; he is on his way to Burgundy."

"No, my lady," Philip frowned, "he would never abandon you; you carry his future in your belly."

"I fear if the king is taken he will be murdered, as my father was," she moaned. "His brother George has a passion for the crown."

"You are safe here, your Grace." He emphasised.

Resigned to her fate, the queen lowered her head and cried softly into her hands.

"Highness," Philip said, trying to boost her spirits and worried that if he delayed much longer he would be caught up in the rioting.

"All the Nevilles have turned against us."

"You are wrong. John will never betray Edward."

"Your devotion is touching, but one day you will see them for what they are."

"I too am a Neville," he reminded her. "I must go now, but I leave the Tower guards with you."

The queen eased herself down into the chair with the help of her servants and was comforted by her sobbing daughters.

"Go if you must," she said woefully, her fretful countenance, proof she was not bearing her predicament well.

"I will send Dr Sergio to you," Philip promised, referring to her physician.

Bowing he gave a sweeping wave before withdrawing.

"Sir knight, I will not forget what you have done for me this day," she called after him.

"Thank you, your Grace," he bowed. "Madam," he sniffed, aiming his impertinent codicil at Lady Hastings.

"Which way?" his esquire asked, as they walked briskly to their horses.

"To the Tower," he said, hurrying to the gatehouse. "And make haste, we don't have much time."

"The rioting is spreading," Ashley warned, watching columns of black smoke rising above the city.

"Here, mah lord," Arbroth offered, holding Clovis' bridle.

"Get on your own horse," Philip said, vaulting into the saddle and drawing on his gloves. "Hurry!" he hissed, as two of his retainers struggled to bring their nervous rounceys under control.

Philip led his men out of the abbey grounds and rode back to London.

Turning north at Ludgate, the horsemen took to the suburbs, utilizing lanes and alleyways to avoid gangs of drunken looters. Keeping the city wall to their right, they rode through Smithfield and Moorfield, and re-entered London at Aldgate. From here they moved swiftly on to the Tower, which was in a state of panic.

Dismounting, Philip sought out Sir John Tiptoft and found him between the Bowyer and White Towers, his calm exterior cloaking an underlying dread.

"My Lord?" Philip bowed.

"Is the queen safe?"

"Yes sir."

"Thank God," Tiptoft gasped, before pacing in agitated fashion, his curly hair wet with the sweat of fear.

"Lord Warwick will be here within the hour," Philip predicted. "What will you do?"

"I want to get on my horse and ride like the Devil," he exclaimed, "but I cannot."

"Then I shall stay...!" Philip bravely declared, drawing his sword.

"No!" Tiptoft countered. "There will be no resistance; the Tower must be surrendered without a fight. Lord Warwick offers mercy to those who do not oppose him."

"My Lord, he will show you no such luxury," Philip warned, sheathing his blade. "Oxford demands your head for that of his father."

"When the first of Warwick's men arrive I will hand over the keys and leave," Tiptoft said. "Now you must go."

Known as 'The Butcher' for his sickening executions as Constable of England, Tiptoft was the king's first cousin by marriage and a committed Yorkist. Eight years earlier he executed the Earl of Oxford's father and brother for treason; now their family was out for revenge.

"My Lord!" a lookout yelled from the Bowyer Tower.

"What?"

"Lord Warwick's standard!" he announced, cupping a hand to his mouth.

"The time has come for me to bid thee farewell," Tiptoft said.

Philip hesitated.

"Go now."

"Come with me, my Lord."

"No."

"What is there here for you but certain death?"

"What would history say of me if anything happened to the old king while he was in my care? When I am relieved of that responsibility I shall leave; now go, and Godspeed?"

Bowing to Tiptoft, Philip hinted for his esquire to gather the men before leading them out through the Lion Gate.

"Which way, sire?" Ashley asked, glancing over his shoulder.

"We'll ride to North Marston," Philip said, urging his men

to greater speed. "We must get out of London before the gates are closed."

Riding north through narrow streets packed with terrified people, some eager to get in, but most anxious to get out, Philip found Moorgate and Cripplegate too well guarded. Turning west in frustration, he rode hard for Aldersgate and arrived in time to see the gates closing, and a crowd of angry citizens being pressed back.

"Open the gates!" he demanded, thrusting a gloved finger at the harassed guards.

"But –"

"Open up, I say, or by God you'll answer to the Earl of Warwick!"

The confused guards dragged the wooden gates apart and a relieved Philip Neville forced his way through the yelling crowd. Clearing the gatehouse he trotted along Aldersgate Street, trying to understand this sudden antipathy towards Edward.

Philip and his retinue stopped at North Marston to rest their horses and re-supply. He knew once Warwick learned he had left London, he would send men in pursuit. Arbroth urged his master to make for the coast and take a boat for Flanders, but Philip was determined to see his son and led the way to Ashby-de-la Zouch.

The Talbot home in Leicestershire lay between Appleby Magna and Ashby-de-la-Zouch. The house itself was a modest country manor set in gardens and woodland. When he arrived Philip dismounted his men and dispersed them into the tress around the house. Squatting in the long, wet grass, Philip, his esquire and Arbroth hunkered down and watched.

"Why do we wait?" Ashley questioned.

"How do ye think we've stayed alive so long?" Arbroth whispered in his ear, stifling a sneeze.

"Shush," Philip hissed. "Wait here."

Standing us, he padded cautiously through the grass, a hand on the handle of his sword. With every cautious step, he listened for inconsistencies among the natural sounds of the countryside.

As he approached the house, the door opened slowly and he instinctively made ready to draw his blade. He was only stopped from doing so by a voice he knew.

"You're safe here."

"Show yourself?" Philip demanded just to be certain.

"Take your ease, dear friend," Francis Talbot smiled, his skinny face materializing from behind the door. "Praise God you are safe. Come in, but keep your men around the house; Warwick's people ride this way each night looking for Edward's men," he warned, shaking Philip's hand.

"'Tis good to see you," Philip gasped, noting how his face looked pale and drawn, and his goatee was almost thread-bare. "You look ill?"

"I've not been well since my sister…" He twitched, lowering his head. "You know she was always embarrassed by her hands, said they were too big." He sighed, looking at his own hands. "George has Isobel's blue eyes." He added smiling. "And your temper."

"I miss her," Philip said. "How is Margaret?"

"I am most fortunate; she has all the strength I lack."

"I cannot tarry long," Philip warned, glancing around. "I wish to see my son."

"Yes," Francis nodded. "Come in."

"Keep your eyes open," Philip told his esquire, before following Francis. "Where is Margaret?" he asked, as Francis led him to a tiny room.

"Tamworth,"

"Oh," he said, entering the nursery.

Tiptoeing into the small, candle-lit chamber, Philip spotted a wet nurse seated in front of the window with a babe in her arms.

"Give him to me," he demanded, rudely.

The nurse frowned at Philip's dusty attire and looked at Francis, who nodded, and she unwillingly handed over her charge. The infant sensed Philip's unease and grew agitated. When he started to cry, Philip didn't know what to do.

"Take him," he urged, offering the baby to Francis.

"He's your son," Francis insisted.

"Please," Philip whined, as the crying rose to an irritating pitch.

"He senses your distress," the nurse frowned.

"'Tis plain you have no idea how to care for a baby," Francis sniggered, folding his thin arms over his chest.

"Perhaps… but he is coming with me."

"Surely you jest?" Francis gasped, unfolding his arms and looking horrified.

"He's my son."

"You would take him now?"

"I would."

"You must not do this… for the child's sake, and my wife's sanity, he is all we have to remember –"

"And what do I have?"

"But you did not want the burden?"

"I'm taking him," Philip confirmed, lifting his son and looking into his wandering blue eyes.

"My Lord!" Ashley hissed.

"What?" he answered sharply, holding the infant close to his chest.

"Riders coming!"

"Bring the horses and round up the others."

"Please," Francis implored, as Philip turned to leave. "I beseech thee not to do this –"

"Enough!" Philip hissed hurrying outside as his men rode up.

The baby became more irritated and started to cry louder.

"Take the child!" Philip told Arbroth, passing him to his bemused retainer and straightening his stirrup.

"You'll break our hearts," Francis pled. "I am begging you, for the sake of my sister."

Closing his eyes, Philip rested his forehead on the curve of his saddle and ground his teeth. Releasing a gasp, he stared angrily at Arbroth, who without a word handed the child to Francis.

"Let's go!" Philip barked, hauling himself in the saddle and snatching the reins from his groom. "Before I change my mind."

"Thank you," Francis said gratefully, holding the whimpering infant tight, as Philip thundered into the woods in a flurry of horse hooves and flying mud. "God go with you."

"Mah lord?" Arbroth said casually as they followed a path through the underbrush.

Too angry and upset to speak Philip put a finger to his lips to silence his retainer.

"'Tis for the best, sire," Ashley dared.

Philip's flushed cheeks pulsated with rage, and his companions said no more.

Carefully avoiding enemy patrols, Philip sought a safe haven until the furore died down. Rather than risk the lives of his men, he dispersed them to their homes, his armourer and young Warren returned to London with the servants, leaving him with only Arbroth and Ashley.

"Mah lord, where do we go?" Arbroth questioned, watching their friends ride away.

"Norwich."

"Norwich?"

Still peeved at leaving his son with Francis, Philip urged his much-reduced party on.

They rode to Norwich by way of Leicester and Peterborough, covering the distance in less than five days. Fearing he might be recognised, Philip sent Arbroth to town for information. While he moodily squelched through wet, muddy woodland, his esquire squatted over the embers of a smoky fire trying to dry his damp clothes. After several hours Philip drew his sword and looked hard into the trees. Concerned, Ashley padded over to the horses, their nervous snorting irritating Philip.

While the boy tried to muffle the animals he adjusted his eyes to the fading light and saw movement in the underbrush.

Glimpsing the unmistakable wild hair of his Scottish retainer, he sheathed his sword and relaxed.

"About time," he gasped in relief. "Where have you been?"

Sliding from his panting rouncey, Arbroth ignored the question and tossed a sack of meat and vegetables at the esquire.

"See what ye can do with this, laddie."

The boy caught the greasy, bloodstained sack and dropped it.

"Noo there's gra-ititude for ye."

"Never mind that," said Philip. "What did you find out?"

"Henry o' Lancaster's been released and Lord Warwick is ready ta place tha croon back on his daft head."

"You've been drinking?" Philip growled at his slurred explanation.

"Ah have indeed," he grinned, rocking on his heels.

"You fool! What if you were followed?"

The Scot shook his head and put a hand over his heart. "Ah give ye mah word," he exclaimed.

"You Goddamn…" Philip hissed, his angry retort curtailed

by a rustling in the woods. "Shut up," he hissed, drawing his sword and turning to his esquire. "To horse."

Ashley leapt into the saddle and Philip feverishly made a grab for the reins, but as he put foot to stirrup he tripped over a tree root and accidentally kicked Clovis, causing the animal to whinny and bolt. Holding onto the reins for dear life, he was dragged through the brush, his feet bouncing over the ground forcing him to drop his sword. Clovis eventually stopped but before Philip recovered several pairs of hands grabbed his arms and held him secure.

"What the –!" he yelled.

"You are my prisoner," a knight wearing the livery of the Earl of Warwick announced, signalling for his men to release him.

"What do you mean by this outrage?"

"You serve Edward of York," he said, flipping Philip's cloak open with the point of his sword to reveal the silver rampant Lion badge, sewn on the breast of his murrey and blue doublet.

"Who are you?" he demanded.

"Sir Bernard Astley, the Earl of Warwick's man," he explained, his lips curling back from his stained teeth to form a mocking grin. "Henry is now the king and the usurper Edward has fled from these shores."

Philip tried to snatch a sword from one of his captors but Astley slashed at his wrist.

"Damn you!" he grimaced, slapping a hand to the injured limb.

The tip of Astley's blade had split Philip's glove and sliced the skin open.

"You've cut me!" he whined through gnashed teeth. "You son-of-a-bitch."

"Search him," Astley commanded.

One of his men came forward, padded him down roughly and removed the dagger from his boot.

"What now?" Philip sneered, nursing his bleeding hand.

"We ride back to London," Astley said, his shocking blond hair, blue eyes and sandy beard reminding Philip of the Nordic race who conquered much of England hundreds of years ago. "His lordship will decide your fate."

Once mounted, Philip adjusted his seat while Sir Bernard and his men formed a double line.

"Now you stand still?" Philip huffed, patting Clovis' neck and licking blood from the back of his hand.

Clovis gave a gentle snort and looked around at him with indifference, and Philip was given a piece of rag to bind his wound.

Closely guarded during the journey, Philip found no opportunity to escape and when the Tower loomed in sight he struggled to control his composure, for he knew his life was in the hands of his vindictive cousin and his Lancastrian cronies. Philip was locked in an apartment in St Thomas's Tower, a water-gate on the south wall overlooking the Thames. When the door was slammed shut behind him he thumped the stone mantle above the fireplace out of frustration.

"You pays for any damage!" a guard shouted through the door.

"It stinks of shit in here!" he bit back.

"Then you should feel at home," the guard chuckled, walking away.

"Yeh, you're in the shit anyway," a second guard added.

"Piss off!" Philip yelled. "God-damned turds."

Relieving himself in the latrine, Philip sat on a stool near the fire to mull over his fate.

Several days later, Philip was drawn to the window by the sound of cheering coming from Tower Hill.

"What's happening?" He shouted, hurrying to the door and hitting the woodwork to attract attention.

The guard on duty grudgingly opened the door.

"Well?" Philip asked.

The sluggish guard blew snot into his hand and wiped it down the wall.

"Lord Tiptoft's 'ead's come off," he smirked, tracing a cross in front of his own face. "Oxford's done 'im in."

Shocked by the news, Philip stumbled back several paces.

"You're next, m' Lord," he said.

Philip sat on a chair and dropped his face in his hands.

"I wish to see Lord Warwick!" he demanded, as the guard left and locked the door.

"Aah, is lordship's too busy for the likes of you."

"Then take a message to *his highness* and tell him his cousin wishes to speak to him."

The guard peered through the metal grill and scoffed.

"Now why don't you stay quiet and wait for the axe like a good fellow?"

"Do as I say!" he snapped, showing him a silver coin.

The guard pressed his face closer.

"Where did you hide that?" he sniffed. "Give it 'ere and I'll see is lordship gets your message."

"Do you take me for a fool?"

The guard muttered something under his breath and left.

Three days later John Lord Montague paid Philip a visit on his brother's behalf.

"My Lord!" Philip gasped, gripping Montague's hand as he entered the chamber, "'tis good to see a friend."

"Are you well, cousin?" Montague asked, looking around the chamber.

"Yes... yes, is Richard with you?"

"No, he's helping Henry choose his new council," he explained.

Philip glared at the inquisitive guard until he left.

"Bring us some food and wine," he demanded, turning to Montague. "Why am I being treated like a common criminal?"

"You are fortunate; Oxford demands that you follow Lord Tiptoft to the scaffold."

"For what reason?"

"Your loyalty to Edward."

"I took an oath to serve the king…" Philip insisted. "As did you, my Lord… and Richard."

"You know and I was true to Edward yet look how he repaid me," Montague countered. "And what have you got to show for all your years of devotion and sacrifice?"

"I care nothing for advancement," Philip lied. "Or reward."

Montague looked surprised.

"Join us and the Nevilles will be invincible."

"I'll not betray Edward for Henry," Philip announced boldly.

Amused by his confident stance Montague covered a grin.

"You find my situation humorous, cousin?"

"Calm yourself," he said. "The thought of my brother bending his knee to Queen Margaret tickles me."

"He must hate Edward very much to degrade himself so."

"Edward does not value our years of service," John explained, "He humiliated us before the Woodvilles."

The guard returned, accompanied by a servant bearing a tray of food and a jug of wine. Without a word the servant entered the chamber, laid the tray on the table and filled two goblets with wine before bowing courteously to Lord Montague.

"Get out," Philip sneered, turning to John. "What is to be my fate?"

"Richard does not want your life."

Philip sat back in his chair relieved and indicated the food.

"No, I have so little time," Montague said. "But you must remain here until London is secure."

"My Lord, you must not serve Henry," Philip dared, ravenous after Montague's comforting words.

"I have made my bed, now I must lie in it," he said, ready to leave.

"Farewell, my Lord," Philip said, raising his wine in salute as Montage reached the door. "John, help me escape," he whispered. "I would sooner die in exile than live under Lancaster's rule."

"Then you're a fool."

"Queen Elizabeth is about to give birth and a male child is foretold. When Edward learns of this he will come home and defeat Henry, and all who have betrayed him will suffer."

"I leave for the north soon," Montague said, reaching inside his tunic. "Here," tossing him a purse. "Ask nothing more of me."

Philip downed his wine and placed the empty cup on a table.

"For the sake of our friendship, I beg thee not to do this."

"I'll never turn my back on my brother again," Montague vowed. "If you see our cousin Edward, tell him when we next meet it shall be on the field of battle."

"Farewell, my Lord," Philip said.

"Godspeed," Montague ended, rapping on the door to be let out.

With his cousin's footsteps echoing down the stairs, Philip walked to the window and looked out at the river. Craning his neck he caught sight of a head stuck on a pole. The severed noggin had been boiled in salt and cumin, and the neck dipped in tar before being spiked. Through the distorted glass he recognised the bloodless, gaunt features of Sir John Tiptoft and shuddered. Shortly after Philip left the Tower and fled from London, Tiptoft had a change of heart and fled, but was caught in Huntingdonshire and brought back to London for trial. Found guilty he was imprisoned in the Fleet Prison before being hauled to Tower Hill for execution.

During his time at the Tower, Philip ingratiated himself with Sir Geoffrey Gate, the new constable, but escape was always uppermost in his mind. He asked for an hour a day to exercise in the fresh air and his request was, surprisingly, granted, but he was closely watched and did nothing to arouse suspicion. One day after Mass he returned to his chamber and worked out a plan. Several days later he befriended a friar, who came every evening lately to pray with him and hear his confession, but Philip had a reason for his sudden need of spiritual consolation.

By gaining the constable's confidence, Philip was able to tease information out of him on the situation beyond the Tower. On October 13 he was told Henry of Lancaster had been released from the Tower and crowned king. Three weeks later he was informed Queen Elizabeth had given birth to a son, reinforcing his hope that Edward would return soon, and the need to escape now became an obsession.

One Sunday in late November, Philip attended Mass at St John's Chapel in the White Tower. After the service he dined with the constable and was escorted to his chamber. With daylight fading, he asked a guard to fetch friar Mortain, the monk who prayed with him daily. When Mortain arrived Philip led him into a partitioned part of the room and both men knelt before a large cross. After a few minutes Philip said he was desperate for a piss and left, and the monk continued to pray alone. Grabbed from behind, Mortain found himself wrestled to the ground. When his habit was pulled up over his head he tried to yell, but Philip clamped a hand over his mouth.

"Stop…" the monk gasped, biting his finger. "Why are you doing this?"

"Sorry father, but my need is greater than yours," Philip apologised, binding the monk's hands and feet with a length of rope.

"I should have known," the trembling friar griped, as Philip pushed him close to the fire. "I could cry out."

"But you won't," Philip smirked, heaving several logs into the flames.

"No," he grunted, closing his eyes to avoid hot embers flying in his face. "May God forgive you?"

"I doubt he will."

Looking out the window at the overcast sky, Philip sat at the table and stared at his warped reflection in a thin piece of polished steel. He then began altering his appearance to look as much like the monk as possible. Having been shaved earlier he used a watered solution of clay to tone down his skin colour. Producing a handful of black hair, trimmed from a horse's tail, he thickened his eyebrows and shaped a fringe which was stuck to his forehead with hoof glue. Using soot thinned with red wine, he dabbed it lightly under the eyes and filled out his cheeks with stale bread. When he was finished, Philip looked at the round-faced friar, then his own reflection, and back at the frowning monk before nodding approvingly.

"You befriended me for one reason," the monk huffed.

"Do you think I enjoyed listening to all that sanctimonious bluster?" Philip sneered, removing his footwear while the Benedictine looked on in disgust.

When Philip's brother Thomas came to London disguised as a monk, he gave himself away by wearing boots. Determined not to make the same mistake, he rolled his hose up above the knee, pulled on the habit to cover his doublet and set his bare feet in the sandals.

"I could be a monk," he grinned, making the sign of the cross at the shivering friar, dressed only in a pair of grungy braies. "Ah," he remembered, stuffing the pillow and boots under the habit. "Farewell, my son."

"*Misereatur vestri omnipotens deus*," the friar responded, which translated to 'May Almighty God have mercy on you'.

Philip cracked the door and peeped out into the passage. Drawing the hood up over his head, he crossed his hands and pushed them into the wide sleeves of his habit. Tiptoeing down the stairs, he walked out into the cold rain; listening for the curfew bell as he shuffled slowly to the gates.

"Don't ring," he hissed, glancing up at the sky. "Please God."

At the first set of gates he was lazily acknowledged by the sheltering guards before passing through, but at the Middle Tower he was stopped by a more conscientious watchman.

"Leaving before Vespers, father?"

"I am unwell, my son," Philip groaned, leaning against the wall and urging.

The guard quickly ushered him out.

"God bless you," Philip gasped, making the sign of the cross as the curfew bell began to toll.

"Yes, yes father bless you too, just go."

The Tower gates were locked between sunset and dawn, and with his hose beginning to unroll, Philip spat out the soggy bread and hurried through the Lion Gate.

"Made it," he gasped, as the heavy doors were slammed shut behind him.

Once clear of the Tower Philip removed the pillow and boots, stripped off the habit, tied it over his tunic and kicked off the sandals. His first night of freedom was spent at a noisy inn near London Bridge and next morning he purchased a hackney. Fearing capture, Philip rode swiftly to the Kent coast and took passage aboard a merchant ship bound for the Low Countries. After battling contrary winds and seasickness, he stepped ashore at Alkmaar and made his way to Bruges.

Chapter 18

FROM THE MOMENT he arrived in Bruges, Philip Neville was coldly received, because of his association with the Earl of Warwick. At first, Edward welcomed his cousin and praised him for escorting his family safely to sanctuary. Philip was fed and armed, but that was as far as Edward's generosity went and the money given to Philip by Montague soon ran out, leaving him penniless. During his time in Burgundy, he wrote to his mother in France asking why she never told him Michael was alive. There was no reply.

King Edward was not as close to his brother-in-law Charles as he believed; with familial ties to both York and Lancaster Burgundy dithered, his vacillation encouraged by Edmund Beaufort. The young brother of the dead Duke of Somerset had served Burgundy for several years, but when Edward arrived on the continent he prudently vanished. In December King Louis renounced the Treaty of Peronne and declared war on Burgundy, an act that tipped the duke's hand. On the last day of December 1470, Charles gave Edward money, troops and ships to help him regain the throne.

For six months the Earl of Warwick governed England through the re-crowned Henry VI, who sat passively on the throne and allowed his kingdom to be ruled for him. During his time in France, Warwick had pledged to support Louis if he went to war with Burgundy; now the French king demanded that support. Fearing Edward's return, Warwick's navy patrolled the channel, but when a squadron of Breton merchant ships was spotted the fleet gave chase, leaving the way clear for Edward. With the Channel open and the weather calm, he set sail for England with a tiny army on 11 March 1471.

The York-Burgundian fleet bounced helplessly in the tempestuous North Sea as it fought to enter the mouth of the Humber. Standing on the forecastle of the *Anthony*, Edward held on to the rigging with both hands, as the prow dived into the troughs and rose on the swells. The breaking waves buffeted the vessel and threw freezing water in his face, but he remained on deck, as an example to his men. Nearby, Philip Neville, soaked to the skin, seasick and convinced he was going to drown, prayed hard. At first, the voyage from Flushing to the Norfolk coast had gone smoothly and after dropping anchor at Cromer, scouts went ashore to reconnoitre the area. They returned with bad news: the Earl of Oxford was in Norfolk raising troops for Henry, so Edward sailed up the coast to Yorkshire and into bad weather.

Having survived the violent storm, Philip stumbled out of a small boat near Ravenspur, a market town on a spit of land curving down into the mouth of the Humber. Pale and trembling he splashed out of the shallows and tottered up the beach to the cliffs. Shivering in the long grass, he removed his boots, tipped out the water and rubbed his cold hands together. Once on terra firma, Edward watched his scattered army of 1200 Englishmen and Flemings stagger out of the surf. Cold, wet and hungry, they dropped to their knees and thanked God for delivering them from the fierce waters of the North Sea. After unloading supplies, the ships sailed away, leaving the tiny Yorkist force isolated and apprehensive. A fine sleety drizzle was falling but Edward denied his men the luxury of fire; instead, he raised the blue and red quartered royal banner and knelt with his nobles to give thanks. With prayers over, he sent for his cousin.

Removing his wet, floppy cap, the bedraggled, queasy knight presented himself to the king, who was being helped out of his wet clothes by two esquires of the body.

"Your Grace?" he quivered.

"Well cousin, we are here and here we shall stay."

"Yes, sire."

"Are you acquainted with this country?"

"Yes, your Grace," Philip answered, drawing his short, saturated cloak around his body to keep out the biting wind.

"Then ride to Kingstown and announce me. I will gather the army and follow you."

"We number so few to conquer a kingdom," Philip sighed, looking at the men shivering in small groups up and down the beach. "Do we march to London?"

"We are too weak for such a bold enterprise; we must bide our time and build our strength," Edward replied, waving him off. "Now go."

Philip bowed and left to carry out his orders.

Commandeering one of the few horses available, and with an escort of four men-of-arms, Philip followed the north bank of the Humber to Kings-town-upon-Hull, twenty-five miles to the west.

As he approached the town Philip found his way barred by the swollen River Hull, which tumbled into the Humber from the north. As he waited on the icy river bank, a delegation rode out demanding to know his business, though by his exposed livery they had a fair idea.

"I am Sir Philip Neville," he answered boldly, "and I am here on the king's business!"

"What does King Henry want?"

Philip looked at his companions, huffed and raised his eyebrows.

"*King Edward,*" he clarified, "Seeks permission to enter your fair city."

The cagey town representatives looked to their spokesman, who declared:

"Hull is for King Harry; therefore we must respectfully refuse your request."

"You deny the rightful king-."

"No," he countered, looking over his shoulder at the walled city nestled conveniently between the River Hull and the north bank of the Humber. "But we dare not oppose the Earl of Northumberland."

Philip growled his disappointment and turned his party around.

"We can do nothing," one of the civic leaders called after him, "but we shall not interfere with your progress."

Philip waved away the offer without looking back.

Next day he rendezvoused with the king on the road to Hull. Sensing bad news, Edward halted the column and rode forward to speak with his cousin, accompanied only by his chamberlain. Philip trotted out and they met on the slush-covered road.

"Your Grace, Hull refuses to recognise you as king," Philip explained, alighting from his horse and examining the animal's bloody fetlocks. Whilst riding through deep puddles of frozen water the weight of his horse broke the thin icy surface, creating sharp edges that lacerated its lower legs.

"Don't tell me, they fear Northumberland?" Edward guessed.

Philip nodded and Edward accepted the news with a disappointed sniff.

"John Neville no longer bears that title," he said.

"But his very name commands a great following in the north."

"So be it," Edward frowned, rubbing his chin on the back of his hand.

"What now, sire?" Philip questioned, flapping irritating snow from his face.

"Lord Hastings suggests I am here only to claim my Dukedom."

"But –"

"'Tis a falsehood," Edward assured him. "We ride to York."

"You should avoid York, sire," Philip warned.

"Allow me to finish."

Philip soaked up the gentle reprimand, and Hastings took over from the king.

"When we reach York," he began, his falsetto tone irritating, "his highness will proclaim his allegiance to King Henry."

Philip deliberately ignored the lord chamberlain and remounted.

"'Tis a pretence," Edward reiterated. "To buy time for our friends to join us…But know this, I would kiss Henry's arse to get my crown back."

"You take a great risk, sire," Philip counselled, acknowledging Edward's brother Richard, sitting his horse at the head of the army. "York is for Henry."

"I have no choice."

"Your Grace, we must make haste," Hastings urged.

"Sire, the people of Hull will not oppose your progress," Philip assured him.

"Get them moving, Will," Edward told his chamberlain, looking up at the dark sky.

Philip fell in beside his young cousin Richard and the army sloshed its way north-westwards in nervous silence.

To reinforce his false claim, Edward removed the royal banner from its pole and replaced it with the House of York standard. The cross of St George next to the staff and the fly divided lengthways, half murrey, half blue. A silver falcon with gold fetterlock and six white roses, underlined by the motto '*Dieu et mon Droit*', was emblazoned on the fly.

By the feast day of Edward the Confessor, 18 March, Edward was only three miles from York when a galloping rider forced him to halt.

"Sire, I am Thomas Conyers, Recorder for the city of York," he announced, doffing his hat and bowing from the saddle.

"What do you want, Mr Conyers, Recorder for the city of York?" Hastings asked flippantly.

"Your Grace, York is hostile to you," Conyers explained nervously, his warm breath freezing before his face.

"I come to York to claim my dukedom, nothing more."

"Sire I beg thee –" Conyers pled.

"Enough!" Edward snapped, angrily clicking his tongue against the roof of his mouth and waving his men on. "Move aside."

Conyers moved his horse to the side of the road and sat in silence while Edward's army made its ponderous way to York.

The closer they came to the city, the more uneasy Philip became. Less than a mile from the city, Edward was met by two more riders who informed him he would be well received in York. Encouraged by this unexpected turnabout, Edward increased the pace until he arrived at Walmgate Bar, its twelve foot high, six foot wide doors studded with broadhead nails.

"Open up in the name of Edward, Duke of York!" his standard bearer demanded, trotting up to the outer gates and flaunting his long, tapering standard. "I hold in my hand a letter from the Earl of Northumberland supporting his grace's claim!" he lied.

There was a moment of quiet before a warden appeared on the parapet above the gatehouse.

"His Grace may enter but he must be accompanied by no more than twenty armed retainers. Food and fodder will be provided for all your men and horses!"

"They insult my brother!" Gloucester snarled at Philip.

While the mounted detachment rode through the yawning gates, Lord Hastings dispersed the infantry around St Lawrence's Church close to the gatehouse.

Trotting along Walmgate, Edward and his bedraggled escort became objects of curiosity to those who ventured out into the cold, wet streets. Philip rode behind the king as they moved between narrow, rows of crooked tenements on their way to the River Foss.

"Lord Percy's house," Richard of Gloucester said, pointing to a beautiful manor on the north side of the street.

"He died there after Towton, cursing the Plantagenets," Philip revealed, nudging his chin at St Denys' Church, opposite the Percy house."

"He was a fool."

"Yes, your Grace," Philip sniffed, urging his horse up and over Foss Bridge, where the column was forced to push its way through cursing fishmongers, unloading fish from uncooperative mules. "Now he's a dead fool."

Once clear of the bridge, Edward trotted passed the Merchant Taylors Hall and the Carmelite Friary before riding along St Saviourgate, but the increasing crowd slowed progress.

"Sire, these people have great fondness for you," Philip whispered, noting how some looked at Edward with indifference yet cheered openly for Richard.

"My brother has little time for the people of York."

"They have no time for him, your Grace."

"King Harry," Edward shouted, raising a gloved fist. "King Harry!"

His example was half-heartedly echoed by his escort and boisterously taken up by the masses.

"Did I hear right?" Philip gasped, irritated by Edward's declaration.

"My brother must convince them he is here to claim only his ducal rights," Richard explained, acknowledging those who called out to him with a friendly wave. "See, he wears the Prince of Wales feathers in his hat."

"I hope it works," Philip sniffed, "or our heads will crown the Micklegate before sunset."

As they proceeded along Petergate, Edward continued to voice his support for Lancaster.

Edward and his escort eventually arrived at the gates leading into the Minster grounds. Dismounting and accompanied only by his chamberlain, he walked to the South Transept and stood before the doors. Handing his sword to Hastings, he removed his hat and entered the cathedral alone. Sliding gratefully from the saddle, Philip removed his riding gloves and rested his numb backside against a stulpe, one of the bollards placed to stop carts entering the Minster Precinct. Leaning back, he looked up and tutted at the gargoyles spaced out along the Cathedral walls.

"Huh," he shuddered, his eyes drawn to the hideous stone sculptures.

"They reflect the power of the Church over evil," Gloucester explained. "Do they bother you that much?"

"When I was a child my father warned me that if I disobeyed my mother when he was away, those... things would haunt my dreams, and they did."

Richard patted his shoulder reassuringly.

"I wish one would fall on his head," Philip grinned, as William Hastings walked back through the mesh of wooden scaffold shrouding the central tower.

"I know you despise the lord chamberlain but he is my brother's dearest friend."

"He's a cunning knave who plays both ends against the middle," Philip said, slapping his sides for warmth. "I apologise, sire... I have been cold since we left Burgundy."

Hastings suspected Philip was denigrating him to the young duke and joined the king's banneret. The lightly bearded, dark-eyed standard bearer looked uncomfortable, as the two men were not on good terms.

"It is said the Duke of Exeter and Edmund Beaufort are in England," Hastings declared, his tone provoking.

"Fear not, *my Lord chamberlain*: when we meet them on the field of battle they'll rue the day they set foot on English soil," Philip called out, unable to restrain himself.

"If we don't recruit this army, and quickly, it'll be us who'll rue the day," Gloucester prophesied.

"Your Grace, Exeter and Beaufort will never serve Lord Warwick," Philip exclaimed.

"I hear your brother has risen from the grave and pledged his sword to Henry," Hastings smirked. "Now he'll have to die all over again."

Philip pushed himself off the stulpe and advanced on Hastings, forcing him back against a wall. Grabbing the chamberlain's scrawny neck with both hands, he contracted them around his throat and snarled in his face like an angry dog.

"I'll kill you for that!"

"Leave him!" Gloucester yelled, grabbing his shoulders, but he was not strong enough.

Philip held on, as a red mist blurred his vision and he squeezed until Hastings' eyes bulged hideously and his face turned purple.

"Stop!" Gloucester shouted, as Lord Rivers came to his assistance. "Release him I say."

Philip loosened his grip but deliberately dug his nails in as he withdrew, gouging the flesh.

"You've cut me!" Hastings squealed, dabbing his neck and looking at the bloodstains on his fingertips. "Look!"

"I will…" Philip hissed, dribbling spittle, before a guard announced the king's return.

Having thanked God for his safe arrival, Edward left the Minster to rejoin his companions.

"What's happening here?" he demanded.

"Sire, this knight has laid hands on me, me a royal councillor!" Hastings screeched, patting his neck with a handcoverchief and levelling an accusing finger at Philip. "Such an offence is treason… I demand justice."

Edward looked to his brother for an explanation but he turned away and Philip wiped the spit from his chin.

"What's this all about?" he fumed, looking at Philip.

"Your Grace?" he gasped innocently.

Before Edward could reprimand him, Gloucester stepped forward.

"Sire," he whispered, cocking his head at the bemused crowds. "This is not the time."

"I'll deal with you later," he muttered out of the corner of his mouth.

"But your Grace –" Hastings whined.

"My Lord Chamberlain, tonight we dine with the mayor," Edward announced, before turning to Philip. "You will join the army outside."

"But sire –" Philip objected, only to be cut off by Edward fawning to the crowd as they pressed forward to touch his person.

While Edward soaked up the adoration Philip mounted his horse, bowed to Gloucester and returned to Walmgate.

That night Edward was wined and dined by the high and mighty of York. Several days later, when he led his army out of the snow-dusted city, he was cheered part of the way. Edward and Hastings had discussed the best way to punish Philip for his assault, but Edward's brother protested on Philip's behalf, reminding him that their cousin had always been loyal to the House of York. Lacking knights, Edward postponed making any decision and marched his army to Sandal Castle near Wakefield.

Outnumbered and in the heart of Neville country, Edward took a roundabout route to avoid Pontefract Castle, where John Neville Lord Montague was rumoured to be waiting in ambush. When the white walls and towers of Sandal Castle came in sight, the army was much relieved. As they rode up the angled passageway and rattled over the drawbridge spanning the dry moat, Philip turned to his cousin Richard.

"I always felt safe here."

"Sandal is my mother's favoured residence," Richard announced, pointing to the bleak countryside below the castle, where the Yorkists were slaughtered in December 1460. "Down there is where Somerset foully murdered my father, and my brother Edmund."

"We lost many good friends that day," Philip said as they rode through the bailey, remembering the rotting heads of his uncles and cousin, spiked above the Micklegate in York, after Towton.

Sandal Castle was built on high ground, its massive barbican protecting the Great Tower. Numerous buildings, stalls and lean-tos filled the limited, 'U' shaped bailey, causing severe over-crowding, but the fortress was still a dominant symbol of Yorkist power.

Edward dismounted and led his lords to the Great Chamber for a private council, while Philip stabled his horse and joined several knights at a nearby ale stall. Fearing Warwick's brother would move against him, Edward wasted no time working out the next phase of his plan to reclaim the throne. For some inexplicable reason, Montague remained at Pontefract, ten miles to the east, his lack of initiative a boost to Edward's confidence.

Before a drop of ale touched his lips, Philip was ordered to attend the king. Dragging his feet, he headed for the Great

Tower and went up to Edward's private apartments on the second floor, only to be refused access.

After a lengthy wait, Anthony Lord Rivers came out.

"My Lord," Philip offered, grinding his teeth, for he had taken an intense dislike to the king's brother-in-law since the day at Woodstock, when he sided with Lord Somerset, against him.

"Walk with me," Woodville commanded.

The two men tripled down the stairs and out into the inner bailey.

In his late twenties, Lord Rivers, the queen's brother, was generous and considerate but predatory in his pursuit of opportunity. Along with his father, he fought against Edward at Towton but changed sides shortly thereafter. His handsome features bore the scars of several jousting injuries and one of his front teeth had been knocked out. To prove his faith Lord Rivers wore a hair shirt next to his skin.

"Lord Warwick is raising a great host against us."

"What can we do," Philip huffed, "My Lord?"

"It is the king's wish that you go your cousin, Lord Warwick, and tell him Edward will forgive his transgressions and offers him clemency; if he accepts, the king guarantees no harm shall befall him."

Philip's jaw dropped, for he knew such a mission could only end badly for him.

"Is it the king's wish that I do this thing?"

"It is; and you go alone, one man will draw less attention," Rivers explained, the gap in his teeth causing a whistle to accompany his words.

"Is this Lord Hastings' suggestion?"

"No," he snapped.

Philip knew Warwick had lost patience with him for siding with Edward and dreaded meeting his kinsman again.

"This is signed by his Highness," Rivers said handing him a

letter stamped with Edward's seal. "Give it to Lord Warwick and no other."

"I'll need a miracle," he groaned, staring at the thick, red wax seal.

"Then you'd better pray for one," Rivers suggested, walking away.

"My horse is lame, my Lord!"

"Then pick another."

"Cod-head," Philip snorted under his breath.

Chapter 19

PHILIP RODE BACK to York alone, a heavy cloak concealing his livery coat. When he arrived at Claremont Hall, he washed and changed into a black doublet and hose. Next morning he set off south, refreshed but pessimistic, and after spending an uneasy night at a Rotherham inn, he rode on to Sheffield Town. The further south he rode the more doubt chiselled away at what little confidence he started with, forcing him to stop every few miles and scrutinise his surroundings. Dozens of men and women travelled up and down the highway, yet he grew more and more wary that he was being followed.

"Something's afoot," he warned his fine palfrey, patting its warm, damp neck before touching spur to flank. "I believe Hastings has set me up… one day I'll get even with that spineless toad."

Near Sheffield, the sky turned dark and heavy and then the heavens opened. By sunset cold rain was pelting his face mercilessly, soaking his clothes and deadening his senses. Struggling to see in the darkness, he knew he must stop soon. Wet through and shivering, he turned off the main road and splashed down a muddy, waterlogged lane until he came across a low building. As he dismounted something made him look back, dabbing his blurry eyes he peered hard through the curtain of rain but saw nothing. Leading his steaming horse through a broken-down wall he approached the building.

"In the name of the king!" he shouted, poking his head through the door-less entrance, "Anyone here."

Tying his palfrey to a bush Philip entered the dark, single story hovel, its dirt floor covered with wet, rotten straw.

"Shit," he swore, as his head collided with a desiccated rabbit, tied to a roof beam to keep it away from rats. "What in God's name!"

Looking up, he saw rainwater pouring through several large holes in the thatch, and then heard the distant dull thud and splatter of horses. Dragging his palfrey inside, he swung the saturated cloak from his shoulders and unsheathed his blade. Not his usual sword, the weapon made a sharp, rasping sound as it cleared its scabbard, causing the horse to snort nervously and lash out at the crumbling wall with its hind legs. Philip placed his cloak over the animal's head to calm him.

"Easy," he whispered, stroking the stallion's neck.

The horse settled down and Philip took up a position behind the doorway.

Soon he heard the metallic jingle of horse furnishings mingled with the cadenced thump of hooves.

"Where did he go?" A voice called through the rain.

"Dunno."

"Better stop here for tha night; we can't follow him in this."

"Aye."

Pressing his back against the wall, Philip knew someone had sent these men after him and held his breath. Cold sweat formed on his face, his mouth dried up and fear generated wind in his stomach. Unsure of their numbers, he squeezed his cheeks together and released a squeaky fart, and prayed they couldn't hear.

"Leave them!" one of the strangers growled, meaning their horses, as he jumped from the saddle and dashed for the shelter of the building, they were his last words.

As he stepped over the threshold, Philip's sword swung

through the air and smashed into his face beneath the nose with a loud crack and he fell backwards. Reaching for the man's belt Philip pulled him inside and threw him to the floor, blood pouring from the ugly wound.

"They need feeding!" his companion called out, unaware.

Philip grabbed the man lying at his feet by his legs and hauled him away from the door before cutting his throat with a ballock dagger.

"Come and help me!" the second man shouted angrily, struggling with the baulking horses.

"Do it yourself!" Philip growled, hoping the sound of the rain would aid his mimicry.

"What?" he bellowed, rushing in. "I'll teach thee-!"

Before he could finish, Philip thrust his sword hard into his side.

Shocked, by the unexpected attack, he staggered around the dark room, tripping and stumbling over scattered furniture, and fell heavily.

"Treacherous bastard!" he gasped, believing his companion had attacked him.

"Who sent you?" Philip demanded, squatting on his chest and shoving a dagger to his throat.

The wounded man looked shocked and struggled to breathe, and Philip grabbed a handful of his soggy beard.

"Answer me..." he yelled, pressing the sharp point against his jugular. "Who sent you?"

With the last of his strength, the wounded man forced his head up and spat in Philip's face.

Sleeving saliva from his cheek, he smashed the man's nose with the pommel of his dagger. "His name," he repeated, grabbing the dirty neck of his tunic.

"Piss on you," the man choked, well aware he was drowning in his own blood.

"You black-hearted dog."

The dying man made a frenzied grab for the silver crucifix round his neck, but Philip's thighs prevented him from reaching it. Snatching the cross from its chain, he swung it just out of reach.

"Please…" he gurgled.

"You want it?" Philip taunted, dangling the religious symbol in front of his eyes.

Spitting blood and fighting for air he managed a feeble nod.

"Then give me a name."

"Lord…" he coughed harshly, "Lord kiss-my-arse."

His head flopped back and when Philip saw the dark liquid trickling from his mouth, he knew his time was up.

Standing, he slipped the dagger into his boot, retrieved his sword and looked outside. Satisfied there were no more he dropped the crucifix on the dead man's chest and checked the first body for life; there was none. Removing the cloak from his horse's head, he went outside and searched the two horses for food. Laying his meagre fare out on one of the dead men's chest he snacked on a piece of cheese, rye bread and wine before curling up in his wet cloak to sleep.

Waking with a jolt, Philip shot up and stared at the darkness through the open doorway, but there was nothing but the rain. Moving to the door he poked his head out.

"Sweet Jesus," he trembled, looking into the blackness. "I don't like what I can-not see!"

The cold rain cooled the sweat of fear on his face and calmed his nerves. He had been dreaming of a dark shape pursuing him through the forest and no matter how fast he ran the shadow grew until it engulfed everything. The nightmare was so intense it scared him awake.

Calming down he looked up at the moon through a tear in the clouds and gauged the time at between three and four of the clock. Dragging a broken piece of table to the doorway, he sat down and tried to sleep. As his heartbeat slowed and his head grew heavy, he heard a noise inside the cottage but convinced himself it was nothing. The unmistakable slurping thud of excrement falling out of his horse's arse came as a moment of comical relief.

"Phew…" he grinned, resting his back against the door frame and dozing off.

Early next morning, Philip's eyes snapped open to the thrum of pigeon wings. Stretching his arms, he fixed his gaze on several trapped birds frantically seeking a way out through the roof.

Scratching his scalp, he massaged his neck and yawned. Blinking at the body near his feet, he pursed his lips and spat out a gobbet of foul-tasting phlegm before robbing the two corpses. He found several coins and a handful of raisins wrapped in a piece of rag.

"Nothing much," he coughed, grabbing his cloak and leading his palfrey out.

Taking a quick look at the two horses belonging to the dead men, he looked at the fine stallion that belonged to Lord Hastings and smiled.

"Lord Rivers told me to take a horse," he chuckled, imagining the uproar that must have followed his departure from Pontefract.

Stepping into the bright, spring morning hurt Philip's eyes and as he hauled himself into the saddle he blinked as raindrops dripped off the trees and splashed his face. Nudging his horse up the muddy lane in the direction of the main road, he greedily scoffed the raisins, only to discover the material used to wrap the dried fruit was a filthy handcoverchief.

"Goddamn!" he growled, tossing it away and spitting out what was in his mouth. "Filthy Bastards!"

His horse looked around to see what all the fuss was about and trotted on.

Philip cursed William Hastings and jerked the reins, forcing his palfrey to pick up the pace. The warm weather gradually dried his clothes and the cheery warbling of sparrows in the hedgerows relaxed him.

After three days Philip arrived at Warwick and rode through the town to the castle. Built on a high sandstone bluff, the fortress was strategically located above the River Avon, its gatehouse protected by a dry ditch and formidable barbican. Philip followed a flanking wall that ran along the outside of the wide ditch, north and east of the castle, and as he approached the barbican, he was surprised to find the drawbridge up.

"Halloo!" he called out.

Several faces popped up on the battlements.

"I am Philip Neville, cousin to the Earl of Warwick!" he shouted.

"I know you, my Lord," a ventenar countered, leaning through one of the embrasures. "What is it you want?"

"I wish to speak with his lordship!"

"He's not here."

"Where is he?"

"Leicester."

"Leicester?"

"Edward of York had proclaimed himself king and marches on London."

"Do you know where Edward is?" Philip asked, confused by the news.

The ventenar shrugged his shoulders.

"Then I am bound for Leicester," Philip announced, wearily turning his horse and trotting away.

Needing oats for his horse, he made his way to Coventry, a short ride from Warwick.

The red sandstone beneath Coventry's recently lime-washed walls was already coming through in patches producing an unsightly pink stain. Riding through the Greyfriars

Gate and along Warwick Lane, he was overawed by the number of armed men in the city.

"Why so many soldiers?" he asked a young flower seller.

"Lord Warwick has come," she smiled, offering him a yellow bloom from her basket.

Philip accepted the daffodil, which he stuck in his horse's bridle and thanked her with coin before trotting on.

In the narrow confines of Pepper Lane, he weaved his way to a group of foul-mouthed archers.

"Where can I find Lord Warwick?" he demanded.

The archers ceased their crude banter and eyed him in an unfriendly manner.

"What business do you have with his lordship?"

"I bear a message from the king."

"You look like a beggar to me," a centenar huffed, eyeing his dusty, rain-stained attire and the foamy horse between his legs.

"Even 'is 'owse looks done in," another appended.

"I have ridden far to see his lordship," Philip hissed. "Where is he?"

"Whitefriars," the centenar scoffed, pointing. "That way."

Philip headed for the Carmelite Priory of the Whitefriars and spotted soldiers wearing the white and red livery coats, of Henry Holland Duke of Exeter, his distinctive ear-of-wheat badge prominent, and their presence disturbed him. Exeter was a devoted Lancastrian who hated Warwick intensely; Philip believed an alliance with such a man would be his undoing.

"The lamb has lain with the wolf," he told his horse as he approached Whitefriars.

"I wish to see Lord Warwick," he announced, dismounting before the red-brick monastic gate.

"Philip?"

"Harry?" he chirped up, recognising one of Warwick's secretaries. "Harry Wheeler?"

"Yes."

"'Tis good to see a friendly face."

"You risk your life coming here," Henry Wheeler warned him, looking around guardedly and lowering his voice. "Lancaster's men are everywhere."

"I have a message for his lordship."

"He is in counsel."

"I must see him."

"I'll take you to him but I warn you, he is in bad humour and your presence will only aggravate him."

Philip allowed his weary horse to gnaw on a patch of grass while he accompanied the fast-walking secretary to the abbot's lodgings.

"Exeter's men?"

"Those of us who serve the white bear resent this nefarious alliance."

"Is Exeter here?"

"No, he's still in Newark with Oxford, but they are coming. So are Montague and Clarence."

"How can Edward hope to win against such odds?" he hissed.

"It's a sad day when those who fought to put Edward on the throne now conspire to destroy him."

"Very sad."

When they arrived at the abbot's lodgings, Wheeler entered first.

"I'll tell his lordship you're here."

While he waited, Philip pondered how Warwick would react.

The door to the abbot's lodgings opened and a dozen knights marched out, their pained expressions indicative of a very toxic council.

"His lordship will see you," an esquire announced, crooking a finger at Philip.

Brushing trail dust from his tunic, he thanked Harry and stepped into the lion's den.

"Be on your guard," Harry warned.

"My Lord," Philip greeted his cousin as he entered, bowed and handed his sword to the guard.

An esquire standing behind Warwick sniffed haughtily at the dishevelled visitor, whose clothes and boots were stained with dried mud.

Bent over a table covered with papers, Richard was busy examining a map and ignored his cousin at first. Resting his fists on the table he slowly looked up.

"Cousin... come, let us embrace," he smiled, moving around the table and opening his arms.

Warwick's icy kiss felt like the kiss of death and Philip was unnerved by this unexpected show of affection. Looking at his kinsman's face he clearly saw the deep worry lines etched on his pale face; his grey-flecked hair and unshaven chin, evidence of the stress he was under.

"I bear a message for you, my Lord," Philip revealed, breaking the embrace and offering the letter, "from the king."

Warwick took the epistle but baulked when he recognised Edward's seal. Snapping the wax, he unfolded the paper and read the contents. Returning to his chair, Richard tossed the note on his desk, clamped his fists together under his chin and contemplated a moment.

"I know I have gone too far," he said ruefully, staring at the letter. "Edward talks of fellowship and mercy, yet I know in my heart he will never forgive me."

"My Lord, the king seeks only reconciliation."

Warwick stopped him with a raised hand.

"I have placed the crown on the head of a fool and allied myself with Louis of France and Margaret of Anjou. I executed the queen's father and brother, and married my daughter to his brother… against his wishes. Would you forgive me?"

"The King makes this offer in good faith."

"My Lord, I suspect a trap," the esquire whispered in Warwick's ear.

Philip glared menacingly at the pompous youth, while Richard shuffled through the papers on his desk, looking for something.

"I have made promises to those who have joined me. I cannot now betray them. If we succeed, all will be well; if we fail, we go down together."

Philip sensed discouragement in his tone.

"My Lord you have this chance to make everything right."

"Sire, you have a great host with more men on the way," the esquire interrupted. "Edward has nothing to oppose you."

"Numbers count for little if one has the confidence of the lords," Warwick groaned. "I lack such luxury. If I do not march soon, Edward will gain the advantage."

"Go to him, my Lord," Philip pled. "He has always held you in high esteem."

Warwick stared into space and unconsciously wiped his nose on his cuff. For a moment Philip believed he would accept the king's offer but a heavy rap on the door snapped the Earl out of his gloom and he signalled for the guard to open the door.

A distressed messenger entered the chamber and bowed sharply.

"My Lord, Edward of York approaches with an army," he exclaimed, wiping sweat from his eyes.

Leaping to his feet, Warwick screwed up Edward's letter and chucked it in the fire behind him.

"My cousin talks of mercy and comes dressed for war," he barked.

"My Lord…" the messenger dared.

"What?"

"York has forced Exeter to abandon Newark and is in hot pursuit."

Floored by the news, Warwick paced rapidly to and fro, rubbing his chin intensely and glowering at his cousin.

"What of Clarence?"

The messenger looked down at the floor.

"So Edward has no army?" Warwick growled at his esquire. "I want every man inside this city," he told the courier. "Find Exeter and tell him to join me here at once," he added, stabbing a finger on the table, "If he has not lost his nerve."

The messenger bowed and left.

"If Edward comes we'll meet force with force," he boasted, confidently.

"*When* he comes, my Lord," Philip said wryly.

"Stay here and fight at my side," Warwick offered.

"I cannot," he refused, shaking his head.

"You know… if not for me you would never have escaped from the Tower?" Warwick revealed, staring knowingly at his surprised kinsman. "You are a fool if you believe Sir Geoffrey did not know you were using friar Mortain for your own ends?" Warwick smirked. "Your very nature makes you so easy to manipulate. His suspicions were roused when you asked to see a priest, though your hostility to the clergy is notorious."

"Nevertheless, I can-not betray my king," Philip confirmed, peeved by his cousin's disclosure.

"Your king… What has Edward done for you that you stand by him so passionately?"

"My Lord, I have delivered the message… Permit me to leave."

"No!" he barked, banging his fist on the table. "You have seen and heard too much. You will remain here. Give me your word you'll not leave the city and I'll spare you the indignity of prison."

"You have my word, my Lord," Philip sighed, bowing respectfully.

As Philip left Warwick passed his esquire a shifty nod.

"Shadow him, Mr Shelby," he said, "and don't let him out of your sight."

"He won't see me, my Lord," the esquire said confidently.

"Oh he will," Warwick smirked. "And when he does, give him this," he added, handing over a purse.

Philip sensed he was being followed the moment he left the abbey. Leading his palfrey through the streets, he headed for the Bull Inn on Smythford Street. After securely stabling his precious horse, he entered the hostelry through its low doorway. An ideal stopover for travellers, the Bull Inn served food and drink. Handing over the last of his money for a jug of wine, Philip sat reading the names gouged into the table-top and wondered where he was going to sleep. With so many soldiers in town, The Bull was packed with men dressed in a variety of colourful livery coats, ranging from the plain white of Sir John Conyers to the green and red of the city militia.

As he decanted the wine from jug to cup, Philip spotted Warwick's esquire trying to act inconspicuous.

"Mr Shelby," he called out, "join me."

The red-faced esquire shuffled over to the table, disappointed at being caught.

"Here," Philip said, grabbing another cup from a passing serving girl.

"My Lord," the perturbed youngster pouted, reluctantly accepting the wine.

"Don't feel bad," Philip declared, raising his cup and looking around. "Good health!"

"Good health," Shelby echoed in a subdued voice, "Sir, I must protest…"

"His lordship sent you to watch me," Philip smirked. "How many are you?"

"Four."

"Where are they?"

"Outside."

Philip suddenly whipped the dagger from his boot and threw himself over the table. Grabbing the back of the esquire's head he wrenched it down hard against the tabletop and pressed the blade into his neck.

"I could cut your throat," he threatened, "and you would bleed out before they could reach you."

The terrified teenager yelped and struggled to break free until Philip let him go. Slumping back in his chair, the esquire held his throat and panted.

Slipping the dagger nonchalantly back in his boot, Philip sat down and glowered at the shocked patrons on the next table.

"What are you looking at?"

The men wearing the livery of Sir John Scrope of Bolton looked away and Philip scoffed at their timidity.

"I am to give you this," Shelby trembled, placing the purse on the table.

"Did you shit yourself?" Philip grinned, turning his nose up.

The esquire shook his head but his blushing face told a different story. Philip took the purse and tipped the contents into his palm.

"Thank his lordship for me."

The boy nodded and tried to control his fear, while Philip downed the rest of his wine and dragged a cuff across his mouth.

"I fear Lord Warwick will regret his new allies," Philip said, standing up. "You'll find me here on the morrow."

Shelby watched him walk up to the innkeeper.

"A room," Philip demanded.

"Money," the innkeeper shouted above the noise.

"Take it out of that," Philip chirped, slamming the purse on the counter.

"You see what a little money can do, Mr Shelby!" Philip shouted. "It can turn a miserable bastard into a happy one."

Chapter 20

FOR A WEEK Philip could do nothing but watch events unfold around him. From the city wall he saw King Edward's slow approach and witnessed Warwick's mounting frustration, and he grinned when the king challenged Warwick to single combat and he refused. However, Philip's heart sank when the advent of Lancastrian reinforcements forced Edward to withdraw, yet he felt a pang of remorse for Warwick when his son-in-law, George, went over to his brother, the king.

Philip's spirits soared when the king brought his army back and challenged Warwick to settle their differences in battle, but the earl would not be tempted. Philip's euphoria waned next morning when Edward packed up and marched south. Fearing the king would take London; Warwick put his army on the road and went in pursuit, praying Somerset could hold out until he arrived.

Despising Warwick, the Duke of Somerset was only waiting for Queen Margaret to arrive from France, but when he learned Edward was on his way he hastily abandoned London. The Yorkists entered the city on the eleventh to a rousing welcome. The old king was dispatched back to the Tower and hundreds of relieved Yorkists spilled out of sanctuary to greet their saviour.

To cap Warwick's frustration, he was told his brother, Archbishop Neville, had sought a pardon from Edward. There was some good news: Margaret of Anjou was expected within days and Thomas Fauconberg, the bastard son of Edward's dead uncle, Lord Fauconberg, was raising an army in Kent to support the Nevilles. Given time, Warwick would command an invincible force; but Edward dashed his plans by going on the offensive.

While Warwick's army tramped through St Albans, Philip, riding under guard, contemplated his chances of escaping. Before leaving Coventry, he begged his cousin to release him, but Exeter and Oxford advised against such a move. Not wishing to antagonise his new, though somewhat sceptic allies, Warwick denied his request and Philip found himself closely guarded.

As the Lancastrians marched to Barnet, mounted prickers roving ahead of the column came pounding back and reported that Edward's vaward was close. When Philip heard this, he passed his guards a smug grin. The prospect of fighting against the king put the fear of God into many of Warwick's men and Philip saw more than a few lower their heads and discreetly cross their chests. Determined to join his liege lord, Philip knew he must escape.

Warwick sent a detachment on to Barnet and positioned the rest of his fifteen thousand men on high ground less than a mile from town. Exeter shifted to the left, Montague held the centre and Oxford moved to the right. The encampment was set up in the nearby village of Kitts End and before Warwick's pavilion was up, mounted couriers came and went with frenzied regularity. While foot-soldiers filtered into line, Philip remained in the custody of the Duke of Exeter. With four men-of-arms watching his every move, he sat on a boulder observing a cannon being set up across the St Albans Road.

The master gunner cursed and threatened his grunting,

perspiring minions as they dragged a huge red bombard into position.

"Why is your gun painted, master gunner?" Philip asked, curiously.

"To keep away the rust!" he growled, whacking a gunner on the back as he slipped in the mud. "Get up!"

"Huh," Philip sniffed, craning his neck for any sign of Edward's advance.

The sweating gunners suffered an unrelenting barrage of expletives and thumps from the master gunner, which made Philip chuckle.

Lord Warwick and a score of lords and knights rode to a nearby hillock and looked towards Barnet and Philip was able to observe the differences between the three most important nobles. Warwick looked cadaverous and his animated posturing and fluttering eyes were indications of the turmoil tearing his soul apart. His brother, Lord Montague, appeared vaguely quiet and aimlessly kicked at the ground with the toe of his boot, while the flashing eyes and aggressive posturing of the powerful Duke of Exeter showed his eagerness to fight. Philip tried to eavesdrop on their conversation but the acoustics were against him and as they left, the sound of hammering drew his attention back to the guns being brought up. Many were light pieces, easy to manoeuvre and quicker to load and fire than the bulky bombard which marked the centre of the battery. Quickly bored, Philip slid off the rock and strolled back to the main camp.

In and around the hamlet of Kitts End, tents of every shape, size and colour were going up and the rapid sound of mallet striking peg echoed over the fields. Baulking horses were dragged to the horse park, cooks cursed each other and coughed as they prepared food over densely smoking fires, and soldiers queued at forges, waiting to have their weapons sharpened. As he wandered through the noisy camp, Philip glanced over his shoulder and smirked impertinently at the guards shadowing him. With little to do, he walked from one end of the line to the other, mentally appraising the defences, counting troops and gauging their moral fibre.

With darkness descending, Warwick's advance detachment came running up the hill from Barnet, having been driven out by Edward's van. The alarm was sounded and Warwick ordered the fires doused and everyone to be ready. He also instructed the master gunner to fire his cannon at intervals throughout the night. This pointless tactic not only kept the Yorkists awake but Warwick's men as well.

Philip deliberately worked his guards hard, walking them from Enfield Chase on the left over to the St Albans Road and back again. During his progress, he would stop and chat with several acquaintances, which only infuriated his flustered escort. Finally he found a dry, if dangerous, spot under a powder wagon and lay down to sleep. Shutting his eyes, he tried hard to ignore the odour of sweat, smoke and horse shit permeating the air. Opening his eyes, he peeped out and grinned when he saw the guards still there. Folding his arms over his chest, he shifted his head to make himself comfortable and dozed off.

A ventenar bellowing at some unfortunate wretch woke Philip and he crawled out from under the wagon, groaning and coughing. Straightening up, he stomped around to rid his joints of arthritic stiffness.

"Gentlemen," he sniffed, addressing the guards.

Snorting mucus back into his throat he spat it out and shivered uncontrollably from the sharp chill in the air.

"What o' clock is it?" he asked, the boom of a gun clearing his fuzzy head.

"Nigh on midnight," one of the guards obliged.

Scratching his shoulder, Philip ambled towards the torch-lit front line, shadowed by his guards.

Near Exeter's position, he noted the weariness on the faces of his escort and knew it was time to go. Suddenly Philip found himself confronted by the Duke of Exeter, who loomed out of the darkness accompanied by several knights. One of the duke's companions lifted his lantern and shone it into Philip's face.

"Where are you going?" Exeter boomed.

Philip nodded curtly at the towering nobleman whose vindictive hatred for the Nevilles now flashed intensely from his dark eyes.

"Why is this, this spy at liberty?" he demanded, pointing at Philip. "Put him in chains, at once"

Despite being married to King Edward's sister Anne, Exeter was a staunch Lancastrian.

"Do you hear me?" he barked, striking his fists together.

"Yes, your Grace," the guards cringed, bowing apologetically before pushing Philip on.

"What's up with him?" Philip scoffed.

"He's been like this since he found his wife was being bedded by another… Now move."

"I need to take a piss," Philip groaned, holding his balls.

"Then piss."

"Not here," he growled, nudging his chin at an embankment topped by a hedge. "There."

The guards lit several torches from a fire and escorted him to the embankment on the far side of the Great North Road, which circled Enfield Chase. When he reached the bank, Philip unhooked his tunic ready to lower his hose.

"I have to shit as well."

One of the guards pushed his torch forward.

"You want to watch?" Philip snapped. "Grab some leaves and I'll let you wipe my arse."

"Make haste," one of them hissed angrily, hinting for his companions to turn their backs.

Plucking a handful of wet leaves Philip went through the motions, and then he was gone. Scrambling up the bank on all fours he dived through the hawthorn hedge, somersaulted out the other side and landed awkwardly.

"Where did he go?" one of the escort hissed.

"We'd better find him or we'll lose our 'eads."

Philip remained face down in the mud holding his breath as flaming torches appeared above the hedge. It was now that he felt stinging pain prickling his face and hands, caused by lacerations received when he propelled himself through the hedge.

"There!"

Philip lay still as flickering orange flames bobbed along the embankment before disappearing. Rising slowly, he dodged and ducked his way blindly down to Barnet. The sound of his own heavy breathing covered the rustling of the long grass as he stumbled on until he blundered into a group of archers. Believing them to be Exeter's men, he froze.

"Who the ell er you?"

Alarmed by his sudden appearance, the bowmen stood up and moved cautiously around him, deliberately drawing their swords.

"Ee's a spy."

"Slit is throat –"

"Wait!" Philip gasped, thrusting a hand out as he tried to think.

"I'll fetch his grace," someone suggested, when a loud discharge from one of Warwick's cannon increased his anxiety.

"His grace?" Philip panted, his heart thumping against his chest.

"The king's brother."

"Praise God," he gasped, dabbing perspiration from his scratched face. "I am Philip Neville, cousin to his grace."

"Take him to *his cousin*," a guard said suspiciously.

The Yorkist archers marched Philip to Richard of Gloucester.

After initially driving Warwick's men out of Barnet, Edward divided his army into three wards and advanced quietly through the darkness, to take up positions as close to the enemy as they could without being seen. Halting three hundred paces from the Lancastrian line, King Edward ordered complete silence and prohibited fires to be lit under pain of death. Unaware the Yorkists were so near, Warwick's artillery continued firing, aiming at where they assumed Edward's army was camped, but most of the gun stones flew harmlessly overhead.

The archers took Philip to a torch-lit marquee and led him inside.

"Hello!" the young Duke of Gloucester said, amused to see his cousin alive.

Philip's eyes adjusted to the faint light of a candle guttering on the table, and gave the young Duke's features a sallow, ghostly hue.

"Your Grace," he said, observing shadowy movement near the back of the pavilion.

"How did you get here?" someone asked.

Philip thought he knew the voice and peered into the darkness, but couldn't be certain.

"He's Warwick's man –" another warned.

"Enough," Gloucester cut them off.

"I was a prisoner of Lord Warwick's but I got away," Philip revealed. "I have information that will help the king win his battle."

"What information?" Anthony Woodville, 2nd Lord Rivers since his father's execution asked, the deep jousting scars on his face revealed by the pale light.

"What I have to say is for the king's ears only," Philip insisted.

"Then tell your king what you have to say," Edward demanded, stepping into the light.

"Your Grace," Philip smiled, bowing awkwardly.

"When you failed to return I feared for your life," Edward announced. "'Tis good to see you, I need every loyal man I can get... Come."

Philip joined the king and his commanders near the back of the pavilion as several smoky lanterns were held over a sketch of the area around Barnet.

"Tell me what I need to know," Edward said, while his lords shuffled in closer and leaned over the table. "This chart makes no sense."

"Your Grace, Lord Warwick has chosen his position well," Philip began, "but he trusts Exeter not a jot. If you offer him the chance he will disband his army."

As Edward pondered Philip's words, his brother George feared he might heed their cousin's advice.

"My Lord you must not –" he objected.

"You say this?" Edward gasped, "You whom I have forgiven so much?"

The Duke of Clarence sheepishly edged back out of the light and Gloucester yelped as hot wax dripped on his hand from the candle he held.

"How does his line stand?" Lord Rivers lisped, as Richard angrily threw the candle to the ground.

"They occupy this ridge... Oxford is here," Philip explained, pointing to the area left of the St Albans Road. "Montague holds the centre," he added, waving a finger over Kitts End. And Exeter is to his left."

"And Richard commands the reserve?" Edward said contemplatively.

"Yes, sire."

"They have much ordnance?" John Lord Howard commented, the loud bang of a cannon prompting his interjection.

"They have guns spread along their entire line, my Lord."

"Your Grace, do you trust this information?" Ralph Hastings intervened.

"I thought you were in sanctuary," Philip scoffed, "my Lord."

"Enough," Edward hissed. "I have no reason to doubt my cousin."

Gloucester licked the reddening skin on his hand and raised his eyebrows at Philip.

"What is their strength?" Edward asked, scrutinizing the map.

"They number some fifteen thousand?" Philip guessed.

"We hear he commands almost thirty," Edward mused, rubbing his chin.

"An exaggeration, sire."

A brief silence filled the tent and Edward pointed to the map and spoke to his young brother.

"Richard, your men will face our dear brother-in-law, Exeter."

"I look forward to it," the eighteen-year-old responded gleefully.

"Will?" he said, addressing Hastings. "You face Oxford… here."

Hastings nodded and glanced at his brother Ralph.

"I'll take on Montague," he revealed. "George…?"

"Sire?" his sulking brother chirped up.

"You will be at my side."

He responded with a disappointed huff.

"Where I can keep an eye on you," Edward added. "My Lords, we attack at dawn… To your beds, gentlemen."

The assembled nobles bowed and shuffled out, each with their own thoughts and concerns.

"Brother?" Edward said, tapping Richard's shoulder.

"Sire?"

"Reunite our cousin with his men."

"They're here?" Philip asked, surprised.

"Yes, tomorrow you fight with Richard...and may God grant us victory."

Gloucester motioned to one of his esquires.

"Your Grace?"

"Take this knight to the Scot who fleeced you yesterday."

"Yes sire," the teenager frowned, "This way, my Lord."

The esquire led Philip down a muddy path through creaking trees and scrubby brush. With no fires allowed, only an occasional shaft of moonlight, piercing the cloud, helped them negotiate their way. They finally came to a halt and the esquire pointed at hundreds of dark shadows laying or sitting on the ground.

"You'll find your thieving Scot down there," The esquire said, walking away.

"Wait!" Philip hissed, but he had already been swallowed up by the darkness.

"Be silent," an alert centenar growled.

"I seek my retinue," he whispered, cupping a hand to his mouth.

"Who are you?"

"Sir Philip Neville."

The centenar thought for a moment and shook his head.

"Did they come from London with the king's brother?"

Philip nodded, but wasn't certain.

"Then they be over there," he said, pointing into the darkness to where the St Albans and Great North roads converge.

Philip zigzagged carefully through groups of slumbering soldiers and was cursed by those he stepped on. Despite Edward's order that no fires were to be lit, many of the soldiers huddled together around tiny lanterns, which gave off a weak, pale yellow light. Philip pulled off hats and examined faces, but saw no one he recognised.

"Master?"

The familiar Scottish twang brought a smile to his face.

"Arbroth?"

"Aye, mah lord, 'tis me."

"Good to see you," he said. "Where are the others?"

"Here, and every one of 'em drunk," Arbroth grinned, pointing to a circle of sleeping forms. "We knew ye'd come and have brought yer armour and horses, but there's no' much food."

Several men stirred beneath their blankets and carped at the disturbance.

"Shad ap," one of them groaned.

"Damned ye –" Arbroth countered.

"Leave them be," Philip said.

"We thought tha worst," Arbroth revealed, grabbing a blanket and finding a place for Philip to lie down. "Here."

"Me too," Philip yawned, curling up inside his blanket on the damp grass.

"We have your armour, my Lord," his page confirmed, edging up on one elbow.

"Good boy," Philip smiled.

Chapter 21

HARNESSED IN PLATE armour and wearing a linen tabard bearing the king's colours over the breastplate, Philip Neville stood alone, several feet in front of his men. The dense, ground-hugging fog that had rolled in overnight exaggerated his isolation and heightened his awareness. With his visor open he breathed softly and listened, but there was no sound; even nature seemed to be sleeping this morning. To alleviate the dryness in his mouth, he tried to generate spittle, and the desire to run became overpowering.

The cold, moist air gave that time just before night turns to day an eerie, indistinct quality. With dawn breaking through the dark grey sky, the shadows behind him began to take on form and he soon heard whispered words passing between the men.

Philip woke an hour before sunrise and after a shared breakfast with his cousin Richard, he returned to his own retainers. Once armoured, Philip addressed his company, regretting the time they had been apart but praising their constancy. He told them to do their duty and promised much plunder when the fighting was done. Each man then withdrew into his own thoughts, some praying for protection, others for a quick death.

Drawing his blade from its scabbard, Philip kissed the crossbar.

"Take your men to the right, my Lord," a grave-voiced esquire advised.

"I can barely see my hand," Philip commented, looking down at the splayed steel fingers of his gauntlet.

"It hides our weakness; you'll find a space in the line."

Philip sent his page to the rear and led his twelve retainers in the direction of the low embankment, between Enfield Chase and Hadley Green. Philip's men-at-arms wore a mix of armour salvaged from old battlefields, while his archers sported a quilted brigadine and sallet.

"My Lord, I have a strange premonition of doom," Ashley Dean moaned, blinking nervously as one of Warwick's cannon boomed.

"Stay close," Philip urged, as an unseen gun-stone whistled over his head.

"I can't stop shaking."

"You'll do good," Philip said encouragingly, hinting for his Scot to watch the lad.

Arbroth passed the teenager a paternal wink while securing a red, painted sallet to his own head.

"Put your men in here, sir," a sergeant offered, forcing open the line, "Make way here!"

"Philip nodded his gratitude and hurried his men into the gap.

"Archers ten paces forward," the sergeant commanded, muffling his voice before turning to Philip. "Sir Richard Ratcliffe is to your right, my Lord."

Philip's archers unsheathed their bows and moved out, only to be consumed by the mist. Once his men-at-arms were in position, Philip took several steps forward until he stood alone between the archers and the main line.

"See anything?" a knight asked, hiccupping from an excess of wine and grimacing at the sour bile burning his stomach as he came up beside Philip.

"Nothing."

The doom-like quality of the mist, thickened by dark layers of gun smoke persuaded Philip to close his visor.

"By the saints!" he gasped, as the inebriated knight at his side was thrown violently backwards by an arrow slamming into his exposed face.

Sensing Edward's army was closer than he anticipated, the Earl of Warwick had ordered his bowmen to advance and shoot into the mist.

"Watch out!" a Yorkist archer yelled, his stark warning relayed worryingly up and down the line.

The shock of unseen arrows whizzing out of the darkness, to hit and bounce off his armour, frayed Philip's nerves. Fortunately, they were mostly broadhead arrows, deadly against brigadines but ineffective against plate armour. Philip knew this was not going to be like other battles he had fought. At St Albans, Towton and Hedgeley Moor he could see his enemy; today he couldn't even hear him.

"Don't run," he told himself.

Boys carrying sheaves of arrows now flitted past him on their way to re-supply the archers.

"Notch… aim… loose!"

This order given by the Yorkist captains to their bowmen was reassuring, yet Philip sought protection from a higher source.

"*Mea culpa, ideo precor beatem mariam simper virgini et te pater orare pro me ad dominus deum nostrum…*," he prayed.

"No quarter!" someone shouted, echoing Edward's order to take no prisoners.

"Amen," Philip hissed.

The disjointed blare of Yorkist trumpets was followed by the fire of their artillery and the crack, crack of Burgundian hand-guns.

"Forward!"

The command froze the blood in Philip's veins and every nerve in his body tingled with anticipation.

"God help me," he groaned, crossing his chest, as the rest of the army came up on either side of him.

Without waiting for the artillery to cease firing, the Yorkist men-at-arms advanced into the mist and through their own archers. With sword in hand, Philip tramped through the wet grass and waist-high gorse until he saw wraith-like figures moving about in the clammy whiteness ahead. Stumbling over a crumpled body, he looked up and spotted someone pounding towards him out of the fog. Instinctively raising his sword, he parried the blow from a soldier wearing Exeter's red and white livery.

"Shit!" he grunted, deflecting the strike and slashing at his opponent's elbow. "Take that."

The billman screamed and disappeared back into the smoky miasma and Philip watched in disgust as a dozen terrified Yorkist soldiers dropped their weapons and broke.

"Come back, you dogs!" he bellowed, stopping several and punching them back into the fight. "Stand your ground, God-damn you!"

"King Henry!" Warwick's army chanted in unison. "King Henry."

"God is our right!" Edward's men countered with competitive verve.

"Look to your front!" someone warned, and the two armies blundered into each other with a loud clatter of arms and armour.

Intoxicated at the prospect of slaughter, Philip's fear vanished and with a sense of invincibility he hacked away at Exeter's retainers. His sword opened arteries, smashed limbs and spilt entrails; yelling at the top of his lungs encouraged his bloodlust and blotted out the crack of breaking bones.

"Sweet Jesus," he coughed, sustaining an unexpected blow to the head.

Fortunately, the padding in his helm absorbed most of the impact but he was momentarily stunned and blood dripped from his nose. With his ears ringing, he staggered backwards.

"Fuck!" he gasped, lifting his visor to wipe stinging sweat from his eyes, "Oh shit."

Returning to the fray, Philip used not only his sword as a weapon but his head, shoulders, fists and feet.

The loud clanging of weapons and clatter of armour blended with agonising screams of wounded and dying men, and the cold, inert fog added to the chaos. Glancing to his right, Philip briefly spotted the embankment through the mist and knew the Yorkists were gaining ground.

The rich, meaty smell of freshly spilt blood fuelled Philip's killing frenzy and he became insensitive to all pleas for mercy. Setting his sights on an opponent armed with a battle-axe, he taunted him, until he lumbered forward, swinging his axe. Philip dodged the blow and countered with an upward thrust of his sword. The point caught his opponent under the armpit but the strike was weak and the mail gusset deflected the attempt. Side-stepping, the Lancastrian swung his weapon in from the side and the heavy head struck the steel skirt protecting Philip's abdomen. His armour absorbed the blow but threw him off balance; fortunately, the axe-man went down, brutally killed by one of Ratcliffe's men.

"You cunt!" Philip cursed, as traumatising pain shot through both hips. "Bastard…" he groaned, stomping on the dead man's face before limping away. "Ohh, by God's blood –"

Fearing his hip might be broken, Philip gingerly made his way to a tree and eased his agony by resting against the trunk and raising and lowering his leg until the throbbing subsided to a bearable level. Bursting to urinate he suddenly let go and grimaced at the sensation of warm piss running down his leg and into his shoes. Grateful his thigh was still in one piece, Philip walked back to the din and anarchy of battle. Stepping over mangled bodies and pools of bloody entrails, he made his way to the front.

The Duke of Gloucester and his banneret appeared out of the mist, his frayed red and blue, swallow-tailed standard drooping in the listless air, its silver rose and boar concealed in the folds.

"Your Grace?" Philip said, recognising his cousin despite his bloody armour. "Are you wounded?"

"It is not *my* blood…" Richard laughed hysterically, opening his visor to reveal a face flushed with a lust for war. "We're pushing them back on their own camp. If we can break their flank, the day will be ours."

"Yes sire," Philip nodded, infected by his enthusiasm.

"Forward!" The duke insisted, pointing his sword at the enemy. "Everyone… forward."

On the Yorkist left the Earl of Oxford had smashed through Hastings' line, but instead of turning in against the centre, he pursued the fugitives down to Barnet and beyond. Fortunately for Edward, the fog masked this disaster and the rest of the army fought on unaware.

The pressure on his left, Oxford's disappearance and the lingering mist forced Warwick's line to swing from east-west to northeast-southwest, exposing his camp at Kitts End. During a mutually agreed lull in the fighting – to enable both sides to catch their breath and remove some of the dead and wounded – Philip spoke to his Scot.

"Any of our men hurt?"

Arbroth shrugged his shoulders.

"Where's Ashley?" Philip blew, every muscle throbbing.

"Back there," he affirmed, pointing to the rear. "Tha laddie's lost his nerve."

"Let's finish it," Philip panted, as trumpets announced the truce was over.

Booting a bloody, dismembered limb like a football, he saw a bemused swordsman standing motionless in the fog. Wearing only a sallet, Philip saw an easy kill and readied himself. Suddenly the Lancastrian appeared to snap out of his confusion and charged. His sword thwacked Philip's shoulder with a loud clang and skewed off the pauldron. Before he could recover, Philip slashed at his midriff. Staggering to a halt the swordsman dropped to his knees and yelled desperately as his intestines burst out of the tear in his stomach.

The vile stench steaming off the twisted entrails permeated Philip's visor and he retched. Turning aside, he fumbled to open his visor but the vomit was already gushing out of his mouth. A disgusting mix of semi-digested food and stomach fluids splattered the inside of his sallet and he blindly tripped out of line, thumping the visor up.

"Fuck!" he choked, snorting and spitting.

Slipping on the damp grass, he fell heavily and as he went down, the Yorkist line buckled under pressure and Philip found himself under a pile of tumbling soldiers.

"Goddamn it!" he shouted, as his visor was kicked closed and he was pummelled mercilessly by a clutch of Lancastrians who had broken through.

Drawing his elbows in, Philip tried to protect himself, but when a boot stomped on his helm he knew he was in trouble.

"Help me!" he screamed, as his head was pounded and he remembered St Albans.

Alerted by the desperate cry, Arbroth launched himself at the three men attacking his master.

"Get off him, ye English bastaaaards!" he roared, slashing away with sword and dagger. "Ah'll slit yer throats!"

Several Yorkist men-at-arms joined in and Philip found

himself being kicked and trodden on by friend and foe as they fought over him.

"Sweet Jesus!" he spat, grateful for his armour.

Suddenly the word 'treason' echoed loud and clear and the momentum of battle slowed.

Using his knees and elbows, Philip forced himself up and pulled a davit of grass from his visor, while Arbroth and his companions finished off the assailants. The harrowing experience sent Philip into a fit of trembling and it took a moment for him to compose himself.

"We are betrayed!"

The warning rippled along the Lancastrian line and men on both sides looked for the source.

Sir Richard Ratcliffe, his armour dented and bloodied, pointed to the enemy.

"There!" he yelled, excitedly.

Exeter's men hesitated and looked at each other in fearful bewilderment.

The cry of treason went out after the Earl of Oxford returned unexpectedly with part of his command. During his absence the Lancastrian alignment had changed dramatically and Oxford unwittingly rode to where he assumed Warwick's right was. In the fog Oxford's star and streamers banner was mistaken for Edward's sun and streamers. Believing they were being flanked, Warwick's archers loosed a volley at Oxford's men. Before the mistake could be rectified, shouts of betrayal rent the air and Oxford's men broke. Encouraged by the hesitation in the Lancastrian line, Edward's army released its pent-up emotion in one uncoordinated yell and charged.

"My Lord!" one of Gloucester's knights called out.

Philip raised his visor and pointed to himself.

"Me?"

The knight hobbled over and revealed his face.

"Roby?" Philip said, surprised to see his old esquire. "Are you hurt?" he exclaimed, noting Harrington's limp.

"A horse fell on me… I fear my leg is broken."

"You and horses," Philip tutted.

"Lord Warwick's life is to be spared."

"Praise God," Philip cried.

Harrington limped away, and Philip threw himself back into the fray with one purpose: to kill as many of the enemy as possible.

"His grace is down!" one of Exeter's retainers yelled.

This exclamation and the dissipating mist further panicked Warwick's demoralised army, and the men in Gloucester's Battle, sensing victory, took full advantage.

"Die!" Philip screamed, using the scent-bottle pommel of his sword to knock out an opponent's teeth, "You shit-arse."

Slapping a hand to his mouth the injured man tried vainly to staunch the blood staining his jack.

"Get out of the way!" Philip spat, kicking him aside, the blood pumping through his veins amplifying the rapid beating of his own heart.

"No prisoners!" Ratcliffe reminded him.

Philip heard nothing as he continued to cut, slash and stab.

Gloucester's men pressed on, killing anyone in their way. Philip raised his visor to spit but caught a herald watching him and drew it down before moving on. Spotting Warwick's great banner, he hurried to keep up with those converging on the enemy camp.

Forcing himself on, Philip tried hard to reach his cousin first. Joining up with several of his own retainers, he led them through the enemy baggage park, ignoring frenzied clusters of archers, who were dragging Lancastrians from hiding places and slaughtering them. The badly wounded had their throats cut; others were forced to their knees and executed with a blow to the head.

"Where is he?" Philip yelled, looking around as his helmet was removed.

"My Lord!" one of his men-at-arms cried, pointing to a great oak tree in the middle of the baggage park, its lowest branches brushing the ground.

Free of the constrictive sallet and its bloody, vomit-tainted lining, Philip gulped in fresh air and wiped his flushed face.

"Who are those people?" he questioned, seeing a dozen soldiers milling around the oak.

"Lord Cromwell's men," Arbroth answered. "Mah lord!" he replied, pointing at Warwick's richly embroidered tabard on the ground.

"Get away from there!" Philip bellowed, staggering through the muddy grass as fast as his weary legs could go.

The scavengers snatched what they could and scattered.

"Oh, cousin," Philip panted, coming upon Richard's partly-armoured corpse.

Slumping to his knees, his eyes teared up and his heart was fit to burst.

By taking his reserve to help Exeter, Warwick tried to stem the rout, for a while his presence helped, but in the centre his brother John came under increasing pressure. The situation went from bad to worse and Warwick fled. Reaching the horse park he attempted to mount but exhaustion had taken its toll and he was caught by Cromwell's men and dragged to the ground. Maddened by the death of their lord, Cromwell's retainers butchered the Earl and stripped his body of armour and jewels.

"Look what these curs have done," Philip groaned, ignoring the stink of fear-discharged piss.

Warwick had been stabbed in the face and neck, and once his ornate breastplate was removed, a dagger was plunged deep into his heart.

"Lord Warwick is to be taken alive!" one of the king's men yelled to anyone within hearing.

"Too late," Philip muttered. "Find me something to wash his face with," he snarled, closing his cousin's glazed eyes.

"Mah lord," Arbroth responded, handing him a rag.

Dabbing the cloth in the morning dew Philip wiped the blood from Richard's forehead and cheeks.

"Oh, tha dirty swine have killed his little dooggy," Arbroth exclaimed, pointing to the butchered remains of Warwick's faithful hound Mongo, lying in the long grass close by.

"Why did you betray us for one who cares not a fig for your sacrifice?" Philip lamented, examining Richard's injuries and spotting his mangled, bloody hand. "They've cut off his finger and taken his father's ring."

Crossing his chest, Philip leaned over the body, kissed Warwick's still warm lips and laid the rag over his face.

"Stay with him," he told Arbroth.

The Scot frowned in disappointment.

"You'll get your share," Philip hissed, as he struggled to his feet.

"The King!" someone announced.

Accompanied by his brother George, nursing a head wound, and a sombre Lord Hastings, Edward approached the tree. Towering above everyone, his silver armour gilded with gold, dented and bloodied, and his quartered royal tabard torn. Edward was the very embodiment of a warrior king.

"Your Grace," Philip bowed, as the church bells down in Monken Hadley chimed in celebration of Christ's resurrection.

Sheathing his sword, Edward looked sadly down at Warwick's body and Philip bowed and took a step back.

"It grieves me to see my poor cousin like this," Edward groaned, tracing a cross on his chest. "Who is responsible?"

"Lord Cromwell's men," Philip retorted angrily.

"Hang every mother's son –" Clarence suggested, outraged at the sight of his father-in-law lying in the dirt.

"Have a care, brother," Edward cautioned.

"Sir Humphrey is dead, sire," One of the royal heralds intruded, glancing at his list and pointing to the name 'Sir Humphrey Bouchier, Lord Cromwell' written in the deceased column. "Um, your Grace?" he added reluctantly.

"Well?"

"I fear Lord Montague's name will soon be added to my list."

Philip cringed at the news and his head drooped.

"'Tis said he wore your colours beneath his clothes and was about to betray his brother," the herald informed the king.

"He would not do such a thing," Philip dared, glaring at the herald.

"I know you loved them both, as I did, but it is finished now. Richard's heart was ruled by vanity and he has paid the price, though I would give a king's ransom for it not to have ended so…" Edward sighed, looking at the sky as a light drizzle began to fall. "This rain will wash away all the blood spilt here this day."

The eighteen-year-old Duke of Gloucester, bleeding from a gash on the forehead, joined his brothers and was shocked at the butchered remains of his kinsman.

"Do we have prisoners, worth a ransom?" Edward asked.

"A few, sire," Richard answered, his tattered tabard and blood-splashed face evidence of his bravery.

"Send them to London, with yokes about their necks."

"Your Grace?" Hastings intervened, embarrassed by his own poor performance.

"What is it, Will?" Edward asked intolerantly.

"Henry has gone."

Edward closed his eyes and groaned out of frustration.

When Warwick departed from London back in March to

pursue Edward, he left the old king behind. Having entered London a month later, Edward removed the crown from Henry's head and sent him to the Tower. Rather than risk an attempt by those Lancastrians hiding in the city to free Henry, Edward took him to Barnet, where he was rescued by Oxford when he broke Hastings' left flank.

"I will ride back to London," Edward said, addressing his chamberlain. "Rest the army here for a day and then disperse the men to their homes."

"Yes, sire."

"You will stay here," Edward told Philip. "Find Montague's remains and bring them both to London. They shall be laid on the pavement outside St Paul's, for all to see that the mighty Earl of Warwick is truly dead... I want no more rebellion."

"Your Grace," Hastings cut in, "Somerset and Margaret are still at large; we must raise a new army and crush them immediately."

"Sire!"

"Jack," Edward beamed, looking around and spotting his mud-splattered friend Sir John Howard. "You look like you've been run over by an elephant."

Though much older than Edward, John Howard was one of his most loyal servants; he was fair of face with greying hair, and had a passion for fighting.

"I fell in a ditch, sire," he gasped, his voice and gestures excitable, "but I have the old king."

"Is he in good health?"

"Yes, your Grace," Howard assured him. "He keeps repeating that he warned Lord Warwick not to fight his battle on such a holy day."

"What of Oxford and the other traitors?"

"Exeter is dead; the rest have fled."

"Your Grace," the portly Sir Edmund Grey interrupted, sweat coursing down his grimy face as he joined the king.

"Sir Edmund?"

"Sire," he puffed, indicating a party of horse. "Your escort."

"Very well," Edward said, sheathing his sword. "Come, gentlemen."

Grey passed Philip a grudging nod of recognition and he reciprocated with a curt nod. Ten years ago, on the eve of Towton, Philip insulted Sir Edmund and refused to apologise and he never forgot it.

As the king and his companions rode away, Philip glowered at Sir Edmund.

"Fat turd," he muttered before sending Arbroth to secure a wagon for Lord Warwick's body, then dispersed his men to locate Montague. "You'll find him where the fighting was fiercest!" Philip called after them, pointing in the direction of the St Albans road.

"I'll fetch the horses?" His esquire said, his staring eyes having witnessed such unspeakable acts of inhumanity that his young mind was unable to shut them out, and he fled the field.

Ashley looked to have aged ten years in the last few hours, but he was not alone. Many a man picked his way aimlessly over the cluttered field, vomiting at the ghastly sights, or stared into space, traumatised by the magnitude of the slaughter.

While his ashamed esquire slouched off to the Yorkist horse park near Monken Hadley, Philip waited for his men to return. He was exhausted, his mouth had a bitter tinge and his jaw ached from unconsciously grinding his teeth during the intense fighting. Removing his gauntlets, he examined his helmet and huffed at the damage and vomit staining. When he looked up, he saw hundreds of soldiers returning from the enemy baggage park, staggering under the weight of so much plunder.

Philip watched as numerous priests came to the field, offering absolution to those who could pay, while heralds and their pursuivants booked the dead and wounded nobles. For Philip the saddest sight was the injured horses, some standing with a leg missing, others with horrific, gaping wounds, shrieking from pain and waiting for someone to come and put them out of their misery.

"Where did you find that?" he asked, catching sight of his Scot dragging a horse and cart.

Arbroth shrugged his shoulders.

Grateful for his ability to procure almost anything, Philip passed him a gratuitous smile.

"Here they come," Arbroth said, jerking his chin at the men stumbling through the drizzle carrying a body wrapped in a blanket.

"Put them in the cart…" Philip commanded, unable to look, "gently!"

"It is done," Arbroath finally announced.

Philip was distressed at the two bodies lying on the rough bed of the wagon and covered with a blanket, their stockinged feet exposed to the rain.

While they waited for the horses, Arbroth handed him a cup of wine.

"Here, mah lord," he said, unbuckling the strap of his own sallet. "Two of our people are missing."

"They'll turn up," Philip said confidently, downing the wine. "Aah," he shuddered. "Tastes like piss."

"The horses!" one of Philip's men-at-arms said, pointing.

"Right," he said, punching his breastplate, "help me out of this."

Once his armour was removed, Philip washed his scratched, bleeding, vomit-crusted face and dabbed his swollen eyes. Wearing only a damp, sweat-stained doublet and piss-stinking hose, he delicately mounted and rode to Barnet. Shivering from the severe pain in his thighs, he drew the woollen cloak close to his body and looked back. With the fog gone and rain falling heavier, he saw soldiers and locals scavenging the dead and wounded. Glancing up at the sky, he observed hundreds of birds circling overhead, drawn to the area by the scent of death. Soon dogs and pigs would come to feast on the carrion.

Chapter 22

NEWS OF A Yorkist disaster, spread by stragglers from Hastings' battle, drew a veil of despair over London, but when Edward arrived triumphant, the gold crown on his helmet glittering in the sunlight, gloom and ambiguity were replaced by euphoria. King Edward rode through cheering, grateful crowds to St Paul's, where he stopped and gave thanks to the Almighty for his victory. Philip Neville's solemn little convoy entered the city almost unnoticed the following day. At St Paul's, he had the bodies of Warwick and his brother carried inside and placed in crude coffins, despite the king's command they be left outside on the pavement. Six of his knights were sent by a forgiving King Edward to guard the remains while Philip and his weary men returned to his residence in the Strand.

"My head aches," he moaned, falling heavily into a chair and regretting it.

"Oh my," he gasped, closing his eyes to the pain in his head and rubbing his swollen thigh.

Arbroth disappeared and returned later with a poultice, which he handed to Philip.

"What's this?"

"'Tis one o' Lady Joan's cures."

"What's in it?" Philip scoffed, sniffing the bundle.

"Barley, betony, vervain and 'erbs, all boiled up."

"Huh," Philip sniffed, laying the poultice delicately on his throbbing head.

After a few hours rest, the pain subsided and he washed off the stink and blood from his bruised body before retiring to bed.

Charged with guarding his cousin's bodies, Philip returned to St Paul's next morning. Yawning deeply, he scrunched up his face, causing several of the scabbed over scratches to crack. Warwick and his brother lay in open coffins, their ghostly faces exhibited for all to see. The coffins rested on trestles in the Crossing, beneath the tower, where the nave and quire converge with the North and South Transepts. The area was illuminated by hundreds of candles and a dozen priests sang a Mass for the souls of the two brothers. Their bodies would remain on show for two days before being sent to Bisham Abbey for internment.

As he looked desolately at Richard's pallid and slashed face, Philip remembered the years growing up with the four Neville brothers. A slight smile raised the corners of his mouth as he recalled an incident when, as a young page, he hid in one of the stairwells of Middleham with Thomas, sniggering at the booming voice of Lord Salisbury threatening retribution on those responsible for adding salt to his wine. His thoughts flashed forward to the exciting days of the fourteen-fifties when he and John roamed across Yorkshire beating up Lord Percy's retainers. As he stared at his cousin lying in a roughly-hewn box, he massaged his chest to rid himself of the heart-ache.

The monotony of standing guard and watching lines of morbid spectators shuffle in to look at the body of the once mighty Earl of Warwick forced Philip to go off and explore the cathedral. Limping up the nave, he looked at the high-arched ceiling, an act that sent a sharp jolt shooting up his neck.

"Ouch," he groaned. "Son of a –"

Turning round near the west doors, he ambled back to the Crossing, rubbing his upper thigh. When he reached the Tower, which supported the massive spire, he walked into the quire and stopped at an elaborate Chapel next to the High Altar. Standing before the alabaster effigies of John of Gaunt and his first wife, Blanche, their hands pressed together in prayer, Philip gazed admiringly at the beautifully crafted tomb. The duke's head rested against a pillow, his feet on a lion, while his displayed lance, shield and helm reminded visitors of his achievements.

"You see what your legacy has done," Philip muttered, referring to Sir John's Beaufort's descendants. "Bastards all."

Stretching out his fingers, he touched the cold effigy of Blanche.

"You must not," a priest warned.

Surprised and embarrassed, Philip returned red-faced to the Crossing, where for the next five hours he stood in sombre repose.

Despite his great victory at Barnet, Edward believed Warwick's death would only strengthen the cause of Lancaster. From his network of spies he learned that Margaret had sailed into Weymouth, where she was waiting for Somerset and Devon to join her. With his troops fought out and disbanded, Edward ordered the raising of a new army.

Once the bodies of Warwick and his brother were removed to Bisham Abbey, Philip returned to his home.

"Mah lord," Arbroth announced, as he slouched in, "we are ordered tah Windsor."

"Windsor," he gasped. "For what purpose?"

"Tha king is raising a new army."

"So soon?"

"Aye?"

"We must rest," he groaned, rolling his eyes. "I don't mind

the fighting but we should celebrate our victory in the taverns, yet we are commanded to pray and fast."

"That'll be tha queen," Arbroth sniffed.

"Has Mathew come back?" Philip asked, referring to one of his archers who failed to return after Barnet.

"No… and he's no' with tha wounded," Arbroth confirmed. "He must be dead… Tha man would no' come home."

"Send his share to his family."

"They say Exeter survived and has taken sanctuary, but tha king'll soon have him oot o' there."

"We should have searched the battlefield and cut off his goddamned head," he scoffed. "I'm going out."

Arbroth knew Philip was off to Bankside.

"I'll be back, before curfew," he lied, shaking the apathy from his mind.

Philip rode his rouncey along the Strand, passing through Temple Bar and along Fleet Street and the closer he came to London Bridge the more he thought of what lay ahead.

"Mah lord?" someone called, intruding on his private thoughts.

"Oh God," he groaned, recognising the voice and reining his horse up near the west end of the busy Fleet Bridge. "What do you want?"

"We must go tah Windsor," Arbroth insisted, turning his nose up at the stench blowing off the river. "And we must go now."

"Why?" Philip growled, using rein and spur to control his restless horse.

Arbroth gave a brooding, silent warning against disobeying the king.

"We'll go tomorrow… tell them you could not find me."

"Ah cannah do it, mah lord," he whined, "'tis an order from tha king."

"Does anyone ever listen?" Philip huffed. "I need to... Oh, this is bollocks!"

"Mah lord?"

"Go!" Philip snapped, waving him away and circling his horse ready for the return journey. "Goddamn you," he snarled, the lustful image of Portia's nakedness withering into disappointment. "Get out of the way," he barked, forcing his horse through irate pedestrians. "Codheads."

After celebrating St George's day with a great feast, King Edward was ready to leave Windsor Castle for what he hoped would be the final confrontation. In and around Windsor's Lower Bailey, several thousand soldiers jostled for space alongside carters, armourers, pavilioneers, cooks, minstrels, barbers and the numerous other services needed to sustain an army on the march. There was also an artillery train, spare horses, supply wagons, camp followers and mobile forges. Assembled in the upper Bailey waiting for the king were his lords, knights and esquires.

It had taken Philip two days to collect his retainers, horses and equipment and ride through lashing rain to Windsor. For the next four days he performed his knightly duties while his armourer oiled and buffed the armour and the horses were roughshod.

On the cold, damp morning of 24 April, Edward and his brothers attended a private Mass in the Royal Chapel while his lords and knights waited patiently. Relaxing in the saddle, Philip was contemplating the forthcoming campaign when his thoughts were interrupted by Thomas Vaughan. Time had not been kind to poor Sir Thomas; his wife had passed away after a long illness and he was looking all of his sixty years. His short beard had turned grey and his leathery, lined features seemed painfully gaunt, yet he still exuded an aura of optimism. Shortly after the Smithfield tournament, Philip had fallen out with the Welshman over his support for the

Woodvilles, and the last time they spoke, he gave Thomas a choice: him or them. Thomas' refusal to choose between them was enough.

"Philip?" Thomas chirped, edging his horse up next to Clovis and squinting at the leaden sky.

"Thomas," he sniffed guardedly.

"The rain is holding, but it will not last" Vaughan commented. "I see the king's chamberlain is here... and Sir William Stanley," he added, acknowledging both men with a courteous nod.

Philip let out a disapproving murmur and flicked the reins loosely over his palfrey's twitching ears and forelock. As knights-of-the-body, both men wore the king's murrey and blue livery, yet Thomas had received ample reward for his service. He had been Treasurer of the king's Chamber and an ambassador in the negotiations for the marriage of Edward's sister to the Duke of Burgundy. Philip received money to rebuild his manors but his star had not risen beyond that of royal bodyguard.

"I hope this will be the last fight," Thomas announced.

"Well I don't," Philip responded boorishly. "I've been a soldier these twenty summers, I know nothing else –"

"I have fought on so many fields I cannot rid myself of the stench of death, it follows me everywhere. I have lived three score years and my poor wife is dead, my back aches relentlessly and I cannot close my eyes without seeing the faces of those I have killed."

"This war must go on until all our enemies are dead."

"What then?"

"There'll always be another war," Philip quipped with a caustic smirk.

"Why have you set yourself on such a destructive path?" Thomas asked, his tone laced with regret.

"I have a passion to wear the blue mantle of St George," Philip sighed.

"Why?"

"My father was murdered, his father before him was accused of treason in the Southampton plot, and my brother fought for Henry of Lancaster," Philip explained, touching his grandfather's ring beneath the leather riding glove. "If I can win the right to wear the blue mantle, all the wrongs done to my family will be righted."

Thomas shook his head.

"Gentlemen!" an usher interrupted, exiting the Royal Chapel. "Edward, by the Grace of God, King of England and France, and Lord of Ireland!"

As Edward walked out of the Chapel, pulling on his riding gloves, his beautiful caparisoned courser was run over for the Groom of the Stirrup to hold the strap ready for him. Sweeping back his long blue velvet cloak edged with fur, Edward hauled himself into the saddle while his nobles bowed their heads.

"Thank God," Philip muttered, nudging Clovis several paces forward, eager to get away from Thomas.

The King took his place at the front where he was joined by his banneret.

"Forward!" he commanded after a tense moment of silence.

The banneret shook the folds of the quartered royal banner loose and Edward watched it unfurl in the breeze. Crossing his chest, he led his lords and knights through the gateway north of the Great Tower and down into the lower Bailey. Minutes later the royal army rattled over the drawbridge and snaked its way west, beneath low, dark, forbidding clouds.

After ten days' hard marching, Edward managed to trap Queen Margaret in Tewkesbury with the Severn at her back. During the night of 3 May, the mood in the Yorkist camp, three miles away at Tredlington, was one of sober reflection, passionate praying or dreaded anticipation. With all the village buildings occupied, Philip sat under a hedge close to a roaring fire chatting with his retainers over cups of ale. Every man knew battle was imminent and mulled over his thoughts and fears. An order had been issued by the king that any noise would not be tolerated, the penalty for violation being forfeiture of armour for a noble and the loss of an ear for the common soldier. When one of Philip's men fell back and laughed raucously, he knocked him out with a pan to the kisser. Looking through the hypnotic flames, Philip noticed his esquire staring into the fire.

"What's up with him?"

"He's no been tha same since Barnet," Arbroth offered.

"Keep him out of it tomorrow."

"He'll forget soon enough," Arbroth replied, massaging his jaw.

"And what's wrong with you?"

"Every time ah fight ah break a tooth, at this rate ah'll have none left by Christmastide," he moaned, shaking his head and counting the remaining teeth with his tongue.

"Philip Neville?" a messenger whispered, approaching the group.

"Here," he answered, anticipating a reprimand for his noisy retainer.

"The king asks that you attend him."

Expecting to spend the night guarding his cousin, Philip snatched up his sword and followed the messenger.

"What does his grace want at such an hour?" he asked, the odour of damp grass tickling his nose.

The messenger said nothing as he led the way to a well-lit manor house.

Standing at the entrance was a guard who thrust his hand out to stop them.

"This knight is here at the king's behest," the messenger confirmed. "Step aside."

"He must leave his blade outside."

"Here," Philip sneered, unbuckling his belt and wrapping it around the scabbard. "Look after it."

The guard took the sword but before he could enter a voice from inside commanded him to wait. After a moment the door opened and Edward appeared wearing a long, plain woollen cloak, its hood drawn up over his head.

"Your Grace?" Philip bowed, perplexed.

"Cousin," Edward answered, coughing harshly in the damp air, "Walk with me."

Amused by Edward's attire, Philip snatched back his sword and buckled it around his waist.

The King and his cousin walked inconspicuously through the smoky encampment.

"Your height will give you away," Philip warned, confused by the disguise.

"I find sleep difficult before battle," Edward revealed, stooping to conceal his great height, "so I go over my plans in my head and try to put myself in my opponent's place."

"We will win the day, sire," Philip boasted. "I am certain of it."

"If it be God's will," Edward said. "My Lords are confident, but I want to know what the common soldier thinks, so I walk among them and listen in on their conversations."

"Why do you care what they think?" Philip sniffed, looking around at the thousands of sleeping forms huddled close to collapsing fires, some asleep others awake.

"Most of these men come fresh from the plough and tomorrow many will die for me."

"Stay!" a watchman commanded, stepping out from behind one of the wagons that circled the camp. "Give the watchword?"

"Step aside," Philip snarled. "This is the –"

"God and St George," Edward cut him off, keeping in the shadows. "The watchword is God and St George."

The sentinel stepped back and allowed them to continue.

"Get to your beds," the watchman commanded.

"We shall take impertinent impudent advice," Edward answered, moving on.

Coming across a soldier sitting alone before a smouldering fire massaging his bare feet, Edward stopped and looked at his sleeping comrades.

"Is it fear that keeps thee from thy blanket on such a cold night?" he asked, placing a comforting hand on the man's shoulder.

"Piss off," the bearded man-at-arms growled, glaring at Edward's hand until he withdrew it. "I've got an 'eadache if it's any of your business."

Philip made to chastise the soldier but Edward warned him off with a frown.

"Avoid strong drink and fish," he advised, "keep warm and your pain will ease."

The soldier rolled his eyes and shook his head.

"Where is your home?" Edward asked him.

"Devonshire," he growled. "'Ave marched the last three leagues without shoes."

"You have come a long way to fight for your king?"

"I was ordered by my Lord to march and if I die tomorrow who will feed my family – *the king*?"

"Buy a pair of boots," Edward said, handing the man a coin before walking on. "And tomorrow, fight well for me."

"Who's that?" the surprised soldier asked Philip, staring at the silver coin in his palm.

"The King, you knave," he hissed, hurrying after his liege lord.

Stopping near a flat-bedded wagon, Edward placed his foot

on a wheel hub and peered out into the black vagueness of the night. In the distance he saw an orange glow reflecting off the low cloud.

"Margaret's camp?" Philip wondered aloud, listening to the plop, plop of rainwater dripping from the trees after a recent downpour.

"Aye," Edward confirmed. "I have less than five thousand men," he added pensively, resting an elbow on his knee and leaning forward.

"We are used to being outnumbered and they are good men."

Edward pondered a moment.

"The day before the battle at Mortimers Cross, three suns appeared in the sky," he explained. "Being Candlemas, my army fell to its knees wringing their hands and wailing that the apparition was an ill omen. I chastised them for their defeatism and told them they were wrong, that it was a good sign, for the three suns represented the Holy Trinity, and confirmed God was with our cause. Their confidence was restored and we went on to win the day."

"And tomorrow we finish Margaret once and for all."

Stopping occasionally, the king chatted with any soldier who appeared troubled.

After walking completely around the camp, Edward bade his kinsman good night.

"Your men fight with Richard on the morrow, but you will not be with them," the king told Philip.

"Your Grace?" He gasped.

"Fear not," Edward smiled. "You will be on the hottest part of the field."

"I would rather be at your side."

"You will obey my command."

Philip bowed as Edward walked away, trying to guess the role he was to play in the forthcoming fight. On his way back,

Philip passed Will Hastings, his bony arms around two maidens, and nodded begrudgingly.

"Lucky bastard," Philip grouched, as he watched them enter the king's billet. "I hope you catch the French pox."

Saturday 4 May

Philip Neville stood beside his snorting courser on a thickly wooded hill, concealed amongst the trees of a Deer Park belonging to the monks of Tewkesbury Abbey. Careful not to reveal his position to the enemy, he watched King Edward's army forming up into three battles. Several horse lengths behind him were two hundred well mounted knights and men-at-arms. Sir Maurice Berkeley, commanding the detachment joined Philip as he studied the activity below.

"The ground is too wet," Berkeley commented, testing the spongy soil with his armoured foot

"It's worse down there," Philip said, pointing to a hedge at the bottom of the hill.

"Then we must be wary lest our horses become mired."

"Careful my Lord," Philip warned, looking up at the sky, "or the sun will strike armour and give our position away."

"I hope this works," Berkeley said ominously, edging forward for a better view of the two armies squaring up to each other below.

Philip stared hard at Berkeley's back and sneered at his lack of confidence.

The Yorkist army had been up since dawn and after absolution and breaking their fast, the knights, archers and men-at-arms listened to a passionate address by the king before setting off for Tewkesbury. Richard of Gloucester, commanding the vaward, approached the town as the Abbey bells tolled the hour of Prime. Margaret's Lancastrian army had taken up a strong position behind a series of thick hedges, running east to west along the southern end of Gaston Field. Their flanks were protected by two streams, the Swilgate on the left and Southwick Brook on the right. Edmund Beaufort, calling himself 'Duke of Somerset', commanded Margaret's forces and took personal charge of the right wing. The ground between the two armies was criss-crossed by muddy ditches and high hedges, and where the line was vulnerable the Lancastrians planted rows of sharpened stakes. Unable to cross the Severn, Margaret had no choice but to fight here.

Recovered from his Barnet wound, Gloucester led his men to the left and lined them up opposite Somerset. Edward took the centre, facing Sir John Wenlock and Hastings shifted over to the right, looking across at the Earl of Devon. The Yorkist artillery was spread amongst the three battles and the archers and hand-gunners were out front. Fearing an ambush, Edward dispatched two hundred of his best mounted men under Sir Maurice Berkeley, a red-headed knight with a high forehead and sickly complexion. This detachment rode along a hidden lane that led to the Deer Park, half a mile to the west. If no ambush was discovered there, Berkeley was to wait for an opportunity to strike any enemy formation that threatened his left flank. Before his cavalry rode away Edward told Philip to watch Berkeley.

A sharp bang from one of Edward's cannon echoed over the intervening space between the armies, breaking the tension and marking the opening of hostilities. The rest of the Yorkist artillery fired a disjointed salvo and gun-stones, varying in weight from three to three-hundred pounds, arched into the Lancastrian position. Hundreds of scared rabbits suddenly darted from their burrows and raced haphazardly across the fields. Thick, black gun smoke soon began to settle in the lanes and ditches, and after a period of threats and jeers from both sides, the Battle of Tewkesbury was under way.

Philip and his companions eagerly watched archers and hand-gunners shoot at each other.

"Look there," Philip exclaimed, his eyes tracing the trajectory of a gun-stone fired from a Yorkist bombard.

The huge limestone ball smashed into a tree near the Lancastrian centre, splintering it into nothing.

While Philip stood admiring the bombard's destructive power, a fellow knight edged his horse up and indicated movement behind Somerset's line.

"Cavalry?" Philip surmised, looking to where his companion pointed

Berkeley tugged at the bevor protecting his neck, exposing his prominent cheekbones.

"What are they up to?" he mused, a hint of sour wine on his breath.

From their vantage point Philip and Sir Maurice watched a large body of enemy cavalry trot into Lower Lode Lane and ride towards the Deer Park.

"They've seen us!" Berkeley panicked.

"Wait," Philip said, grabbing his arm.

Reaching a junction, the Lancastrian horse dog-legged into a second lane that took them away from the park.

"The King cannot see them," Berkeley surmised, "If they continue on their course, they'll pass beyond his left and hit him in the rear."

"Somerset is leading them," Philip smirked, spotting Beaufort's banner, a golden portcullis on a field of white. "Good."

"To horse, gentlemen," Berkeley commanded, spitting to remove the foul taste in his mouth.

"Here," Philip said, mounting and calling for an esquire to bring his lance.

Taking hold of the ten-foot-long, painted lance, he held it point up and waited for the order to charge. Leaning forward in the saddle, Berkeley watched Somerset lead his column to a bare hillock in Gloucester's rear and form his men in a double line.

"Why do we wait?" one of the knights complained.

Berkeley ignored the grumblings and patted his courser's neck.

"*My Lord*?" Philip hissed, incensed by the delay, but Berkeley would not be rushed.

Down below, a satisfied Somerset launched his attack against Gloucester. Having exposed themselves and taken far too long to line up, the Lancastrians gave Richard time to react.

Before leaving on his flanking manoeuvre, Somerset had issued orders for his centre battle to charge forward when he struck Edward's rear. Commanding this part of the line was Warwick's old friend, Sir John Wenlock, who for some reason did not move. His failure to advance allowed Gloucester to concentrate on Somerset and after a brief clash, he forced him to retreat towards the Deer Park. With a high thick hedge around the park, Berkeley knew if he charged too soon, his formation would break up before making contact. Philip failed to understand and thought Berkeley had missed the opportunity.

"Wait," Berkeley insisted, aggravated by Philip's intolerance.

"My Lord," he pled, thrusting a hand out dramatically as Somerset's horse broke into the park through gaps in the hedge. "There is the enemy!"

"Yes," Berkeley growled, slamming his visor down. "And now we shall attack him!"

Philip muttered a short prayer, crossed his chest, closed his visor and lowered his lance.

The Yorkist cavalry trotted slowly out of the woods and moved down the hill. Gripping his lance between vamplate and graper, Philip couched the weapon tightly under his right shoulder and leaned forward. Hotspur went from a trot to a half-gallop and a tingling warmth fuzzed Philip's senses. Moisture was sucked from his mouth and he felt light-headed. When he saw Somerset's men milling around in the muddy bottom, anticipation became so strong he could hear his own heart beating. The expectation of combat induced an emotional thrill that could only be released by a demonstrative yell which was taken up by the rest of Berkeley's men.

"Come on!" he roared, urging his fourteen hundred pound, chestnut courser into a full charge. "Kill every mother's son."

The sound of two hundred horses hammering downhill was akin to the low rumble of thunder and the ground trembled beneath the pounding hooves. Focusing his strength into the point of his lance, Philip urged his charger to even greater speed. The courser's dark mane streamed wildly, its ears stuck out and every muscle bulged. Somerset tried to meet the threat but many of the horses were mired in the mud.

With the bright sun reflecting off their armour, the York-ist cavalry smashed into Somerset's line and the effect was devastating. Lances splintered off plate armour and men and horses were bowled over and over each other. Unhorsed riders, unable to get clear, were crushed by the weight of Berkeley's warhorses and blood burst from ruptured arteries, staining the grass. Philip thrust his steel-tipped lance against the breastplate of an opponent, but it skidded off. Pulling his reins to the right, he circled his charger back in position. Looking up, he saw a mounted knight, his bassinet missing its visor. Levelling his lance, jabbing his spurs in Philip drove his excited courser forward.

"Die!" he screamed with a wide-eyed leer, ramming the tip of his spear into the knight's face. "Damn you!"

The point entered his opponent's mouth, shattered teeth and bone and burst out the back of his head. Lifted in the saddle, the knight was grotesquely impaled on the lance, his limbs flaying in the air. Unable to extract the weapon, Philip could only watch as it bent and broke with a sharp crack, splashing him with flesh and blood.

"Son of a whore!" he spat, tossing the broken lance away.

Though dead the knight stayed on his horse which galloped on, its lifeless rider wedged in the saddle. Philip was unable to prevent his own charger stomping on a screaming wounded man and the stink of his hot blood hit Hotspur's nostrils, causing the stallion to snort in terror and rear up onto its hind legs. Several wounded horses tumbled to the ground, their ear-piercing shrieks merging with the screams of men whose bones were crushed by flaying hooves, but Philip eventually brought his horse under control.

Catching sight of Edward's army surging toward the Lancastrian line, Philip drew his arming sword. Swinging his reins to the left, he rode to the aid of a colleague, only to see him cut down before he could reach him.

"Damn!" he shouted in frustration.

Attacked from two directions, Somerset's horse broke and fled and the fighting in the Deer Park petered out. Those Lancastrians who were captured quickly gave up a gauntlet or piece of armour as a sign of submission. Berkeley's success was carried on by Edward, who smashed through the Lancastrian barricades half a mile to the east. To keep the momentum, Berkeley urged his cavalry on and Philip rode his panting courser along the hedge, looking for a break. As the last of Somerset's horse disappeared through a hole in the enclosure, he nudged Hotspur towards the gap.

"Come on," he hissed, forcing his hesitant horse into the hedge.

Having negotiated the prickly barrier, Philip jumped him over a brook. On the far bank he fell in with a mass of Yorkist horse and foot which merged to pursue a part of the Lancastrian army fleeing through a meadow. Hemmed in by a high hedge on one side, and Southwick Brook on the other, the lush meadow soon became a slaughter pen. Looking to the right, Philip spotted a knight on foot he recognised from his dull armour and plodding gait.

"Thomas?" he called, drawing back on the reins and opening his visor.

Resting exhausted against a tree, the knight lifted his own visor to reveal flicking red eyes.

"They're finished!" Philip shouted, pushing his feet down in the stirrups and lifting his arse off the saddle.

"Yes…" Thomas Vaughan puffed, pointing wearily to the Avon. "We'll end it… there!"

"Take my horse?" Philip offered, concerned by Thomas' fatigue.

"No!" he coughed violently, shaking his head. "Go on…"

"Good luck to you," Philip sniffed, trotting away. "Run, you cod-heads!" he laughed, cantering towards the River Avon, slicing off an archer's hands at the wrist as he begged for his life.

Dropping the bloody blade to his side, Philip rode up to a billman tearing at his livery coat.

"Hello," he smiled, coldly.

The man spun around and the blood drained from his terrified face. Before he could speak Philip brought his sword up, cleaving his chin in two and cutting off part of his nose. The fugitive fell rasping and gurgling, his blood splashing the budding buttercups carpeting the meadow. Extending his sword arm out, Philip rode on, deliberately clipping the head, face or shoulders of fleeing Lancastrians. With every hit his heart-rate increased and he laughed at the sheer terror on their faces.

"Bollocks," he hissed, accidentally striking down one of Lord Hastings' men.

The weight of his warhorse knocked several of the enemy

into the blackthorn hedge that separated the meadow from Gaston Field. The sharp sound of bones snapping as Hotspur's iron hooves trampled the dead and dying was music to his ears. Reaching the Avon, Philip followed the narrow river until he came to the Abbey wall. Drawing up his blood-splattered courser at the Abbey's flour mills, he opened his visor and looked around. The constant wailing of dying and wounded men began to fray his nerves, but he was too tired to care. Dismounting, he examined Hotspur's bloody chest and forelegs and spoke sweetly in his ear.

"Easy, boy."

There were several superficial lacerations on the animal's neck, chest and flanks, and sweat steamed off into the air, but there were no serious injuries.

"You're good," he said, patting his neck. "We're both good."

Overwhelmed by sudden fatigue, Philip laid his head on the worn velvet saddle cover and breathed deeply. A wide-eyed fugitive pounded past him, tossing away anything that might retard his flight, but Philip was in no shape to chase a rabbit.

Physically and emotionally drained, he dragged his trembling legs through the marsh grass and slumped down on the river bank. Still armoured, he lay on his back laughing and fighting to keep his eyes open. In the background he could hear the screams of women being attacked in Tewkesbury and closed his eyes, his laughter diminishing to an infrequent chuckle. Snapping his eyes open, he sighed deeply and concentrated on a curlew in the sky above him. Before the bird had passed from view he was asleep.

Chapter 23

WHILE PHILIP SLUMBERED in the eye of the storm, a number of Lancastrian refugees, fleeing the battle, sought sanctuary in the nearby Abbey Church. King Edward followed them inside and a brawl took place in the nave, defiling the Holy Sanctum. The abbey monks meanwhile, were in the quire offering a mass for the souls of the dead, when the clatter of weapons and screams of injured men echoed off the cathedral's high walls. Suddenly the quire door flew open and a priest entered, blurting hysterically that soldiers were violating sanctuary.

"Mah lord," Arbroth shouted, finding Hotspur, bloodied and alone, and fearing his master might be hurt.

"Whaat?" Philip groaned, angered at being woken as he struggled to raise his head above the tall grass. "Get this off me," he gasped, thumping his helm.

"Ah have news," Arbroth gleefully revealed, detaching Philip's sallet from its gorget.

"Well?" he hissed, indifferently.

"Tha day is ours."

"Thank God," he yawned, frantically scratching his red, itchy neck. "What of our people?"

"Light wounds, nothing more. They're plundering Tewkesbury."

"They can have it."

"Lord Somerset and some o' his men have claimed sanctuary, in there," Arbroth explained, pointing at the great abbey, before pulling off Philip's tacky, bloody gauntlets and undergloves, "and tha king has gone in after them."

"Look after my horse," he said, determined to be in at the finish.

"Aye."

Drawing his sword, Philip limped the short distance to the abbey, passing a number of blown horses and bewildered soldiers suffering severely from fatigue and post-battle trauma.

Passing through the gatehouse and cemetery he crossed his chest before entering the abbey church. Walking up the nave between two rows of vividly painted pillars, Philip carefully stepped over a body lying in a pool of blood. Moving on, he acknowledged several Yorkist knights and esquires he knew, slumped exhausted on the floor, their backs to the wall. As he approached the screen that divided the nave from the quire, he could clearly hear an argument going on.

Moving through a door in the screen, he saw the king standing near the high altar in heated conversation with Abbot John Strensham. The elderly ecclesiastic, his white surplice speckled with blood, was pleading with Edward to stop the slaughter and show mercy. Philip walked in as quietly as his armour allowed.

"Your Grace," the white-haired abbot begged, his willowy hands clasped together before his thin, ashen face, "these men are under God's protection. For the sake of your immortal soul, I ask you... I beg you, do not violate his house."

With his arms crossed superciliously over his blood-stained breastplate, Edward towered over the diminutive cleric, his long, damp chestnut hair stuck to his sweaty head.

"My Lord abbot," he sighed, "these men who seek refuge have betrayed their king. By law they have no right to sanctuary."

"And you have no right to allow it," Gloucester added forcefully.

"But your Grace..." the abbot stammered, fearing the abbey could lose its royal patronage if he antagonised the king. "Please, show mercy."

"I'll withdraw my men, but these traitors must not be allowed to remain within these walls," Edward said, looking around and raising his voice. "I offer pardon to anyone who will leave this church now!"

"Brother," Gloucester objected strenuously. "You cannot show weakness, these dogs must pay –"

Edward silenced his brother with a raised hand, and the abbot reluctantly agreed to the king's terms.

Strensham and his black-robed monks stepped back and several Lancastrians gingerly came out of hiding. The king signalled his escort to search the abbey for those still in hiding.

"Philip," Edward smiled, spotting his cousin, "this is a house of God, put away your sword... What do you want here?"

"*I am one of your knights*, your Grace," he reminded him, sheathing his blade.

"Search every corner and alcove!" Edward commanded, before addressing Philip again. "Maurice did his duty?"

"Yes, sire," he confirmed.

In the background the sound of the sacristy door being pummelled drew Philip's attention in that direction. After a brief scuffle, the door was forced and the king's men returned, shuttling two captives before them.

"Why Edmund Beaufort, what a surprise," Edward sneered, recognising one of the prisoners. "You will pay for your family's treasonous ways."

"Your Grace..." the Abbot gasped. "You gave your word."

"My Lord abbot," the king countered, his temper rising, "I offered pardon to those who came out of their own free will."

"The House of York never keeps its word," Beaufort huffed.

"Your brother gave me his word, once," Edward explained, "and then betrayed me... I'll not make that mistake again."

The bare-headed duke, his dark hair, face and armour plastered with blood and gore, stared hatefully at Edward and spat.

"Take him away," Edward fumed, as the gobbet hit the floor between his sabatons.

Beaufort's arms were seized and he was hustled out.

"Michael?" Edward sniffed, recognising the second prisoner.

Watching Somerset's departure with a satisfied smirk, Philip heard the name and jerked his head around.

"I am Gilbert de Auberoche," the prisoner muttered with an accent, keeping his head bowed, his long hair so matted with blood that it draped over his eyes, concealing his grimy, sweat-streaked features.

With his armour badly damaged and head low, Philip failed to recognise him at first.

Edward looked at his captive kinsman, expecting a plea for mercy.

"You are no Frenchman..." he said, looking into his blood-shot eyes. "Are you – cousin?"

"And you are no king," Michael parried. "Cousin."

Edward rolled his eyes up into his head and sighed.

Two years younger and five fingers shorter than Philip, Michael Neville was a die-hard Lancastrian. The sight of his body floating in the sea off Bamburgh, seven years earlier, convinced Philip he was dead. Barely alive, Michael was rescued and taken to Holy Island, where he was nursed back to health by the monks. Fearing capture and still weak, he made his way slowly to the southeast coast and secured passage aboard a ship bound for France.

When Michael appeared before his mortified mother, he persuaded her not to reveal he was alive. To avoid questions, he grew his hair, lost weight and took a new name. Later, he left France with another who despised the York-Neville faction, Edmund Beaufort. The pair rode to Bruges and offered their swords to Burgundy's son, Charles Count of Charolais. Six years later, Michael and Edmund returned to England, believing Warwick's invasion would pave the way for Henry's return. At Tewkesbury Michael fought on while the rest of Margaret's army fell apart, before fleeing to the abbey.

Floored at coming face to face with his brother, Philip stared at him with mixed emotions ranging from sadness and frustration to relief and anger. Michael had saved Philip's life at Bamburgh, but now he was powerless to intervene, and feared he would be forced to watch his brother die a second time. Resigned to his fate, Michael balled his fists, straightened up and glowered insolently at his captors.

"There is nothing left to say," Edward said, turning to his guards. "Get him out of my sight."

As he was pushed past Philip, Michael stopped and drew the hair away from his forehead, allowing the brothers to make eye contact. Through the dirt, Philip saw the healed scar Michael received at Towton and shook his head.

"Move!" the guard insisted, pushing him on.

Michael scoffed at Philip before being shoved in the back.

"Sire," Philip gasped, as his brother was led out, "I humbly beseech you to spare his life."

"Why should I?"

"I thought him dead all these years and though Lord Warwick told me he lived, I did not believe it until now... Please, your Grace, grant him mercy."

"You witnessed his contempt and heard his defiance," Lord Hastings intervened. "He will never change."

"He has been influenced by the Beauforts," Philip said, ignoring the chamberlain.

Edward glanced at each of his companions for advice, but only Richard spoke up.

"Brother," he said, "our cousin's misguided loyalty has never swayed. Many have changed their coat to receive your good graces and switched back when fortunes wheel turned against us."

"Your Grace, you must not show weakness," George countered, urged to speak out by Lord Hastings. "We have won a brace of victories; Henry is our prisoner and his heir is dead. You must wipe out every last vestige of Lancastrianism or we will never have peace."

"Enough. Today we thank God for our success and tomorrow the prisoners will be tried and those found guilty will be executed," Edward vowed. "You may go," he told Philip.

His cousin bowed and backed away, his spurs scratching the orange and black tiles. Disillusioned with the king's broken promise, the Abbot lowered his head and led his monks out.

"I want them kept apart," Edward told his chamberlain, meaning the Neville brothers. "They are not to speak to each other."

"As you wish, sire," Hastings said, receiving a whispered message from one of his retainers, which he was loath to relay to the king. "Your Grace... Margaret has eluded us."

Edward groaned at the news and his face flushed.

After the destruction of her army and the death of her son Prince Edward, rumoured to have been killed by Gloucester, Margaret fled.

"I want her found and quickly," Edward warned, punching his fists together. "She must not be allowed to leave England."

"Your Grace," William Stanley intervened, holding the king's helmet. "Allow me?"

"Um... Philip could go with Sir William," Hastings suggested. "That way he'll be out of our hair."

"My Lord chamberlain, you know there is no love between them," Richard warned, meaning Philip and Stanley.

"Margaret will cross the border or head north," Edward said, frowning at Hastings before addressing Lord Stanley's brother. "You will cross the Seven into Wales and Philip will ride north."

Stanley acknowledged the order with a deep bow and Hastings sent a messenger after Philip.

After an evening spent gathering his retainers, Philip Neville set off to scour the country north of Tewkesbury. For almost a week he searched but found no sign of Margaret. Riding into Worcester for news, he learned that Edward was in the city earlier but had left for Coventry. While he rested his horses, Philip was told the Lancastrian nobles taken at Tewkesbury had been tried in the market place and those found guilty were beheaded. Anxious to know his brother's fate, he interrogated several Yorkist messengers, and was relieved to hear that he was on his way to the Tower. Philip also wanted to know why the king was in Coventry, and was told that Margaret's northern supporters had risen on her behalf.

With his men and horses refreshed, Philip set off for Coventry.

"Somerset has been executed," he told his esquire as they trotted along the road.

"Yes, my Lord," he confirmed. "It is said the army went on a drunken rampage in Tewkesbury."

"Such is war," Philip sniffed.

"Mah lord!" Arbroth called out.

Philip looked over his shoulder and saw his Scot swaying

in the saddle as he trotted forward dragging Clovis along. Offended by his breath, Ashley urged his horse on.

"Tha boy's too sensitive," Arbroth slurred, wiping his mouth.

"And you're nothing but a drunken fool," Philip growled, flapping a hand in front of his face. "You dare come to me in such a state… What is it you want?"

"Narry a thing," he beamed, snorting snot from his nose.

"Then draw back and stay there until you sober up."

Arbroth's head drooped at the reprimand and he pulled back. The gentle plodding gait of his horse, the relief that Michael was safe and the warmth of a spring sun brought on a bout of weary contentment and Philip struggled to stay awake.

Not far from Coventry the column ground to a halt and Philip snorted awake and sat up straight. Squeezing his cheeks together he yawned and rotated his aching left shoulder.

"Why have we stopped?" he mumbled, wiping slaver from his chin and resting his hands on the pommel of his saddle.

"Coventry, my Lord," Ashley announced, pointing up the road. "No more than half a league."

Shaking the dullness from his head, Philip massaged the back of his aching neck and urged his rouncey into a trot.

King Edward's army was camped outside Coventry, in an extensive orchard not far from the Greyfriars Gate. Sliding from the saddle, Philip made his way to the king's pavilion, which was marked by the huge quartered royal standard fluttering from its centre pole.

"What is your business here, sir?" an esquire demanded, stepping out between two guards.

"My business is with the king," he answered brusquely. "So step aside."

Spotting his livery badge, the esquire signalled for the guards to admit him.

Before he entered the luxuriously decorated timber and canvas marquee, Philip met William Stanley coming out.

"Will?" he gasped, surprised.

"Philip," Stanley acknowledged. "His grace is in fine humour today."

"Good," he sniffed, pushing past him.

Once inside, Philip found himself in an atmosphere of heated excitement, but he was unable to see over the heads of so many.

"Cousin!"

Philip looked for the source of the greeting.

"Your Grace?" he responded, waving at Gloucester.

"By St George, this is a day of mixed tidings," Richard said cheerfully, taking him aside.

"Where is the king?"

"He will not see you now."

Philip rubbed his itchy head, flustered by the noisy crowd.

"The rebellion in the north is over," Richard revealed, "and Margaret is our prisoner."

"Stanley?" Philip frowned, as several couriers rushed past with letter satchels, bowing to the Duke as they went.

Richard's silence confirmed that William Stanley was responsible for Margaret's capture and Philip's confidence faltered.

"I have other news, grave news," Richard said dourly. "Our bastard cousin Fauconberg lies off the coast of Kent with a fleet," he explained. "He intends to attack London."

"We'll never get there in time."

"No, but I am commanded to take fifteen hundred picked men and ride south," Richard announced. "Lord Rivers must hold on until we arrive."

"Count me in," Philip offered.

Richard looked out of the tent at his cousin's retainers sprawling on the grass.

"Your men look all in –"

"Your Grace," he interrupted. "I beg you, let me do this."

"I shall speak to the king."

Philip nodded gratefully.

"Choose only those who can ride and your best horses, and assemble them in that field," Richard said, pointing to a line of trees on the edge of the orchard. "We leave within the hour."

"Yes, your Grace," Philip said confidently, returning to his companions.

For two days the Duke of Gloucester pushed his men along the old Roman road to London. By the evening of the seventeenth he was camped beyond Barnet, where the air was still so heavy with the stench of decay that his men had difficulty keeping their nervous, whinnying horses from bolting. Next morning Richard received word that Fauconberg was attacking the capital and an order from the king to wait for him. Rather than disobey, Richard sent Philip and fifty mounted men-of-arms on to London, and prayed the city could hold out.

By the time Philip arrived at Islington, most of his company had fallen out from fatigue and he was forced to ask for volunteers to ride the last mile. Six came forward, but his own men could not even mount. Before leaving, he ordered his esquire to help him into his armour.

"And saddle Clovis,"

Ashley brought the sumpter bearing his steel suit to a piece of wasteland, where Philip was dressed, but with time of the essence, he chose only partial armour. Upper leg and lower arm pieces were tied on and as his page fumbled with the ties, he lost his temper.

"Enough!" he hissed, while his cursing groom ran Clovis over.

"What's up with you?" Philip asked, noting Daniel's limp.

"He stepped on my toes, sir," his groom moaned.

Pushing his foot through the stirrup, Philip mounted. "Hurry them on," he told his esquire, shaking his head at those asleep.

Ashley and Arbroth watched with foreboding as Philip rode the last mile to London without them, before they collapsed on the grass.

When Philip led his six weary companions through Aldersgate, a wagon was suddenly wedged in behind, cutting him from the others. Alerted by the rumbling wheels, he looked back but as he did so a two-wheeled cart was dragged across his front, effectively trapping him in the gateway.

Three villains armed with daggers leapt from a doorway and before Philip could react they were on him, stabbing at his armoured legs and crowding his horse. Clovis reared in panic, his muscular body falling against the wall and crushing one of the assailants against the stonework. Struggling to free his blade, Philip fought off a second attacker with hands and feet, until Clovis's legs gave out and both horse and rider crashed to the ground. Slipping his feet from the stirrups, Philip pushed himself away from the thrashing hooves and briefly saw his men sitting calmly on the other side of the barrier.

"Help me!" he commanded.

There was no reaction.

"Bastards!" he spat, rolling under the cart.

Crawling out the other side, Philip scrambled to his feet and was hit in the back of his head but he felt no pain. Freeing his sword he slashed the nearest attacker above his eyes. Blinded by the blow, he screamed and staggered off while his confederate lunged in, slicing and stabbing at Philip's head and chest.

"I'll castrate you!" Philip yelled, "You cunt."

"What are you waiting for?" he countered.

But he delayed too long and Philip slashed at his throat. Slewing away he choked and gurgled as he tried to staunch the blood squirting from the yawing gash.

Philip's men finally dragged the cart aside and belatedly came to his rescue.

"Gutless knaves!" he spat, while a plump woman waddled over from a second-hand clothes stall to bandage his head.

"Our horses would not move," a mounted archer apologised, while Clovis was helped up.

"Lying dogbolt," he barked, wincing from the pain. "You God-damned cowards!"

Out of the corner of his eye, Philip saw the lone survivor huddled against the wall nursing his face and shrieking.

"Who sent you?" he demanded, pushing the woman away.

The man mumbled something and Philip, paced impatiently, spitting dust.

"My Lord!"

Philip turned to see one of his men slitting the wounded man's throat.

"I wanted him to talk!" he snarled, about to strike the archer with the pommel of his sword.

"Ee would a killed ye," the archer countered, pointing to a dagger near the dying man's hand.

Philip screamed his frustration and angrily wiped his sword on the archer's jack.

"Where is Lord Rivers?" he asked the crowd, which had gathered to watch.

"On the bridge," someone offered, pointing in the direction of the river.

Philip picked up the reins and led his party down to the

north bank of the Thames, on foot, delicately touching the bulging lump on the back of his head.

As he approached the north end of London Bridge, Philip noticed clouds of black smoke swirling up into the sky from a score of smouldering buildings, on the opposite end of the bridge.

"What happened?" he asked, aiming his question at a soldier fleecing a corpse.

"Where've you bin?" the looter scoffed, surprised by his comment.

"I have come from the king."

"We fought a battle 'ere," the soldier said proudly. "The rebels burned the gatehouse and some of the houses on t'other side, but we raised the drawbridge; when they couldn't cross their ships fired on the Tower and they attacked Aldgate."

"Did they break through?"

"Nah, Lord Rivers drove 'em off."

"Where are they now?" Philip demanded, looking over the river at Bankside to see if the brothels were still standing.

"Gone."

"Gone where?" he asked, relieved to see the Rose intact.

The soldier shrugged his shoulders and continued to plunder the dead man's pockets.

"Who commands here?" Philip snapped, the lump on his head throbbing.

"The Queen's brother," said a gunner sitting astride a cannon. "Lord Rivers."

"And where is *his lordship*?"

"Here."

Philip turned and came face to face with Anthony Woodville washing his hands in a bucket of water, held by a servant.

"My Lord," Philip bowed.

"Philip," Rivers responded, moving his lips to hide his missing front teeth. "You come too late and with too few men," he lisped his glowing, red face and bloody armour evidence of the hard fighting.

"The King will be here soon," Philip announced.

"Hum?"

"Will the rebels attack again?"

"No, they're returning to the rat-holes they came from," Woodville revealed. "What happened to you?" he asked, noting the blood-stained bandage around Philip's head and his torn, dirty tunic.

"Nothing," he huffed, glaring angrily at his escort.

"I need you to escort my prisoners to Southwark," Rivers said, wiping his face with a towel and indicating a group of dejected, closely guarded rebels sat in a circle. "And scout the road towards Blackheath."

"I must go to the Tower –"

"I command here, you will obey my orders," Rivers said, throwing down the towel and walking away. "We lack horses."

"Get them up!" Philip barked angrily, waving at his escort to get the prisoners on their feet.

Snorting heavily, he cursed Lord Rivers under his breath before following his men, as they urged the captives towards the bridge.

Chapter 24

LEAVING HIS PRISONERS at the Marshalsea in Southwark, Philip sent his men to reconnoitre the Blackheath Road and returned home. A physician who came to treat his wound gave him an anaesthetic of henbane, hemlock, opium and briony and sutured the deep gash on his head. Combined with exhaustion, the potion put him into a deep sleep. Next morning he woke with a strange gurgling sensation in his stomach and just managed to grab a pot and pull down his braies. The briony in the anaesthetic worked like a laxative and while nature took its course, he pondered this latest attempt on his life. Wiping his backside with cotton rags, he washed his face and cleaned his teeth.

After breakfast Philip rode to the Tower still suffering from guts ache and entered the great fortress just as the gates were unlocked.

"I am on the king's business," he declared, offering his sword.

The startled warden at the Middle Tower accepted his blade and motioned for the portcullis to be raised. Lowering his head, Philip couldn't wait for the barrier to crank fully up and trotted down the outer ward to the Garden Tower, where he turned into the inner ward.

"Where can I find the constable?" he asked a passing guard.

"Why, there," he replied, pointing at the twin-towered

Coldharbour gatehouse, abutting the southwest corner of the White Tower.

Philip dismounted carefully and watched an elderly man exiting the gatehouse, his legs so bent it looked as if he was riding an imaginary horse. Well wrapped against the unseasonably morning chill, the constable walked with the aid of sticks.

"He can barely stand," Philip gasped, groaning at the pain in his stomach.

"Is lordship's nigh on semty," the soldier explained. "He suffers with is bones but fights like a lion."

"Huh," Philip sniffed, unimpressed.

"Two days ago 'e stood on the wall waving 'is stick in the air, daring the rebel ships to fire at 'im."

"My Lord," Philip said, turning to the constable and leaving his horse to graze. "I am Sir Philip Neville."

Sir John Sutton, Lord Dudley, lifted his heavy head and eyed the early morning visitor suspiciously.

"What do you want at such an ungodly hour?" he huffed.

"I come from the king," Philip lied, noticing Dudley's heavy eyelids and trembling, blotchy hands. "I wish to interrogate one of your prisoners."

"Which one?"

"Michael Neville."

"Oh, him," Dudley mused, shaking his head. "A contemptible knave who openly abuses the king's name… I fear he will not be long for this world."

"He is my brother," Philip tutted. "I know what he's like."

"You are the king's man?" Dudley sniffed, noting his doublet.

"Yes," Philip hesitated. "His highness is on his way from Coventry; I came on ahead with his grace the Duke of Gloucester."

"Where is Richard?"

"He waits on the king, three leagues from London. I was sent to inform Lord Rivers of his coming."

"Let us walk," Dudley smiled, taking his arm for support. "His grace is to replace me when he arrives."

"Yes, my Lord."

The two men strolled to the Chapel, Philip holding back so as not to tire his frail companion.

"Many years ago I served King Henry's father and bore his standard at his burial," Dudley revealed pensively. "I know that one day soon I shall be attending his funeral."

"My Lord?"

"Edward cannot permit him to live; Henry knows this and spends his days at prayer… I do not condone murder but I know what must be done to put this kingdom in order."

Philip recalled his conversation with Henry as they rode together from York, and was saddened at the idea that he must die.

"Today is the Sabbath… I go now to pray for the old king," Dudley wheezed, unhooking his arm from Philip's as they approached the Chapel of St Peters. "It won't take long. Stay and dine with me and you can tell me all the news."

"I must humbly decline, my Lord," Philip apologised. "But what of my brother?"

"He's a fool to himself," Dudley said, placing a hand on his shoulder. "You can do nothing for him but pray for his soul."

"But –"

"My orders are explicit no one is to see the prisoners…now good day, sir."

"My Lord," Philip sulked, returning to his horse while Dudley shuffled to the Chapel.

"Say one for me, old man," he muttered, picking up the loose reins and leading his rouncey away. "Come on."

Walking back through the passage through the Garden

Tower, Philip carefully felt the stitches on the back of his head and slipped on the worn cobbles.

"Shit!" he swore, losing his balance and instinctively grabbing a passer-by to prevent falling. "Forgive me, madam…" he apologised, regaining his footing. "By the saints!"

"Philip," she yelped, equally surprised.

"Why are you here?" he snapped, disgust twisting his features.

"The queen refuses to leave this place until the king comes for her," Elizabeth Hastings explained, crouching down to the little girl at her side. "Are you hurt, my Lady?"

The child pouted and shook her head.

"This is the Princess Mary," Elizabeth announced.

"My Lady," Philip said, forcing a smile and bending to kiss the five-year-old's tiny hand. "You have no escort?"

"We are safe here."

"Henry has many friends in many places… Tell the queen she must trust no one."

"Can we see the lion?" The young princess whined, tugging Elizabeth's dress.

"Tomorrow…" she promised, raising her faint brows and looking at Philip. "You know your brother is alive?"

"Yes, I met him at Tewkesbury."

"He is here.…"

"I know."

"All these years I thought he was dead –" she gasped.

"I too believed it."

"Michael is the reason you are here?" She suddenly realised. "I can help you."

"Where is he?"

"Those prisoners brought in after Tewkesbury are held in the Beauchamp Tower," she revealed, lowering her voice. "Michael was caught plotting to rescue Henry and removed to the Salt Tower."

"What can you do to help me?" he sneered.

"I'll take the princess back to her nurse..." she said, frowning at his curt response, "Meet me here in one hour."

Philip nodded grudgingly and Elizabeth led the child away.

After stabling his horse, Philip walked up the steps of the inner south wall, passing several workmen busy repairing a damaged section. Moving through the Lanthorn Tower, he peered over the wall and noticed large wine casks filled with earth, placed at various points.

"What's that?" he asked, glancing furtively at the next tower on his route, the Salt Tower.

"His lordship put 'em there to strengthen the walls," a mason answered, his hair and face dusted with a layer of fine dust.

"Clever," Philip said, continuing his unhurried stroll.

Paranoid he was being watched, Philip walked straight through the Salt Tower and out the other side, lest he give himself away.

Moving along the battlements, he followed the walkway north towards the Martin Tower. Climbing to the top, he looked up at the polished blue sky and closed his eyes, allowing the wind to blow through his hair, but the barking of angry dogs, scrapping on Tower Hill, shattered the peace.

"Curs-sed mongrels," he muttered, leaving the tower and loping back towards the Garden Tower, stopping on the way to chat with several men-of-arms.

When he heard the Chapel bell toll the hour of Terce, 8 a.m., Philip said his goodbyes and went back to the Garden Tower.

"Here is your pass," Elizabeth puffed, having hurried over from the royal apartments. "The queen remembered what you did for her," she said, handing him a folded note and drawing several strands of loose hair off her damp forehead. "I must be seen with you."

Philip took the pass and nodded his appreciation, though it galled him to do so.

"Wait," he insisted, as she was about to leave.

Peeking furtively out, he drew her forcibly into the damp, vaulted passageway and pressed her back against the cold wall. Her confused, blue eyes flashed in the low light, while the smell of her scent and the odour of sweet almonds on her breath mesmerised him. As he held her arms he noticed tiny beads of perspiration on her forehead and her bosom pressing against his chest. Breathing heavily, she wound her arms around his neck and they kissed passionately, a reaction he didn't expect.

"I must go," she gasped, releasing her hold.

"You have set my heart aflame," he moaned, licking her sweetness from his lips. "I would –"

"I cannot," she panted, trying hard to compose herself.

"My heart aches –"

"Not only your heart," she blushed, breaking free and hurrying away.

"You damned fool," he hissed, condemning his own weakness and storming off in the opposite direction.

Striding up the steps to the south inner wall, he ground his teeth and deliberately scuffed his boots as he made his way along the ramparts to the Salt Tower.

At the narrow doorway, Philip showed his pass to a guard.

"I am here to see the prisoner."

"Dunno bout that," the guard said reticently, examining the queen's seal before leading him in and down the spiralling steps to the basement. "Spose it's awright."

Chained to an iron ring, rusted into the wall, Michael Neville sat on the cold floor, dressed in a tatty, stained shirt, soiled hose and torn stockings. His long hair and beard were caked with old, dry blood and he hadn't washed since Tewkesbury. Except for sacks of stored salt and a pot, the room was empty.

As the key grated in the lock, Michael expected the worst and held his breath.

"Stand back m'Lord," the guard warned. "When I brought 'is food yesterday 'e threw the pisspot at me."

Philip stepped aside and the guard pushed the door open.

"Michael?" Philip called, cautiously entering the dark, foul-smelling chamber.

"Who's there?" Michael demanded, his words bouncing off the stone walls.

"Your brother?"

"Get out, *brother*!"

"You arse-face," Philip retorted, screwing up his nose at the foul air while his eyes adjusted to the darkness.

"Unlock these and I'll show you what an arse-face can do!" he bit back, rattling the manacles and lunging from his squat position, only to be brought to a jolting halt by the short chain.

The guard chuckled as Michael lost his balance and fell back into a sitting position, their fraternal antagonism amusing him.

"'Ee curses the king and applauds the death of Lord Warwick," he revealed, sparking the single candle, as Michael angrily kicked at the dirt.

"Leave us," Philip commanded, the disturbed dust bringing on a coughing fit.

"I cannot."

"Here," Philip spluttered, pulling the ring from his middle finger. "Perhaps this will change your mind."

The guard snatched the gold band and left, hacking up dust from his throat.

"Have you come to gloat?" Michael asked.

"Don't talk like a turd."

"Then what is it you want?"

"We are brothers."

"Brothers," he huffed.

"There's no time for this shit," Philip said impatiently, glancing back at the door. "I'm here to get you out."

Michael guffawed and the guard poked his head round the door and the swirling dust cloud settled.

"Your cause is finished," Philip confirmed, angry at his responses.

"No, brother, there are many others, living in exile just waiting to take our place."

"Somerset has been executed, your king and queen are prisoners, and their only son is dead"

"You're a fool, you've wasted the better part of your life seeking revenge on those you believe murdered our father, but you are wrong and always have been, and that, dear brother is the extent of your loyalty."

"You sound like our mother."

"One day you will know the truth and it will tear your heart out."

"You must urry!" the guard hissed.

"What's the plan?" Michael sniffed, scratching his lousy hair and deliberately rattling his chains. "A dead horse?"

"Nothing so refined," Philip smirked. "Is there one here who can be bribed?"

"You forget I've been locked in this shit-hole for more than a week."

"Shush," Philip insisted. "Let me think."

"Take your time," he huffed. "I'm not going anywhere."

"It must be tomorrow."

"Tomorrow," Michael gasped. "Impossible."

"I'll find someone to unlock your chains and leave the door open. Make your way to the outer wall and climb over, then hide in the moat until dark. I'll fetch a boat and wait offshore, when you hear the curfew bell look to the river, when you see a flickering light swim out to it."

"I won't work," Michael said emphatically, running a dirty finger pensively over the deep scar on his cheek. "There are many boats at night and far too many lights'"

"You prefer to stay here in your own piss and shit?"

"What if something goes wrong?"

"Let me worry about that."

Michael scoffed at his answer and ended the discourse by looking away.

"Why did you play dead all these years?" Philip asked.

"To save my life," he explained.

"My heart has been heavy with guilt these seven years."

"Good," Michael smirked.

"Why?"

"Edward is a usurper."

"Henry's grandfather stole the crown in the first place."

Michael pouted.

"Be ready," Philip snapped, shaking his head slowly as he turned to leave. "Before I go there should be peace between us."

"When was there ever peace between us?"

"Have you forgotten those days in France, with Lord Talbot?"

"Yes..." Michael recalled, "Before you were seduced by our cousins."

"You chose your road, I chose mine."

"You must go..." the guard whined.

"How is my new-born nephew?" Michael asked as Philip reached the door, his tone less abrasive.

Philip looked at his brother sitting degraded in the dirt, and was overcome with sadness.

"When you reach France, tell our mother she has a grandson, named for our father."

Michael sniggered and dragged the stiff, tacky hair from his eyes.

"What happened at Bamburgh was no fault of mine," Philip said.

Michael bent his leg up and rested an arm on the knee.

"The monks who treated me told me I was out of my mind with fever," he explained. "But our paths have crossed since Bamburgh, and I could have killed you."

Philip looked confused and Michael continued.

"When I was able to walk I joined a group of lepers. I wore their rags, shared their rations and put up with their stinking sores and complaints all the way to Canterbury. When I reached France I changed my name so no one would know me."

"You were on the Doncaster road?" Philip gasped, pointing accusingly. "You should have made your presence known."

"And be taken?"

"I would not have betrayed you –"

"Huh," he scoffed. "I saw that toad Arbroth shit himself."

"My Lord!" the guard pled.

"Until tomorrow," Philip said, making his way out and up the stairwell, only to be called back by the guard, as he locked the cell door.

"Here," he whispered, handing Philip his ring.

"But why?"

"I could never explain how I came by such a thing... and they would suspect me."

"Listen," Philip said, gently forcing the ring back on his own finger. "I'll give thee a handsome purse if you do one thing for me."

"No," the guard gasped fearfully, having overheard the conversation, "the risk is too great."

"Quiet," Philip insisted, ignoring his plea. "Find a length of rope and hide it in his room, and tomorrow before curfew unlock his chains and leave the door open."

"No..."

"You must do it tomorrow-."

"I can-not –"

"Hush," Philip snarled, grabbing his jack and pushing him up against the wall. "If you refuse I'll denounce you as one of Henry's spies –"

"You would do such a thing?"

"You have a family?"

He nodded vigorously.

"Then do as I say and no one will know you had a part in it," Philip promised. "Betray me and it will go bad for you and your family. When my brother is free I'll send you the purse."

The distressed guard grudgingly agreed and Philip made his way back to the stables.

An hour before sunset next day, Philip and Arbroth rode to Fish Wharf, not far from London Bridge and easily bribed several boatmen to take them downriver to a point not far from the Tower. While the ferrymen used their oars to keep the vessel from drifting, Philip struggled to spark a lantern in the wind.

"Curfew, mah lord?" Arbroth announced, as the bell in the southwest corner tower began to toll.

"I can hear it," Philip said, looking at the light from the torches along the wall reflecting off the dark water and distorting his focus. "Now we can do nothing but wait," he said, as Arbroth aimed the lantern at the Tower, opening and closing the shutter.

The final clang of the bell told Philip the Tower was locked down for the night and the four men in the bobbing wherry stared anxiously at the north bank.

For almost an hour they waited and finally, Philip snatched the lantern and blew out the candle.

"God help him now," he sighed, looking ruefully at the silhouette of the Salt Tower.

"Mah lord –" Arbroth said quietly. "We canna stay here."

"Alright…take us back."

Next morning, Tuesday 21, the Feast of the Ascension, Edward entered London through Bishopsgate. Wearing gleaming armour, and accompanied by three dukes, six earls, sixteen barons, the mayor and aldermen of London, and dozens of knights, his arrival had all the pomp and splendour of a returning Roman emperor. Secreted amongst his escort was the captive Queen Margaret, her bowed, pale face covered. Applauded all the way by a euphoric crowd, Edward soaked up the adoration like a sponge.

When he arrived at the Tower, Edward enjoyed had a tearful reunion with his wife and children. The constable greeted the king and informed him of his cousin, Michaels, constant haranguing and Edward's brother George asked what should be done about him.

"I wish someone would rid me of such troublesome relations," he sighed, wearily rubbing his temples.

George excused himself and made his way to the White Tower.

While Edward and his queen rode to Westminster, Philip was at home playing tables with his esquire but his mind was not on the game; he could not understand what had gone wrong the night before.

"Has the king sent for me?" he asked, eager to speak on Michael's behalf.

"No my Lord," his esquire confirmed, conscious of his concerns.

"Huh…" he sulked.

"Will you go to him?"

"When I am summoned," Philip sniffed, moving the wrong piece.

"You are in error, sir," Ashley dared.

"Oh," he mused, withdrawing the disc. "I cannot sit here all night."

"What will you do?" Ashley asked, aware the game was over.

"Try again," he frowned. "What o'clock is it?"

"Two hours tah sunset," Arbroth interjected, entering the parlour and glancing out of the window.

"Nothing will happen tonight," Philip said confidently. "I'm going out."

"Mah lord?" his Scot said, smiling at Ashley; both knew he intended going over to Bankside.

Draping a cloak over his shoulders, he left the house and walked along a narrow lane that dipped under the Strand Bridge and headed for a landing place on the Thames.

While Philip waited for the ferry to Southwark, Michael sat in the basement of the Salt Tower, wondering why he was still there. Suddenly the thump of heavy boots coming down the steps gave him hope.

"About time," he whined, extending his manacled arms out as the door opened.

Six grim-faced guards marched into the basement. Three of them grabbed his arms and a fourth unshackled his legs. Jerked to his feet, Michael was roughly dragged out of the chamber.

"What's this?" he gasped, digging his heels in. "Where are you taking me?"

Without a word, they pushed and pulled him up the winding steps, but he struggled so violently two of the guards tumbled back down the coiling stairs, their helmets striking the stonework.

"Get off me!" Michael shrieked, punching and kicking. "Goddamn you."

"'Old 'im!" a frustrated guard yelled, striking Michael's head with the base of his poleaxe. "Stay still… you bastard."

Momentarily stunned by the blow, Michael fell out onto the parapet and grabbed for one of the merlons. The guards tried to prise his fingers free and the poleaxe-man came to the rescue again, the flat iron blade smashing his fingers.

"You dog-fuckers!" Michael spat, releasing his grip. "I'll kill you all."

Carried along the rampart, Michael was forced through the Lanthorn Tower and down a set of steps, to the inner ward. Weak from lack of nourishment and exhausted from being chained up, he was dragged over to the Green. What he saw waiting for him sent an icy shiver down his spine. A stocky, thick-necked giant, dressed in black and wearing a hood, stood on the Green holding a large-headed axe, his laced-up sleeveless leather jerkin revealing extremely muscular arms.

"No!" Michael shouted, resisting with renewed energy, for he understood what it meant.

Several guards rushed over to help their colleagues restrain the prisoner, but Michael refused to stay down. The axeman watched amused as the prisoner bit and punched his way to the block.

"Carry him, you fools," he groaned, twisting the long axe handle and glancing up at the sky. "For God's sake!"

Fighting for his life Michael felt no pain as he was kicked, thumped and stomped on.

"Damn you to Hell…!" he snarled, biting down on a finger thrust in his mouth. "Bring that bastard Edward here!" he coughed, spitting out a chunk of flesh.

"He bit my thumb off!" one of the guards yelped, slamming his fist into Michael's face.

Screaming obscenities and spitting blood, Michael was dragged to the execution block set up on the Green between the west wall and the White Tower.

"This is not happening…!" he spluttered, as his head was forced down onto the block. "I am not ready to die."

"Stay!" A brute of a guard insisted, grabbing his greasy hair and pressing his head down.

Worn out by his efforts, Michael's cheek hit the recess cut out of the block; but he was not finished yet. As those holding his arms relaxed their grip, he made one last superhuman effort. Forcing his head up, he thrashed his chained arms and unleashed a chorus of expletives.

"Bastards!" he coughed, discharging a liberal amount of blood and spittle. "Fuck you… and fuck the whores who gave you birth."

"He fights like the Devil," one of the guards gasped, nursing his bleeding chin.

"Do you want a confessor?" another asked.

"Go to Hell!"

Gagging for breath and blinking sweat from his eyes, Michael spotted the king's brother George and focused his accusing gaze on him. The twenty-one-year-old Duke was observing from behind a tree, but Michael knew him by his dark, wavy, shoulder-length hair and aquiline nose.

"Coward!" he screamed at him, the veins in his neck bulging. "Take heed, cousin… When your time comes you will die screaming like a bitch on heat!"

Puffing deeply, Michael knew the end was near; turning his head to fit snugly in the recess, he finally relaxed.

"Give me a crucifix," he asked calmly as the executioner stepped forward.

One of the guards snatched the cross from his own neck and held it to Michael's mouth.

Trembling, he pursed his lacerated lips, kissed the silver crucifix and blinked his gratitude.

"You see," he grunted, with a wicked leer. "Tell your prince I go to the grave with a smile on my face!"

As Michael whispered a final prayer the guards slowly released his arms and stepped away. A shaft of light suddenly pierced the dense cloud and hit the wet grass, making the dew glisten.

"Kyrie Eleison, Christie Eleison," he gasped, closing his eyes. "Amen."

The axe swooped down, his head came off and Michael Neville was dead.

Chapter 25

HAVING SATISFIED HIS carnal cravings several times during the night, Philip fell asleep and woke refreshed. Bidding Portia a joyful farewell he walked out of the Rose with a confident bounce in his step. Filling his lungs with air he looked up and saw a well-dressed gentleman coming towards him.

"Sir Philip Neville?"

"Yes?" the man responded cheerfully. "I am Henry Marlowe; I have come to take you to his grace the Duke of Gloucester."

"Am I arrested?" Philip asked, cagily, his early optimism gone in an instant.

"No sir."

Philip accompanied Marlowe back to St Mary's Landing where they boarded a boat.

As the vessel was rowed upriver, Philip tried to keep a lid on the fear percolating in his stomach and threatening to explode inside his over-thinking mind.

"Why does his grace wish to see me?" he asked. "And how did you know where to find me?"

Marlowe's silence convinced Philip that the Tower guard he tried to suborn had blabbed, and he rubbed his sweating hands together to stop them shaking. By the time the boat bumped against the landing stage, Philip's face was awash with panic-induced perspiration. Stepping onto the pier, he heard the palace clock strike eight and his legs refused to move. Nauseous from worry, he struggled to compose himself as followed Marlowe to New Palace Yard, before being ushered into the Great Hall.

When the doors closed behind him, Philip felt a terrible sense of isolation and an invisible icy hand gripped the back of his neck. The words "Come in, cousin" from the far end of the hall snapped the tension. Narrowing his eyes, he could see a shadowy figure slouched in the high chair behind the king's table.

"Sire?" he said, walking up the hall and recognising his kinsman. "Your Grace."

Richard hauled himself up out of his seat, moved stiffly around the table and stepped down off the Diaz, while Philip bowed his head.

At five feet eight inches tall, the king's youngest brother was a fearful warrior, though out of armour his poise seemed awkward. Richard's tanned face was crowned with a mop of thick, brown hair which levelled out below the ears and several healed battle scars were prominent on his chin and forehead. Well-read, pious and headstrong, his affable personality shone from a pair of dark, attentive eyes.

"Philip," he smiled, putting him at his ease. "You smell like a brothel." He added, his smile transforming into a grin.

"Yes, sire," he answered awkwardly.

"You are predictable," Richard sighed, wagging a finger at him. "Whenever there is a crisis, the lord chamberlain knows where to find you."

Philip wanted to disparage the king's chamberlain but he thought it prudent to say nothing.

"I have something to tell thee that will break thy heart," Richard said sadly, crossing his chest. "Your brother Michael is dead."

"No," Philip gasped, unable to comprehend his words. "It cannot be...how?"

"The King made a comment but his intent was misconstrued," Richard revealed. "And Michael was executed."

Philip's heart dropped to the bottom of his stomach and a humming noise filled his head.

"Was there no trial?" he blurted.

Richard shook his head.

"This reeks of the lord chamberlain's handiwork," Philip whined, pacing rapidly to and fro and grinding his teeth.

"No, not him."

"Then who?" Philip rudely demanded.

"It was not the king's intention to execute your brother," Richard explained. "But what is done cannot be undone."

"My God," Philip rasped, rubbing his temples to ease the sharp pain shooting through his head. "As easy as that."

"I must accept part of the blame."

"You, your Grace? I don't understand."

"Had I taken up my post as Constable of England earlier, Michael would be alive."

Philip looked at the floor and shook his head.

"There is something else," Richard continued. "You are to be arrested."

"By the blood of Christ," Philip spluttered, outrage replacing distress. "What have I done to deserve such a fate?"

"You openly offend my brother's councillors and show contempt for the Church."

"Hastings –" Philip snapped.

"Not only him," Richard interrupted, miffed by his antagonism and lack of respect. "His brother Ralph and his wife, Edmund Grey, Lords Rivers, the Bishop of Durham... Must I go on?"

Philip sighed woefully.

"The King had no choice," Richard continued. "He needs

the support of all his lords and bishops if he is to bring peace and tranquillity to this war-weary realm. You are an outdated curiosity who has no place in a kingdom earnestly striving for peace."

"Your Grace, I beg thee, intercede on my behalf."

"I cannot, it is known that you plotted to free Michael and rescue Henry."

"'Tis a falsehood," Philip gasped.

"The guard you bribed revealed your plan to Lord Dudley," he said, producing the pass from Elizabeth. "Do you still deny it?"

Philip's jaw dropped.

"This is the queen's seal, but she has no knowledge how it came into his possession," Richard explained. "The Lady Elizabeth is arrested." He went on, dropping the pass on the table behind him, "And your servants are being questioned. Do you deny you spoke intimately with Henry when you rode together from York?"

"My God, I showed a broken man a little compassion," Philip responded. "He was in my custody for ten days... I did try to free my brother but there was no plot to rescue Henry, I swear it."

Richard put his hands behind his back and took several steps, tapping his lips as he did so.

"I believe you, but if you are caught you'll not live to see the summer out," he warned. "The ports are being closed as we speak to stop the Kentish rebels escaping. Because of our kinship I'll not stop you, but you must leave now."

"I am exiled?" he gasped, his dream of wearing the garter finally over.

Richard's stony silence gave him his answer.

"What of my servants?"

"They will be set at liberty, I give you my word."

"And my property?"

"You show no concern for your son?" Richard frowned, surprised.

Embarrassed by the duke's criticism, Philip drew his collar away from his tacky neck.

"The Talbots care more for your son than you do… Leave him with them, I shall look to his education and well-being," Richard promised.

"Your Grace," Philip bowed, "I'll need time to –"

A look of impatience from Richard cut him off.

"There is no time. As we speak a warrant is being drawn up for your arrest," Richard said. "But beware of Ralph Hastings, he blames you for what has befallen his wife and is out for blood."

"Better men than him have tried to kill me –"

"Enough!" Richard barked, before softening his tone. "Make your way to Burgundy. I will write my sister, Margaret, she will help you when you arrive. I can promise no more. I shall speak to my brother the king when the time is right. You must go now, and Godspeed."

Philip thanked his cousin and left, his footsteps echoing through the hall. Richard watched him leave and turned to an esquire, who entered from a side door.

"It is done," he said, "though I like it not."

"'Tis for the best, your Grace."

"Perhaps, but wherever he ends up he'll find no cure for what ails him."

Early next morning Philip, suffering severely from a hangover, Arbroth, his esquire and one servant set off for London Bridge. Philip's warhorses were on their way to York, while his armour, weapons and other necessaries essential for the journey were loaded on a pair of sumpters. The four men cantered in sombre silence through a misty, chilly morning, each lost in their own thoughts.

After three days they reached Winchester, where Philip and

his esquire spent two anxious nights at the Star Inn. Arbroth went on to Southampton alone to check if the port was open. When he returned, he told Philip that Southampton was heavily guarded. Moving on to Poole, they were disappointed to find it shut up tighter than Southampton, forcing them to ride another thirty miles, to Dorchester.

Though Henry's armies had been defeated, Philip sensed he was in territory sympathetic to Lancaster's cause. Arbroth went on to scout Melcombe Regis, a town on the coast, nine miles south of Dorchester while Philip and his companions sought lodgings at the Greyfriars Monastery. With the Prior absent his friars were reluctant to let the strangers in; it was only after his esquire explained they were fleeing Yorkist persecution that they were granted sanctuary.

Shortly after arriving at the monastery, Philip learned of Henry's death. When he asked what happened, he was told by a monk that the old king had fallen into a malaise since the loss of his son and died of a broken heart. Believing Philip was Henry's man, the monk, who revealed these sad tidings, told him that many believed Henry was murdered on Edward's orders and that his brothers performed the dastardly deed. Philip played his part well, cursing Edward and threatening revenge.

After supper, Philip and his esquire were shown to an apartment known as 'the king's chamber', while his servant was lodged in a small room. Before Philip could wash the layers of sweat and dirt from his body, there was a knock on the door.

"Who is it?" he asked, soaking a cloth into a bowl of tepid water.

"Me, mah lord," his Scot answered.

"Come in."

"Melcombe is open; ah saw nay one soldier," he chirped, entering the room, "and coonted ten ships in tha harbour."

Philip passed his esquire a relieved smirk and Arbroth continued.

"Ah took tha ferry over tah Weymouth and spoke with several o' tha Capt'ns. Two'll tah take us, but they canna leave till tha day afta tah-morrow."

"Where are they bound?" Philip asked, scratching his bare sides. "Goddamned horsehair."

"Ah dinna ask."

"Tomorrow we ride to Weymouth, but we'll need a place to stay there," Philip said, using a piece of white soap to wash the grime from his face. "I don't trust these monks."

"Aye," Arbroth agreed, fondly patting the dagger in his belt before leaving.

After washing, Philip collapsed on his uncomfortable pallet and fell asleep.

As the priory bell tolled the hour of Prime, Philip awoke and went to the window. Stretching his knotted muscles he looked out furtively, snorting back the mucus in his nose. Tenderly touching the lump on the back of his head, to make sure it was still going down, he belted on his sword and briefly stared at a painting of St Francis of Assisi on the wall.

"Get up," he hissed, nudging his sleeping esquire with his boot.

"I'm awake," Ashley moaned.

Philip paid a visit to the Lavatorium and cleaned his teeth; when he finished he stretched his lips back and ran his tongue over the incisors.

"Better," he sniffed, heading for the refectory.

Philip found his companions seated at a rough table, dining on cold fish, bread and watered wine. Cocking a leg over the bench, he sat opposite Arbroth and was served a trencher of food by a monk.

Philip mumbled his thanks and downed the wine in one gulp, shuddering at its bitter taste.

"I wouldn't give this food to my horse," he whispered, leaning over the table.

Philip's esquire covered a smirk and rubbed his unkempt hair.

"When you're done here go and get the horses ready."

"Aye," Arbroth acknowledged, picking up the fish with his fingers and scooping it noisily in his mouth.

"Where's Mosby?" Philip asked, referring to his servant and frowning at his retainer's manners.

"Packing," Ashley answered, shaking his head.

"When we reach Melcombe, you'll return to London," he told his esquire, tearing off a piece of bread. "Plead my case with the king if you can do so without risking your life."

"But my Lord –" Ashley protested.

"There's no reason for you to share my exile," he said, chewing slowly and staring down at the table.

All three continued breakfast in silence.

After thanking the monks with a very small donation, Philip left the priory and rode through Dorchester.

"What a dung heap of a town," he commented, turning off onto the Weymouth road.

Philip and his esquire stayed a short distance behind Arbroth as they rode to the coast. Halfway to Melcombe, Philip uncharacteristically abandoned caution and spurred his rouncey into a gallop. Distracted by the sprouting spring foliage encroaching onto the old Roman road, he turned a bend and suddenly jerked back on the reins. Sitting his horse in the middle of the road was Arbroth.

"Not far noo, mah lord!" he said cheerfully, pointing at the dark river Wey meandering its way down to the coast.

Squawking gulls, circling overhead, and a salty tinge in the air confirmed his statement. Philip angrily shooed his Scot on before standing in the stirrups to look back up the road.

"Are we being followed?" his esquire asked, glancing nervously over his shoulder.

"No…" Philip frowned, observing a convoy of carts in the distance, moving slowly along the road. "Not that I can see…."

Riding down the low-lying peninsula between the Wey and the sea, the four men approached Melcombe Regis.

"I'll miss Cherrylips," Philip sighed out of the blue.

"She's a whore, my Lord," his esquire said, horrified.

"But she was a good whore."

"Why Cherrylips?"

"You're too young to know such things," Philip grinned.

"I know about women," he protested.

Arbroth leaned across and whispered in the teenager's ear and he blushed.

"My Lord," he gasped.

Crossing the town ditch, the four men cantered along St Mary's Street, their approach observed by curious locals, who put their heads down and went on with their business.

"What's up with them?" Philip huffed.

"Sickness has broken out in parts of the kingdom again."

"So?"

"It is said the great pestilence entered England through Melcombe," his esquire explained, referring to the awful plague of 1348 that ravaged the country, "and they fear its return."

"Oh?" Philip said, before accosting a fisherman. "We seek accommodation."

"Maidenhead Inn," he sniffed in an almost incomprehensible dialect, pointing down the street. "That way."

"Where's the harbour?" Philip asked his Scot, as they rode on.

"End o' tha street, mah lord."

Drawing up next to the hostelry, its upper floors leaning

dangerously out over the street, Philip dismounted and tutted at its squalid façade.

"Sell the horses and book passage for two," Philip told Arbroth.

The Scot nodded and waited while Mosby unloaded the sumpters.

"Tah where?" he asked, taking the reins from Mosby.

"Anywhere but France," Philip said, looking at the building's dilapidated state. "What a shit-hole."

As he entered the dingy inn, the few customers seated at tables followed his progress with palpable resentment.

"We need a room," Philip sniffed, removing a coin from his purse and placing it on the counter, while his esquire and servant dragged in weapons and weapons, wrapped in waterproof cloth.

"How many?" the lazy-eyed innkeeper asked, leaning on the counter.

Philip raised four fingers and the innkeeper took the money.

"Upstairs," he grunted.

As Philip shuffled up to the first floor, his nostrils were offended by a pungent odour of mildew.

"My God…" his esquire coughed.

"It'll do," Philip grimaced, opening the door.

The room was small and musty with mouldy, water-stained walls, and a heavily-discoloured straw mattress on the floor.

When Arbroth arrived later, he was shocked at the state of the place.

"Mah lord!" he gasped. "We'd be better off in a pig-sty."

"If I can put up with it, you can," Philip said. "Did you sell the horses?"

"Aye… They would only pay eight poonds."

"For six good animals," Philip moaned. "What about a ship?"

"There are two, one bound fer Ireland, t' other for Portugal; they'll both take us fer ten poonds."

"Ten pounds!" Philip gasped.

"Ten poonds *each*," he corrected.

"Might as well be ten thousand," he moaned, shaking his head.

"How much money do we have?" Ashley asked.

"Twelve pounds."

Shrugging off the bad news, Philip sent his servant to buy food, and Arbroth out to the town limits, to watch for pursuit.

While Philip and his esquire rested, a large body of cavalry wearing the dark red and blue livery of Sir William Hastings, and commanded by his brother Ralph, galloped into Dorchester. Infuriated by the intrigue between his wife and Philip Neville, and her arrest, Ralph begged the king for permission to lead the pursuit and bring him back. Convinced his cousin was too shrewd to be caught, Edward granted his request. Hastings rode his men hard but reached Dorchester too late. Believing his quarry would head for the nearest port, he sent scouts fanning out towards the coast.

Arbroth returned to the Maidenhead at midnight with nothing to report. That night Philip and his men slept fully dressed, their weapons close. As dawn broke, Philip woke to the sound of muffled voices downstairs. Moving to the door, he opened it slightly and put an ear to the crack.

Despite the early hour, one of the detachments sent out by Hastings reached Melcombe and was searching the inns. When they arrived at the Maidenhead, they forced the innkeeper to open up and demanded to know if there were any strangers staying there. The yawning manager hesitated until threatened with violence.

"Broken door," he snorted, glancing at the stairs.

"How many?"

"Four."

The captain drew his sword and motioned for his men to follow.

Closing the door gently, Philip tiptoed through the room, nudging his men awake. Philip and Ashley snatched their swords and Arbroth his ballock dagger, and all three crouched in the blackness. The creak of boots on the stairs told Philip their pursuers had caught up and he licked his lips as adrenalin coursed through his body. A deathly silence filled the room when the door squeaked open and Philip held his breath. Tightening the grip on his arming sword, he tensed his body, ready to pounce.

Several shadows slip furtively into the room and then all hell broke loose in an orgy of noise, confusion and violence. Releasing his fear in one loud scream, Philip lunged forward, thrusting his sword at the nearest silhouette. The point pierced the man's chest, skewered between two ribs and punctured a lung, but momentum carried Philip on and he tumbled over his victim. Looking around, he saw indistinct figures clawing at each other, their curses turning to cries when inflicting or sustaining an injury, and blood-curdling screams penetrated every corner of the inn.

"Kill them all!" Philip yelled, grabbing somebody by the throat and squeezing. "Arbroth," he gasped, belatedly recognising his retainer's wild hair and releasing him.

"Aye," he spluttered, with a brutal cough. "It's me!"

It was over in the blink of an eye and the silence was deafening.

"Ashley?"

"Here?" his esquire panted.

"Mosby?" Philip called, but there was no response.

"Ah cannah see him," Arbroth hissed, massaging his throat.

"Did we get them all?"

"Not quite," Arbroth growled, finishing off a wounded man.

"I want one alive," Philip said, as the dying man let out a final breath.

"Too late," Arbroth sneered.

"You jug-head," he cursed, tripping over a body to reach the window and throw open the shutters for air. "I need to know if there are others."

As several nesting pigeons scattered in a flurry of flying feathers, dawn's pinkish, blue light cast an eerie glow on the macabre scene in the room. Looking around, Philip recognised the livery of Lord William Hastings and was overcome with rage.

"Where's Mosby?" he barked, licking blood from his lips.

"Ah have found him," Arbroth retorted, pointing at a body curled in the corner of the room.

"Craven curs," Philip spat, kicking the nearest corpse so hard it jarred his knee. "Sons of bitches," he groaned, holding onto the window and closing his eyes to the pain. "That's my bad leg."

"Lord Hastings' men," Ashley confirmed, joining him at the window.

"They're scouts," Philip warned, stepping back. "When they fail to return more will come… Leave everything but your weapons."

"But, mah lord…yer armour –?" Arbroth objected.

"Forget it."

"We can carry it –" Ashley offered, reaching for the harness.

"Leave it, I said!" Philip growled, anxious to get away.

All three wiped their weapons on the bedding and hurried downstairs, where the innkeeper sat anxiously biting his black nails.

"You told them," Philip said, pointing his sword at him.

"No, m'Lord…" the tippler quaked.

"Gutless turd," he sneered, sheathing his blade. "Let's go."

The three men left the inn and walked quickly to the river, their progress attended by the echoing bark of a dog.

"You'll have to come with us," Philip told his esquire. "England won't be safe for you now."

Ashley knew he could not stay behind after his involvement in the killing of the Lord Chamberlain's men.

Reaching a crossroads, Philip cocked an ear and picked out the distinct rumble of horses.

"Which way?" he demanded, the strain showing in his flashing eyes and deeply furrowed brow.

"Here," Arbroth said, turning right and heading for St Nicholas Street.

In the faint early morning light, the usually vivid blue waters of the Wey looked dark and ominous, and the foreshore stank of rotting waste.

Looking over at the harbour on the opposite side of the river, Philip was crestfallen when he saw only a single ship at anchor.

"Where are the others?"

"They were here yesterday, mah lord," Arbroth gulped.

"Great," Philip fumed, looking at the thick rope stretched over the river. "The ferry?"

"Aye."

"Horses!" his esquire warned.

"Go," Philip commanded.

The three men ran to the edge of the quay but there were no ferrymen at such an early hour.

"What'll we do now?" Ashley whined.

"We'll take it," Philip said, turning to his Scot. "Grab the rope."

The thick, hemp cable, attached to a post on either bank, was used to haul the ferry from Melcombe to Weymouth and back.

Jumping into the stern, Philip listened as the horses drew nearer.

"Thay're almost here," Arbroth grunted, struggling to drag the flat-bottomed boat through the water. "Help me, laddie."

Ashley took hold of the rough rope and both men heaved for the Weymouth shore.

"Look!" he yelped, pointing to the ship.

Philip snapped his head around to see the merchantman raising her sail.

"Put your backs into it," he urged, as a body of horsemen spewed out of St Mary's Street and spread along the Melcombe shore.

A dozen archers leapt from the saddle and removed their bows from the protective oilskin bags.

"Have a care!" Philip shouted, ducking to avoid a chaotic volley of arrows.

Riding his black palfrey up to the edge of the quay, Sir Ralph Hastings, wrapped in a fur-lined cloak, watched as the ferry ground into the shallows on the far shore.

"Made it," Philip's esquire panted, blowing on his sore hands.

"Cut the rope and sink her," Philip said, leaping onto the limited beach.

Arbroth drew his dagger and feverishly sawed until the fibres parted and the rope splashed into the water. By now arrows were falling thick and fast, and hitting a number of houses in Weymouth High Street.

"Lend a hand!" Arbroth shouted at Ashley, struggling to lift a large boulder.

While his men smashed out the bottom of the ferry, Philip and Hastings glared at each other across the narrow stretch of water.

"Mah lord!" Arbroth gasped.

Alarmed at the sound of the ship's anchor being wound up,

Philip urged his companions on. Aggravated at not being able to give his nemesis a bloody nose, he settled for a two-fingered salute.

"You black-hearted dog!" he shouted, baring his teeth. "Piss on you!" he added, spitting deliberately and bolting for the harbour, jeered along by Hastings' men.

"Get this ship out of here!" Philip demanded, running up the gangplank after his men and coming face to face with the flustered captain.

"I am master here and I decide when we leave," he snapped, his arms crossed over his puffed-out chest.

Philip's relief turned to disappointment when he saw the condition of the merchantman.

The *Holy Ghost* was an old clinker cog, high-sided and round-beamed, built of overlapping oak planks and caulked with lamb's wool. A single mast supported a square sail amidships and her crew numbered sixty seamen and soldiers; for protection against pirates, archers could be crowded into fore-and after-castles.

"Where are you bound?" Philip asked, while half-a-dozen sweating seamen heaved at the windlass.

"Fifty pounds," the captain retorted, eyeing his unwanted passenger with disdain, "or I go nowhere."

"You'll get your money," Philip growled, touching the handle of his sword. "Damn your eyes."

When he saw the anger in Philip's eyes and his blood splattered tunic, the captain glanced at the royal troops lining the Melcombe shore.

"In the king's name," one of Hastings' lieutenants bellowed, "I command you to lower your sail!"

"I dare not defy the king."

"If you do not, they will seize your ship and cargo," Philip warned, while the crew dodged flying arrows and looked to their captain for orders. "Make a decision, and make the right one or I'll spill your guts all over this rotten deck."

As more and more arrows thudded into the ship's side, the captain's hesitation evaporated.

"Secure the anchor!" he yelled, cupping a hand to his mouth and pointing to the open sea. "And take her out."

The bulky cog creaked, cracked and groaned as she turned until the sail caught the wind and she moved slowly out of the harbour.

Ralph Hastings and a dozen horsemen cantered along the north shore, keeping pace with the ship as she bobbed towards the Channel. The archers running alongside continued to shower the *Holy Ghost* with arrows, forcing her crew to stay down. Unable to do more than watch, Hastings's men-at-arms hurled insults or bared their arses at the departing cog.

"Thomas Talbot," Philip gasped, recognising one of the nobles riding with Hastings. "Bring me a bow," he commanded, making his way to the stern and climbing into the after-castle.

Arbroth snatched a warbow and arrow bag from a surprised archer and handed it to his master.

Ignoring the arrows zipping past his head, Philip set his feet firmly on the deck, placed a thirty-two inch ash arrow against the bow and drew the string to his right cheek.

"Can ye do it?" Arbroth questioned.

"My Lord!" his esquire objected.

"At Sheriff Hutton I was known for my skill with the bow," Philip bragged, as the goose feathers tickled his skin. "But that was a long time ago."

Bending his body, he looked down the shaft and swung the bow until the arrowhead pointed straight at Talbot.

"You threatened me at York." Philip mumbled, recalling the day Thomas Talbot reluctantly handed over Henry of Lancaster to him.

"Aim true, mah lord," his Scot whispered.

Shifting slightly to the left Philip unexpectedly changed the target and focused on Hastings. Adjusting the bow to allow for wind and timing the rocking of the boat in his head, he took careful aim and the muscles in his right arm bulged from the strain as the hemp was stretched to its limit. With all the misery Ralph and his brother caused him over the years flashing through his mind; Philip narrowed his eyes and released the two fingers holding the string.

The arrow shot over the water and hit Ralph Hastings in the upper chest, knocking him out of the saddle. Thomas Talbot and several others jumped from their horses and rushed to their fallen commander.

"You've killed him," Talbot yelled, "Bastard!"

Philip closed his eyes and released a long gasp of gratification.

"My Lord, you have done murder," his esquire said, harshly.

"They can only execute me once," he sniffed, passing the bow to his Scot.

At the point where the river empties into the English Channel, a gust of wind suddenly filled the sail and sped the merchantman on its way. Philip steadied himself as the ship bounced through the swell, and stared at the vast emptiness ahead.

"My Lord?" his esquire dared.

"What?" Philip snapped, already contemplating the consequences of his impulsiveness.

"Nothing," Ashley sulked, leaving the after-castle.

The cog sailed past Portland Isle and the gut-wrenching heartache of exile now hit home. At the thought of leaving his beloved England and his son, Philip's eyes misted and his mouth twitched.

"We are in God's hands now," he said, as cold sea-spray splashed his face. "If I ever return, I will be tried for treason."

"Tis you who have been betrayed, mah lord," Arbroth responded, "by a king ye served faithfully."

"Yes," Philip mused, watching the shrinking coast and sleeving salt water from his face. "I have bled for this king and done all he has asked of me," he added. "I have no reason to reproach myself."